Rereading the Revolution

Rereading the Revolution: The Turn-of-the-Century American Revolutionary War Novel

Benjamin S. Lawson

Bowling Green State University Popular Press
Bowling Green, OH 43403

Library of Congress Cataloging-in-Publication Data

Lawson, Benjamin S.
   Rereading the revolution : the turn-of-the century American
Revolutionary War novel / Benjamin S. Lawson.
      p. cm.
   Includes bibliographical references and index.
   ISBN 0-87972-817-5 (clothbound). -- ISBN 0-87972-818-3 (pbk.)
   1. Historical fiction, American--History and criticism. 2. United States
--History--Revolution, 1775-1783--Literature and the revolution.
3. American fiction--19th century--History and criticism. 4. American
fiction--20th century--History and criticism. 5. War stories, American--
History and criticism. I. Title

PS374.H5 L37 2000
813'.08109358--dc21

                                                        00-025233

Cover design by Dumm Art

For Mary

The Poets light but Lamps—
Themselves—go out—
The Wicks they stimulate—
If vital Light

Inhere as do the Suns—
Each Age a Lens
Disseminating their
Circumference—

—Emily Dickinson

CONTENTS

ACKNOWLEDGMENTS

The traveler feels both relief and gratitude upon reaching journey's end: relief at reaching the anticipated destination, and gratitude to those who helped and encouraged along the way. *Rereading the Revolution*, especially, has profited from the assistance of many librarians who aided in the tracking down of once-popular books which have become obscure titles and which are unavailable at any one location. Interlibrary-loan staffs have, thus, been crucial for my research, and I would especially like to thank William Davis and Faye Lewis of the Dougherty County Public Library (Georgia), Dorothy Carver of the Albany State University library (Georgia), and Rebecca Fausey of the Hancock County Public Library (Ohio). Also helpful have been the library staffs of Indiana University, the University of Pennsylvania, and Bowling Green State University.

National Endowment for the Humanities summer seminars for college teachers have provided time, opportunity, and facilities for research, not to mention fruitful intellectual interchange that inspired insights in this book. Credit is due the directors of those seminars: professors Jay Martin of Claremont McKenna College, Michael Wood of Princeton University, and Peter Conn of the University of Pennsylvania. The provocative if sometimes contentious sessions of the School of Criticism and Theory (then housed at Northwestern University) no doubt lent a greater sophistication to my critical views. Semesters spent teaching at the University of Helsinki and University College London furnished their own germane perspectives from a distance which perhaps makes American culture seem a more easily perceived and unique phenomenon. Certainly, national dimensions of any culture emerge clearly by contrast: we understand who we are partly by understanding who we are not.

I have learned other salient lessons about the dynamics of culture-specificity by being a long-time faculty member at Albany State University. More generally social lessons as well as more narrowly academic ones are not missed by those upon whom little is lost—to paraphrase Henry James. Administration and faculty have taught well, generally without their knowing it; students have not suspected that they all along were teaching as well as learning. Perhaps differences within individual societies sometimes enact and illustrate the same dynamics of definition as more broadly national and cultural ones. The faculty and staff of the Department of English and Modern Languages have been supportive in recognizing that scholarly enterprises conjoin with teaching in communicating humanistic values to students. The computer science and word-processing centers have been most helpful. Finally, I would like to thank Alma A. MacDougall of Bowling Green State University Popular Press for her constructive and meticulous (re)reading.

INTRODUCTION

The need of Americans to recapture and appropriate supposedly defining national moments seems at times so compulsive that memorializing becomes part of a doubled social and cultural commentary whereby the memorializing itself is memorialized. They celebrate past celebrations. Recent and frequently simple and jingoistic bicentennial celebrations (clearly not cerebrations) of the independence, the constituting, and the Constitution of the United States have included commemorations of the centennial. The 1876 Philadelphia Exposition has been reexamined largely because 1976 was both a bicentennial and the centennial of a centennial. The Centennial Exhibition of 1876 "revived interest in everything Colonial" (Novak 183). Eight million Americans in Philadelphia after the Civil War used the timeliness of the occasion to recall—to remember *and* to call forth again, to evoke in the present—the glories of an earlier war. If the recent and divisive Civil War had left America with animosities and painful private memories, a spur to reconstructing would be positive visions of past and national enterprises.

Yet the great exposition's principal purpose was to extol the technological wonders of the present, of a latter-day, altered, and "improved" world. Paradoxically, a single event signaled both an indulgence in nostalgia and a validation of progress, both continuity and change being present to the minds of visitors. The title of a national homily like Archibald Willard's popular *The Spirit of '76,* painted for the centennial celebration, takes on an unintended but appropriate ambiguity, for the flag-waving spirit depicted and the artistic mode which communicates it are clearly those of 1876 rather than 1776. (A more genuine modernism, however, suffered under the scrutiny of the polite and pious: Thomas Eakins's *The Gross Clinic,* for example, was denied hanging space.)[1] Whereas the happenstance of the date may have called forth the response to history, the nature of the response was conditioned by and in terms of—if oftentimes purportedly and on the surface in contrast to—the whole contemporary scene. Responses are always "readings" of the present rather than a past whose supposed spirit is a present conjuration. Since media sometimes seem to be messages in the unavoidable though "unspoken" nuance of audience perception in any case, commemorators delude themselves in the thought of getting it right. Where texts are con-

cerned, the nature of modern mass-market publishing, the look and avail-
ability of books and attitudes about their assumed functions—these and
other factors affect messages which are inevitably embedded in moments.

By 1976 Americans were again turning their attention to the Revolutionary War and its aftermath, necessarily pursuing interests and
employing interpretive strategies available in the period of the bicentennial. But by this time the erudite had long found special reason to inter-
pret earlier interpretations, to study the history of history, and even to
believe that presumably originating events as well as books about them
possess a common textual status. As Roland Barthes puts it: "the only
feature which distinguishes historical discourse from other kinds is a
paradox: the 'fact' can only exist linguistically, as a term in a discourse,
yet we behave as if it were a simple reproduction of something on
another plane of existence altogether, some extra-structural 'reality'"
(153). Postmodern interpretations of interpretation have become a new
mode *of* interpretation, but perhaps as era-specific as any other. The late
twentieth century had rendered history self-conscious, placed it in quotation marks, meta-morphosed it. Ineluctably, we also include in our
accounts of the eighteenth century what we think the nineteenth century
thought about the era nearly as much as we examine the senses in which
the one century was a precursor to the other. We "read" backwards as
well as forwards, and we cannot always be aware of the precise origins
of our impressions and images; many arise during the periods intervening between the subject of our study and the time we study it. As far as
we are concerned (can we be concerned any further, even if we, too,
prove ultimately and unwittingly naive?), the past must always and per-
force be a function of the mind of the present, of what has "gotten
through" and remains available to us in the present. "As far as I am concerned" could preface every statement we make.

Any notion of the true "pastness of the past"—as T. S. Eliot called
it—is thus subverted by the very nature of knowing. Any desire to recall
the past becomes itself a characteristic of the present, whether or not
suggested by the occurrence of national anniversaries. As Raymond
Williams and Michel Foucault variously have it, consciousness and
knowledge possess social determinants.[2] Although epistemological theories and theories of narrative structuring are thus equally applicable to all
texts—historical and literary, written and otherwise—we must still
account for reasons why texts are called forth at all and why they
express particular, even paraphrasable, perspectives. Our theories
explain texts already written, events already consummated. The ground-
(ing) and "epistemological innocence" which history—the written record
as well as actual events—has lost has been paralleled by literature's

losing the false isolation and exceptionality of the "creative." If decon-struction has been an assault on "the privileged realm of historical fact," it has made all texts equally (a)historical. Following upon and not alto-gether denying the concept of the atemporal text, the new historicists have (re)placed it in and with "the social, ideological, and material matrix in which all art is produced and consumed" (Greenblatt 429). Thus, "The deconstructive interest in the problematic of materiality in signification is not intrinsically ahistorical" (Michaels 28). If knowable cultural context cannot be ontologically prior to texts, the interplay itself of text and context at any moment defines discourse as era-specific. All interpretation responds to linguistic, political, ideological, and ethical constraints. In this sense the new historicist turn is toward endowing the linguistic construct with a temporal dimension. The project of a recent study of American literary history, for example, is "to ground textual analysis in history; and more than that, to make history a central cate-gory of aesthetic criticism" (Bercovitch viii-ix).[3]

The effect of recent theories is to invest fictions of all types—the novel, history, popular culture—with equal, if limited, powers of refer-entiality:

It is this very separation of the literary and the historical that is now being chal-lenged in postmodern theory and art, and recent critical readings of both history and fiction have focussed more on what the two modes of writing share than on how they differ. They have both been seen to derive their force more from verisimilitude than from any objective truth; they are both identified as linguis-tic constructs, highly conventionalized in their narrative forms, and not at all transparent either in terms of language or structure; and they appear to be equally intertextual, deploying the texts of the past within their own complex textuality. (Hutcheon 105)

If the facts, what Murray Krieger has dubbed "raw materials" (339ff.) which can only be known as and if they are presented, together with accounts of the facts constitute history, then only the latter is ultimately knowable, uncomfortably distanced by the nature of discourse from what we feel we want to learn—"reality" outside language. Our encounters are with written texts which typically we would not have read at all were it not for our innocent interest in facts. Hayden White, especially, has treated the issue of narratology, of the shared purposes and structures of history and fiction (in their old-fashioned and separate generic defini-tions). To White, those who made fetish of fact "did not realize that the facts do not speak for themselves, but that the historian speaks for them, speaks on their behalf, and fashions the fragments of the past into a whole whose integrity is—in its *re*-presentation—a purely discursive one," fragments "put together in the same ways that novelists use to put together figments of their imaginations to display an ordered world" ("Fictions of Factual Representation" 28). Or, as Daniel Aaron puts it:

All fiction is a kind of history writing; all historians and biographers, and auto-biographers too, employ fictional devices; all storytellers, whether they think of the past as a visitable place, a usable cache loaded with analogues for their times, or an equivalent of a Hollywood spectacle, are affecting the way it is per-ceived. And how the past is perceived can influence the course of history—an idea that once was more widely entertained than it is now. (60)

Any text is comprised not only of a questionable correspondence to external realities but also of an inner stylistic and narrative coherence. Fiction is thus not the antithesis of fact, and facts themselves relate to one another only with "the aid of some enabling and generically fictional matrix" which "itself implies or entails a specific posture before the world which is ethical, ideological, or more generally political" (White, "Fictions of Factual Representation" 34-35). Brought up against the fact of language, history and the novel may be drained of referentiality with-out losing the force and effect of an era-specific cultural commentary, however much this commentary is divorced from totalized readers' con-trol or from validity and verification of meaning.[4] Self-contained works may not be fixed in the ontological ultimate, and may still function as the real *pen*ultimate constituted by written cultural expression.

As intertexts and "art forms" the novel and history have developed along parallel, sometimes intertwining, courses and have defined each other and in part created and responded to a zeitgeist which is always redefining the nature of each. Ultimately, Donald Pearce's statement in *Para/Worlds: Entanglements of Art and History* that "great historical art is obviously transhistorical" (4) means precisely that all fictional art is historical, graced with the same chances of passing beyond culture, nar-rative, and language to realms of universality. By reason of major cur-rent epistemological and narrative theory, the notion that history alone deals with a preexistent and otherwise knowable order of actuality becomes moot.[5] Clearly, these views take on a special significance and complexity when applied to a hybrid genre like the historical novel, a form which seems to encroach on the prerogatives of history, like history to treat a past subject while reacting to the modes of thought and feeling peculiar to the moment of composition. If writers are to us guileless in differentiating between these forms, they have certainly been assertively self-conscious in drawing distinctions between the raison d'étres and objectives of history and of historical fiction. The common-sense thinking of earlier times that the genres are obviously distinct becomes itself an aspect of that cultural milieu, of how the world was viewed. In writing of discrete forms we are thus inserting a diachronic element into our arguments and thereby attempting to define those eras which we are investigating. At the same time we silently obviate the need for our own critical disclaimers by passing over repeated reminders that *now* we posit commonalities in narrative. Even later commentators who find in all written texts a common base write of differences, affected as we all must be by "the mind of the past"—Emerson's phrase for "books"—and by the additional problematic effects of minds since that past. As Dominick La Capra writes, we should reduce texts neither to the status of "documentary symptoms of contexts" nor to that of the isolated formal artifact (7). Present theory cannot be "pure," but must be tangled with all that has affected it. With these presuppositions we attempt to delimit historical fiction and to examine a possible subtype, subject, and chronological development.

A cogent definition of historical fiction results from a combining and adapting of nomenclature employed by Warner Berthoff: "pastoral is a branch of fiction dominated by nostalgia for the imaginative satisfactions that, in the perspective of economic disorder, certain benign myth-constructs are remembered as providing; the chronicle-novel, on the other hand, moves in the direction of certified history and the kind of credence owing to that." The impulses of audience and authors simultaneously to embrace both sentiment and fact can be seen to lead to the creation and consumption of a single genre which in Berthoff's terms would be the "pastoral chronicle-novel," a form which partakes of the mythic because the purpose of myth is not so much explanation as "recovery, preservation, organization, continuance" ("Fiction, History, Myth" 269, 281). Imaginative romancers—contradistinguished from realistic novelists who manipulate perceived contemporary facts which would seem therefore intrinsically verifiable—make "this disparity an even more pronounced condition of their writing by wedding their unrealistic fictional form to the investigation of history" (Budick 2). The very type of fiction which purports to deal with the past makes the slightest use of "certified history" in its move to "benign myth-constructs." But from its beginnings early in the nineteenth century historical fiction became a popular form which expressed not a derived, dual, and unsatisfying vision compounded of the disparate claims of history and literature, but rather a unified and intellectually and emotionally satisfying vision. The dilemma which William Spengemann finds in our idea of American literature—being forced "to choose between America and literature, between nonliterary history and ahistorical literature" (140), is resolved in the genre. Others, in fact, have provocatively suggested that novels dealing with the present scene are historical, too, in the sense that they portray a "period" in social and historical context (Barnes 214). Perhaps the privileged realistic novel itself "was in a sense engendered by the Romantic historical novel, adopting from it a historical perspective to represent the contemporary world" (Baumgarten 179).[6]

In Western societies the historical romance owes its very existence to the world made possible by those French and American Revolutions which so frequently become the subjects of the romances. The idea of change and the specific changes in notions about the nature of fiction and history—and the interplay between philosophies of history and of art—eventuated in the development of a distinct genre with a new form and function. For a relatively short period of the nineteenth century—from the birth of the modern historical novel with Sir Walter Scott until the beginnings of a "scientific" historiography—the romancer was considered a historian, the historian a romancer. In this way, "Historical writing and historical novel writing influenced each other mutually" (Hutcheon 105). Not only did the historian and the historical novelist write homological narratives in their attempts to impose order upon the past, the past itself was considered somehow, intrinsically, more "romantic" than the present (Budick 3). The choice of subject, per se, seemed to call forth romantic treatment. Certainly, American narrative historians of the time like George Bancroft, William Prescott, John Motley, and Francis Parkman appeared to regard "romantic conventions not as meaningless stereotypes, but as effective ways of communicating a message that all their literate contemporaries would understand" (Levin, *History as Romantic Art* ix). As late as 1898, Charles Kendell Adams, otherwise questioning the old history, could reverse the expected order by citing the Revolutionary War novel *Hugh Wynne* for documentary evidence of political activity in Philadelphia (Morgan 79). It seems evident from their grand, sometimes nationalistic, celebrations of the Americas that, while they understood the techniques and theories of the modern English and French historians, they admired and emulated no one so much as Scott (Levin, *History as Romantic Art* 11). The significance of concepts like the idea of progress could be similarly asserted with similar authority by William Gilmore Simms or James Fenimore Cooper, Parkman or Bancroft.

Although all human societies possess a sense of tradition and a sense of responsibility for transmitting those traditions in some manner, written history has come to seem so specialized and scholarly that general, even if otherwise educated and sophisticated, readers have turned to memoirs, biographies, diaries, and the historical novel to satisfy their craving for a national, therefore a personal, identity (Renault 315). The period examined in this study witnessed the growing divergence of academic Euro-American history from romantic narrative convention, the simultaneous birth of scientific history and notable rebirth of popularity of the historical novel. "Romantic narrative history" became fragmented and discredited as it split into history—as an empirical scrutiny of impersonal economic and social forces—and into romantic narrative. In a sense, then, the romantic and quasi-fictional historical novel claimed the ground vacated by a no longer academically fashionable narrative history and by an avant-garde and naturalistic fiction which was following European historians like Leopold von Ranke to a faith in inductive methods and the adopting of models from the physical and social sciences. In its own terms, the historical novel could still be both traditional history *and* literature. Von Ranke himself may have been consciously reacting against the influence of Scott's romances (Weinstein 264). For a time academic history and experimental and naturalistic creative literature would be held to similar "scientific" standards, and both gradually parted ways from romantic narrative fiction. Popular fiction and popular history continued to offer the delights of an easily understood vision and version of the past. (It goes without saying that the phenomenon was affected as well by the growth and democratization of readership coinciding with the rise of publishing itself as an educational and entertainment industry which implicitly challenged the authority of old institutions of culture, yet succeeded by promoting and thereby perpetuating a basically conservative English-language tradition which still held sway.) But a platitudinous history for the masses might still be faintly suspect because illegitimized by the standards of what professional history had otherwise become, whereas an unabashedly fictional narrative could not be faulted on this basis and could still furnish something of real history commixed with invention, personalism, and love interest. Neither did the common reader often understand or appreciate the bleak challenges and cerebral satisfactions offered by Zola's experimental novel.

Well before 1900 American writers themselves had begun to speculate on the uniqueness of historical fiction. In his 1845 plea for native materials William Gilmore Simms wrote that "it is the artist only who is the true historian. It is he who gives shape to the unhewn fact, who yields relation to the scattered fragments,—who unites the parts in coherent dependency, and endows, with life and action, the otherwise motionless automata of history" (*Views and Reviews* 36). By the turn of the century, the historical romancer Robert W. Chambers concluded that

"Romance alone can justify a theme inspired by truth; for Romance is more vital than history, which, after all, is but the fleshless skeleton of Romance" (*The Maid-at-Arms* vii). Later, but in the same strain, Hervey Allen noted that the historical novelist, in creating the illusion of having lived in the past, appeals not only to the intellect but to the imagination and emotions as well (120). Again, in 1964, Shelby Foote, both historian and novelist, stated that, though both try to re-create the past for their readers, "to make it live again in the world around them," "the historian attempts this by communicating facts, whereas the novelist would communicate sensation. The one stresses action, the other *re*-action" (220). Norman Mailer allowed for a medium mixed on a basis other than shared textuality in *Armies of the Night,* his "History as a Novel, the Novel as History." More recently, Thomas Fleming has emphasized the point that historical novels should be neither dull repetitions of the old facts or "voracious imaginations" consuming reality (20). In this American tradition of commentary the events of the historical novel include not simply or arbitrarily historical events, but, rather, a re-creation of them in terms of personality and its perspectives. Although the genre seems to surrender both that freedom from the actual valued by theorists from Aristotle as the mark of poetry's superiority over history and that authenticity granted to "real" history, it finds recompense and rationale in a unified and positive agenda (see Baumgarten 177, Daspre 238). Not a failed melding of quasi-fiction with quasi-history, by 1900 the form could find proponents as dedicated as the American novelist Winston Churchill, who spent three years researching and writing *The Crossing,* just one of his historical novels.

A *re*-creation of the past, historical fiction is a recreation, a pasttime, of the present which balances readers' expectations of a measure of invention with more than a little convention (see Cawelti, "The Concept of Formula" 87). Even when undertaking an elucidation of the structure of the historical novel, the critic must simultaneously consider that its perceived significance arises from the dynamic interplay of form and content with periodization, genre tradition, and the force of culture and history itself—literary history not least of all (Baumgarten 175). The specific sense that fiction can and should make of social and political history has been variously understood. Ernest Leisy maintains that, in producing an illusion of the past, "the historical novelist is interested less in the many subtle causes of events than in how the spirit of an age is reflected in a place and in a people" (7). Similarly, Hervey Allen finds a major difficulty of the historical novelist to be "the shaping of the whole story into a design that is part of a grand pattern of historical events, pregnant with important meaning" (120). The search of fiction for ways to make the past come alive yet somehow, in its own terms, to replicate the historical account is an ongoing one for those novelists for whom the historical circumstances are more than backdrop. Harry Henderson concludes that "perhaps the strongest element shared by the historical novel and conventional history is an informing social vision, a vision which projects fairly explicitly an image of social structures and the relations among them" (13). To the historical novelist Rafael Sabatini the period novel may lean either to the side of the historical happenings or to that of the imaginary, but the invention should be "set against a real background to which story and characters must bear some real and true relationship" (36). The story itself must satisfy and must possess some inescapable correlation to a past milieu; the action that develops in the fiction must reinforce the action that envelops it, and vice versa.

As dramatization of earlier texts, one of historical fiction's increasingly important functions became what Robert Frost called, in speaking of poetry, a "momentary stay against confusion" ("The Figure a Poem Makes" 394). Somewhere in the past, people want to believe, existed moments of heroism, when the great deeds of our ancestors must have had a profound influence on a simpler time, a text easily understood. By 1900 there existed an especially acute antiquarian desire "to recapture the physical details of an age slipping rapidly beyond the blur of hazy reminiscence" (Kammen 163). The confusions of the present make one long "to go back to something that is fixed and stable, to rest one's soul in an age in which the problems and perplexities of our day play no part." "The historical novel satisfies a desire for national homogeneity. It helps us realize the sacrifice for ideas and ideals, the sweat and blood that have made democracy work" (Leisy 3-4)—to quote a scholar whose tone resembles that of the historical romancers about whom he writes. The novels are, therefore, exemplary. Discussing Harold Frederic's Revolutionary War novel *In the Valley,* written shortly before the period covered here, Stanton Garner says that the author "sought the symbols of the past which might explain the present" and that "his impulses were epic, a search for cultural roots" (18-19). Though a myth of an earlier era is in the making, this imaginative vision is being offered up as a new reality calling for the appreciation, even emulation, of the present. Such a vision can be at least psychologically convincing, a revivification which comes as the real thing fades away.

The second of the periods when historical fiction nearly dominated the American literary scene was at the turn of the twentieth century. James Woodress writes of a "torrent," a "flood tide," of historical fiction which challenged the aesthetic assumptions of the realists (385-86). Richard Altick mentions that "American historical romances were especially in demand" (224). Once again, as in the few decades following the War of 1812, enthusiasm for the historical novel made itself known.[7] The melodrama and grand heroic posturing of the costume romance more than held their own against the philosophical, social, and psychological analyses of the realistic or naturalistic novel. The time was one of rapid change and disruption, in a world increasingly beset by modern problems. Urbanization, industrialization, immigration and emigration, Populism, unionism, suffrage movements, economic depression and the closing of the frontier all left their marks on American life and art. The Civil War and the Spanish-American War not only provoked thoughts of an earlier conflict but also promoted a national self-consciousness during an era of a more general crisis in consciousness. As did the Philadelphia "century of progress" Exposition of 1876, the Chicago Columbian Exposition of 1893 coupled present accomplishment with a sense of roots— no thought then that Columbus had invaded rather than discovered America. But a major economic depression was in progress (as was the case in 1876), and the great dynamo which inspired Henry Adams also brought to him a comforting and contrasting vision of a pre-Columbian Virgin. Reinterpretation of the nation's roles seemed necessary; reassessment of American values was demanded. The question of an American identity, writes a recent anthologist, "acquired a new urgency at the end of the nineteenth century, when the cultural, racial, religious, and economic disparities among the peoples of the nation intensified and registered themselves more visibly on the national consciousness" (Lauter 2: 850).

In the midst of these myriad pressures and influences "the Revolutionary period in particular provided an image of energy and purpose which the later nineteenth century otherwise lacked" (Martin 83). As an inevitable fallout from the anxieties of the time, the genre's popularity has its roots in the nostalgia resulting from the desire to "escape from the painful realities of industrialized America" (Kammen 165). As Steven Marcus views it, the historical novel then was one byproduct and expression of the new historical consciousness "that these new conditions of permanent transformation evoked" in a culture which possessed little visible material culture from the distant past (167-68). Historical fiction answered a need: "when people read historical fiction, one of the many things they are doing is exercising their yearning for an older and simpler world, a culture in which these martial notions of courage and honor and a right side and a wrong side still held firm" (182). Even a supposed modernist of the time, Charles Ives, could see the pastoral and the patriotic as one: the present, he wrote, is the "seed of 1776 gone soft."[8] William Dean Howells theorized that the historical romance was sentimental and escapist, a mindless "relief from the facts of the odious present" like what he took to be the "shameful imperialism" of the Spanish-American War which he attacked so viciously in "Editha" (Kartiganer and Griffith 398-99).

A sometimes hysterical ethnocentric and nativist Americanism accounts in part for the popularity, context, and content, of these novels and for what might at first glance strike one as an odd and inappropriate Anglophilia. For many descendants of the old immigration who considered themselves the folk of the founding fathers, xenophobia went hand in hand with the asserting of a pseudoscientific Anglo-Saxon racism. The challenge to an Anglocentric and monolithic value system represented by the thought of an evolving and empowered multi-ethnic America eventuated in a conspicuous rebirth of the related phenomena of anti-Catholicism, anti-Semitism, and anti-radicalism, forms of insecurity, bewilderment, and resentment (see the early chapters of Bennett). America was either to become a new land by absorbing if not assimilating the hundreds of thousands of new immigrants predominantly from Southern and Eastern Europe, or cling to an old identity and cohesion by the implementing of programs like that of the Immigration Restriction League of 1894, a Brahmin campaign for literacy testing. Naturalization and Americanization seemed one answer, exclusion another (see Hofstadter 178-81). Seen in this light, legislative restriction of immigration, Revolutionary War novels, and the founding of self-declared patriotic ancestral societies become cultural manifestations of the exclusionist approach. The Sons of the American Revolution and the Colonial Dames, for example, were founded during the 1880s, while robber barons were building their ersatz English castles. "Many Americans soothed their fears of losing status by joining various old-American or pro-English societies to which they laid claim by devout researches in genealogy" (Strout 140), a craze for pedigree-searching which "swept the nation" during the 1890s (Kammen 165). Thus did plutocrats indicate their distance from workers oftentimes already separated from them by language and religion as well as wealth, race, or national origin. In an 1898 high society novel of contemporary New York, Constance Cary Harrison, author of the Revolutionary period *A Son of the Old Dominion*, has a character address the fad: "With this Revolutionary—Sons of the Cincinnati—Colonial Dames business all over the place, patriotism may be 'in' again next year" (*Good Americans* 8-9).

Immigrant-phobia had been naively dramatized as the other side of Anglophilia in novels of the 1880s like John Hay's *The Bread-Winners* (1884) and Richard Grant White's *The Fate of Mansfield Humphreys* (1888). While John Fiske waxed "ecstatic over meeting all the great

swells of the Athenaeum Club," Thomas Bailey Aldrich poetically protested in "Unguarded Gates" against America becoming "the cesspool of
Europe" (Commager xxxvi). Criticism and literary history like "Francis
H. Underwood's *Builders of American Literature* (1893), Henry C.
Vedder's *American Writers of Today* (1894) and Barrett Wendell's influential *Literary History of America* (1900) promoted the 'genteel tradition,' canonizing a literature of high ideality, Anglophilism, and,
according to its detractors, benign irrelevance to the realities of American life" (Reising 14). London seemed to be the cultural capital of the
Western world, and by 1900 American writers and artists were more
integrally part of the intellectual life of that city than at any other time in
American history (Commager 589). Reaction to conditions and events
late in the century led to America's old establishment increasingly
throwing its lot in with England's and maximizing its difference from
the lower orders of the Continent. The old establishment's naïvete con-
joins with its insecurities: "Unaware of his own 'hyphenated' characteristics as a nostalgic Anglo-American, the Yankee was dangerously
vulnerable to hostile suspicions of the foreign ties of immigrants from
other countries" (Strout 134). Greater frequency of transatlantic travel, a
growing democratization of Great Britain, and a perception that America's new imperialist ventures were undertaken under the aegis of Anglo-
American civilization rejuvenated bonds between the countries (witness
the Anglo-American League of 1898) and furthered a "reversal of both
America's traditional hospitality to immigrants and her policy of isola-
tionist anticolonialism" (Strout 134, see also Bailey 437ff.). Old-line
Americans' apprehensions about change were obviously and ultimately
not nearly so innocuous as the sign under which the Anglo-American
labored, according to the Henry James of *The American Scene* (1907), a
man disoriented by a United States transformed during his absence: "The
Old Sweet Anglo-Saxon Spell."
    Yet, in spite of ties of history, culture, and language, the American
"also inherited a historic hostility to the British oppression which had
provoked so many American symbols of patriotic pride from the Declaration of Independence to 'The Star-Spangled Banner'" (Strout 134) and
which still could seem arrogantly aggressive in its imperialism. During
the post-Civil War generation the resulting ambivalence appeared most
"complex and paradoxical, for there was a curious combination, in these
years, of fierce resentment and almost obsequious veneration" (Commager xxxiv). The New World continued to define itself by difference
from the Old; England and America continued rival nations. But at the
same time cultural debts were openly acknowledged. The period had in
fact begun with Northern antagonism toward the British aristocracy for

their backing of the Confederate cause and their threatening to intervene in the war over the *Trent* affair. Many Southerners complained that Britain was not supporting them actively enough. In 1895 the United States again confronted the British, in an international incident stemming from an old dispute over the border between British Guiana and Venezuela. Reasserting the Monroe Doctrine of 1823, American Secretary of State Richard Olney proposed that the issue be referred to arbitration, an example to many Englishmen of unwonted and unwanted American interference. President Cleveland received much jingoistic support for recommending that the United States superintend the running of the boundary line and even fight to maintain it. Apparently encouraging the Venezuelans, the U.S. government facilitated the signing of a treaty between Venezuela and Great Britain which submitted the dispute to an arbitration board, whose decision was not handed down until October of 1899. America had enhanced its prestige as a great power and in the end, ironically, had improved its relations with Great Britain, which, "alone of the European powers, was ready to cheer America down the slippery path of imperialism" (Bailey 449). Having again asserted its strength in relationship to Great Britain, "by 1897 the country was definitely recovering from the Panic of 1893 and from the Venezuelan scare, and prosperity was going to its head" (Bailey 451).

By the 1890s, then, as a recent history textbook has it, "expansionist sentiment and national assertiveness began to re-emerge" (Unger 597). (Re)assurance was sought that what was right for old America was right for others. New Western states were being added to the Union; the frontier was declared officially closed in 1890, the year of the Battle of Wounded Knee. Acquisition of further territory would now be at the expense of lands outside the continental United States. However, the protests of Mark Twain and William Dean Howells of the Anti-Imperialist League notwithstanding, the intervening of American forces in a Cuban revolution was not generally perceived as an altogether selfish and ruthless imperialistic scheme. Spain could be accused of such designs, in both Cuba and the Philippines; England could be as well, in 1776 if not in 1898. A strain of innocent altruism runs through an American colonialism which saw opportunities to extend the political, social, and economic benefits gained from America's own eighteenth-century rebellion *against* colonialism. Historical novelists presented new evidence that these blessings were real and worth the sacrifice. Few in the contemporary nation stressed self-interest in the protecting of American lives, property, and trade. While Great Britain "was conspicuously friendly to the United States during the crisis with Spain," continental European powers almost all thought the United States guilty of unprovoked aggression against Spain (Bailey 465). As William Randolph Hearst and Joseph Pulitzer continued to whip up public sentiment against Spain, especially after the sinking of the *Maine,* diplomacy failed and President McKinley was pressured into sending a war message to Congress. Might the sun never set on *either* the British *or* the American empires? "As a result of the war with Spain in 1898, the United States became an imperial power and discovered in Britain a sympathetic partner in world politics" (Strout 143). Also in 1898 the earlier successful revolt of the American faction against the monarchy of Queen Liliuokalani led to the annexation of the Hawaiian Islands, a land increasingly seen as strategic in the Pacific. It is as if Americans in essentially conservative cultural expressions like novels of the American Revolution could lay claim to a glorious present and future by validating an Anglo-American past. America joined with the "mother" country in celebrating Victoria's grand diamond jubilee in 1897. Albeit a sometime rival to England even in the present, America was carrying forward the torch of an English heritage. America was supplanting Great Britain as an international power, and felt few national cultural anxieties of influence—to give Harold Bloom's phrase a new application—because England was associated with an old world whose very function was to *be* a heritage, therefore no real and present threat. This temporal dimension to the relationship between England and the United States allowed ambivalence and voided genuine antagonism.

The 1884 founding of the American Historical Association, marked by contention about the role of the scientific in the new history, was shortly after followed by reappraisal of the British influence and of the American Revolution (Van Tassel 929). The "Whig Conception" of a George Bancroft, whereby the Revolution was characterized as a classic struggle for liberty, was being faulted by professional historians as too simple and chauvinistic (though still promoted by a few, British among them, even after the turn of the century). A new generation of American historians, molded by new conditions, "demanded a more objective reading of the American past. After 1890 two new tendencies in Revolutionary scholarship profoundly altered the traditional interpretation" (Greene 4). The first of these, especially, furnished written texts parallel to the cultural ones just mentioned, for to the "Imperial School" the Revolution could be understood only when considered as an episode in the history of the British Empire. For the most part, the British had had ample reasons for their policies; too many American colonists had been provincial and self-seeking. According to Jack Greene, these revisionists were "thoroughly caught up in the general movement toward Anglo-American accord that gained increasing vigor in the decades immediately preceding World War I" (4). The other tendency, the so-called Progressive Conception, stressed the economic and the social and saw in the colonies the seeds and sorts of divisions which conspicuously culminated in the Progressive Era. The Gilded Age was all too familiar with the issues of disenfranchisement, corruption, and special interest projected onto the Revolutionary generation most famously by Charles Beard after the turn of the century. As could be guessed from earlier argument on other bases, novels of the Revolution functioned in the popular mind as a combination of what historians have dubbed the Whig and the Imperial conceptions. Available to and easily apprehended by the layman, these books interfused a staple American nationalism with a pro-British and therefore "anti-American" stance surprising only to those rare readers unconscious of more recent British-American détente. Far from desiring to project a tawdry present onto the past (the Progressive historian's ploy?), mass-market romancers found and formed an audience by projecting a hypothetically heroic and assured past onto a doubtful and uncertain present.

The historical novelist's longing for the past, reasons for this longing, and her or his drive to reproduce it are characteristics of the present, as we have glimpsed. Again we see that history as actual events and history as the written account are separable only in their abstractions; our reading of the late-nineteenth-century texts of both sorts reveals similar hermeneutic mechanisms at work, mechanisms at once both source and manifestation. Phenomena and ways of dealing with them seem time-specific but also of a piece as now-perceived human expression. To say that these novels are "about" 1900 as well as 1776 is not so much to furnish ontological ground as to problematize "about" as a word which now must suggest "what are they doing?" as a dynamic of perception equally applicable to the actual, to "hard history," and to imaginative writing. Whether or not authorized beyond what is available to discourse, they carried the weight of authority to their makers and audiences. Thus, we are not really modifying our argument to take close looks at how these books are representative reactions to particular domestic and foreign issues of their times and reactions to reactions like social upheaval and other books. Much fiction of all sorts appears a response to particular and troubling issues of the Progressive Era. That all was not well with America seemed to be demonstrated by urban crowding, "the shame of the cities," strikes, unionism, the plight of the poor, Populism, the women's suffrage movement, crime, race and immigrant relations, the Depression of 1893, and written texts dealing with these problems.

Between 1860 and 1910 the number of American towns with populations of over fifty thousand grew from 16 to 109; in the decade before

1890 Chicago more than doubled its population (Hofstadter 174). As we have seen, this growth was attributable not only to movement from the country to the city and to natural population increase, but also to the influx of the many non-Protestant, non-English-speaking peoples. To the adherents of "high-toned moral imperatives of evangelical Protestantism" like the self-styled prophet Josiah Strong—who pre-dated the more well known Billy Sunday by a generation—the city itself represented a new and necessarily corrupt way of life: "The first city was built by the first murderer, and crime and vice and wretchedness have festered in it ever since" (qtd. in Hofstadter 176; Strong's words are taken from the 1898 *The Twentieth Century City*). The capitalism of the Gilded Age was being challenged; the hysteria with which the authorities reacted to the Haymarket protesters in 1886 attests to the government's insecurity. (Recall that the publishers of mass-market books like historical novels struggled too for success in a market economy.) The historical romancer Paul Leicester Ford reported being deeply disturbed by the social unrest of the 1890s (Kammen 338). If there was growing fear of revolution, presenting images of an earlier "necessary" revolution was a means of allaying that fear to the extent that the earlier revolution was seen to eventuate in a democratic government responsive to the people. The present was furnished a positive model of American virtue, a reason why American traditions were worthy and why departures from them were to be deplored. In a sense the American historical novel thus served as an analogue to the settlement worker—most often herself or himself of Anglo-American Protestant heritage, unlike the ward boss, who was likely to be of new immigrant stock (Hofstadter 182)—as an agent of Americanization. Instead of criticizing the corruptions of national values, these writers' approach was to portray those values in an earlier time, when they existed in a "purer" form. The historical novelist's enterprise was in this way the other side of muckraking, a conspicuous avoiding of muck which in its own way suggested something amiss and to be avoided. While Lincoln Steffens wrote of "Tweed Days in St. Louis," David Graham Phillips of "The Treason of the Senate," Charles Edward Russell of "Lawless Wealth" and "The Tenements of Trinity Church," Rheta Childe Dorr of "What Eight Million Women Want," John Spargo of "The Bitter Cry of the Children," William E. Walling of "The Race War in the North," Upton Sinclair of "The Condemned-Meat Industry," and Edwin A. Ross of "The Suppression of Important News" (Swados), historical romancers depicted a fantasy eighteenth century in which deep-seated pre-industrial political and social ills were minimized and laid at the door of the occasional corrupt and licentious Tory or the atypically unruly American mob. The books are aspects of the spirit of the time, not "about" a reified spirit; authors' calculated avoidance and at times overt comment show that this fiction cannot be "really"—for us or contemporary readers—a refuge from turn-of-the-century America, no matter how perceived by earlier Americans whose minds we cannot enter.

Perhaps most intriguing about these novels is their implicitly and simultaneously declaring both independence from and dependence upon Great Britain, its political and social structures, its literary traditions. Partly, the paradox comes of "America's perennial love-hate relation with Europe and all of its attendant feelings of cultural inferiority and moral superiority, or parricidal guilt and newborn innocence, of nostalgia for the old home and the urge to destroy it" (Spengemann 99). On one level American Revolutionary War novels would seem to demand a celebration of the patriots, the rebels, and a condemnation of the British. However, in novel after novel English culture is presented as basically valuable and normative. One particular reason for this view has already been posited: "the rapprochement between England and America at the opening of the twentieth century" (Morgan 180). Another is the intrinsically and, in 1900, pointedly conservative ideology of these writers and their constituency. Although these novels may represent a movement away from French-influenced naturalism, an escape from the modern in literature, as works in English they must be read with the thought in mind that "even the most original and idiosyncratic works of American literature were written in a European language by persons steeped in transatlantic culture and whose idea of literature itself was based primarily upon European poetry, fiction, and drama" (Spengemann 103). In the end, attention must always be paid to the overarching issues of the nature and autonomy of an American literature itself.

To the student of genre, the very following of the conventions of the historical romance might seem to dictate a certain interpretation of history whereby reconciliation with Britain is preordained and unavoidable. Not only is the form historical and fictional, belonging to both the past and the present, it is also British and American as well as political and erotic. The hybrid genre must respond both to the (British) conventions of the romance and to the necessity to integrate (American) "history" into the text. Since documentation and dynamics of this point will be furnished by the analyses of particular novels, suffice it here to say that the truly democratic American hero could not very well be the traditional wealthy, aristocratic, dashing hero of the *historical* romance. On the other hand, telling the historical facts—as they were conceived—sometimes would distort the expected course of the fictional narrative, undoing it as the plot of a historical *romance*. The very genre was Anglo-American;

especially in novels about revolt from England the form's elements seem
to work at cross purposes (we should keep in mind, however, that in literature as in botany a hybrid is a real if new strain, capable of propagating itself). To follow the formula writers had to assign the protagonist
characteristics of British heroes or, alternatively, had to employ a British
male love interest as a temporary stand-in for the eventual and appropriate American hero, the effect being a temporally blurred picture of an
Anglo-American hero. The presence of a truly egalitarian American, no
matter how praised in the platitudes of the time, would constitute a challenge to the formula itself. In addition, fictional characters would unduly
disturb history by performing truly significant actions. Strategies of integrating and working out these tensions—or their continued presence—
between the fictional and the historical, the aristocratic and the
democratic, the British and the American, romance and adventure,[9] past
and present, make for the particular quality of turn-of-the-century American Revolutionary War novels as an episode in the history of a genre. A
vision of American rebellion is, ironically, being communicated in a
genre the European tradition of which is being too slavishly followed.

History has another history. Because actual figures from the past
were popularly viewed as outside narrative, they were considered always
available icons beyond authorial control, not consumed by love or fiction. In serving both fiction and history, which they must in historical
fiction, the heroes of history by necessity are prevented from carrying
out roles as altogether historical personages or altogether fictional creations. They are shut off from any unitary being by the demands of the
form; their meaning in history precludes their fulfilling a fictional role,
and the constraints of romance void their historical reality. Historical-fic-
tional characters like Nathan Hale must abstractly embody those American virtues made available to American heroines only in the persons of
"invented" fictional-historical characters. To allow the hero of history to
succeed in love would violate his political meaning and the presumptive
separation of history and fiction. The merging of the two types of discourse requires the erasure of the historical hero, even as it calls for the
fictional and the historical to correspond and comment upon each other
in significant and revelatory ways. In a world imagined more fictive
than historical, figures like Hale are rendered impotent and homeless.

On the other hand these figures are validated in history: in a compromise maneuver the author is forced to show them eventually disappearing into history while fictional heroes serve as their surrogates.
Presence in history is absence in fiction. The oftentimes pathetic and
malleable male fictional protagonist loses force by having to substitute
for two others: the hero of the British romance tradition and the hero of

American historical tradition. Whatever revolutionary spirit they possess, the heroes of history are forbidden from becoming embodiments of that spirit in a novelistic world like *Brinton Eliot*. They must serve novelistically as spirit alone, since they embody, inhabit, and represent a presumed world of "history" and will not be there at novel's end to garner rewards and spouses. Therefore, "in many historical novels, the real figures of the past are deployed to validate or authenticate the fictional world by their presence, as if to hide the joins between fiction and history in a formal and ontological sleight of hand" (Hutcheon 114). Historical figures are there by not being there, by being conceived as figures of history rather than fiction. The stranded fictional romantic protagonists are not there by way of being others. Unthinking acceptance of the formula, in addition to antiquarian interests and a defensive posture toward the present, eventuated in the writing of conventional novels which could scarcely dramatize radically new perspectives. Following the convention empties the text of the possibility of strong statement. These novels of the Revolution are, thus, far from revolutionary.

Another typical textual manipulation involves the use of the sorts of contrived familial symbolism and metaphor which had long been employed to explain the issues of the war. The idea that America was an insubordinate child and Britain the sometimes misguiding parent was common even in the eighteenth century; "the device of the divided family, the best and most economical means for depicting the American Revolution as a civil war" (Ringe 358). (It goes without saying, also, that the trope had been made timely by the interference—in almost the physicist's sense—caused by the Civil War's falling between the subject and the composition of these novels.) A related method of illustrating divided and dividing loyalties arises from the contemplation of future possible families. Commonly, two men—one of distinctly American sympathies (though we have seen the limits of this possibility), the other stereotypically British—compete for the hand of a technically American woman who has not yet committed herself to either man, or to either cause (the terms in Civil War novels would be "Southern" and "Northern"). The woman becomes in these cases less simply the American than America, groping toward a realization of her destiny. Flexible and tractable half a century after Seneca Falls, she defines herself through relation to the Man and thereby fulfills the expectations of historical romance and the turn-of-the-century conservative ideology of (male) vested interest.[10] As will be highlighted and made graphic in discussions of particular novels, for her the War for Independence recasts but preserves the status of dependence in a new (American) family. She is permitted only brief flings of tough-minded, independent action. Less frequently, the hero rather than the heroine is the one who finds his way by fits and starts. Although Michael Kammen possibly goes too far in stating that literary treatments of the American Revolution serve as national rites of passage, he is on safe grounds in his conclusion that a "theme common to the genre as a whole involves the myriad ways in which love and politics intersect" (179). These fictions are imaginatively convincing to the extent that conventional love plots are made to serve the purposes of a symbology of the Revolutionary (not revolutionary) struggle. Or, to quote Philip Fisher, in the historical novel "the local moment and events so completely embodied the larger national or social struggle that the plot could be read as a coded version of the larger social world" (15). As revelations of the ways in which "history" becomes image inseparable from it, the novels become not merely popular entertainments, retrograde, overly sentimental and romantic Americana in the age of realism, but significant works which reinterpret the Revolution and present new perspectives on and for the late eighteenth, nineteenth, and twentieth centuries.

Much of the intent of the present project is suggested and subsumed by its title. Most obviously, it investigates the nature of turn-of-the-century written texts of a particular popular genre and finds in these texts distinguishing and meaningful relevance for their time. What turn-of-the-century agendas were manifested (if in other fashions like ancestor worship as well) by the great vogue and the characteristic narrative strategies of these books? Why did the reader of 1900 want to turn again to the Revolution? In a related sense the books themselves are re-interpretations. It has, in any case, become a critical commonplace that every reading is a rereading, since reality can be apprehended only through cultural (con)texts, written or otherwise. Every interpretation is also affected by earlier interpretations, so that a true diachrony vis-à-vis single past events like the Revolution becomes illusory. The appeal of the period nonetheless exists for the present even while we have come to feel that the event "itself," whatever can be known of it, has been defined and mediated through texts available and functioning in our own milieu. We confront past eras in part by construing the modes whereby those eras confronted and construed still earlier moments. We are not only reading (or misreading) again, but reading in new ways; in so doing we understand the naive pretense in affecting the belief that history ended in 1906. "American Revolution" becomes a (pre)text for our explanations and our wanting to explain—an excuse as well as an already existing cultural discourse. Like those recollecting the Philadelphia Exposition, we include in our bicentennial celebrations a centennial celebration of the centennial.

To image the temporal and cultural embeddedness of the historical novel—and at the same time to suggest that every novel is a historical novel—I depict, at the center of concentric circles, the developing action (a world fictional, although defined and limited by the nature of language, the history of its own time and genre, etc.). Surrounding this action and bearing reciprocal influences with it is the enveloping action, the historical epoch of the setting. But this is only evidently the history the novel is "about." Beyond, outside, later in time lie larger circles: the interim between the enveloping action and the moment of writing (at least fifty years, some have said, for the formula historical novel); the moment of writing; the date of publication; the time of our reading, and of our rereading; our sometimes belated and evolving interpreting and reinterpreting, based upon our memory of the book and oftentimes affected by others' readings. (Some circles, of course, may be concurrent, as when we read the book immediately upon its publication.) Other things being equal, the further apart these circles, the more distance the book has from us and the more likely it will be read as merely a cultural artifact. The other things that are not equal include our consuming drive still to evoke for certain texts the mystified sign of "universality." By the time the novel gets through to us, as it were, these moments if not more have mediated and modified its meanings. The poem, writes Wesley Morris, as a "process recurs again and again in each succeeding generation of readers (perhaps in each individual reading), binding the present not only to the past, to the moment of the poem's creation, but to all of the intervening time between creation and reading" (212). The very fact of holding in our hands a hard-cover, ornate, gilt-edged volume, nevertheless faded, fragrant, and dusty, speaks to us of time's effects, just as the physical qualities of early film and photographs affect our notions about the times portrayed more than we recognize. Like the antiquarian book collector and binder, we re-cover texts. Though significance springs from the nexus of time and place, time is here the instrumental dynamic once we posit written expression of a single culture as our subject. Even figuring the temporal in a spatial diagram becomes appropriate, since doing so is a means of making the notion present, simultaneously now and here. Like our subjects, which cannot really be separated from our readings of them, our interpretation even of time is a tangible text of the now.

Consequently, both our desire to read texts and our approaches to them—the latter without the former a chimera—demark our present. Our interest(s) in turning to these books at all, our critical methodology—our agendas, in other words—create the force of a comma after the "rereading" of "rereading the revolution," "the revolution" in apposition to "rereading." The late twentieth century, not the late nineteenth century, has expanded the canon for scholarly investigation. These are some of the books salvaged from the margin since 1906. The American Revolution indubitably and intrinsically fascinates as a distinguishing national moment, as it did a century ago, but the modern scholar comes to it freighted with new, yet still pre-, conceptions, including those images inherited from the decade after 1896. More or less recent interpretive strategies determine what we are capable of discovering in those texts which we now feel worthy of study. In addition to revisionist histori- ographies, historical-sociological literary critical schools affect our read- ings: feminism, African American and other ethnic studies, increasingly analytical approaches to popular culture. All these approaches have grad- ually developed methodologies which have, in turn, been modified by the conclusions of a poststructuralism which has made possible a new historicism broad enough to include consideration of phenomena of tex- tuality and the intertextuality of the novel and history, history and his- tory, the novel and the novel. This project of cultural studies is aptly summarized by Vincent B. Leitch:

To begin with, the combined effect of feminist, ethnic, and leftist criticism was to force recognition that literary texts were fundamentally documents and social events, having sociohistorical referents. Second, the projects of structuralism and semiotics demonstrated that texts were shaped by social codes, conventions, and representations, which rendered defunct the idea of literary autonomy. And, third, the rise in importance of the mass media and popular culture over the cen- trality of the literary classics compelled critics to admit the crucial formative and educational roles played by these new discourses. (404)

Although in these ways definitive, present paradigms—as is usual in our historical/critical commentaries—nonetheless remain unspoken. We simply take for granted that a book like *Rereading the Revolution* is really "about" the time of its own writing as well as the times of its sub- ject and the subject of its subject.

Arriving at a sensible and revelatory organizational scheme in pre- senting these historical novels posed a challenge. What could be learned from treating them in the chronological order of their Revolutionary War subjects? In the order of what modern historians consider pivotal moments in the struggle, thereby perhaps emphasizing the centrality of General Burgoyne's surrender at Saratoga and the combined American and French attack upon Yorktown? Could the books be placed in sepa- rate groupings as responses to what are now viewed as British colonial policies like the enforcement of the Navigation Acts or the regulation of western expansion (see E. James Ferguson 125, 180)? Should they simply be taken up in the order of their publication dates, even though all the novels appeared in the span of ten short years? (This would concentrate thirty-five of the forty-eight novels in the period from 1897 until 1902 and six in each of the peak years.)

It has finally seemed least fallacious, least imposing of eighteenth- or twentieth-century paradigms, to figure a regional component into the turn-of-the-century genre, "our literary decentralization" mentioned at the time by Howells in *Criticism and Fiction* (Lauter 2: 531). (Some of the novels have a range of settings or are set partly at sea.) Revolutionary War and prewar activities themselves were, in fact, localized in some instances, and squabbles of local vested interests among the colonies are often noted by historians. Within the resulting units, each of comparable length, I have retained a chronological order by author. As George Dekker has written in *The American Historical Romance,* "regionalism and the historical romance tend to go together" and "in the historical romance regional fiction achieves the heroic and historical dimensions of epic" (100, 108). More recently, Eric J. Sundquist has it that, "as a literature of memory, local color often has elements of the historical novel" (Elliott 508). Although the vogue of local color writing had begun to wane by 1890, regional fiction still implicitly asserted, if it for the most part had rendered innocuous, real sectional differences in traditions and interests which had been brought to a head in the Civil War. Howard Mumford Jones devotes an entire chapter of *The Age of Energy: Varieties of American Experience, 1865-1915* to regional definition and difference, noting that, "although the half-century moved toward nationalism and uniformity, that movement was continually slowed or checked by tensions among various regions and bickering segments of the American people" (49). Antiquarian and regional impulses coalesced in the local color movement; "its tendency," to Benjamin T. Spencer, had been "to insulate literature from the dominant social currents of the national life" (235). In large part, a nostalgically recaptured past would be a regional past for an era of new and powerful homogenizing tendencies of communication, transportation, and attendant effects of an urbanization foreign to those of the old American provinces. The rural seemed to be going under to an urban whose advanced artists issued notions of realism. Intuitively, we react to "urban local color story" as a contradiction in terms for the late nineteenth century. Certainly, we view Hamlin Garland's Midwestern realism and H. B. Fuller's use of the city as new directions in American regionalism. In these historical novels the Revolution is generally melodramatized with a great specificity of place in a time more thoroughly rural than their present. They thus fulfill at once "a need for space and a sense of the past," motives which, according to Jack Salzman, "dominated the popular imagination at the turn of the century" (Elliott 566). Noting the local in these chauvinistic romances allows us, at least, to perceive one more major strand in American literature written three decades after the national reunion perhaps only superficially signalized by the end of the Civil War. Even the much-desired Great American Novel, noted Edward Eggleston and others, could appear only in sections by separate authors dealing with their separate sections of America.

Revolutionary War novels of this period have provoked surprisingly little critical discussion. Even Herbert F. Smith's *The Popular American Novel: 1865-1920,* for example, scarcely mentions historical fiction and cites no American Revolutionary War titles. Most serious exegesis has come by way of adjunct to treatments of "greater" books by the few canonized authors like Sarah Orne Jewett. Yet the vogue was immense, a measure itself of significance to a culture. Lowbrow and highbrow writers alike responded, and responded in similar fashion, to the impulse to memorialize the Revolution. On the model of genetics, the author becomes the gen(r)e's way of propagating and perpetuating itself. Although anticipated by novels like Harold Frederic's *In the Valley* (1890) and followed by the sequels of Robert W. Chambers, the preponderance of American Revolutionary War novels of this era falls between 1896 and 1906. I have avoided those many books which were advertised as juvenile fiction, though I have retained the trilogy of "girls' novels" by Amy Blanchard for other reasons and to illustrate that, apart from scant obvious treatment of adult love, the juvenile books share much with the adult fiction. I have also, partly in an attempt to make a large subject manageable, not addressed self-declared biographies of notables like John Paul Jones and George Washington (though, again, in their operative effects fiction and fact merge in the reality of presentation, and a definitive line between the two is impossible to draw).[11] Determination of the difference between biography and novel has been based upon whether a significant fictional plot functioned independently from the details of the historical figure's life as they were understood at the turn of the century. To communicate something of the very tenor and tone of these books, their actual uses of language as well as their paraphrasable subject matter, I make substantial use of direct quotation, particularly since most of these novels have never been reprinted and remain nearly unavailable. Plot summary, also, serves to clarify how the times made sense of the subject. The discussions of specific texts are not intended as mere footnotes, but rather as stagings of unique thought and nuance as well as reinforcement for previous arguments. In allowing the novels to speak for themselves, as it were, both individually and as embodiments of a formula, I hope to make my representation carry the force of presentation, while in candor acknowledging our earlier point that every presentation *is* a re-presentation, just as every reading is a rereading.

The landing of the
British troops in Boston
After Paul Revere's print

Chas. Edw. Hooper, illustration for Allen French, *The Colonials* (New York: Doubleday, Page, 1902), p. [161]; see pp. 53-60 below.

NEW ENGLAND

New England's name itself seems to signal a dependence, or, at least, an independence defined historically in terms of difference from an Old England from which had come characteristic regional institutions like the Puritanism of the founders. Yet the old stock had proven capable of radical innovation in its intellectual life, "movements" as well as "establishments," to employ Emerson's terms. It is fitting, then, that these New England novels possess a patina of the old-fangled in keeping with the aura of remembrance evoked through portrayals of maiden aunts in the contemporary local color tales of Mary E. Wilkins Freeman, Rose Terry Cooke, and Sarah Orne Jewett. Fitting, also, that one of these books, John W. DeForest's *A Lover's Revolt*, is as anomalous as any discussed in this volume, provocative in its atypicality. The happenstance of DeForest's book being chronologically earliest is propitious in that it allows an initial glimpse at the possibilities of the genre and at the same time proves how much of a piece most of the other books are, how potent, in other words, the force of a literary convention which overrode distinctions between highbrow and lowbrow.

Not that social challenges to the colonial establishment were unknown even at the time of the Revolution. If, for example, turn-of-the-century female and African-American characters are typically subjugated in fiction, their real-life counterparts in the eighteenth century sometimes voiced their complaints, linguistically if not actually empowered by the rhetoric and ideology of the oppressor. In an epistolary set-to with John on March 31, 1776, Abigail Adams, for example, likened male tyranny to foreign domination: "If perticuliar care and attention is not paid to the Ladies we are determined to foment a Rebelion, and will not hold ourselves bound by any Laws in which we have no voice, or Representation" (Lauter 1: 930). Without representation, exploitation would seem especially taxing. The advanced guard of 1900 continued the rebellion in better organized, more coherent and conspicuous movements. "From the 1890s, then," summarizes Cecelia Tichi, "the new woman had a recognizable identity, one derived largely from the rational, analytical demystification of the 'fair sex'" (Elliott 591). That latter-day daughter of New England, Charlotte Perkins Gilman, was in the 1898 *Women and Economics* to spell out a program for women's social, political, and economic liberation, and by 1915 to imagine a utopia altogether without men.

27

The "muscular Christianity" of 1900, though, equated Anglo-Saxonism and *Mani*fest Destiny with the aggressively male as well as the white (just as women's rights had been linked earlier with abolitionism and many led in both causes). This is the retrograde agenda in the preponderance of the Revolutionary War novels. But in 1777 itself, seven years after the death of Crispus Attucks in the Boston Massacre, nearly a year after the Declaration of Independence, the African-American Prince Hall drew explicit parallels in petitioning for freedom and for his destiny: "They can not but express their astonishment, that it has never been considered, that every principle from which America has acted in the course of her unhappy difficulties with Great-Britain pleads stronger than a thousand arguments in favor of your [African-American] Petitioners" (Lauter 1: 687). Other turn-of-the-century instances of these national hypocrisies will be cited in due course. In the midst of obvious social agitation one hundred and twenty years after the Bostonians Adams and Hall, how much greater must seem a studied avoidance of these social and political issues, so great that the choice of this formulaic genre itself signals an avoidance.

*   *   *

The novel which presents the general pattern of these novels in the most stark and symbolic—almost psychosexual—terms is John W. DeForest's *A Lover's Revolt* (1898). The title indicates its approach. It is not quite true that "the military tactics of the Battle of Bunker Hill seem to interest him [DeForest] more than his tale of lovers divided by war" (Haight xx), but rather that the romantic tale seems to disappear because it embodies the issues of battle. DeForest's much earlier quasi-realistic treatment of the Civil War—*Miss Ravenel's Conversion from Secession to Loyalty* (1867)—is here replaced by romantic and patriotic images meant to revive American feeling for an assured and national ideal depicted in terms of the Revolution but relevant to the country reunited after the Civil War. *A Lover's Revolt* describes a period of British occupation of Boston, includes the battles at Lexington, Concord, and Bunker Hill, and ends with Howe's withdrawal and the insanity and death of the young "heroine." The impressionable Huldah Oakbridge goes too far the way of the British ever to return; rape rather than marriage becomes the correct metaphor to describe her characteristic predicament. She is taken outside—and takes herself outside—permissible "national" limits.

Thomas Paine's rhetoric of hysteria is reborn. (In the 1776 "Common Sense"—though the appeal here was to emotion rather than common sense—Paine had expressed fears that the children in American homes housing British troops might be uncertain of their fathers.) When the British Captain Moorcastle (note the name) forces a kiss on Huldah, her resistance is "the faint struggle of a colonial against English domination" (22). In her very passivity she is partially responsible for the tragic outcome. At ease with American men, she feels like a child with Moorcastle. Too much impressed by a title or a uniform, she outrages her "puritan" relatives by declaring that she intends to join the established Church of England. She recovers from an illness she contracts as a nurse only to wander off confusedly in search of Moorcastle—and drowns. She had been heard muttering that Moorcastle, predictably a gay deceiver, was her husband, even though she had just accepted the proposal of a Lieutenant Eastwold (again, the name suggests Old England). Moorcastle had already sailed back to England.

When, in his pursuit of pleasure, the pompous and condescending Moorcastle first seemed successful with Huldah, Asahel ("Ash") Farnlee, the young American protagonist, had quickly withdrawn from competing for her. Uncompromising rather than cowardly, he thereafter goes his own independent patriot way, not interacting to any significant degree with either Huldah or Moorcastle. Eager to be offended, as it were, he feels his manhood and self-respect threatened and considers his not—as does his father—a legal or political revolt but rather a social one. The obviously insecure Farnlee rebels against being belittled by the proud British. Whenever Americans are considered insignificant, as when Moorcastle forgets his name, Ash instantly has a psychologically compelling reaction which results in his becoming a stern and pitiless partisan. He rejects both "British domination and provincial sycophancy" (174). The mercy he shows Moorcastle early in the novel is not characteristic; by the final chapter he rides away in anger from Huldah, coldly ignoring her helpless condition as though femaleness itself were an affront to his manhood (to the degree that yielding, stereotypically associated with women, becomes the American vice). We are told that Ash's heart had gone to George Washington ("an incarnation of nationality"), "gone beyond the reach of woman" (278). National virtue has become so embodied in a (male) figure from history that DeForest is taken quite outside the bounds of the expected course of fiction in which a new if not novel dispensation toward history is embodied by the terms of marriage of fictional hero and heroine. Here the mythology of men bonding in American nature (cf. Cooper, Melville, and Twain) again finds expression.

In DeForest's radical scheme the American woman is victimized by the British but is exiled altogether from a (male) American world. This definition of nationality seems particularly parochial, defensive and irresponsible, in 1898, when the "woman question" received wide publicity and women were making conspicuous gains in public life. Wyoming had just become the first women's suffrage state in 1890 and the push for the ratification of the Nineteenth Amendment to the national Constitution was well under way. For male writers to flee to the Revolution was to flee sometimes intractable women, but also to seize an opportunity to belittle women as too tractable and therefore constitutionally colonial. Theodore Roosevelt became the image of both American leadership and the manly; even the most assertive women were still not men. In DeForest's novel, manhood has taken on its narrow, prototypically American meaning:

In short, there was no longer any question of divine right; not even much interest in the question of British rights for Americans; but a burning interest in the question of equal manhood. The faction of Uncle Fenn was practically dead; the faction of old Squire Farnlee was mortally ill; the faction of young Ash Farnlee prevailed. (277)

The bootlicking Uncle Timothy Fenn had always believed that everything English was sacred. He dies, "like an empire in convulsions," as the American forces enter the city. That death disables meaningful participation in the present: "The Oakbridges were so busy with the poor old Tory body of death that they missed seeing Major Asahel Farnlee ride past on the staff of His Excellency, his black eyes sparkling and his dark aquiline face flushed with triumph, an incarnation of the coming republic" (416). As if this were not enough, DeForest adds a one-page sequel, enjoining us to make the Revolution meaningful by continuing to insist on a social and cultural independence. The author has pursued his theme so far that he has broken the constraints and conventions of historical fiction itself, and in the end resorts to overt nonfictional commentary upon present history. A title as complete as that of *Miss Ravenel's Conversion from Secession to Loyalty* might read *A Lover's Revolt from Subservience to Aggression*. Huldah Oakbridge is victimized by the British/aggressive and never converted to the American/aggressive, and the hero revolts from love itself. Lovers give themselves, and conventionally give themselves to women. But aggressiveness was key to a contemporary American imperialism which could be viewed as an appropriate carrying onward not only of eighteenth-century British colonialism but also of Victorian British imperialism. (DeForest did not pursue the complicating thought that in conventional fiction "loving" a man, in this case Farnlee's "loving" George Washington, perhaps put his protagonist in the role of a woman, a role to many in his audience weak and aberrant.) James F. Light is right in asserting that the tale insists that love is possible only among equals (171); the statement need only be qualified with the addendum that heterosexual love is rejected as intrinsically a pairing of unequals.

Women writers also struggled to understand and fictionally embody issues of the Revolution which had come to them, though neither they nor any other of the male writers quite violated conventions to the extent of DeForest. The hero of Mary Imlay Taylor's *A Yankee Volunteer* (1898) is a Massachusetts man who volunteers, but hardly a volunteer to an altogether partisan or unique Yankee faith. The spirit which motivates John Allen places him somewhere between the egalitarian American and the aristocratic British, even though he early on becomes a Continental soldier. (To validate his tradition and to give it a "factual" justification, the narrative purports to be the journal of the present namesake's great-grandfather.) Allen's engagement in the military provokes the domineering and aggressive Tory Sir Anthony Talbot to break off Allen's engagement to his equally Anglophile daughter, Joyce. The question of whether John and Joyce will marry furnishes whatever suspense the plot possesses. Who will change? Will John's career in the adventure plot take him emotionally or intellectually away from an unreconstructed Joyce too far for him to be reintegrated into the love plot? Major complications arise with the appearance of an all-too-appropriate other possible mate for John, and an upper-class British soldier for Joyce. Who will marry whom? The answers to these questions illustrate the value system and popular literary conventions which inform novels of this type.

When John Allen departs for the American Congress meeting at Philadelphia, where he will serve as clerk for his reserved and dignified magistrate father, he leaves behind a Joyce Talbot who already believes that he is a traitor to his king and may therefore be a traitor to her. She will now be often in the company of her brother—himself a British soldier—and the gentlemanly British subaltern Francis Beresford. The troublous journey to Philadelphia includes a brief stay at Boston's Old South Meetinghouse, where Judge Allen and John see notables Dr. Warren and Samuel Adams and where they join forces with the redoubtable rough-hewn crafty veteran Ephraim Minot, who serves as the unassuming common American in this book. Soon, back in Massachusetts, the provincial Congress calls upon young Allen to head a regiment, a rustic motley crew drilled by Minot to give them the discipline necessary in what Judge Allen considers the most bitter of all wars—a civil war. On separate occasions Dick Talbot and Sir Anthony, Joyce's brother and father, excoriate John for what they believe to be his intransigence and traitorous behavior, and challenge him to duels, neither of which eventuates. Allen becomes an examiner of passes and persons as Tories—including the Talbots—pour into Boston and patriots flee the occupied city. General Gage declares martial law in Boston and clemency for rebels who lay down their arms; American forces invest Bunker and Breed's Hills. During the famous British cannonading and charging of the hills the patriots hold their redoubts for a time but soon retreat. Minot providentially saves Allen from a bayonet, Charlestown burns, and Washington arrives to take command of a now more experienced and disciplined force.

John's commitment to the cause and to military protocol is tested when Minot captures Dick Talbot. Dick's oft-mentioned facial resemblance to Joyce makes him her proxy and creates for John, even in her absence and despite his dislike for her brother, a troubled conflict between love and duty. Prescribed punishment usually would be death for a soldier taken when not in uniform, hence considered a spy. The narrative has gone out of its way to emphasize this theme common in "war novels." Allen opts for duty but is relieved of an unpleasant dilemma by Ephraim, who has already released Dick to British lines because he knew John really did not want to harm him. Still sensitive to the demands of honor, John confesses his non-deed to Washington, covering for Minot since the underling had acted in his behalf. Circumstance again saves Allen when General Putnam brings word that the American authorities have learned of Minot's role in the episode. This fact, along with the Allen family's reputation for honor and John's apparent good intentions, leads Washington to allow him to return to the American lines, though not yet to active duty. The stern general has nonetheless noticeably cooled toward his sometime escort. Deus ex machina in the persons of Minot and Putnam cannot mitigate the force and consequences of Allen's having responded to the requirements of the love plot in freeing Richard Talbot; Allen cannot hereafter altogether align himself with the embodiment of American martial spirit, although he is promoted to captain after saving a young soldier's life (his finally becoming a major puts him on a level more nearly commensurate with that of Joyce—more a marital than a martial consideration).

Joyce, on the other hand, still considers Allen a traitor to the *British* cause even as she begins to speak of herself as one so base as to love a rebel. When the Continental army retakes Nook's Hill and Boston, John escorts the Talbots to their Marblehead home, protecting the family from hostile patriots. (Equally despicable and rowdy rabble of the king's army have already looted their Boston home. Later, Allen's characteristic gentleman's view is again provoked, and he ridicules a disorderly camp of "soldiers and others of the lower classes" [315].) The colonists seem to be losing their tolerance for a king who, with his ministers, has subverted the rights of the British as well. When Sir Anthony dies, buried by patriots, Dick Talbot automatically becomes "Sir Richard." Following the Allens' discovery that the Talbot women have removed to Halifax with Richard's army, John's father remarks that when a woman loses her "tyrant" she usually cannot rest until she finds a new one. Undisciplined lower orders of any stripe or nation are scorned; women in particular are viewed as needing to depend upon (male) figures of authority though they may have their brief flings of democratic independence: their careers in life and love will be determined by their "natural" acceptance of having, socially and politically, second-class status in a hierarchical society—and acceptance of being in a romantic costume romance.

Allen receives orders to join his regiment in New York, where he meets the "gentle and tender" (248) Dorothy Wayne, a distant cousin reared by Quakers, old-fashioned and a patriot. (Of Puritan ancestry, John is to that extent also outside the mainstream of the Church of England, thus in a retrograde view perhaps in "need" of reconciliation with the normative tradition of the mother country.) Minot and John get wind of British bribery and conspiracies even before the British fleet itself arrives from Halifax and the bloody battle on Long Island is fought. The fighting and troop movements are described in as much detail as nature was earlier in the novel. Allen falls, unconscious, of bullet and bayonet wounds, and later awakens to find himself recovering in New York, tended by Dorothy. She tells him that the Americans have lost Long Island but were able under cover of fog to fall back to the city. Dorothy continues to inform John of military affairs and to take care of him, growing atypically spirited in her talk of the patriot cause and disconcerted by John's talk of Joyce Talbot. Before the Continentals retreat further to Harlem Heights and British ships attack up the Hudson, Allen is removed to King's Bridge.

When a nearly recovered John receives word from a self-effacing Dorothy that the Talbots are in New York, he and Minot scheme to visit Joyce. Rowing with muffled oars and avoiding the British authorities, Allen arrives at her home just in time to overhear Beresford proposing to her and belittling him. When John reveals himself, the men exchange words but not blows, Beresford promising not to stoop to the office of informing against a man who is not there in a military capacity. The lovers also quarrel, each jealous of the other (Joyce has met Dorothy). They reconcile, however, before Dick Talbot and another soldier appear. Allen avoids further trouble because the hot-tempered and changeable

Talbot, offended at being ordered to do something so beneath his dignity as to be a spy—and perhaps finding some logic in his new cause—deserts to the Americans.

John fares no better than the Americans, who withdraw from Forts Washington and Lee, when his reconnaissance mission ends with his being taken prisoner and interrogated by Cornwallis. General Howe offers John a bribe in return for his disclosing Yankee positions and strength. His refusal to take the bribe results in his being placed in solitary confinement, living conditions not so foul as those of most American prisoners held in New York. (Dorothy, whose grandparents had once befriended Howe's brother, has intervened in John's behalf.) As John's "good angel" she now selflessly promises to bring Joyce to the prison. Beresford has unfortunately been placed in charge of the prison, but does allow an interview between John and Joyce. Although she still considers Dick a turncoat and is told by John not to jeopardize her position for his (John's) sake, Joyce remains silent when Ephraim Minot, disguised in a British uniform, furnishes John with a red coat and escapes with him to a boat and Hoboken. They find that conditions have not improved for the American forces, suffering and dispirited, who fall back through the Jerseys. Brighter days are finally signaled by Washington's heroically leading the army across the Delaware to defeat the Hessians at Trenton and by Minot's and Allen's being rewarded with promotions.

The title of the book's last chapter indicates just how thoroughly and unconsciously novelists like Mary Taylor accepted archaic social/political views and popular literary formulas. Dorothy designs the denouement of "A Royalist Surrenders" by arranging for the Talbot women to pretend to be her attendants at the home of friends of her parents near the battlefield where Dick and John oppose the British. Joyce and John are brought together by an unbelievably forgiving Dorothy, a Dorothy whose love for Allen is not really secret but who has turned pander. The lovers are to wed in the Philadelphia of the Declaration of Independence and, apparently, to forget Dorothy. The logic of John's marrying the more truly American girl goes by the boards, defeated by the constraints of romance and nostalgia for the mother country. The sincerity of John's earlier praise for the patriots' singleness of purpose and his damning the Tories as worse than the British seems obviated by his act of marriage. In fact, Allen's previously becoming a "determined Whig" (65) resulted from his feeling rejected by Joyce; being accepted makes him consequently and considerably less a patriot. She had told him that he would join her and the Tories if he really loved her. Nothing has changed, yet John does join her—and Joyce now announces that she has become a rebel, too, for the love of him. Fantasies of love preempt liberal ideology. The narrative grows ever more unconvincing and inconsistent. In her natural simplicity, in her not becoming a stereotypical romantic heroine, despite (actually because of) her representative "American" qualities, Dorothy must be discarded. Only a marriage with Joyce Talbot can mark a reconciliation with England; only a marriage of star-crossed lovers can make melodrama of drama. Not only a royalist but also a Yankee has surrendered.

That Ellen Olney Kirk's *A Revolutionary Love-Story* (1898) departs from the usual narrative pattern of these texts is attributable more to its following an alternative convention than to its being truly original. This tender tale turns tragic after misunderstanding and coincidence in the lives of the fated lovers. The jealous and Iago-like villain's machinations stem from personal considerations which bear little organic relationship to the Revolution and, indeed, the apparently anomalous denouement comes well after the close of the war. The initial situation seems much like that in other books of its kind; the ending strikes one as the arbitrary, if standard, conclusion to a sentimental and unhappy romance. Whereas a certain English narrative tradition feeds into and reinforces a broader gesture of social and political compromise with the "mother country" here as in most of these novels, in this case the fictional outcomes on first reading appear to defeat the notion of embracing a conservative Anglo-American ideal. But even if the book does not culminate in the "right" marriage, the usual mode of asserting the birth of a new American family which nonetheless encompasses the old, in many other ways the novel does suggest the dual, Old and New World vision.

A Revolutionary Love-Story is set in a New England town with an Old England name: Saintford-on-the-Sound. The lovely, young, richly attired Cicely Farrington has two brothers and a father, John James Farrington—called "the squire"—who "wore an air of exile" and, as a local wag puts it, was "born three thousand miles from his native land" (7). After "more than a century in the Connecticut colony, the family had retained not only the traditions of high life in England" but, on a reduced scale, "many of its forms" as well (6). The patriot hero himself, Sidney Marrable, voices a standard sentiment that equates personal chivalry with political aristocracy: "Though I don't believe in kings, you are my princess, my queen" (53). The incipient Romeo and Juliet plot can be scrapped after British soldiers rough up the Reverend Dr. Daggett, ex-president of Yale and kinsman of the Farringtons, and pillage the Connecticut coast. Even "Squire" Farrington is convinced that England is now the enemy, capable of the same "gross licence" (31) of which he had earlier found only the rebels guilty. No longer torn between Sidney (patriotic fervor) and her father (Toryism), Cicely's dilemma ends and her fate appears a foregone conclusion. (In reality she and Sidney had in any case already come to a mutual romantic understanding.) She discovers (American) self-sufficiency and the virtues of work during the hard times of the Revolution, when her father's failing health dictates that she must supervise the farming, spinning, and weaving. Although Cicely does not wear the simple "patriotic homespun" (3) urged by the Continental Congress, she does make do with her mother's old, albeit once fashionable, clothes; she inherits an English love of tea, but she now makes an American version from local herbs. Cicely's experiences have made her, if not an American heroine, certainly the Anglo-American heroine meant for a Sidney Marrable, who is at once an enterprising democrat and a courteous, gentlemanly soldier.

The logic of the book's plot is rather arbitrarily defeated by happenstance and by the schemes of cousins of Cicely and Sidney. The slightly crippled Morris Marshall, a relative of the deceased Mrs. Farrington, envies both Marrable's success with Cicely and his physical grace. A brevet major though noncombatant, Marshall spends his time working to thwart the military plans of the British and the personal plans of Marrable. In both public and private life Marshall appears to live by his notion that the truly American (if nineteenth-century, anarchic, Western, and manifest destinarian) impulse is "for freedom, for room to expand each at his own need and in his own way" (30). Marshall's own need leads him to use his home-front jobs as messenger and head of a committee of safety to court Cicely. He lurks in the shadows during a nocturnal tryst of Cicely and Sidney, later promising Cicely to tell no one but secretly hoping that Sidney will die in the war. Marshall prevents another meeting of the two and fails to pass along an oral message meant for Cicely (she happens to be absent, tending her ill father). He then steals a letter which Cicely had sent to Marrable, a letter apparently incriminating and imprudent because of its too-frank avowal of love. This stolen letter is delivered to Cicely's pretty young rival, Sidney's cousin Ruth Gentry, who all the while has been promoting her own chances with Sidney. His valor at Valley Forge, wound sustained at Princeton, and leadership displayed at Stoney Point enable Sidney to become a member of General Washington's staff, a captain, and finally a lieutenant-colonel. His success with Cicely has, however, fallen victim to misunderstandings resulting from wartime separation, bad luck, and miscarried or intercepted messages.

After the war ends Cicely's brother James marries in England, and New England gossip—never borne out—has it that there Cicely also will

marry one of "their titled relations" (131). (The American/British coun-
terpoise in the Farrington family is maintained, however, because the
other brother, Bicknell, a patriot soldier, had been mortally wounded.)
Cicely returns from England to find Sidney already married to Ruth
Gentry, whom Cicely has been led to believe he actually loves. The
pathetic remainder of Cicely's life is summarized in a very few pages.
Increasingly frail, she continues to spurn the older Morris Marshall
despite his gaining "fresh wealth and greater honors" (131). (His prosperity in spite of—or because of?—his American amorality perhaps
serves as a commentary on the Gilded Age.) After her father dies and
James's family returns to Connecticut, she becomes a "dependent sister
and maiden aunt" (132), skilled at handicrafts. When Cicely is thirty-six,
Sidney, now a successful government official, discovers Marshall's and
his own wife's earlier treachery and insists that Cicely has always been
the one woman in his life, a life ruined by others' sins. But forms are
maintained in a joyless stoicism which anticipates the New England
dreariness of Edith Wharton's *Ethan Frome* (1911). The sickly and selfless Cicely fashions an ornate christening gown for Sidney and Ruth's
next child, requesting also that it be named for her if it is a girl. It's a
boy: "Thus Cicely's last wish, like many another that had lain near her
heart, never came to pass" (137-38). Even before the son is born, Cicely
dies from a melodramatically fatal illness contracted on that "treacher-
ous spring day" (137) when she had delivered the gown.

The only sense in which this love story is in the end revolutionary
stems from its not being a tale of successful love at all. It does not revolt
from convention: touching tragedy, syrupy sentiment, and preposterous
pathos represent a norm in popular fiction. Events seem arbitrary and
unmotivated because of secret subterfuges. Neither is the book especially Revolutionary, since its culminating scenes follow the War for
Independence and bear little intrinsic relationship to it. Marrable had
joined the staff of George Washington and his Farrington "princess"
learned an Americanness during the war, but their polemic significance
is diluted in the loss of a marriage which would symbolize the constituting of a new—but notably still Anglo-American—New England.

Among the books by the prolific Amy Ella Blanchard are several
romances based on various episodes in American history, including three
on the Revolution. Blanchard was generally considered a girls' novelist,
and these novels do clearly stress polite and moral behavior, Christianity,
and a simply interpreted American patriotism. In the first of the Revolutionary War books, *A Girl of '76* (1898), didactic point is made even of

clothing: plain homespun signifies a traditional American virtue, whereas silk, satin, and lace are both sign and cause of the frivolity and worldliness of the British—not to mention unmentioned Gibson girls. A girl of the eighteenth century was taught to show "reverence and respect for her elders" and experienced something "very unlike what a girl of to-day might expect from a parent" (126); not interrupting elders is "an example of politeness which it might not be so easy to find nowadays" (170). Emphasis is placed throughout on appropriate conduct for the young, and the narrative is almost preoccupied with the role of women, as though a self-conscious stand for tradition were being made in the face of the changing mores of 1898.

A Girl of '76, dedicated "to the memory of my Revolutionary sires and especially to that of the little fifer, Amos Blanchard"—significantly, to males—has few surprises in its plot and is told in a straightforward and predominantly monosyllabic style. The fact that Elizabeth ("Betsey") Hall fishes tea, left floating after the famous tea party, from the waters at Charlestown belies her actual dedication to the American cause. The thirteen-year-old lass, in this opening scene, is dutifully following the orders of her imperious and temporarily Tory grandmother. Betsey has ample chance to display her true colors in the narrative which follows. With her grandmother she tricks some British soldiers into not stealing the Halls' ox; she helps hold up a Tory courier for a possibly important dispatch. Betsey later cooperates with other patriot girls in preventing some British sailors from repairing their ship. When her Tory nemesis finds her in possession of a letter to General Washington, she literally eats her words—the document itself. Although briefly feeling its attractiveness, Betsey shortly thereafter rejects the lifestyle of her Tory cousin and finds herself singing a solemn Yankee psalm at a glittering Tory party. Her father and her boyfriend, Amos Dwight, have meanwhile marched off to the war and undergone the requisite number of injuries and narrow escapes. Washington retakes Boston. Betsey marries Amos after having rejected a young British soldier she had earlier treated for a wound and after sending off another suitor to the war as unworthy of consideration except for his willingness to fight (he is immediately killed). Aunt Pamela Porter, who has lost her husband in the war and unofficially adopted Amos, gives her home to the newlyweds and arranges for Betsey's father, Stephen Hall, to establish himself in his new East India trade business and to hire Amos.

The particular methods Betsey employs in her youthful military and "political" exploits illustrate the book's simultaneous (and confused) concern with the issues of age, gender, class, and sex. On the one hand, she must mature and achieve for herself and the nation the independence demanded by the plot; on the other hand she must discover her role as a woman in the establishment of a new American family (i.e., ultimately, dependence). Betsey's declaration to her mother that she wants "to be a little girl as long as you think best" (249) is immediately balanced by the Declaration of Independence ("Britain's offspring is child no longer" [253]) and by a marriage which marks the end of girlhood but not the beginning of independence.

She asserts herself as a "man," but assertiveness itself is portrayed as a male trait which must be abandoned by one who becomes a woman, a wife. Her independent action achieves dependence. "Oh, to be a man!" (46) she sighs, and longs for the chance to fight the redcoats or to be a fifer. Even Amos wishes at one point to dress the fifteen-year-old Betsey as a boy and take her with him to war. She had in fact already been a transvestite in order to confiscate the Tory message. (In a sense her search is for the proper clothes—neither ostentatious women's garb nor men's dress.) She frightened away the would-be ox thieves by impersonating an entire patriot platoon by playing the fife, unseen by the Tory wrongdoers. The unconscious male sexual symbolism appears even more parodic in the scene when Betsey and other American girls prove themselves worthy and equal opponents of the British by exploding a favorite tree because the enemy sailors were planning to make a ship's mast of it! (The girls of '76 and Amy Blanchard were nothing if not naive.) Personal dependence, however, becomes a precondition for national independence, and one cannot remain a man forever. Finally, we are left with an image of the woman making clothes for the man. Amos is preparing to return to war and, in what is intended as a tender and touching episode, Betsey knits socks for him: "And she handed the stockings to him, hoping he would not notice two wet spots upon the gray yarn" (159)—tears at the prospect of his departure, but also tears of happiness and contentment. Blanchard's tone precludes the subversive possibility that her now-married protagonist still desires to engage the enemy; she wants only to oppose the enemy by marrying and supporting a man who in turn engages the enemy.

Known primarily as a late nineteenth-century Vermont regionalist, Rowland Evans Robinson wrote two short novels which belong to the present category: *A Hero of Ticonderoga* (1898) and *A Danvis Pioneer* (1900). Each of these books is less than a hundred pages in the reprint edition and each is a local color treatment, with large doses of dialect, of pioneering, hunting, and farming in early upper New England. The Revolution figures only briefly and incidentally as an—albeit important—event in the larger story of the settling of the region and the formation of a regional lore and character.

Despite its title, only the final twenty pages of *A Hero of Ticonderoga* describe Revolutionary War goings-on. Nathan Beeman becomes a hero only at the conclusion of a tale of frontier life near Fort Ticonderoga. Nathan's father, Seth, had homesteaded in the area under a grant from the province of New Hampshire which is soon contested by a claimant to the same land who holds title under the authority of New York. Ethan Allen's Green Mountain Boys oust the "Yorker" but, after the accidental death of Seth, this claimant's morose brother works for a period as a hired hand and eventually exacts his revenge by managing to become Nathan's new father. This stepfather chops down a huge tree in which Nathan is perched, thinking he has thereby eliminated his hostile son, but Nathan escapes and moves in with Job Carpenter, an old woodsman and veteran of the French and Indian Wars. At novel's end a forgiving Nathan returns home to help his mother care for the now-pathetic stepfather, Silas "Toombs" (really Graves), who is suffering from terminal palsy.

Rumors of war have been heard only intermittently until after Nathan's leaving home (in a chapter called "Rebellion"), when the protagonist's personal situation becomes more and more obviously an image of a national war for independence. The nation as a whole is sometimes the protagonist in these maturation tales. Enlisted in Ethan Allen's militia, Nathan "felt himself suddenly leaping to manhood" (272). Silas Toombs is, it goes without saying, the sole suspected Tory for miles around. "'Yorkers,'" as Job has it, are in any case "next to Reg'lars for toppin ways" (244). Nathan, who as a boy had often visited Fort Ticonderoga, joins the flotilla commanded by a sometimes bickering Ethan Allen and Benedict Arnold and is able to lead the Americans into the fort to a bloodless victory. This exploit gains Nathan more fame than his later participation at the loss at Hubbardton and the win at Bennington.

The usual conciliatory gesture to Britain is communicated in Nathan's boyhood enjoyment of touring the fort and, especially, of seeing the well-mannered and beautiful wife of Captain William Delaplace, its commander. Mrs. Delaplace seems to Nathan instinct with romance (love and a glamour of position, power, and polish). She gives Nathan a coin and maintains to her husband that the Yankees are "like our own people," "they surely show close kinship with us," whereas Captain Delaplace feels "they are a turbulent, upstart breed" (237), "bold and self-reliant, and impatient of control" (238). (We had just been informed that helpfulness and self-reliance were necessary virtues on the frontier.) The dual heritage, English and American, is preserved and passed along to later generations, to the present owner of the farmhouse which stands on the site of the Beeman's log cabin. In the novel's last words:

Within the house, upon a pair of massive moose horns, rests the old flintlock once filled with beans, "good enough for Yorkers," and later loaded with a leaden death message for Tory and Hessian. Cherished with as fond pride by its fair possessor, is a worn pocket-piece—the silver shilling given her ancestor by the beautiful lady of Fort Ticonderoga. (287)

Not the final chapters, but the middle ones of *A Danvis Pioneer: A Story of One of Ethan Allen's Green Mountain Boys* (1900) contain episodes set during the Revolutionary War. Although Robinson seeks to validate the historical worth of the fictional protagonist's career by connecting to history in the novel's subtitle, actually the wartime scenes constitute less than half of an already short book. And the Revolution does not function greatly as motive for a main character who claims he goes to war more for adventure and love of action than out of patriotism. Otherwise, Robinson goes over much the same ground of landscape and event here as he had in *A Hero of Ticonderoga*.

This time it is Josiah Hill who is on his way to the frontier to stake a claim, only to find he has been given a false deed by an unscrupulous lawyer and his land has been claimed by others under a New York grant. The lawyer, Anthony Capron, marries Hill's promised bride back in Connecticut and Hill continues as a hunter and trapper with the woodsman and veteran Kenelm Dalrymple. Hill joins the Green Mountain Boys shortly before the surrender of Ticonderoga and accompanies Ethan Allen to Montreal, from where he must soon after rejoin his regiment. His further adventures find Hill serving as scout on Lake Champlain, being captured by Indians and immediately thereafter freed, and befriending American military men. One dying soldier at the Battle of Hubbardton, Torrey, enjoins Josiah to take care of his family, not knowing that his wife has already been killed by Indians. But Hill does find the remainder of Torrey's family and soon marries the daughter, Ruby. Three characters from earlier in the book too coincidentally reappear, including Anthony Capron, who turns up among a group of captured Tories.

After the war Josiah returns to pioneer life under a Vermont charter, and becomes a noted woodsman, marksman, and hunter as well as farmer and family man. The final chapter of *A Danvis Pioneer,* "The Apparition of Gran'ther Hill," seems really a separate and self-contained local color story and tall tale, effective in its humor and use of dialect, about how the vigorous Josiah's impossibly long life leads to premature reports of his death and his being taken for a rejuvenant or a ghost. Little is made of the ideology of the Revolution beyond comments like that of the homespun frontiersman that, although he is rightfully Sir Kenelm Dalrymple of Dalrymple, he prefers the "tol'able free life" (66) he has as an American. Josiah Hill has quite inadvertently achieved the position of "patriarch of a populous town," "a founder of the Republic of the Green Mountains," noteworthy as pioneer and Green Mountain Boy. (The image may suggest the nature myth of the medieval Green Knight.) He outlives his contemporaries and arrives at such an old age that his role in the past "loomed large to his vision, and lost nothing in the telling" (117). His listeners—and Robinson's readers in 1900—had not been there; they have only Hill's inflated telling. Robinson's text thus unleashed from ascertainable verisimilitude takes the place of deeds. For a belated audience Hill's and Robinson's stories free themselves to assume the status of myth. Once again, as in the conclusion to *A Hero of Ticonderoga,* we are left with valued relics of the past in and for the present.

What may very well most strike the modern reader of *From Kingdom to Colony* (1899) is that its author can seem so oblivious to the deep contradictions in the book's themes, plot, and characterization. Mary Devereux simultaneously celebrates and protests British treatment of America and the British hero's treatment of the American heroine; Devereux's narrative is strained to a breaking point in its attempt to accommodate romantic plot and praise of all things British, on the one hand, and a democratic ideal and American independence, on the other. Although the action of *From Kingdom to Colony* takes the reader beyond the battle at Lexington and briefly projects forward to an achieved independence, the book begins with a dedication to the author's father followed by a prologue which describes the family's Old World roots. The first Devereux mentioned is a Norman nobleman honored by William the Conqueror. Next appears the 1639 Bromwich Castle household of Sir Walter Devereux, whose youngest son carried out the plan to migrate to the wilds of an America where "we shall be the head of our name in this new land,— the same as our brother Leicester here, in old England" (6). (One again recalls the desperate genealogical searches of newly founded American "patriotic" societies during the 1890s.) Marking the only meaningful difference for the family in America is the fact that the wife must work a bit, despite the presence of a faithful black servant and his Indian wife.

In a suggestion of a future opposition to England, however, the Devereuxs rout a gang of British marauders. With the family estate secured, we pass over a century and arrive at chapter 1.

The novel shifts to July of 1774 and to the Marblehead home and lands of the present patriarch, Joseph Devereux, grandson of the American immigrants, who has hung the family arms and seems to belong to the days "of his ancestors" (55). Dorothy ("Dot"), the sixteen-year-old daughter, possesses the expected combination of "high spirit, strong courage, and a pure, tender heart"; she is "impetuous, laughter-loving, and somewhat spoiled" (51). Her brother John is in love with her friend Mary Broughton, just as John's frank and stalwart friend Hugh Knollys is in love with Dot. The household is rounded out by old Aunt Lettice and Aunt Penine, both of whom have "the old-time reverence for King and Parliament" (58), and by Dot's little cousin "'Bitha." The family feels increasingly uneasy at colonial protests against the mother country's economic policies, impressing of American fishermen and quartering of British troops in American homes, and unfair representation in Parliament—political problems, which, Mary concludes, "we girls cannot rightly understand" (41). They are ready to give credence to the Indian Moll Pitcher's dire prophecies of future conflict.

Dot is drawn into these problems—and appreciates getting to do more than bake and churn—when she is assigned the duty of giving a light signal to American boats attempting to smuggle firearms and powder from Boston. (Aunt Penine meanwhile is caught eavesdropping and planning to subvert the American plan; she is eventually sent away to her brother's home.) As Dot and Mary relax in the "Sachem's Cave" just above the sea, they are confronted by a youthful British officer who falls backwards to the rocks below when forced from the cave by a hostile Mary. Dot, however (although her cave, too, has been violated—and will be again), feels a fascination and sympathy for her people's supposed enemy, tends the injured man's lacerated head, tells him her name, and discovers that his is Cornet Kyrle Southorn (a hint of a post-Civil War Cavalier myth?). Even though the responsibility of lighting the signal lanterns falls to the peddler Johnnie Strings, Dot surreptitiously dresses in her brother's clothes to participate in the nocturnal adventure. When the girls see Strings tussling with someone, Dot warns the approaching Americans of danger by seizing the lanterns and throwing them into the sea. As Johnnie flees, the disguised Dot talks to his opponent (Cornet Southorn, of course), whom she tricks into a brief captivity in a sheep-house. Her brother later declares that she has been as brave as a man. As a woman she is victimized by the British and by men—by the hero, in other words, of a romantic novel; but as a "man" she asserts herself by capturing the British, the man, the hero. Her force is finally undone by her being caught up in the ambiguous feelings about king and colony of her author, who ultimately must also make her a conventional romantic heroine—dependent and "female." Dot's father defines this British/male aspect of the equation when he says the British have been guilty of "overbearing and insolence to us as a country as well as individuals" (178). The author's naivete and confusions lie in her including—but sometimes apparently not including—women in this category of "individuals" who should therefore oppose insolence, even after we enter a more largely American world.

When Dot visits her old nurse, she is told of Moll Pitcher's statement that she is beloved by an Englishman and that the affair will create sorrow. No sooner does she start home than she is detained in the woods by Southorn, who has figured out that she it was who had locked him in the shed. He assaults her, kissing her hands and lips, declaring her his "sweet little rebel" (203). Dot slaps him, determined never to speak to him again but soon defending him to Hugh. Southorn spies on her at the wedding of John and Mary, and, during a fracas in town between the Americans and the British, he abducts her, forcing a loyalist minister at gunpoint to marry them. Dot says she detests him and feels herself a traitor, but finds herself signing the marriage register, becoming Southorn's "own little wife" (245). She immediately languishes of "brain fever" but does not faint until—and this for the first time in her life—Southorn's detachment receives orders that it must vacate Marblehead. Catastrophes multiply as Dot faints again when Southorn bids her farewell and asks her forgiveness, her father suffers a seizure after being told of Dot's plight, and Aunt Penine lies fatally ill. Before John goes off to the scene of conflict after the battle at Lexington, Dot tells him she loves Southorn but not his cause—though it would seem more sensible, considering Southorn's deeds, to embrace the British rather than the male if a wedge is to be driven between the terms "British" and "male." Feeling guilt as well as sorrow, she attends at the pathetic death of her father.

Returning from a final visit to Aunt Penine, Mary and Dot find shelter from a storm at the Gray Horse Inn, where George Washington and his staff happen to be housed. The girls are immediately struck by the charismatic Washington's "self-nobility, self-reliance," a "supreme control" of himself and thus of others (306). Washington, repeatedly said to be paternal in his reactions to Dot (thus a replacement for Joseph Devereux), writes for her a promise of aid. Dot soon uses this paper to negotiate the release of Southorn, who has been lurking nearby apparently to see her rather than to spy on the Americans. The general perceives their mutual love and releases Southorn, who now owes both life and honor to

Dot, with the proviso that he be exchanged for an American captive of the British. After Dot tells him that she has loved him from the start, Southorn recognizes her conflict between love and duty and acknowledges that he has been a brute, a brute with now only a half-hearted devotion to the British cause. John Devereux and Southorn are reconciled; Washington blesses the young couple, who are now to return to ancestral England, enjoining Dot not to forget her native land. Southorn has determined to resign his military position when he arrives in his Devonshire hills, and promises Dot that they will often visit America after the war.

All the while Hugh Knollys has been unbelievably selfless and self-effacing, true son of a mother who invests George Washington with all the power and awe others associate with King George. It is Hugh who delivers Dot to her lover, escorting her to Cambridge, from where she is to go with Southorn to England. Hugh, "utterly unmanned" (359) by Dot's preference for Southorn, nonetheless refrains from disconcerting her by declaring his love. Dot, for her part, explains to Southorn that Hugh is merely a childhood playmate for whom she has only sisterly feelings. When the crazed patriot Farmer Gilbert, believing Dot a British spy, tries to ambush her in the forest, a trailing protective if disquieted Hugh deflects his aim. Offended by any imputation against her or her family's patriotism (and however much we may see his point and remember quite a different response to the British "gentleman's" harassment), Dot slashes Gilbert with her riding whip, recalling to Hugh the "impetuous, wilful Dot of bygone days" (370). Despite his long-suffering and various manly American heroics, however, Hugh is finally so unimportant, so incidental, in the author's scheme of things, that he is expendable. He warrants only one more brief mention: he is killed in a later skirmish of the Revolution, soon followed in death by his mother. Dot never learns that he loved her. So heavy is the weight on the Anglo side of the Anglo-American formula that the unfortunate democratic American love interest does not stand a chance. "Self-nobility" divorced from power of office or Old World associations is not enough.

Moll Pitcher's predictions of doom have evidently been evaded as final arrangements are made for Southorn's being exchanged for Captain Pickett and for Southorn and Mistress Southorn to sail for England. Dot wonders aloud what he must have thought of her dressing as a man and slapping him (she is after all now an obedient wife and obsequious Anglophile). Southorn responds that her aggressiveness showed him how aggressive he would have to be in order to gain her—another instance of a woman's independent action leading, paradoxically in an American war for *independence,* to dependent status. As the ship sails away she thinks of her "old home" and realizes that she is reversing the route of her seventeenth-century ancestor Anne, who had declared to *her* husband that she would be unafraid and happy as long as she remained with him, despite going to "a new home in a strange, far-off land" (379). 'Bitha grows up to marry Southorn's nephew, over the protests of the simple Johnnie Strings. And Cornet and Dot visit Mary and John in America every summer.

Dorothy Devereux has joined the former British officer even though he was the "enemy," indirectly responsible for her father's death, and guilty of what amounted to rape. All these shortcomings are excused. "But there is another story," that of Marblehead's "fisher and sailor soldiers" (380). Having gone so far in validating a British norm, it is as if Mary Devereux must now reclaim, in a final three-page rhetorical disclaimer, legitimacy for her book as an American Revolutionary War novel. For this reason the last section of the book serves as a contrast to the prologue, which had set the action in an antiquated and aristocratic Old World context, and seems to defeat the logic of the entire earlier fictional plot. Suddenly we are presented simple commoners as models of American patriotic virtue, commoners who went on to cross the Delaware with Washington and bravely oppose the British at Trenton, becoming thereby a "hallowed memory" which should endure "down the long vista of years between their day and our own" (382). Only once earlier had reference been made to their example, "the priceless jewel of our national history for all time" (171). Freed from the burden of a European past or having to function as heroes of romantic narrative, these loyal and unassuming American folk helped to achieve independence and create a new nation. The unmentioned Hugh Knollys finally receives his due; individuals like him are allowed to be heroes of American history, but not the heroes of British history or of conventional historical fictional discourse. His worth can be asserted but not dramatized. This is why, on balance and at best, Mary Devereux can progress only from kingdom to colony, never to political or cultural nationhood.

Sarah Orne Jewett's contribution to this literature is her only post-*Country of the Pointed Firs* novel, *The Tory Lover* (1901). Larzer Ziff finds this book a relative failure, evidence that Jewett's forte did not lie in this popular formula which was nonetheless powerful enough to find in her yet another practitioner (291). Clearly, the novel lacks those elements of realism, local color, and close character study for which she is generally known (stories like "The Flight of Betsey Lane," in which the lively protagonist startles her matronly peers by taking a holiday at the Philadelphia Exposition). Even the Maine setting of much of the book is not rendered in especially loving, convincing, or detailed fashion. The opening scene at Colonel Jonathan Hamilton's estate presents the general terms, the typical pairs of historical/fictional concerns: politics and love, England and America, Tory and patriot, gentlemen and the "mob of rascals" (30), parents and children. Jewett's manipulation of these counters is the substance of a work which strikes us as essentially conservative and not all that different from the usual historical romance of the time. A contemporary reviewer declined to review the book, pleading "we all know what it is about" as another installment of a genre which has "flooded the market during the past few years" (Holly 195-96).

Gathered at Colonel Hamilton's country house in Maine in October of 1777 is a group of patriots, "men of a single-hearted faith in Liberty that shone bright and unassailable" (7). Despite the obvious opposition to England, there is more Anglophilia than Anglophobia in the book. Mary Hamilton, the patriot heroine of the novel and the mistress of Hamilton house, which has "a look of rich ancestry" (14), fears that the Tory family of her boyfriend will suffer at the hands of patriot rabble. British and American, Tory and patriot, present a united front against any such uncouth and uncontrolled behavior. After the "wild and lawless" (257) patriot mob surrounds Madam Wallingford's home, demanding that she sign an oath of allegiance to their faction (she does not), it is routed by Sons of Liberty. The motto of one of the last chapters is "License they mean, when they cry Liberty" (368), a motto applied here to the unruly patriots only. One feels an authorial uneasiness and a fear of the lower orders. A class-conscious Anglo-American insistence on protocol comes through in statements about the conducting of the Revolutionary War itself: whereas the villainous sailor Dickson is guilty of "common piracy and thievery," the war, though likewise violent, is dignified by instances of "law and order" (112).

The onetime Tory lover discovers the American way. But in her very search for the American hero, Mary Hamilton simultaneously discovers the appeal and charms of England. When confused reports come to Maine that Roger Wallingford, who has shipped aboard John Paul Jones's *Ranger,* has been injured, imprisoned, perhaps killed, Madam Wallingford and Mary sail to England to ascertain his true situation and, if possible, liberate him. During the voyage Mary and Madam Wallingford grow closer and together rediscover Old England. Mary even speaks of feeling estranged, belated, and transient in the land of the Indians: "'tis strange to know that a whole nation has lived on our lands before us! I wonder if we shall disappear in our turn?" (294). Mary reacts emotionally to the English countryside, where she is befriended by Tory and patriot sympathizer alike. In a heated debate she maintains that the Americans have been so patient with British injustices because, although denied rights as English people, "our hearts were English" (314): "We are not another race because we are in another country" (315). The war began simply "like some angry quarrel sprung up between mother and child while they were at a distance from each other" (319). However much homesickness and rededication to America Mary soon experiences, the reader still is left with the impression that the novel's title is unintentionally ambiguous. Not only does one not know whether the hero or heroine (or someone else?) is a lover who is a Tory or one who loves Tories, one cannot even ignore the seeming logic of concluding that the title applies equally to Mary Hamilton and to the authorial voice.

In its inclusion of figures from history like John Paul Jones, *The Tory Lover* furnishes another striking example of the necessary confusions attendant on integrating fictional plot with historical context in such a way as to make the one meaningfully comment on the other. The conventions of history writing, in those days long before either metahistory or metafiction, seemed significantly different in kind from the conventions of fiction. The love story appears at times to have little relationship to the Revolutionary milieu, as fiction and history take their separate though sometimes intertwining and/or parallel courses. The figure of the romantic hero blurs as it merges with the hero of history, in this case Captain John Paul Jones. Yet altogether to enter history is to exit fiction; to mark his fictionality the hero must at the same time be demarked from the representative of history. To be the worthy *American* protagonist Roger Wallingford must be identified with Jones (Jones's surface Europeanism also places him rather against the British, as he is Scottish and pro-French, aided by the Duchess of Chartres); he as well as Mary need a measure of conversion to an indigenous national ideal if together they are to represent this ideal. The requisite changes in Wallingford are precipitated by his voyage with John Paul Jones, a voyage which Mary feels will prove to the unconvinced American patriots that Roger is truly one of them. Roger leaves home, security, mother, and Toryism—he had once said, "I could as soon forsake my mother in her gathering age as forsake England now" (157)—as he takes common cause with Jones. He confides in Jones that he has ceased to be a Tory or even a neutral and has now abandoned his earlier principles "for the sake of one I love and honor" (Mary—though we are free to extrapolate John Paul Jones as well), and has independently also "begun to see that the colonies are in the right" (125). Roger's being injured, captured, and imprisoned, his escaping, working, and being rescued (though the Wallingfords' influential British friends had already arranged a pardon) make him a mature, independent adult, therefore the appropriate future husband and American who sails back with Mary to Maine, where he will ever after love her and serve his country.

This voyage recapitulates an earlier one, for the novel had opened with a parallel scene of John Paul Jones's ship arriving in Maine. Although America and glory are said to be Jones's mistresses, from these early chapters he also has eyes for Mary Hamilton. Roger enlists on Jones's ship at Mary's urging, and there the men become great friends (in Paris they together confer with Benjamin Franklin). Mary had asked Jones to befriend and protect Roger, and as a token of friendship—misinterpreted by Wallingford—had given Jones a ring. All "gentleness and courtesy" with women (the romance?), Jones is "imperious" (350) with men (history?). But Jones ultimately sacrifices his own romantic self-interest in being persuaded by Mary that Roger was not plotting against him, as he had been led to believe, and helps to arrange the reunion of Hamilton and Wallingford. Jones must be heroic without being the (fictional) hero. The tangled love triangle shows Jewett struggling to bring together history and romance in a meaningful way, to endow romance with historical significance while not rendering history sentimental. Thus, although apparently overcome by joy and love for Roger after the return to America, Mary is nonetheless "thinking of the captain," who left them in their happiness "and slipped away alone into the dark without a word" (405). He has slipped away into history, pathetically expendable to the love plot.

John Paul Jones as historical icon disappears safely beyond the transmutations of fiction; Roger Wallingford can only be his surrogate. The fictional protagonist is portrayed as one affected *by* history, yet a central narrative line "depends entirely upon that protagonist's encounter with forces of history he cannot materially affect" (Henderson 52-53). The Revolutionary American protagonist's individuality is erased by his having to function as the hero expected in historical romance, but his presence is also canceled by his being merely a stand-in for the "real" heroes of American history. The conventional love story would disappear altogether if even the hero pays final homage to history, normally a male figure (witness *A Lover's Revolt*); the heroine has to settle for history's fictional next-best. The democratic hero in this hybrid genre is thus both necessary and unnecessary. In the romance convention the democrat cannot be the hero. The sacrosanct representative of American democracy must be "historical" in any case. But to be a romantic hero preempts representing national democratic virtues and historical reality.

The entertaining *Brinton Eliot: From Yale to Yorktown* (1902) by James Eugene Farmer illustrates that, when both lovers are already putative patriots, the "problem" becomes a matter of plot and circumstance, and demands a physical separation which must eventually be destroyed. (In other novels, another sort of separation—ideological difference—defines the problem, and thus seems to call for a relatively greater emphasis on theme and character rather than plot and circumstance.) Idea is slighted when it is taken for granted and when action per se furnishes the main interest; attitude must be adduced from situation when authors do not feel compelled to make their characters self-conscious embodiments of ideas. Yet in the end the dispensing of characters' fates amply exhibits the typical conservative bias of the narrative. Our hero progresses from Yale to Yorktown by way of New York, Philadelphia, India, and France, his military career traced along with those of two college comrades; our heroine resists the advances of not one but two rivals to Brinton Eliot, emerging from the love plot unscathed by British or other American suitors. Together, Betty Allen and Brinton Eliot quickly end their sentimentalized romance with marriage in an America which seems excessively Europeanized only to readers not familiar with this literary genre. The real-life democratic American hero again falls out of the picture.

   Brinton Eliot opens with an affectionate and nostalgic portrait of Yale's beginnings, and college routine there in 1770. College authorities admonish classmates Brinton Eliot, Benjamin Talmadge, and the moral, studious, and much-admired Nathan Hale for dancing (Hale, of course, has been led into the misdemeanor by his more fun-loving fellows). The undergraduates otherwise concern themselves with their studies and the advice of Yale notables like John Trumbull and David Humphreys, but are also concerned with recruiting the "best" men for their college societies. College affairs are interrupted by a surprise visit from Brinton's Philadelphia aunt, Mrs. Chauncey Winthrop, who is accompanied by her daughter, Margaret ("Polly") Winthrop, and by the latter's friend, Betty Allen. More disquieting is Brinton's off-campus argument with Benedict Arnold about whether disgruntled New York merchants (like Eliot's father) have the right to sign non-importation agreements. The friends learn more of colonial political problems from Brinton's father during a summer trip to New York. The respite from college continues as Brinton, Ben, and Nathan travel on to Philadelphia, and are taken to a ball attended by Polly, Betty, and Sally Chew of Cliveden. Brinton later rescues the popular Betty near the Allens' country seat, Westwood, by whisking her from her runaway horse even as it plunges into the

Schuylkill. Indebted to Brinton and now paired with him, Betty nonetheless continues to be courted by the British Major George Bingham. Polly seems infatuated with Nathan Hale. The world outside Yale—a world of contention as well as one of love grown more meaningful as the adolescents grow older—having been introduced, the three students return to New Haven for their final two "bright, glad years" (119).

Part 2 (titled also "From Yale to Yorktown") finds Brinton in September1777 aboard his father's merchant ship, the *Flamand,* at Marseilles, having returned from a two-and-a-half-year voyage to Bombay. Excited at the news of revolution in America, young Eliot determines to sell his entire cargo and outfit the ship as a privateersman, but first must journey to Paris to obtain an official commission from the celebrated Franklin, who encourages Eliot and directs him to Beaumarchais and officials of the French government, including several nobles and the indecisive young king, Louis XVI. Plans to smuggle munitions and Baron von Steuben to America are jeopardized by Brinton's arguing with the haughty English ambassador, Lord Stormont. A French noble sympathetic to the British overhears American discussions, and French authorities are finally reluctant to declare a diplomatic alliance—they have already lent informal aid—until the Americans win a decisive military victory. The British embassy orders that Eliot's ship be detained when it discovers that the ship is being equipped with arms and ammunition, and a ruffian in the employ of the ambassador abducts Brinton and threatens him with death. Eliot's old Yale dancing master, the Comte de Sainte-Lucie, providentially appears—disguised as the ghost of a former victim of this French tough—to scare him off. French henchmen of the British fail in attempts to bribe or beat Eliot's men, a French merchant pays Brinton for the cargo from India, and the *Flamand* finally sails off as an American man-o'-war.

Meanwhile, Betty Allen, though a "pronounced Whig" (140), continues a busy round of frivolous activities in Philadelphia, socializing with the likes of Bingham, André, and Tarleton. While Brinton's career is partially controlled by French, British, and American national interests, Betty's career in love is in part manipulated by parental matchmakers. Her father collaborates with the conservative Judge Shippen in promoting a marriage between their children; the judge in fact threatens to call in a ten-thousand-pound loan to Mr. Allen if the marriage does not take place. Mrs. Allen, a social rival of Mrs. Shippen and not aware of the financial dealings, at the same time works at pairing Betty with Bingham, now quartered at Westwood and made even more eligible in her view by his having come into his inheritance as the twelfth Earl of Harborough. Both these suitors ride with Betty to Germantown, exchange insults, and are captured by an American detachment as Betty gallops to safety. The imperious Harborough had already informed Betty that he intends to conquer both her and the colonies. He had also denigrated Edward Shippen as the subservient son of a father who has tried to purchase Betty's favors—and been lashed with a riding-whip for his pains. Now fellow captives, the rivals nevertheless fight a duel in which Edward, a noncombatant in the war itself, falls wounded. Edward recovers at Valley Forge while Harborough returns to his regiment in an exchange of prisoners.

Nearing the colonies, the *Flamand* encounters and forces the surrender of the *Duchess of Cumberland* (symbolically reversing Harborough's determination to conquer the American woman, whose freedom is later purchased with proceeds from the sale of the *Duchess)*, trailing her into Portsmouth, New Hampshire, and selling her. Now a soldier rather than a sailor, Eliot joins Baron von Steuben at Valley Forge as a lieutenant in the Fourth New York, discomfited that "the Forge" seems desperate and sustained only by Washington's inspirational leadership and the German's insistence on strict discipline even in the face of great suffering. From Ben Talmadge, now a captain in the cavalry, Brinton hears the distressing report that Nathan Hale has been hanged as a spy. The recovered Edward Shippen revolts against parental (pro-British) authority by enlisting in Washington's army—which he also hopes will impress Betty. The love plot and the action plot further entwine when Mr. Allen, now also turned Whig, receives ten thousand pounds in a surprise letter from Brinton (who received 52 percent of the selling price of the *Duchess)*, enabling him to dismiss a Judge Shippen who compares his own disobedient son to the rebellious colonies. American troops have defeated Burgoyne and forced the British evacuation of Philadelphia, as Clinton replaces Howe as the British commander in Pennsylvania. France has announced her alliance with the colonies. The young people celebrate at a ball in Philadelphia, where Mrs. Allen promotes a match between Betty and the widower Benedict Arnold (who then marries Peggy Shippen, and soon afterward has his property confiscated when he turns traitor).

Brinton returns to the front at Monmouth, and marches to White Plains. In the Continental storming and taking of Stoney Point, Harborough kills Edward and Brinton kills Harborough in close sword combat. Eliot, promoted to captain, joins the victorious progress of the American regiments through Philadelphia on their way to Yorktown.[1] His rivals so conveniently out of the way, Brinton weds Betty with much ceremony as Washington and the no-longer-Tory Mrs. Allen look on approvingly. Eliot's father has recouped his losses through the *Flamand*'s privateering. Ironic but for the amalgam of the Old and New Worlds with which these novels so frequently end is the fact that Sainte-Lucie's deeds in the (democratic?) American Revolution gain him reinstatement as a French noble, Pompadour's interdict against him voided. Sainte-Lucie's decision to live in the United States saves him from becoming an object of vilification in the more purely social and political French Revolution a decade later, as if the noble from an "aristocratic" Europe can find a haven only in an "egalitarian" America.

The member of the original Yale threesome absent from the joyous denouement is, of course, Nathan Hale. Yet he becomes conspicuous in his absence. In fact and outside the novel a casualty of the Revolution, his reality takes him outside the fictional narrative to a world in which his loss, his sacrifice, becomes his meaning. History must not be tampered with; Hale is after all not the body but the spirit of the Revolution. Like John Paul Jones, Hale and whatever egalitarianism he represents to the historical imagination cannot enter altogether into the fictional world; he remains an icon not incarnate. Though continuing to bemoan Hale's passing, Polly Winthrop marries an unexceptional upper-crust Philadelphian. At the Eliots' marriage feast a place is set for Nathan Hale, and he is hailed because of his absence, because he gave his life for the cause. This saluting of Hale's spirit accompanies a toast to the new United States, with which his spirit is identified. And despite the aristocratic values implied by the marriages, perhaps despite authorial intention, the image of Nathan Hale remains longest in the readers' minds. Because of our knowledge of nationalistic historical discourse, he oddly enough becomes memorable to the same degree that the imagined story before us is forgettable.

The generic title and grand design of Allen French's *The Colonials: Being a Narrative of Events Chiefly Connected with the Siege and Evacuation of the Town of Boston in New England* (1902) belie a rather pedestrian treatment, although the book is a substantial—six sections, seventy-one chapters—contribution to turn-of-the-century popular literature of the Revolution. The novel's manipulation of stereotypical images of America and England resolves itself into a movement from west to east, from the great American forest, to coastal New England, toward— but not quite to—England itself. A subsidiary aspect of this general pattern during the last half of the book is the heroine's returning from England to Boston. Like a swinging pendulum slowing, losing its force, the plot gradually winds down and finds a point of stasis in the center, in the American East. The villain tests the woman's virtue in each of these locales as well: the western wilderness, Boston, and a ship bound for England. The circumstances surrounding her saving herself for the appropriate man communicate the values authorized by the narrative. The fitting situation and the suitable place for her settling down can embody those values only as that fictional narrative—and the enveloping war against England—ends.

Late in 1772, Francis ("Frank") Ellery languishes under what he feels is the boredom of being stationed on the distant shores of Lake Huron and longs for the fashion, gaming, wine, and women of London. Frank's real home, however, is neither England nor the West; he comes from, and is destined to return to, the middle ground: Boston. His position in the family and the family business has been denied him by Thomas Ellery, his mean-spirited uncle, who will serve as trustee until his (Frank's) younger brother, Dickie, reaches his majority. Frank's career as a soldier and his eventual rebirth in the wilderness—soon to gain significance—follow a "drowning" staged in Boston so that he could escape the clutches of his uncle. Before he can locate a guide to take him to Detroit and eastward, Frank's life in the woods is unexpectedly given purpose and romantic interest by a fifteen-year-old white captive of the Pottawottomis who implores him to take her with him. Originally obtained from captivity among the Wyandots, she has lived happily as a "replacement" for the long-lost daughter of the kindly old Aneeb. But now she fears the fate worse than death with an Indian mate, the Panther. The sensitive and understanding Aneeb releases Alice Tudor upon's Frank's petition and his promise that he will ensure the girl's return to Montreal—her soldier brother's post—and eventually to London, her home (she *is,* after all, named Tudor). After a tearful leavetaking from Aneeb, Alice discovers that Frank must entrust her to a young British lieutenant. Her relief at having escaped marriage to a Native American is short-lived, as the lecherous British soldier immediately tries to get her drunk and rape her. Frank, the representative "colonial," rushes to her rescue and scuffles with the officer, slashing his face. The Briton knifes Benjy, Frank's faithful old aide from back east, as Benjy and Frank in the confusion manage to flee. Feeling himself betrayed, Aneeb has already silently disappeared with Alice.

Frank's dilemma becomes whether or not to further befriend Alice. As Benjy dies, he exhorts Frank to eschew a dangerous and uncertain pursuit of the girl—and Frank himself feels the attractions of family and familiar Boston. He nonetheless determines to find Alice, and does so just in time: Aneeb has been hurt and his entourage, near starvation, has encountered freezing weather. Frank's new life with the Indians becomes a demanding yet therapeutic and transforming experience, very much like that of Zane Grey's heroes in slightly later novels like *The Call of the Canyon* and *Wanderer of the Wasteland*. (More about this theme will emerge in my section on novels set altogether in the West.) He discovers and internalizes a Great West as he accompanies an English girl to the East. During these winter months he becomes his new "family's" provider and takes the lead in building a cabin; "body and mind grew. Every littleness fell away from him." "He was white and Indian both" (54). Alice and Frank grow more intimate with nature and with each other: "She emerged from childhood; he became a man" (56). A shortage of game tempts Frank to continue with Alice alone, but the family is still together when it is attacked by a band of Chippewas, including the Panther. Aneeb distracts the attackers as Alice and Frank rush from their burning cabin, Frank injured but managing to kill the pursuing Panther and another brave. Emaciated and out of gunpowder, Alice and Frank struggle onward to the fort, where Frank falls exhausted, but not before telling Alice the tale of his Whig (except for the uncle, Thomas Ellery) family and Benjy's securing of the family silver against Ellery's selling it. (Their unauthorized secreting of the treasure being unlawful explains Frank and Benjy's originally exiting Boston.) A letter from her brother finds its way to Alice, informing her that he plans to leave Montreal for England soon. Soldiers at Detroit, in an effort to convince Alice to join her brother before his departure, tell her that the nearly lifeless Frank has in fact died.

Having been reborn in the West, Frank is now reincarnated in the East on December 16, 1773. Donning a city man's clothes, he finds himself in the midst of Whig-Tory contention. His own brother seems to have betrayed the family's Whig traditions even in these days of citizens' meetings and the Tea Party. Benjy's sister, the faithful Ann, still tends the old stone house, but the adept manager of the Ellery rope-making business, Humphreys, coincidentally dies just as Frank arrives. An altered man incognito, the equally efficient Frank is hired as the new business manager. With his brother, Dickie, at a tavern, Frank offends a British captain named Henry Sotheran (very similar to the villain's name in *From Kingdom to Colony*) by inquiring about a scar on his face (the result, of course, of his attempted rape of Alice). A comrade of Sotheran, Captain George Tudor, Alice's brother, visits the rope factory in hopes of rewarding Alice's supposed savior, only to be told that Frank Ellery had drowned four years earlier. Although he does succeed in smoothing over the disagreement between Frank and Sotheran, George's inconvenient affair with the feisty Whig Barbara Savage meets little success. At least he soon has his sister with whom to commiserate, as he has summoned her to Boston. Though from fashionable London and nearly a casualty of the West, Alice arrives still loving nature, "health and good-living"

(142). But viewed from her arriving ship, Boston seems "peaceful, lovely, almost English" (143).

Alice's first stop is the Ellery home, where she informs the household that Frank had not drowned but rather had died, serving her, in the wilderness. However, Frank soon clears up any mystery by revealing to Alice, Dickie, and George his identity as manager of the rope factory from which he had long ago been ordered by his uncle. The embargo now forces a cessation of production. An oddly attentive and polite Sotheran is shortly afterward told that Frank was his Lake Huron antagonist, but must postpone confrontation with Frank and pursuit of Alice when the British are ordered to their posts at news of a colonial advance. Frank, on the other hand, attends meetings of dissidents at Cambridge. George Tudor meanwhile continues in his roles as mediator between the rivals in love and war and promoter of the match between Frank and Alice (who now publicly declares for Frank). In his (perhaps) rationalization for delaying revenge against Sotheran, Frank links the private with the public: "One single spark might set the country in a flame; all personal desires must be subdued in such a crisis" (164).

Although Thomas Ellery pretends he would have welcomed Frank, he certainly does not welcome the unprincipled and disreputable Crean Brush, the New York Tory who now arrives to blackmail Ellery for hush money on behalf of his sister, secretly Ellery's wife, by whom Ellery has a son. (Little does Ellery know that this very son, calling himself Roger, works in the family business as Frank's assistant.) By the time Brush and Thomas Ellery discover the son's identity, Sotheran has begun to implement plans to use Roger against the Americans. Henry Sotheran has already accepted payment from General Gage to bribe the patriot Dr. Benjamin Church to release proof of the culpability of Adams, Hancock, Warren—and Francis Ellery. Church, a compulsive gambler always longing for success, accepts the deal when Sotheran agrees to cancel his gambling debts in the name of the Crown. To clear his way to Alice, Sotheran also encourages his servant, Tabb, to court Alice's maid, Christine. Happily, the determined Roger, true to Frank and the American cause, cannot be bought; even after Brush forces him to work for Sotheran, Roger merely plays along as a make-believe Tory. Feigning a drunken stupor, Roger overhears British plans to seize American stores and leaders, and burns a confiscated letter written by Frank which pinpointed the location of the munitions. (Sotheran, as a result, is reprimanded by his superior for not passing along this letter and not capturing the patriot ringleaders.)

Book IV, "Concord Fight and Charlestown Battle," carries on the connections between private and fictional affairs, and momentous public and historic(al) events. As the Americans fire on British troops at Concord and Lexington and on the route of their retreat to Charlestown, George Tudor remains troubled by the obligation and gratitude, on behalf of his sister, which he feels toward Frank. An increasing affection for the colonial must be denied when duty (Sotheran) commands him to forbid Frank the Tudor home. (Barbara Savage retaliates by proscribing Tudor's visits to her home.) Frank, knowing that George, Alice's natural protector, would lose a duel with Sotheran, does not disclose Sotheran's secret and inciting licentious past. Sotheran's animosity toward Frank still simmers, not expressing itself in a duel because, as a rebel, Frank is considered beneath treatment as a gentleman. Dickie, partially at Sotheran's urging, has enlisted with Tory volunteers even before his twenty-first birthday, although he soon after grows disillusioned with certain British and Tory leaders, and glimpses his uncle stealing some of Frank's papers. Alice, who has seen both America and England, remains nonpartisan: "She could see both sides" (289).

After Roger reports Sotheran's and his cohorts' plans to fortify Dorchester Heights, Frank heads toward the Heights in hopes that the Americans can fortify them before the British. As the British troops form up in regimental order and the Americans invest Bunker Hill, Colonel Prescott entrusts the valuable but impulsive Dr. Warren to the care of the cooler Frank. The Battle of Charlestown becomes a confrontation of the "splendour of the British array with the bearing of the men of the land" (329). Although both sides exhibit gallantry and valor, the British finally take the redoubts as the Americans exhaust their powder and ammunition. Warren is killed, while our hero suffers from a bloodied forehead— and is taken prisoner. As Dickie watches the distant battle, he acknowledges his emotional identification with the Americans and, when the opportunity offers, cuts Frank's bonds and helps him escape. The brothers reconcile as Dickie runs off to confront Sotheran for conspiring against Frank. Insults lead to sword-play interrupted by Frank, who goads Sotheran into fighting him instead by beginning the tale of Sotheran's attack on Alice. Frank's marginally greater skill prevails, but his foe is spared when Frank twists his ankle.

Both brothers fall into British hands, which furnishes them yet more chances to befriend one another. Dickie is taken for deserting while Frank has been incriminated by letters forged by Thomas Ellery. Frank, albeit shackled, easily escapes by overpowering the marshal, the repulsive and sottish Brush. In Brush's clothes, Frank frees Dickie and together they confront their uncle with proof—accounts hidden behind a secret panel—that he has falsified business ledgers (Humphreys had left the accurate records with Frank). By this time Frank has deduced

Church's guilt and, fearing Church has revealed his (Frank's) where-abouts, eludes pursuit by leading Dickie by another secret passageway to a cellar on the waterfront, whence Dickie takes a boat to safety. At Sotheran's rooms Frank then continues to impersonate Brush, and talks candidly about Church's letter. Seizing an opportunity, Frank reveals his identity and binds an apparently submissive Sotheran. But when Sotheran shouts to approaching friends, Frank must jump through a window and swim to the Cambridge shore. The reunited brothers join Washington as he condemns Church and grants Dickie's request to serve with his brother in the Continental artillery. Howe's indecision allows the Americans time to regroup, Frank and comrades time to return with cannon from Ticonderoga.

In Boston, Sotheran makes himself such a constant companion of Alice that she seems to forget Frank, for which Barbara in defense of the Whig cause angrily reprimands her. Sotheran tries to make himself indis-pensable to Alice, especially after she moves to Thomas Ellery's, with Tabb's help actually masterminding another rape attempt. A drunken Tabb, however, inadvertently reveals to Roger the circumstances of Sotheran's earlier assault. When Roger informs the incredulous Alice, she throws the accusation at Sotheran, taking him by such surprise that he cannot conceal his guilt, though he does offer to reform and marry her. She reminds him of his responsibility for the deaths of Benjy and her Indian friends. Sotheran insists that Alice keep her knowledge of his ignominy secret, both that he can continue his way of life and that George will not have to die in a duel. After an interval of apparent heart-felt affection for her, Sotheran again seems intent on attacking Alice (on page 447, postponed, as it were, from page 32), locks the door, and sends the maid Christine away with the promise that she can marry Tabb. At the crucial moment Pete, one of the former rope-makers Frank has ordered to watch over Alice, emerges from behind the secret panel and, cudgel in hand, chases off the rascal Sotheran.

The historical events referred to in the title finally arrive as Howe decides to evacuate Boston and the Americans fortify Dorchester Heights and bombard the city. A ball all too coincidentally strikes the Ellery house, knocking open the hidden panel and revealing the family plate, jewels, and ledgers for all to see. Brush covets this wealth, just as other Tories loot and create havoc on the days before the final evacua-tion. Although the rope-makers try to dissuade her, Alice determines to return with her brother to what she hopes will be the rural peace of Eng-land. Ironically, her decision follows an argument with George during which she maintains that the Americans have right on their side. Con-verted herself, she converts George. Before he joins his sister aboard the

Elizabeth, George takes fond leave of Barbara, vowing to see her again and to resign his commission now that he understands the issues better. During George's last visit to the Ellery home he witnesses a confrontation between Sotheran and Tabb. Acting on Sotheran's promise that she may marry Tabb, Christine has dishonored and, in her remorse, drowned herself. When Tabb angrily blames Sotheran and begins to tell George of Sotheran's attempts to ruin Alice, Sotheran shoots Tabb. Knowing Alice should have a shipboard protector, George hesitates but is incited into a fight with Sotheran in which he is "fatally" stabbed. Sotheran vows to take George's place aboard the *Elizabeth.*

Apprehensive at George's absence, Alice, along with Roger, supplies herself with food, weapons, and ammunition, and locks herself in her cabin. Brush conspires with Sotheran to leave the rest of the fleet and sail to England immediately: Brush to unload his contraband on Cornish smugglers, Sotheran to escape American justice. Thomas Ellery tries to coax Roger from the cabin by disclosing he is his father, now willing to take him in and care for him. (Part of Roger's rebuttal is that his mother, whom Ellery claims even now to support, has been dead for five years!) Roger angers, distracts, and delays Sotheran by revealing his (Roger's) complicity in a number of military and political American schemes. Meanwhile, Frank has followed George's trail and found the note, written by George in his own blood, that states he has been killed by Sotheran and that the rogue is now with Alice on the ship—and enjoins Frank to avenge both brother and sister. Frank gallops away on one of Washington's horses, obtains the loan of a ship, sails after Sotheran, and boards the *Elizabeth* during the critical moments of Roger's delaying tactics. Frank's men appear to be vanquishing Sotheran's until the experienced Sotheran himself dispatches many of his enemies. The final showdown ends with Frank, cleverly waiting his opportunity, stabbing Sotheran. During the joyful reunion Alice stands before a porthole, backlit "like an image of the Virgin" (501). (The image of a virgin queen was already suggested by the ship's name.)

This icon of the glorified Virgin derives, of course, from European ("Western") culture rather than from the culture of the American West, the Virgin Land.[2] Alice has had her moment as Pocahontas but finds her apotheosis as the Virgin, having survived the onslaughts of Old World corruption (Sotheran) and New World "savagery" (the Panther). (Similarly, the man who carries the name of British kings, George Tudor—almost miraculously, alive after all—marries an American savage.) In reciprocal movements, her career has taken her from England through the East to the West and from the West through the East *toward* England—when traveling stops. (Frank's stint in the West also involves and presupposes what we might call a reflex movement back to the East.) As James M. Cox writes, "as the country drove toward the Pacific, the countercurrent of cultural memory drove east, so that Virginia and New England became almost for westerners what England had been to the colonists" (Elliott 762). Home—a stable center, the peace that follows war—becomes the old Ellery house in Boston, where Alice and Frank are to live and produce children. On the one side, a short-lived experience of the West is viewed as an ingredient imperative in the new American's makeup; on the other side, at least a theoretical knowledge of England enters the formula. A shared destiny had earlier been signaled in a passage about British sympathizers with the American cause. As the final words of the novel have it, revolutions do not always involve rejection: "And while the English people—but not the English king—learned their lesson from their kinsmen across the sea, in America the new republic was rising up" (504).

The first words of the novel, its title, had initially indicated this agenda. "The Colonials" communicates derived, dependent, and provincial status in a way that "the Americans" would not. Although Boston is mentioned in the title and must self-evidently be the one in New England, "in New England" nonetheless concludes the title and imparts more than simply an antiquarian tone. The impulse at work is to view New England only as part of a composite picture with Old England. Frank accepts his inheritance—and his heritage—in his final rebirth as a citizen of an America which was a "new republic . . . rising up" but replete with Anglo-American values and traditions. This dual heritage *could* be suggested at any time in the course of a novel, but in a Revolutionary War novel cannot be embodied or institutionalized until the military conflict that constitutes much of its plot has been resolved in that conflict's public as well as private effects. If the war was truly *against* Britain, perhaps its outcome would be a united state more indifferent *to* Britain.

For the first two-thirds of Charles George Douglas Roberts's *Barbara Ladd* (1902) events do not occur during, nor do they parallel, Revolutionary activities. Then narrative time passes over several years to 1772, when a number of characters do become involved in these activities. Political and personal compromise and restraint are eventually validated, all within the context of a pastoral ideal which would seem a much more pointed and attractive fantasy in 1902 than in 1772. The modern, the urban, the industrial, and the new immigrant are criticized through being sidestepped; they are the implied butt of attack, the center of a target to which attention is drawn by its center being absent. Escapist motives figure as largely here as in futuristic utopias of the time or popular fiction of ten years later like Edgar Rice Burroughs's *Tarzan of the Apes* or Zane Grey's *Riders of the Purple Sage.*

By this last third of *Barbara Ladd* the young and willful title character has moved from Maryland to Connecticut, though she recalls the Old Plantation fondly. Her family, her boyfriend, and her rambles in nature become her absorbing interests. Both her relatives and her acquaintances are divided between Whig and Tory, just as her young man, Robert Gault, is "a loyalist yet alive to the grievances of the people" (243). When she accompanies her Uncle Glenowen on his business trip to New York, Barbara is fascinated by the city and quite swept away by her social successes there (the artificial glitter of high society being primarily associated with the British), while at the same time she longs for the quiet of the rural ways of her Connecticut valley. She argues with Robert, in New York working at his own uncle's office, about his rumored fighting of a duel over a woman, but her jealousy is defused by her discovery that he had challenged a man who had defamed Barbara herself. Their political differences likewise prove ephemeral in following events. Although temporarily attracted by a sympathetic historical character and a fictional one, Alexander Hamilton and the patriot soldier Cary Patten, Barbara finally will find the appropriate and approved public views in Robert Gault.

The American "cause which she held so splendid and so righteous" (315) fails insofar as it is also embraced by those of the "rougher sort" (326) whom she finds so offensive. After her uncle obtains a commission in Washington's army, Barbara returns to Second Westings in Connecticut to find cowardly, unkempt, and lawless patriot rowdies terrorizing her old Tory friends Amos and Doctor Jim, and destroying Gault House (an action soon after followed by the death of Lady Gault, Robert's mother). When Patten had presumed an intimacy with Barbara, she had put him in his place by asserting Robert's status as a gentleman, one who, though a traitor, had acted from motives of loyalty and honor even when this dedication could mean his losing her. Second Westings (suggesting "again, to nature"?) thus becomes the site of the reenactment of a social dynamic practically schematized in earlier writers like Hector St. John de Crèvecoeur and James Fenimore Cooper: the wilderness, away from the corruptions of traditional society, offers the freedom and opportunity for an individual moral regeneration, while at the same time it creates the possibility of degeneration into a wildness of chaotic license. Imposed upon the American land must be a cultural heritage from Europe, just as "Second" deprives "Westings" of grounded originating force; it is where we have been before, the New (new) England where John Winthrop in 1645 distinguished between that civil liberty maintained in a Christian commonwealth and that natural liberty held in common with the beasts. Both Barbara and Robert fault the unworthy King George as a corruptor of Old World ideals. But neither faults the essential values which he imperfectly embodies; neither can tolerate the New World lawlessness of the unruly American mob.

News reaches Second Westings of the Declaration of Independence, the Battle of Long Island and Washington's retreat to New York, and Robert's promotion to the rank of captain of cavalry. Recalling earlier and simpler adolescent days as she walks through the woods and placidly paddles her canoe, Barbara spots Robert himself on shore. He has barely survived the battle at White Plains, has wandered home, and now falls exhausted, injured, and hungry. Barbara and old Mrs. Debby Blue take him to a secluded vacant cabin to recuperate. In the typical move of (re)conciliation, Barbara admits that her love for him overwhelms political difference: "I find I am just a woman, Robert—and in my conceit I thought myself something more. I love my country, truly. But I love my lover more" (375). Practical power and patriotism are not the part of women. But honor need not be sacrificed after all, for Robert now declares that he will no longer fight "for a cause that I felt to be wrong from the day of Lexington" (376). His readiness to give up all for the American cause and honor proves that he will not have to, that he is worthy of love, just as the change in him also means that Barbara can maintain both love and patriotic honor. The lovers' union is made possible by a compromise of the private with the public, her discovery of love and his of a new political perspective; the strands of the story, as well as the lovers, unite. It remains for Robert to hope one day to return with Barbara "to our own dear river and our own dear woods" (376). Surely "our own dear" nature is a tamed and domesticated one, one associated with the couple's past, American to be sure, but surely no locus of confrontation with the non-European and radically Other.

The association of luxury, frivolity, and fashion with British high society often affects characterization to the extent that in these stereotypical images women are viewed as preeminently susceptible to the allure of the over-refined. Wholesome vigor becomes, by implication, characteristic of a manliness identified with nascent Americanness. In these books' own terms, therefore, the democratic American woman supposedly in the making faces the plight of denying herself in order to qualify as a helpmate to the appropriate regular American guy. The American is a man in these cases; whatever is available to the woman comes only through him. He finally asserts his independence, in war and love, in terms of manhood if not in terms of political ideology. By definition, this antiquated machismo must not stem from arbitrary considerations of wealth or class—though he must possess a measure of these as well. But a parallel womanhood does not qualify the woman for membership in the independent American family; she must resign rather than find her independence. In finally spurning high society *and* in finding national and "natural" virtue she is finding a man, and vice versa.

Dwight Tilton's *My Lady Laughter: A Romance of Boston Town in the Days of the Great Siege* (1904) traces this transition in the career of Constance Drake from Toryism to patriotism, from single to married status. The usual—for heroines—temporarily bipartite division of the plot results. John Brandon speaks of liberty itself as his goddess and mistress, whereas in the end Constance loves the *man* who loves liberty. (The "gender" of ideas grows confused, since the *person* who represents liberty is typically male. DeForest had explored the American logic of liberty's being male, taking the notion to its logical and psychological extreme in positing the homosexual at a time not given to candid explorations of the theme or to explicit embodiments of the theme in fictional plots.) John does love Constance, but it is not required that he love liberty *through* loving her; he is patriot from the start, though not essentially anti-British. It is as though the American man knows and preserves the best of an English tradition, superadded to American maleness, while the American woman can fall prey to the worst on her way to embodying national values. (And both are insensitive to those whose heritage places them altogether outside this British, or even generally northwestern European, tradition.) When she is introduced to the poet, playwright, and essayist Mercy Otis Warren, Constance can only wonder "what it could be like to mould men when one was a mere woman," one who spoke with "clear and cultured tones" (73).

In the British world of Boston Constance Drake shines, toasted for her vivacity and wit as "My Lady Laughter." With an arrogant braggadocio soldiers at the coffeehouse celebrate her along with her uncle, Giles Romney—the king's councillor—and the queen's birthday. Although thus affiliated with this upper-class environment, Constance so sympathizes with all the poor of the city that she insists on asking Governor Gage to remedy their plight. The fun-loving girl is also independent and forceful enough to slap a drunken British soldier who tries to force a kiss on her, just as later she is impish enough to substitute real tea for patriot raspberry leaves (her uncle, likewise, had not begun to drink tea until *after* the Tea Party). By the spring of 1775 the note of contention and

Constance's fears for the future have increased. Her democratic impulses and spunk have made her part patriot without her knowing it, but these virtues cannot be fully acknowledged and fully expressed until marriage to a patriot becomes a possibility. At the palatial home of John Hancock, which "resembled the abode of a London man of fashion" (76), both Mistress Hancock and Mercy Warren argue the colonial cause with Constance, who provokes them with hints that she may be a spy for her uncle. Encountering John Brandon—one of those who had intervened after Constance had slapped the offending soldier—on Hancock's doorsteps, she invites him to accompany her to view British maneuvers and target shooting. When Brandon warns her of the dangers of attending, she insists on going (with British Lieutenant Charlton), feeling, in fact, a "certain exhilarating pleasure" (95) in so doing.

The sober John Brandon had declined Constance's invitation because of his duties as a patriot. He has quit his job as usher at the Latin School to devote himself to the cause, and has been chosen to carry important documents for the Committee of Safety. His sister, the plump and pretty Barbara, however, has Tory connections by way of her love for Ensign Cuyler and her friendship with Constance. At the shooting contest Barbara and Constance, with their escorts, witness the impressive performance of a tall and manly but uncouth American sharpshooter named Tobias Gookin. Officers threaten him as possibly an enemy, but Constance takes his part; Gookin sprints away amidst a shower of bullets. Seeing this assault on one who had done no proven wrong and glimpsing another man shot for deserting brings home to the girls the violence and earnestness of the struggle if not the injustice of the British, though even Uncle Romney acknowledges that British soldiers have at times been unnecessarily provoking.

The lightheartedness of Constance's nineteenth birthday celebration is balanced by worry at the two-week absence of John Brandon. Constance and Barbara visit Dorothy Hancock again in search of news, and are redirected to a patriot meeting. Constance all the while pretends to be merely accompanying the distracted sister and vacillates between maintaining that she is still a Tory and that she is not a Tory, "I am but a woman" (135). The more, in other words, she falls in love the less a forceful political animal she can be; for a woman, the transitional stage to becoming an American includes the surrender of any sovereign political standing. In the midst of this patriot crowd being harassed by the British, she listens attentively. Her changing if still inchoate ideological views are being shaped by the man. Not converted earlier by Mercy Otis Warren or Dorothy Hancock, Constance now "had come under the spell of Samuel Adams" (132). The younger Sam Adams reports that Brandon is safe.

But Constance continues to exhibit a stereotyped emotional female fickleness when she learns that John has visited attractive Hannah Adams and sees a love letter by him (she as yet does not know that the missing addressee is "Liberty"). Suddenly in a huff, she denigrates the patriots as "rebels, fools, humbugs" (142). She constantly disproves the comment made by Barbara at a Daughters of Liberty meeting that "there's no politics in love" (147). (At most these women can only be the offspring, as it were, "daughters" of the real thing, Liberty.) Politics and love being determinants of one another provides whatever unity these novels have.

Accusing herself of being a fool, Constance nonetheless is sensible enough not to disclose to the British that Gookin's wagon, which has bowled that of her uncle and herself off the road to Concord, carries munitions for the Americans. Romney castigates their "darkey" Pompey for careless driving and thereby implicitly defines the people whose war this is, defines exclusionary racial rather than gender terms for a world following the Emancipation Proclamation (see later treatments of Southern novels). Always helpful if obsequious, always willing to aid others to become independent, Pompey is made ludicrous by his Roman name and by his colloquial and ill-digested smattering of learning. The more formal learning he possesses, the more an impostor he becomes, as he is caught in the double bind of being damned if he knows and damned if he does not know. The image of the ignorant primitive was no more racist than the image of the black "professor," a ridiculed curiosity, a freak. In Romney's bigoted remarks and in Tilton's basic portrayal of him, Pompey is not only incapable of significant individual achievement, he is by definition incapable of being a true heir to a European tradition which defines America. And the author is very far from knowing or validating non-Western cultural traditions. Pompey exists outside possibility and community. The writer is predictably unconscious of this prejudice and of the senses in which he addresses another war, the Civil War, when he later describes the cannonading preparatory to the Battle of Bunker Hill. While Constance and Barbara witness the firing they are chaperoned by "their sable protector" (and victimized themselves by sexism). But something else strikes them—and it is not a stray cannonball or awareness of Pompey: to "see brothers in race slaughter one another, was hard to endure" (245). Their comment had often been applied even to a conflict a major purpose of which was the freeing of slaves. Analogies between American slavery and British colonialism came more readily to the minds of African-American writers like Prince Hall, even in the eighteenth century.

Constance's plan to take her uncle to their country home near Concord—he is suffering from gout and, now, a sprain—must be altered after their carriage accident and after she learns from General Gage's wife of British plans to move on Concord. Barbara having explained to her that John's note had been addressed to "Liberty," Constance is now willing to order Pompey to write a note about these British military designs, to be carried to the Adams home by their dog. Though she is secretly aiding the American(s), Constance is furnished a pass by a gallant loyalist, Earl Percy. She intends to press on to her aunt's rural retreat at Menotomy, but when her hastily repaired buggy breaks down she is taken by Pompey to the home of her old nurse, Martha Winship. Brandon, a glimpse of whose riderless horse had shortly before brought on Constance a fainting fit, staggers onto the Winship's doorstep, injured and muttering an obviously important message. Jonathan Winship's brother, Ezekiel—their names signal their being good New England rustic folk—arrives with accounts of British troop movements and Paul Revere's ride, accounts then verified by Tobias Gookin's reports of Lexington and Concord. The next morning Constance discovers that John is resting in the Winship's home, but an interview is prevented when Percy's retreating brigade passes by and unarmed Jonathan is shot on his own porch. Constance tries to shield John from the British search, but Lieutenant Charlton finds and fights him, though he chivalrously allows him to escape. Finally, Constance concludes her trip to Menotomy.

Tory Boston is under siege when Constance returns. Gookin, living in secret at the Brandon house, assures her that John, now commissioned, is safe. Her being a fascinating female enables Constance, in effect, to become an American spy in working with Gookin while being privy to Lord Percy's disclosures that the British will soon take Dorchester Heights at all costs. The Americans fire from the hills at the last moment of the attack, and the British, though technically victorious, suffer great losses. Saddened at the many casualties, Constance is nonetheless inspirited by American bravery and the thought of liberty. Her activities limited by the presence in her home of the recuperating Charlton, when the elusive Toby Gookin is injured she takes responsibility to obtain for John some secret dispatches and a copy of Horace (unlike Pompey, John may read the Romans without being rendered ridiculous). On the pretext of a fishing trip, the fencing master and covert patriot Dan MacAlpine procures a pass and crosses over with Constance to Lynn and to headquarters at Cambridge. They see the dignified General Washington but must settle for a consultation with the slovenly General Lee, who lets her deliver the book and papers—they are maps—to Brandon, now a major. Constance explains Toby's fate and her and her uncle's nascent "loyalty to the cause of the land"—and "to you" (290).

Yet Constance still plays two roles; she may be only pretending Toryism, but she does love the luxury of Howe's Boston and she continues to be the toast of British officers despite the atrocities they have perpetrated. At the new British riding school (a desecration—to her—of the Old South Church) the thespian General Burgoyne recruits her for his latest comedy. She is to play "a Yankee girl" in a farce entitled "The Blockade of Boston" (although it is no longer extant, the general did write such a play). The fact that she is already a Yankee girl in a book with a similar subtitle—another fictive world authored from conservative perspectives—emphasizes her chronic role-playing as well as the textuality of *My Lady Laughter*. Her "real-life" roles change; by some she is taken to be a patriot, by others a loyalist. Appearance and reality, American and Tory, text and ground, become terms which cross and blur in a way which deflates any radical or validated social and political commitments. Anglophile, sexist, and racist conventions are reprised, and this only in a story, a story already known because ritualistically and so many times rehearsed. The locus of American ideology, Faneuil Hall, thus desecrated like the American locus of religious faith, becomes the venue for the British farce. So intent, apparently, is Tilton on achieving this effect that—though the iconic status of the "real" but make-believe Battle of Bunker Hill cannot be tampered with—when news of the attack itself interrupts the performance of "The Blockade of Boston" the announcement is at first taken to be part of the play. "The Battle of Bunker Hill" interrupts "The Blockade of Boston"; the Battle of Bunker Hill interrupts the blockade of Boston. In conflating "events" the author has without knowing it placed the force of quotation marks around the terms in even the latter clause. In addition to signaling the notion that all discourse, historical as well as fictional, is textual, we have an instance of a writer who unwittingly calls attention to this textuality.

Having been misinformed that MacAlpine had fallen ill, Constance visits him to find him well and brushing his old friend's, Captain Terence Drake's (her father's), military uniform. When John appears the lovers argue about her having been in the arms of Lieutenant Charlton at the Twelfth Night masquerade (more masking) at the time of Burgoyne's comedy (she had tripped over her skirt and fallen into his arms). Drake's uniform, as disguise, comes into play again when John wears it to the queen's ball, where he intends to gather information about British troop movements while Washington fortifies Dorchester Heights. The crude and licentious Captain Jack Mowatt's suspicions of Brandon are confirmed when Brandon refuses a toast to the king. John is seized, and Constance tries to save him by insisting that he was at the ball solely to see her, not for military reasons. (She has reconciled with him and acknowledged to her uncle her love for John.) But Brandon is soon sentenced to be shot at sunrise the next day. Remaining suspense revolves around whether he will in fact be executed. Constance persuades Lord Percy to grant him a week's reprieve, but it is not extended for a longer period when John refuses to inform on Washington. Admiring this unwillingness to sacrifice honor for love, but blaming herself for his predicament, Constance succumbs to "brain fever." Even when she staggers from her sick bed to suggest to John that, now that the Americans have practically completed investing the Heights, he could conscientiously reveal their plans, he turns down the opportunity. Constance herself, not such a stickler for technicalities, tells Lord Percy of patriot doings and thereby gains for John another, two-week, reprieve.

With the help of Queue, the dog, Constance near the prison fends off the assault of Mowatt and even profits from the event by taking from him duplicates of the prison keys. British authorities decide to evacuate Boston and revoke Constance's prison pass and John's reprieve, gained, they now determine, through Constance's trickery. MacAlpine, Gookin, and she confer on how to prevent Brandon's imminent hanging. She uses her final pass to furnish John the keys and a sword. In the riot and confusion of bombardment and evacuation, he makes good his escape. As the patriots celebrate the British departure and as the siege is lifted, John and Constance decide to marry immediately. What their lives together will be has already been implicitly defined. No further war or love story is required to create an image of a new and independent—actually old and dependent—national character (i.e., family); obstacles simply have had to be cleared away for the lovers to get together.

Constance Drake, niece of the king's councillor, has actively aided the American soldier, but is in the book's conclusion seen "leaning upon the arm of John Brandon with a wholly new air of dependence" (439). "My lady's" future laughter will be much muted. Brandon acknowledges his dependence on Constance no more than she acknowledges her debt to Pompey. In the order of this fictive world Brandon's wearing Terence Drake's uniform communicates the identification of British and American interests by way of the incest motif; everything is kept in the family. (And the word "patriotism" etymologically stems from "of one's father" in any case.) Not so much the aristocratic per se as the corruptions of aristocracy are attacked. Even though Barbara Brandon's beloved Ensign Cuyler has departed with the other invaders, Constance consoles her with the thought that "he'll be back again" (439).

THE MIDDLE COLONIES

Just as the population center of Boston, site of prewar agitation and celebrated battles like Bunker Hill, serves as a locus of action in the New
England novels, in those of the Middle Colonies Philadelphia and New
York share center stage in depictions of the war and its effects. Certain
outlying locales, especially Valley Forge and Monmouth, derive much of
their fame from their Revolutionary War significance, their associations
with a harsh winter or a decisive battle. In texts, these locales are
(re)appropriated as monumentalized moments. It is as if popular expression has long encapsulated an intuitive apprehension of the spatial—that
is, textual—status of the temporal by merging time and space. After all,
we speak of "the course of the war after Valley Forge" without being
struck by the fact that Valley Forge is actually—like a printed book—a
place, not a period or an event. Diachrony seems merely a trope in the
discourse of synchrony. An egocentric and ethnocentric, totalized and
emotionally satisfying control could not be exerted by the old guard over
the contemporary, still not a text, still messy in asserting its own complexity. Ellis Island had not yet become a moment, but rather remained
an unsettling and unassimilated place for the unsettled and the unassimilated. (Ellis Island, in turn, can now be the subject of historical fiction.)
After notable events associated with a locale are assimilated so long that
the place has the luxury of becoming a time, it has been assimilated long
enough to become the subject of the historical romance and the place
which functions in time as text. Contemporary portrayals of Civil War
battles by writers like Ambrose Bierce could still offend through their
graphic horrifics. Normandy, a "real and present danger," had no such
luxury of nostalgia and romance in 1944. Similarly, at this writing the
blood on the Vietnam Veterans Memorial wall has not dried sufficiently
for the war which it memorializes to become the subject of romantic
commemoration, but rather as a living influence alters our views of earlier conflicts in ways partially contravened by the still more recent Per-
sian Gulf War.

　　In other words, if the locus of threat can be distanced and thereby
rendered harmless by making it a (past)time, we can have things our own
way and indulge our fantasies in creating the imaginative worlds of historical fiction, however much we pretend that we are treating a past as
real as the present. Place and the present are less tractable. The present

cannot be the subject of just this kind of romantic treatment not only because it is the intransigent present—no object of antiquarian interest—but also because we feel it is producing its own terms and controlling us. The choice to write is the choice to regulate and legislate, doubly so in the case of historical fiction. The accretions of decades of image-making allow us the illusion of understanding. Without the possibility of this illusion about the present, we conclude that contemporaneity can be a component of analytical and thought-provoking realism only. Sentimental modes of re-creating the Revolution had grown so institutionalized in popular consciousness and literary conventions that little true political or artistic radicalism was available to those who took up the formula. Thus, a historical novel like *The Continental Dragoon* (1898) sidesteps even the issues addressed in another book of that year by a New Yorker: Elizabeth Cady Stanton's *Eighty Years and More: Reminiscences*. Ironically, the idea of actual and present revolution bore antonymous relation toward the Revolution recalled. Stanton's send-up of the Declaration of Independence clearly was an undigestible lump: "We hold these truths to be self-evident: that all men and women are created equal" (Lauter 1: 1897).

*   *   *

Despite its narrator's declaration that he has "no wish to write more history than is involved" in his "own humble fortunes" (477), *Hugh Wynne, Free Quaker: Sometime Brevet Lieutenant-Colonel on the Staff of his Excellency General Washington* (1896), by S. Weir Mitchell, is filled with Revolutionary period personages: Washington, Franklin, Arnold, André, and others. The narrator's fortunes, in addition, are part and parcel of the affairs of the nation. He hopes that his story will inspire patriotism in our time by inspiring imitation of those many magnificent American leaders who resisted unjust British control during the arduous struggle of the Revolutionary years. And Hugh Wynne, of course, gets the girl.

The competition in romance is for the favors of Darthea Peniston, a young American girl who is graceful and basically good, but who has many moods, loves admiration, and "could be carried off her feet at times by the follies of the gay world" (165). The British—Hugh's cousin, Arthur Wynne, in particular—are representatives of this world. Captain Arthur Wynne of the Scots Grays is handsome, well dressed, distinguished, but dissolute. He attempts to usurp Hugh's place not only with Darthea but with Hugh's father as well; two related aspects of Hugh's American heritage must be reclaimed. After Darthea realizes that she has been too much influenced by her Tory aunt, has "had a girl's

Cover of S. Weir Mitchell's *Hugh Wynne* (1896; New York: Century, 1905).

desire for the court and kings' houses and rank" (398), and has been foolishly discontented with simple American ways, she and Hugh together nevertheless have the opportunity to decide whether to accept or reject a family inheritance. The sort of social stability considered best suited to American needs is finally established.

Several people, or points of view, compete for Hugh Wynne's allegiance. He must sort through and decide which are the best of these in order to discover what his true character should be before he can offer himself up to America—the girl who by this period has also discovered her true nature. Among the influences on Hugh is Quakerism, represented by his stern and silent merchant father, which presents a conflict because of its stance on nonresistance and obedience to those whose authority is a function of being a part of God's established order. Restless to be active in the patriot ranks, Hugh finds himself dismissed from Meeting for his outgoings, the letter of dismissal arriving, symbolically, on the Fourth of July, 1776. The situation parallels the fate of Hugh's English grandfather, the first Quaker Wynne, who had been fined and jailed for his beliefs, then released to go to that America later re-formed in Hugh's generation. Hereafter, Hugh never rejoins the Society of Friends, though he mentions that others often spoke of him as a "Free Quaker," one of those who granted that pacifism could be compromised for adequate reason. This critique of Quaker pacifism has an 1896 relevance because of the rising war fever leading to the Spanish-American War in 1898. The coolness of Hugh's father continues; the young man is not released to marry until immediately after the war and the death of his father, events socially and psychologically conflated by the public and private meanings of independence.

Equally influential on Hugh early in the novel is the world of his cousin and his aunt, Gainor Wynne. Aunt Gainor is an Anglican who maintains that trade is beneath the dignity of gentlemen of the English kind—a status she still claims for the Wynnes. Although she holds to these foreign standards and is in this way like Arthur, she also has saving graces. She likes Hugh, is a self-reliant Whig, and feels that the best Wynnes had gone to America. Hugh's participation in Gainor's social gatherings, which many Tories attended, was an additional reason for his being dismissed from Meeting. For a time he is greatly attracted by the worldly circle at Gainor's, but finally rejects it. The occasion of this second break with early influences is an argument which Hugh and Arthur have at one of Gainor's parties.

Hugh's loving and naturally virtuous mother has come to fetch him from Aunt Gainor's. When she is made the subject of a crude remark by Arthur, Hugh strikes him. Although Arthur apologizes, he clearly indicates that he has a score to settle with Hugh. This first confrontation between the two is followed next morning by Hugh's swim in the cold river, which later seems to him "a mysterious separation between two lives, like a mighty baptismal change" (114). As in Harold Frederic's *In the Valley,* the "spell of America" is woven. The family's morning Scripture reading happens to be about the prodigal son. Hugh's rejection of a way of life as well as the terms of his conflict with Arthur, who takes a competing course as a Wynne "brother," is indicated in this manner. Hugh commits himself to the patriot cause, finally becoming a lieutenant-colonel and confidant of Washington. His dealings with Arthur, resulting from this commitment, eventually include his being abandoned, starving and wounded, by him in a Tory prison, being unwittingly made the carrier of a missive to the traitorous Benedict Arnold, and having a sword fight with Arthur in a battle. Arthur's perfidy to Hugh becomes part of the basis for Darthea's disenchantment with him.

After the lovers' quarrels are resolved and neither Arthur nor Hugh's friend, the ineffectual "girl-boy" Jack Warder, attempts any longer to woo Darthea, the final complication becomes whether Arthur will succeed in obtaining the deed to the ancestral Wynne estate in Wales, and with it a possible baronetcy. Arthur had cunningly enlisted the aid of Hugh's now infirm father in this attempt, and tried to ingratiate himself with John Wynne in such a way as to be made his heir. Documents are eventually found, however, to support the American claimants' right to the British heritage. Gainor argues that Darthea should now become "Madam Wynne of Wyncote." Not so much from magnanimity as from a token impulse to define themselves as Americans, Darthea and Hugh agree to reject this heritage in favor of a simpler Americanism. In 1783 they marry, peace is proclaimed, and Washington bids farewell to his staff. The remainder of the lives of Hugh and Darthea, passed amid children and Revolutionary War memorabilia, is serene and happy. This very popular novel itself must have possessed the pleasantly passive and antique appeal of memorabilia to its contemporary audience, while at the same time it called for a renewed patriotism in the living present.

The elements of first-person, retrospective, and Anglophile narrative mutually support and reinforce one another in pseudo-factual accounts of the Revolution like George Brydges Rodney's *In Buff and Blue, Being Certain Portions from the Diary of Richard Hilton, Gentleman of Haslet's Regiment, Delaware Foot, in Our Ever Glorious War of Independence* (1897). The supposed gain in immediacy, the imparting of an aura of the actual, of first-person narrative is largely voided at the price of a nostalgia considered more important. Not only were those "dear old days," they were days spent defending "our blood-right" (205). The "diarist" early on situates himself in place and time, describing the Delaware River valley and referring to himself as having lived "some sixty years as planter, soldier, lawyer, but always, thank God, a gentleman" (7), an English-style gentleman albeit proud of the patriot uniform and "our ever glorious war." The belated journal ploy allows even the narrator to indulge in sentiment and to monumentalize events while thereby suggesting an apparent rationale for the lack of vivid and perhaps unpleasant detail. Hilton, at once participant, eyewitness, and historian, commemorates 1776 and contrasts that "ever glorious" period with 1840 (and, by suggestion, 1897 and our present): "You of the present days of prosperity and peace can scarce know what it was that sixty years ago brought men from their quiet pursuits and sent them to the front" (15). Although, he answers himself, the "grievous wrongs" of Parliament caused the war, with those wrongs "the old vein of Saxon fighting-blood started into life" (16).

Already ambitious of military glory, twenty-one-year-old Richard ("Dick") Hilton listens attentively as Dr. (soon-to-be Colonel) Haslet complains of unjust British laws, taxes, and quartering of troops. After assessing the situation in Philadelphia for himself, Richard obtains a commission as lieutenant and sets out with dispatches for Haslet at Dover. By the way (both en route and seemingly coincidentally), he briefly stops to bid farewell to his lady-love, Kitty Weston. As a symbolic love-tribute which also communicates a wedding of the courtly and sexual, she ties a ribbon from her hair around his sword hilt. (The gesture in the present context becomes an image of the merging—albeit mechanical—of the love and war plots.) Hilton's diary, at times largely an account of camp life, troop movements, and battles, next takes the reader from the heat, boredom, marching, and eventual defeat and retreat from Long Island to the Battles of Harlem and White Plains and the terrible cold of river crossings and forced marches preceding the December attack on the British at Trenton ("at home we kept our Christmas as our fathers used in England" [55]). One of his lungs pierced by an enemy bullet, Richard is taken captive but treated sufficiently kindly by the British (though, of course, he refuses to disclose the whereabouts of American forces). After he regains strength, the enemy allow him to return home on condition that he not actively serve until a prisoner exchange has been effected. A chance meeting with an old compatriot, Tom Forsythe, leads to the recovery of his treasured mare and a reunion with Kitty. Richard doubles the commentary by sharing stories of army life, and announces that after his complete recovery and the exchange he will be promoted to captain.

Before setting out on his next assignment—to scout and to obtain supplies in New Jersey—Hilton is introduced to an English officer quartered nearby. Ned Dwining has become a friend of Kitty and has long been a companion of Frank Caverton, captain in the British Guards and, to Dick's surprise (Kitty had never spoken of being kin to the "enemy"), Kitty's half-brother. Feeling an immediate and mutual antipathy beyond mere jealousy, Dwining and Hilton argue but postpone dueling because of Richard's present public duties. After being exchanged Dick carries to General Washington the news of Howe's forces leaving New York and participates in skirmishes as well as pitched battles at Brandywine and Germantown. He survives delivering communiqués to an American spy, capturing a British scout, and the freezing weather, insufficient housing and clothing—not to mention the dead-horse meat—of Valley Forge. Only word of Burgoyne's surrender and Howe's indecision and dissipation in Philadelphia inspirits the Americans. Forsythe proposes that he and Hilton, to gain military information and entertain themselves, attend the grand Meschianza given by Howe in British Philadelphia. (This celebrated banquet-tournament-ball, a rendering of popular notions of the aristocratic European Middle Ages, further enhances the emphasis on the antiquated, the connections between past and present and Old and New World traditions.)

Disguised en route as a farmer, later as a gentlemanly "Mr. Blake," Richard enjoys the festivities and the company of a Miss Bingham until an argument with Lord Wolton about the merits of the loyalist cause results in Wolton's challenging him to a duel in which Wolton is seconded by none other than Ned Dwining, who, during the ensuing sword fight, recognizes Hilton. Suffering a shoulder injury, Richard summarily skewers Wolton and in the confusion and hurry of his escape inadvertently picks up his opponent's sword. Given a month's leave at home to recover from his wound and a subsequent fever, Hilton is tended by a Kitty contented enough until startled at seeing her brother's sword— Frank Caverton *is* Lord Wolton! (She obviously cannot marry the killer of her aristocratic brother, apparent proof of Caverton's death soon arriving in the form of a letter from Dwining.) A vengeful Hilton trails Dwining in the midst of the dislocations following Clinton's evacuation of Philadelphia, finding that Dwining has been arrested for his part in the duel and then gone over to the Americans. When Richard corners him in a tavern, Ned insists on his own newfound sincerity and reveals that Wolton is in fact alive and has returned to England, where he, too, plans to go after telling Kitty the whole truth.

Dwining, however, continues duplicitous: when Hilton returns to Delaware, Frank Caverton is in fact there rather than in England. A contrite Ned Dwining apologizes by explaining that his love for Kitty rather than a "natural impulse" (192) had caused his insulting behavior, but that his growing appreciation of the patriot point of view has now altered his private conduct toward patriots. Dwining also confesses that in Philadelphia Lord Wolton had been so quick to take offense because he (Dwining), eager to promote a duel and thereby eliminate competition for Kitty, had purposely misrepresented Hilton's response to Wolton's comments. The earlier differences between Lord Wolton and Hilton are thus explained away as a matter of language (another instance, like the circumstance of portions of the "diary" being missing and the subjects of these portions therefore not being present because not present in language, of the narrative's calling attention to its own "mere" textuality and lack of ontological ground). Ned has made a clean breast of it and proves gentlemanly, complimenting Richard for his gallantry and courteousness. So minor do actual differences appear that all is forgiven among the three men and the way is smoothed for Kitty and Hilton to take up "a newer, happier life" (199). Even the American war "against" Britain can be conducted with British weaponry: Wolton tells Hilton to keep his (Wolton's) sword until "this cruel war is over . . . and you and Kitty have an establishment of your own" (197)—when, presumably, Richard may use his own sword, when there are no longer military uses for it. Unaided American potency is deflated. A sexual symbol here suggestive of inbreeding replaces typical familial metaphor and serves both love and war plots.

This incomplete diary—"about" the Revolution, "written" in 1840, "passed down" (as though an object) to 1897 and surviving to the present—concludes by measuring the very worth of the Revolutionary legacy by a quote from Shakespeare, another derived and British text and standard. After the principals (and principles) reconcile, Hilton's later battles are quickly passed over—Cowpens, Guilford Court House, Eutaw Springs, Yorktown—as though now opposition has become too insignificant to describe, these portions of the diary expendable. But this ambiguous lack of language does not tell the whole story or comprehend all issues. Hilton does retain at least memories and in some instances goes out of his way to describe his life in a border state after the Revolution. If he no longer opposes the British, he is entirely capable of drawing attention to another post-Revolutionary difference by using the conflict as a trope to address a war which occurred after his death: "Even as I write, I can see my own slaves coming in from work; if their mental condition were but equal to their physical strength they would soon attain their independence, even as we did; but they are, as Howe was, unequal to the occasion" (124). From our largesse "we"—as exclusionary as it is in *My Lady Laughter*—will have to give them an unearned and undeserved "independence." (Hilton has forgotten that in his war he was empowered by the Other as well, by Wolton's sword.) By the pretense of the 1840 diary the author congratulates himself that, possessed of the "old vein of Saxon fighting-blood," he deserves independence and freedom while the slaves do not; he fantasizes a stable American plantation world and pretends that 1863 never happened. But only the reader of 1897 could understand the paternalism which rewards whites for the emancipation of purportedly unworthy blacks; only the present reader knows to seek meanings of this sort.

Pauline Bradford Mackie's *Mademoiselle de Berny: A Story of Valley Forge* (1897) attests to the continuing allure, even mystique, of the rich, powerful, and titled. Although history cannot be controverted—the British must be routed and, here almost more importantly, the French monarchy overthrown—in the fiction, the interplay of fiction and perceived history can fashion a personal yet popular vision of a range of factions and political and social perspectives. The French Revolution, hidden in the narrative's future, yet furnishes terms and ideology for the American conflict with Britain. However much their actions are attributable to a larger international political agenda, the French do contribute arms and men to the American cause. The French aristocracy at the same time serves as the image of a fascinating but corrupt ruling class, to that extent becoming the disguised yet actual opponent of the very American democrats who find it so fascinating. Viewing England's colonial administration as inept implies little at fault with a basic system of British government which was in part representative and which adapted and survived. The French government, on the other hand, seemed too arbitrary in its uses of power and so out of touch with commoners that it became the victim of an actual social and political revolution, not a mere war for independence. (Only a decade after their own "revolution" many, even most, Americans opposed the excesses of the French Revolution, conspicuous exceptions like Thomas Paine to one side.)

A traditional monarchy can hardly be unashamedly embraced by a modern American, who would be thought an appreciative benefactor of the egalitarian traditions of which the American Revolution had become an iconographic image. Yet, looming in the future of the novel's action are the disquieting uprisings of an unruly and undisciplined French "rabble" and the century-later threat to the privileged represented by a growing number and array of "lower orders" in America: blacks, women, new immigrants. The presence of these orders in 1897 was testing the sincerity of superficially democratic yet conservative and nativistic Americans. Old World—and old immigrant—pedigree would seem a haven from uncertainty and change; whatever lip service paid to the genuinely egalitarian in novels like this results in part from their authors' afterthoughts of inadequacy, even guilt. Writers would not be thought ignorant of the faults of the ancien régime or the realities of the world around them, yet their stories carry the message of an older world. No nod to democratic principles would seem a betrayal of the very principles of the Revolution which their novels were meant to monumentalize.

Their lives marked by "beauty and pleasant ease" (20), Diane de Berny and her blind half-brother Armand, nephew of the British General Stirling, are regaled in Philadelphia while the Americans suffer at Valley Forge. Diane admires the American Richard Heyward but suspects him of being a spy after he "accidentally" drops his tea—drinking tea being considered a test of loyalty to the British Crown—as well as a letter retrieved by Armand's Great Dane. She confiscates this letter, which later mysteriously disappears from her room. When Armand rides off, Diane guesses that he is attempting to return this letter to the missing Richard (now openly accused of being an American spy). Diane and her Quaker friend Rachel Mott in turn pursue Armand. A farmer and a miller report Armand's whereabouts and direction when last seen; a surly Tory Quaker tells Diane that he was heading toward rebel lines. Awakening from a nap in the forest, she is startled to see American troops headed by her countryman, Lafayette, but reassured by discovering that Armand has safely reached the American camp. Her experience of French court society—she also spent time in a convent in France—prompts her to argue that kings rule by right even against the rebuttals of Lafayette.

Amid the desolation of Valley Forge Diane explains her presence to General Washington. Detained at the American encampment for reasons of security, she later hears from Washington that the letter from Richard was in fact meant for her, was personal rather than political. She finds the joy of her reunion with Armand somewhat muted by his insisting that he can very well care for himself. Armand's secretive meetings with Richard have led Diane to suspect that Armand, too, has sided with the Americans. Richard himself suddenly realizes that he had met Diane before—at the court of Louis in Paris when he was in Washington's secret service. Guilty of this forgetfulness and offense to gallantry, he at least explains to her that the need to preserve his life had necessitated his earlier and abrupt leaving of Philadelphia, where the Meschianza is now to commemorate the changing of the British military leadership in the city. These revels continue far into the night. Richard and Armand meanwhile join the Americans attacking a Philadelphia defended by Armand's own uncle. Shortly after these skirmishes end, evidence accumulates that Armand has been acting in collusion with Roberts, the Quaker Tory; Roberts escapes, but Armand is arrested by Heyward himself. Diane pleads her brother's case—his blindness, his playfulness, his not having a father—with Washington just as she had with General Stirling when she thought Armand a patriot. Mindful of discipline and national interest, Washington imposes imprisonment as the most lenient sentence possible for a spy who acted for personal glory and had not even been granted military authorization. Diane falls ill after all the stress and exposure. By the time she recuperates enough to return with Richard to Philadelphia, the city has been abandoned by the British, who are pursued by the Americans across the Jerseys.

Affected by the sincerity and suffering she sees at Valley Forge, though still feeling herself drawn to the artificial aristocratic French world, Diane concedes that Richard's admirable sense of duty had led to his arresting Armand; she and Richard exchange love vows, but she seems willing to live in democratic America only out of deference to him. At her insistence, Heyward helps to bury Roberts, who has been captured and hanged as an example to Tory miscreants. Armand and Diane are freed to join General Stirling in Tory New York, though she and Richard continue to correspond. A short time later Richard and Diane are married by a priest—though Richard is a Protestant—in a tavern near New York. The violent aftermath to the end of the courtship, not the end of the war, serves as the climax of the novel. No sooner is the marriage ceremony over than the tavern is broken into by four Tory outlaws, more "malignant" enemies of their country than the British foreign "invaders" (263), who have been apprised of Richard's presence. With the help of the priest and Armand—and Armand's dog—Richard chases off these villains, but not before they wound Diane superficially and Armand mortally. Armand dies feeling he has proven himself a deserving son of his military father.

Akin to Armand not only in blood but also in physical appearance and a shared "daring spirit and a love of adventure" (36), Diane never really recovers from the loss of her brother. Sympathies of as scarcely an intelligible nature seem to exist between them as between Madeline and Roderick Usher (or the siblings in *In Buff and Blue*). Their world, threatened by both Revolutions, constitutes a reality separate from the normative present in being foreign, Catholic, and aristocratic. Upon the occasions of Richard and Diane's ritualistically biannual visits to Armand's grave, she always feels her arms aching with loneliness for her departed brother. Her identification with Armand perhaps explains the appropriateness of her not having children; hers and Armand's is a closed world, one which for them to carry on is to violate a taboo. If Diane is thus cut off from Richard she is in like manner cut off from the thought of any alliance with her own extended "family" by the fact that the man arranged by her French relatives to be her husband dies by the guillotine, his estate and fortune confiscated. Her uncle, the Abbé de Berny, bemoans her marrying an obscure American and not continuing de Berny tradition. An image of compromise results: although Diane becomes Mrs. Heyward, the author has calculated the appeal of the less mundane and less American "Mademoiselle de Berny" in the title of her book. Here she remains exotic and single.

But "Valley Forge" also figures in the title. Fantasy must be put to one side; history will have its way. Even the good Abbé becomes resigned, and thankful that Diane "was spared the horrors of the French Revolution" (271). At least token acknowledgment of reality must be made; the American and French Revolutions did occur, their outcomes unanswerable. The French had in fact backed the Americans during the War for Independence, notwithstanding the many ways in which France seemed akin to fellow European nations like England, even in the flaws of its old ruling class and errors in its colonial policy. Plot and major fictional characters concede to these sometimes disquieting and confusing facts just enough to suggest the complexity of the past and the thought that America sprang from a series of adjustments. The British General Stirling, for example, after spending a year in England, decides to live with Diane and Richard in America. Armand had fought on both sides though technically on the British; he is killed by a lawless Tory while defending a patriot. His resting place is the great American forest. Both Richard and Diane Heyward had lived among French nobles as well as American soldiers. Position in an old-style European aristocracy becomes no longer available after the fall of the ancien régime—and after democratic reforms in nineteenth-century England and France. Our new American hero and heroine settle for equivalent and available American titles: they later serve their state as Governor and Lady Heyward.

The effect of the unconvincing sentiments and absurd plot of Joseph A. Altsheler's *In Hostile Red: A Romance of the Monmouth Campaign* (1897) is to trivialize the issues of the Revolution. The few indications of any significant difference between the nations at war seem minor, personal and social at most, in the face of the logic of the action and even the force of frequent bald statement. Accommodation cannot be the point or driving motive in a story in which the contending parties are so similar. Characterization, sketchy at best, makes little coherent meaning of any real and important sort in this fast-paced narrative. The disguises and deceptions which surprise and entertain blur any contrasts which could be considered serious reasons for the Revolution. The title itself misleads, as the red uniform per se is far from being considered with true hostility, and much more is made of formula romance than of the Monmouth campaign.

The plot of *In Hostile Red* hinges on the decision of the American Lieutenant Philip Marcel, without definite purpose or permission from superiors, to assume the identity of a British officer and thereby infiltrate enemy forces. He convinces his friend, the first-person narrator, Lieutenant Robert Chester, to join him in switching clothes with their two captives, Captain Charles Montague and Lieutenant Arthur Melville, aristocrats newly arrived in America and carrying letters of introduction. The lark turns sour when American foragers attack them, but they soon join a body of British cavalry headed by Captain Geoffrey Blake and ride into Philadelphia, where they enjoy better food and living conditions. Both Chester (now "Melville") and Marcel (now "Montague") become accepted comrades of the British troops and favorites of the commander-in-chief, Sir William Howe. Only the arrogant and supercilious Reginald Belfort, who considers all Americans outcasts and peasants and who becomes Chester's rival in love, suspects them. Chester and Marcel adjust very easily indeed, and, in fact, have little adjusting to do, since they take offense only when the personal manhood of the Americans is impugned. They develop friendships and acknowledge the bravery and soldierly qualities of the British. The social life of the city seems a great improvement over the hardships of the American camp, and even Chester grows to appreciate it after meeting the beautiful Mary Desmond, Tory daughter of a patriot father. Even coincidence aids them in their masquerade, as when Montague's British cousin turns out never to have met him before. Everything conspires to perpetuate the fraud, not least of all the apparent indifference of Chester and, especially, Marcel. Reemphasizing Howe's recognition of the trauma of fighting against a land of "our own race and spirit" (118) is Chester's identity crisis during a later scene: he "scarce knew whether to consider [him]self English or American" (212).

Chester and Marcel's devotion to their cause revives sporadically in response to the example of the unorthodox frontier-bred partisan Captain William Wildfoot, who early in the campaign tricks Blake's detachment into an ambush and confiscates a British wagon train. (Wildfoot's unprecedented success in harassing the British stems from his brash aggressiveness and the fact that he too is a patriot disguised as a British sympathizer, the servingman Waters whose impertinent knowing looks have been so resented by Chester and Marcel.) Meanwhile, before the British troops move out to engage the Americans, Chester occupies himself with thoughts of Mary Desmond and the antagonistic behavior of Reginald Belfort, whose possessive attitude toward Mary leads to a duel being arranged. The duel, forbidden by Howe, has barely begun when an angry Mary stops it, offended that such a barbaric tradition is being carried on in her name and against the commander's prohibition. (Chester's duel against Colonel Schwarzfelder does not come off either, as Wildfoot kidnaps the Hessian who had developed an antipathy toward Chester.) Chester had earlier noted Mary's wonted haughtiness thawing before an unfortunate American prisoner, Alloway, who had been tipped off not to reveal his acquaintance with Marcel and Chester. When Alloway escapes on a rainy night, Chester gets word to him to elude pursuit by taking refuge in the Desmond home, where two British searches turn up no one. Wildfoot causes further chaos in Philadelphia by fulfilling a pledge to intrude into Howe's very quarters, binding and gagging Chester and a co-worker and racing off into a city whose outskirts are ablaze under rebel fire.

When four thousand British troops leave Philadelphia and news arrives of the French alliance, Chester and Marcel finally recall their all-too-blunted purpose. After cautiously avoiding a sentinel who only appears alive, Chester obtains a stray horse and rides off to warn the Americans of British strength and is overtaken by another rider on the same errand—Mary Desmond. Thus, just when Chester decides to "cast off" his "false character" (220) (though which character constitutes the "false" one remains confused), our feeling that Mary too must be a disguised patriot is confirmed. They ride on together, collide with Belfort, and outstrip British cavalry, barely getting to American lines, exhausted. Having taken the alarm, the Americans fend off the enemy attack; Belfort is captured and Wildfoot discloses his former role as Waters. Mary, most useful as a "spy," returns to Philadelphia, whereas Chester for no apparent patriotic reason chooses to rejoin the British rather than return to the American camp. Both lovers continue their masquerades, but Chester and Marcel eventually steel themselves for the consequences of the etiquette of honor—acknowledging to Howe their true identities. Instead of ordering their hanging as spies, Howe, who has taken a liking to the pair and their adventurousness, exchanges them for British prisoners of the Americans, including Belfort. Now the friends must face Washington for deserting their units. In a rare display of albeit bleak humor, the imposing general leads them into thinking they will be executed—but merely rebukes them.

American troops re-enter and occupy Philadelphia as Clinton succeeds Howe as the British commander. Marcel and Chester halfheartedly pursue British stragglers like Belfort until the whole army pursues the British army from the city. Conversation at the home of the formidable patriot Mother Melrose is interrupted by the appearance of two British soldiers and a Hessian. The Americans present hide but re-emerge when Melrose slaps and draws her sword on the German for denigrating American women. Standing in for Melrose, Marcel defeats the Hessian but spares his life, just as he and his comrades later spare Belfort yet again. Chester serves as courier when Desmond furnishes Washington with gold contributed to the Continental cause. At the Desmonds' home, Mary rebuffs Chester's proposal with the declaration that she cannot marry an Englishman. Undaunted, Chester delivers the gold and reports of skirmishes to Washington. He quickly rejoins the army as it attempts to cut off the British army from its retreat to New York. As the Americans try to maintain their position with cannon, rifle, and musket, the British line presses forward in the surprisingly graphically rendered Battle of Monmouth. Hand-to-hand grappling with sabers precedes the eventual destruction of the American twelve-pounder, though the Americans are technically the victors, having overcome both the British and the premature retreat ordered by Charles Lee (later overruled and reprimanded by Washington). While many become the victims of heat exhaustion, Chester is among those wounded in the furious fighting, knocked unconscious by a grazing bullet to the head.

That the Mary Desmond who tends Chester will now marry him goes without saying, because he has proven himself to be a true American. That the proof of his worth turns out to be the singularly passive act of being struck on the head seems consistent with the logic of a story whose chameleon-like hero maintains that the "constant assumption of superiority" (243) of the British, not ideological difference or ill-considered foreign policy, was the real cause of the war. His "accomplishment" carries no indication of an attitudinal change; it is as arbitrary and lacking in earnestness as the rest of the discourse. That Mother Melrose should have both Tory and patriot sons "did not seem so very strange" (286) to Chester, for the American gentlemen are like the English officers (and unlike the cruel and mercenary Hessians), "mostly honest men serving the cause of their country" (288). The sincere commitment of Mary to the ideals of America seems finally undercut by the author's uncertainty and conservatism and by the effect of Mary's own disguises and being forced by the conventions of romance to join forces with an essentially neutral Chester in a novel whose genre makes it both a tale of love and a tale of war. The lovers' seeming to be Tory but being "really" patriot underscores not just the lengths to which they go for their cause, but also the concept of seeming. The convention of love defeats whatever consistency the logic of war possessed, and Mary must join Chester in his final disguise.

With *Janice Meredith: A Story of the American Revolution* (1899) Paul Leicester Ford, himself a historian, contributed an immensely popular book to the literature about the Revolution. The novel had sold 275,000 copies by the end of 1902 (Altick 224). It opens with its willful and coquettish fifteen-year-old heroine, instead of dutifully preparing for church, reading a love romance very like the one we are reading. The image projects not only a dichotomy between moral consciousness and self-indulgence, but also calls attention to textual convention. A reasoned and sober attitude toward love and toward America comes only gradually and only after Janice has evaded no fewer than four men before marrying the American man whose destiny has all along been a foregone conclusion. And the Meredith estate in New Jersey, with its Edenic/ American designation "Greenwood," for a time falls into other hands before being deeded back to Janice. Through the course of this action, and integrated with the enveloping historical situation, there is once again conspicuous use of metaphor which relates the young heroine to the figures of lover, parent, and land.

To achieve her true identity, Janice must break away from mother and mother country. Her parents are Tory to the end; Squire Meredith is eventually tarred, feathered, and dispossessed, though finally forgiven by George Washington. More importantly, Janice, in the familiar pattern, has to overcome her own bias in favor of aristocracy and the English. We are never certain that the attitudes of her parents completely lose their reign over her. Usually we are simply not told her opinions. Ford does tell us that the Americans, "truly colonial, could not help but think an Englishman of necessity a superior kind of being" (35). Early in the novel Janice is so flattered and flustered by the attentions of Evatt, an Englishman who offhandedly informs her that he is actually Lord Clowes, that she agrees to elope with him. There are two symbolic touches in this chapter: its title is "The Logic of Honoured Parents and Dutiful Children" and her escape with Clowes is prevented by colonial sentries. Despite their "political" influence on her, Janice's parents cannot empathize with her, and "where obedience is enforced from authority and not from sympathy and confidence, there will be secret deceit, if not open revolt" (83). By the time a happy ending is arrived at, George Washington himself makes explicit the parallel between Janice and America as he tries to alleviate the squire's apprehensions about losing a daughter: "You need not fear that the new tie will efface the old one. We have ended the mother country's rule of us, but 'tis probable her children will never cease to feel affection for the one who gave them being; and so you will find it with Miss Janice" (503).

The hybrid and hyphenated character of Janice's ultimately successful wooer, Charles Fownes-John Brereton, suggests that the *altogether* British lover must be misguided and that the mother country must be misguiding. Though from England, he has embraced the patriot cause and has rejected "our old home" (to use the Hawthorne title). In doing so he first becomes an indentured servant working for Janice's father. She is immediately attracted by him and shares many of his misfortunes but she is told (and herself believes) that she must not love or marry a mere servant. Hints abound, nevertheless, that behind the facade is a "gentleman." He feels, for example, that common British soldiers are greater plunderers than officers are. When the disclosure is made that he is actually Colonel John Brereton and he is released from servitude, he becomes a legitimate prospect for Janice. Here again is one type of hero called for by historical romance. He is the hero because of his "American" qualities, but these very qualities are what in a sense make him unheroic. The status and élan associated with aristocracy must also be present in his character, yet by themselves these traits preclude his being genuinely American. Thus the hero, as well as the heroine, oftentimes has a mixture of attitudes; the author attempts at once to make a statement about the American past and to stay within the boundaries of a literary convention. The lovers' quarrel which follows Janice's promise to marry Brereton illustrates the point. They argue about who should receive invitations to the wedding:

> "What? A revolt on my hands already!" exclaimed the officer.
> "'Tis you are the rebel."
> "Then you are my prisoner," retorted Jack, catching her in his arms.
> "You Whigs are a lawless lot!" (383)

His role as romantic hero forces him to play the political enemy.

Long before Brereton accepts Janice's love, he had undertaken a search for parental figures, a search which defines nationality for him. His being a servant to an American Tory suggests the patriotic rhetoric which likened America's role to that of a slave. A tyrant-master is not acceptable as a father. Brereton also fails at first to find a female image of security. In the early chapters he wears a necklace with a miniature of a woman whom Janice takes to be a rival but who is actually his mother. An unrelated age-group peer must be wed, rather than a mother, to form a new nation. Thus, he is soon described spurning this picture and replacing it with one of Janice. Later, Brereton's mother herself, a Mrs. Loring, appears and Brereton's friend Frederick Mobray reveals to Janice that Brereton deserves pity because he is the illegitimate son of this woman and the British general Sir William Howe. In addition, Brereton tells Janice that he is a great-grandson of an English king, thereby validating a "legitimate" heritage. Brereton's finding his place in America therefore includes compromise maneuvers along with specific denials of earlier family ties. Like Asahel Farnlee in *A Lover's Revolt,* he finds his spiritual father in George Washington, the leader with charisma who is both gentleman and democrat. Martha Washington as stand-in for George pleads Brereton's case with Janice. When, in the end, Brereton expresses his love for Janice, he also declares that she is the only one he loves more than he loves Washington. In a single climactic episode he therefore claims wife-father-nation.

Unresolved conflicts between love and duty, America and England, stasis and change, come to a head in Louis Evan Shipman's *D'Arcy of the Guards, or the Fortunes of War* (1899) at the moment when the heroine shoots the hero. Her shooting him late in the novel is not merely an accepted fortune of war, it functions also as an improbable means of allowing the novelist to indicate an acceptance of apparently conflicting terms. Her symbolic—but not actual—killing of her lover is prepared for by all the usual signs of compromise and conservatism. She can simultaneously slay the enemy and accept the lover, even when they are the same person, because her final undiluted commitment need not be to the patriot cause; she nearly kills him, but he nonetheless has "conquered the rebel" (236). In this scheme, the significance of making do with D'Arcy as husband outweighs political disagreement. So conventional a romance is this book that those conventions do not finally have to "compromise" with even the platitudes of an American history. If history overwhelms *A Lover's Revolt* and destroys love interest, here love interest vitiates political statement: the hero does not *have* to embody Americanness of any sort. Partisanship is so muted by an allegiance to a middle way that it makes little difference that in this case the man is an Irish peer and British soldier while the woman's family is staunchly American. This particular image of the Revolution retained enough popularity to be reissued as a play in 1915.

In March of 1777 young John Gerald ("Jack") D'Arcy, having already served a stint in the American war, resides once again in England. The good-humored, lovable, and well-to-do D'Arcy had acquitted himself bravely at Breed's Hill and White Plains, suffering a wound, but has been sent home for injuring another young nobleman in a duel over gambling. As he journeys to London D'Arcy converses with one "Mr. Blunt" about the virtues of the Americans, contending that they are essentially Englishmen and therefore worthy opponents—whereas Blunt feels they are merely rabble. When highwaymen hold up their coach, D'Arcy's skill with the rapier (a gentleman's accomplishment, as are his two terms at Trinity College and his having been secretary at the embassy in Paris) saves both Blunt and himself. Arrived in London, D'Arcy describes his escapade to his surgeon friend Captain Charles Gregory. "Greg" informs him that he (Greg) has been assigned to active duty in America and desires D'Arcy to go along—this despite Greg's feeling the war is "for a foolish king and his mad ministers" (47). Conversation is interrupted by a surprise invitation to supper from the Marquis of G——, a surprise because G—— is an old enemy of the elder D'Arcy and the uncle of the man whom Jack D'Arcy had wounded in the duel. Predictably, the marquis turns out to be the man D'Arcy had saved during the trip to London. A grateful "Mr. Blunt" is now desirous of arranging for Jack's return to America as a member of Cornwallis's staff. (Earlier, the angry marquis had used his considerable influence to prevent D'Arcy's return.)

The scene now shifts to the Philadelphia home of the prosperous Benjamin Towneshend, his son, Edward ("Ned"), and his daughter, Pamela. Pamela, like D'Arcy himself, has lived on both sides of the Atlantic, having been for a time a belle in England. During time off from his duties on General Washington's staff, Edward has reappeared in Philadelphia, where he is romantically paired with his cousin Cynthia Deane. Although a Tory and a Quaker, the Towneshends' neighbor, Samuel Davis, rescues Pamela and Cynthia from obnoxious, swaggering Hessians in a fray propitiously stopped by none other than Jack D'Arcy and Captain Greg. Jack exhibits his superiority to the offended Germans in a subsequent duel. (Thus, twice in this section of the book is the notion of a monolithic "enemy" diluted by their fighting among themselves.) D'Arcy's aid and Greg's rendering medical assistance to Pamela's infirm mother seem not to impress Pamela, who must face them often now that they are quartered in the Towneshend home. A mysterious note from the American camp—actually about Ned's leaving for Philadelphia in disguise—arouses Jack's jealousy. When Jack declares his love to Pamela, she tells him not to speak of the matter again, saying that one of the reasons is that she identifies with her (American) country whereas he has chosen to fight "against people of his own blood, fighting justly" (131).

A dejected Jack is encouraged and relieved when he finds that the incognito visitor is Ned, and—convinced by Pamela that her brother is not there as a spy—orders an end to the British search of the house and helps Ned to escape. A British council of war which plans a surprise attack on Valley Forge degenerates into a drinking bout during which Dacier, leader of the search party, speaks disparagingly of Pamela and is challenged to a duel by D'Arcy—which never takes place because Dacier soon after perishes in battle. After the council disperses, Pamela spots the British attack order and maps still on the table, and determines that she must ride posthaste to warn Valley Forge. Before she can leave, D'Arcy confronts her, his sense of duty now triumphant over his love. Although she has begun to love Jack, her own sense of duty drives her to take up a pistol from the table, shoot him and leave him for dead, and gallop off to warn her brother and General Washington, who are thus enabled to thwart the British attack.

Pamela returns home to find that Jack is unconscious but alive, shot through the arm and side and being cared for by Greg. During the weeks of his convalescence Pamela lends her aid, neither she nor Jack disclosing how he was injured (he explains that his pistol had accidentally discharged). Pamela in her turn feels jealous at seeing among Jack's possessions a miniature of another woman. Once strong enough to travel, Jack plans to sail back to England, telling Greg that no woman could feel more than pity for the wreck of a man. Captain Gregory, however, persists in promoting the match between Jack and Pamela, informing both lovers that they are being foolish and really do love each other, and mentioning to Jack the possible attractions of a pretty estate and Pamela's becoming My Lady D'Arcy.

During their "final" conversation Jack thanks Pamela for tending him during his recovery, maintaining that she need not ask forgiveness for shooting him, since it was merely "a fortune of war." As they talk, on the very brink of separation, they suddenly realize that Gregory is right, that they truly do love each other. The miniature is a portrait of Jack's mother! (just as in *Janice Meredith* and just as the supposed lover-soldier of Pamela had been her brother). Her wounding him and his being wounded suffice to prove their separate national loyalties. She both injures and heals him, shoots him and saves him, marries him yet warns the Americans of the British danger he represents; John both "conquers" and forgives her. Despite these compromises, their marriage cannot signal a new American reality because they remain ideologically separate and parallel rather than united. Having done their duties in the "public" story, they are freed to enjoy the fortunes of love, a fantasy of unity on the bicoastal ground of the traditional romance. They surrender their freight of political meaning. History and fiction are not integrated in a single vision. The original and essential terms of the conflict remain in place, suspended and unresolved.

Adelaide Skeel and William H. Brearley's *King Washington: A Romance of the Hudson Highlands* (1899) pairs so many supposedly contrasting terms that they begin to cancel each other as they emerge, merge, and fade in the reader's memory: the present and the past, the American and the British, the commoner and the noble, the Native American and the white, the male and the female. A successful wooing balances an unsuccessful. Commitment to any one view seems defused. Even the improbable coupling of "King" with "Washington" dissolves into apparent oxymoron (although in the novel Washington himself refutes the title by asserting the superiority of democracy even as many of his admirers insist that he assume leadership in an American version of monarchy). The tenor of "A Romance of the Hudson Highlands" sounds so like Sir Walter Scott that we conclude the genre itself is compromised, despite the book's purportedly dealing with a conflict *against* Britain.

The improbable plot of *King Washington* combines the two love stories with a kidnapping scheme. In the opening scene we are with British officers and their wives at the Morris house on Harlem Heights, where Sir Henry Clinton, Major-General Prescott, and others toast the ladies while the women themselves gossip of Mary Philipse's jilting George Washington in favor of Roger Morris (an event boding ill also in Robert Neilson Stephens's *The Continental Dragoon,* discussed just below). Clinton has received intelligence from one Ettrick that Washington has now established his headquarters up the Hudson at Newburgh, where he could be opportunely seized. When Prescott's half-Indian, half-French aide, Louis Paschal, requests permission to attend the sacred dances near Newburgh, a modus operandi suggests itself. Paschal is to infiltrate the camp, gain Washington's confidence, and lead him into a trap before the American troops fully invest the town.

Near Newburgh, Captain Jonathan Ford takes time out from duties as Washington's aide to court Margaret ("Peggy") Ettrick, daughter of the not-so-secretly Tory family. The appearance of the apprehended Paschal creates problems for both Washington and his aide, complications in the related adventure and love stories. Although actually a British spy, Paschal apprises Washington of British plans to attack near

West Point, information that seems corroborated by the arrival of British ships. The imposing Washington nonetheless places Paschal under Ford's surveillance, which does not prevent Margaret from becoming infatuated with the foreign, dashing, and exotic Paschal. Paschal contacts his co-conspirator Ettrick and sets up as a French teacher for neighborhood girls, fascinating them with his relative sophistication. Jonathan gives Peggy a gift book but by this time Louis declares—albeit equivocally—his affection for her, and Peggy for her part declares she "will never marry a Yankee" (110). Ford, torn between love and duty, places himself still further on Peggy's bad side as an upshot of chancing to overhear her father praying for the king. Even worse from Peggy's point of view, Ford becomes part of a Continental detachment ordered by Washington to dig up a cache of money buried in Ettrick's garden.

Apparent wooing becomes an aspect of military tactics as Paschal, now courting Sallie Jansen, gives her a diamond ring with which to scratch her name on a window the moment Washington arrives at the Knoxes' ball—a signal to the British. Peggy feels rejected and dejected as a result of happening to see the tête-a-tête between Louis and Sallie and not being invited to the ball because of her family's suspected Toryism. The help of the Indians in the kidnapping scheme has been enlisted by promising them their own sacred dance at the Danskamer, the actual permission for which Washington himself grants through hope of gaining an alliance with the tribes. Appalled whites, there to "prevent excesses," look on as "almost entirely naked" (132) dancers, including Paschal, orgiastically celebrate the occasion. A bad omen, taking the form of a snake, materializes from the fire and is killed by Ford. Shortly, further enacting the restraining functions of what he does not know to think of as a European superego, Washington dances the minuet at the Knoxes' ball with "grace, dignity" (164). By the time Sallie etches her name on the glass, Washington and his cohorts have found and deciphered a coded note which leads Washington to the kidnappers' mill, where his accidentally setting the building on fire with a dropped candle prevents the Tories' seizing him. The alarm given, Ettrick and the Indians flee.

Now Ettrick proposes capturing Washington at a dinner party he plans to host, but even the arrangements are interrupted by Peggy's rushing in to warn of the proximity of approaching American soldiers. Having shortly before frightened Paschal off, Peggy faints during the next scene, in which they are alone together (Paschal's familiarly hovering over her leads the bypassing and suspicious Ford to "lose" his faith in love, as Peggy's seemed to have been destroyed by her observing Paschal with Sallie). As she recovers from her swoon, Peggy overhears her father discussing the capture of Washington, attitude toward whom becomes a test case for attitudes about both politics and love. Peggy spontaneously sides with Washington, whom she feels—though he is *not* a king—to be "God's anointed" and at the same time "the veritable personification of American liberty" (234). Mrs. Washington enters the story to advise and commiserate with the troubled Peggy. The girl simultaneously grows to an appreciation of the trustworthy and brave Ford, his person and his politics. Doing her father's bidding, Peggy invites Washington to the dinner but confusedly warns him not to attend; he attends anyway, wary but otherwise unflustered. The signal is given. Ettrick and Paschal draw their guns on Washington, declaring him their prisoner, but Washington declares that, *au contraire*, they are his: Ford and several other soldiers march in to capture the two. The Tory-bribed Indians have meanwhile imbibed too much firewater, and abandoned their role in the intrigue.

As Jonathan and Peggy clear away any last misunderstandings, an important earlier obstacle to their realizing a perfect happiness is retroactively voided by the revelation that Louis Paschal, who at this moment appears dressed as a woman, *is* a woman—Louise Paschal! Peggy could no more have married her than Ash Farnlee could have married George Washington. In her final confession Louise discloses that, all along, she has been motivated by the British General Prescott's promise to marry her if Washington were captured. She had worked as Prescott's groom even after he had turned cold toward her; now a prisoner and perhaps realizing, too, that her mixed blood precludes any possibility of alliance with the now-indifferent Prescott (or with Peggy, for that matter), she evidently poisons herself (which also makes appropriate the associations between her surname and the idea of sacrifice). Touched by sorrow for a fellow woman, Peggy had pleaded Louise's cause with Washington, who had in fact released her to be judged by God alone. Shortly before the deathbed scene Washington, again exhibiting great clemency, had sent Ettrick into exile to Nova Scotia (the family homestead now falls to his sister, Peggy). Jonathan and Peggy marry.

Overt or implied attacks against the tawdry present are paired with a sentimentalizing of a supposedly stable and reassuring past in *King Washington*. Mrs. Washington, for example, possesses "a grace which our own less courtly age envies" (45), while the beauties of the late-eighteenth-century landscape exist where now are "railroad, brickyard, and squalid tenements" (38). Although certainly regal and magisterial in his passing judgments on political, military, and personal problems, the title character neither appears often nor becomes a king; Washington's being named in the title evokes a sacred American image and connects him with yet earlier European images of authority. The mundaneness of democratic principles joins with the glamour of royalty in a book whose initial scene was all-British (this latter authority proves a belated and derived text, too, as a favorite patriotic song of Washington is "No King but God!" [248]). Figures as various as General Knox and Baron von Steuben discuss the advisability of installing Washington as king to forestall mutiny in the army, unavailability of funding, inter-colony squabbles, and so forth. (Alexander Hamilton had, in fact, long argued for an elected monarch. During the troubled times of the story, the period of the so-called "Newburgh Conspiracy," Colonel Lewis Nicola, for many of the reasons just mentioned, had promoted the notion as the answer to colonial difficulties [see Douglas G. Adair, in Greene 408-9].) When Margaret Ettrick tells Washington that he has already played the part of a king, he responds that in America all are king (hence, God?). A democratic monarch would not have seemed a paradox to those contemporary readers—no doubt the only readers the book had—whose identification with the Anglo-American past led them to void logic in their insistence that they were the true Americans—thus rightfully empowered—and the middle way between those who had not been here long enough and those who had been here too long. In other words, many of those inhabitants of the "squalid tenements" also lived outside English text and history, while the Native Americans' wild dance could not be reconciled with Washington's stately minuet.

The setting of Robert Neilson Stephens's *The Continental Dragoon: A Love Story of Philipse Manor-House in 1778* (1898) on the neutral ground north of New York City, foraged and pillaged by both sides, indicates the book's mixed, Anglo-American perspectives. In its simplistic affirmation of British traditions the novel is much less "pro-American" than James Fenimore Cooper's tale of the neutral ground of more than seventy-five years earlier, *The Spy*, which George Washington, at least, invests with something of democratic mystique. To Emily Budick, Cooper had stepped away from the British "to the uneven, intersected surface of America," "the neutral ground of historical, cultural, and epistemological conflict" (17). Whereas Cooper was to some degree discovering American subjects and establishing an American ground for art in 1821, Stephens felt compelled to escape an established and flawed America for the assurances of nostalgia and popular images of an Anglicized America indistinguishable from an Americanized England. Writers of romance in 1900 were no longer self-consciously declaring a cultural independence in, or by the fact of, their writing; a cultural *dependence*

could be expressed even in books superficially about political independence. Considered in their times, Cooper stands on the American side of
neutrality, Stephens on the British side. The world of *The Continental
Dragoon* is neutral not only in its merging America and England, present
and past, but also in its merging its title with its subtitle. Patriot and Tory
lovers can become one only to the extent that the military dragoon story
can become one with the (albeit curious) love story. War must give way
to the establishing of legalized forms for love, and popular literary convention calls for reconciliation in a manor house already suggestive of
Old World forms.

The ease-loving, Tory, upper-class Philipses had taken refuge in the
city in 1777, but now the beautiful Elizabeth Philipse determines to
revisit the country and her childhood home, the manor house and quasi-
feudal demesne whose long Dutch-English history the author recites
(including the ominous story of the Indian prophet who had pronounced
doom for the Philipses and British on the 1758 occasion of Elizabeth's
Aunt Mary marrying Captain Roger Morris in preference to George
Washington). Her suitor and husband-to-be, Major John Colden, sullenly
escorts Elizabeth, upset at the apparent slights of a girl characterized by
"pride, spirit, independence, and intelligence" (26-27), though reportedly
capable of kindness to those of whom she is fond: "her people, her
horses, her dogs and cats, and even her servants and slaves" (137). (No
subtle satirical humor here—the unashamed classism and racism is "disguised" but no less actual and obvious for being projected onto the eighteenth century.) Planning to stay only a week, Elizabeth is joined by her
amorous aunt, Sarah Williams, and her aunt's still-spry old boyfriend,
Matthias Valentine. Soon afterward an unwelcome guest arrives in the
person of Captain Harry Peyton of Lee's Light Horse, in pursuit of Hessian troops and in need of a horse. When Peyton purchases her horse with
Continental bills, Elizabeth tears them to shreds and spurns the captain
as a "dog of a rebel" (91).

A twenty-page personal history of Peyton now interrupts the present
action. It seems that Captain Harry Peyton's ancestry includes Sir
Edward Peyton, of Pelham, and that the family is now prominent in Virginia. Aspiring to become a soldier, Harry trained in England, had a
"fine time in London" (66), and was garrisoned in Ireland. At the news
of unrest in America, his regiment was ordered to Boston, where, already
sympathetic with the Americans, he discovered that not all the rebels
were lawless rabble; many were clearly gentlefolk. His dilemma was
how to desert without impugning his valor and honor. So he waited until
the British were gaining an American redoubt before delivering his letter
of resignation, then fought on the now-losing American side during the

same battle! Advised by Washington to join the Virginia militia, Peyton traveled through New York, where he outpointed a Tory (coincidentally, John Colden) in a sporting duel. In Virginia he in short order became a captain, on active duty when he had chanced to pass Philipse manor house on the trail of the Hessians.

Back in the present, Colden emerges from the shadows to offer his own horse to Peyton. Recognized by Peyton as the duelist who had excoriated him as a "rascally turncoat" (85), Colden claims that he is a neutral (otherwise he would be obliged to take Peyton prisoner). Peyton nevertheless declines his offer, and appropriates Elizabeth's horse as well as her black servingman, Cato. Her discovering that Peyton had been properly taught by London fencing masters extenuates nothing as the saucy Elizabeth tells Colden that she may even begin to love him if he can regain Cato and hang Peyton (her marriage was obviously to be one of convenience). Colden rides off to the south, intending to return for Elizabeth after the week has expired. Meanwhile, a semiconscious Peyton is deposited back at the mansion after a bloody melee with the Hessians. Instead of returning him to his regiment, Elizabeth holds Peyton prisoner and writes a note informing the British of his whereabouts. On the mend, Peyton overhears that Colden is far from being a neutral and is, in fact, a British major.

The romantic farce which follows is marked by unbelievable twists of plot and a laughable and ludicrous (unintended) sexual symbolism seemingly out of keeping with the conscious and typically prudish tone. The personal and erotic share terms with the public and military in the creating of a single story. Peyton has been rendered impotent for active military duty by a slash to his leg—not to mention his sword's having been broken. Elizabeth sees to it that this wound is dressed; and, despite mentioning that Colden is to be her husband, hides Peyton from Colden's squad and tells the British that he has taken the road to Tarrytown. To enlist her continued protection, Peyton feigns that for her he has felt love at first sight, a love-wound. Reciprocating his pretended affection with genuine, Elizabeth has "the feelings of a girl suddenly stormed into love" (159). Although he recognizes that even the maid, a would-be Richardsonian Pamela in her calculations, and the romantic Aunt Sally react to his charms, Peyton nonetheless has troubling dreams of "wild cavalry charges . . . painful crushings and tearings of his leg" (160). Only after he can use "his cane in such fashion that he could carry himself erectly" does the normally imperious Elizabeth begin to feel "a kind of meekness that was new in her demeanor towards men" (171).

When another British patrol passes by, Elizabeth pushes Peyton into a closet, from which he discovers a basement and a secret passageway to

the river. Biding his time and avoiding a premature and dangerous departure, Peyton returns to the house but soon announces that he must rejoin
his men, implying that he should be true to his service and she to her
betrothal. Incensed, shouting that he must be afraid of Colden, Elizabeth
orders Peyton to leave (she had apparently expected him to propose).
Her emotional investment already a loss, she finds from an unwitting
Matthias Valentine that Peyton had only pretended to love her. She vows
revenge by repaying him in kind: she will make him love her, then cast
him aside. "Dressed for conquest" (214) and detaining him, Elizabeth
nonetheless feigns indifference. But now Peyton declares that he does
sincerely love her, as proof of which she demands that he declare allegiance to the king—he will not. Although he does kneel at her command,
she rejects him and leaves, slamming the door behind her. Feeling his
manhood and his political perspectives simultaneously challenged,
Peyton vows to confront the love/war rival, Colden. When the opportunity for a real duel arises, however, Colden dodges the fight by maintaining that Peyton is not a worthy foe—because his sword is broken and he
is a deserter and therefore no gentleman. (Elizabeth, on the other hand,
reconciling herself to circumstances, promotes the duel in the hope of
seeing Peyton further humiliated and Colden's good name vindicated.)
After a parting insult to the Tories, Peyton storms out, "eager to rejoin
the army now to participate in the fighting that would bring about the
humbling of her cause and make it the more in his power to master her"
(249).

Peyton does not get far, however, as Elizabeth's approach-avoid-
ance conflict leads her to order two servants to ambush him and bring
him back to the mansion. He and Colden now exchange insults and the
cowardly Colden strikes the bound Peyton with the flat edge of his own
broken sword. Elizabeth rushes in, restrains and strikes Colden with the
same sword, admits her love for Peyton, frees him and returns his (albeit
damaged) weapon just as Colden's men arrive. Peyton, with the help of
Elizabeth and her servants, fends off these belligerents—for a time by
standing on Colden's sword!—until Elizabeth pushes him outside. He
breaks into the house to continue defending her. Colden's lunge at him
misses and, when Peyton gains the upper hand, he takes mercy on
Colden. Hate and anger apparently expended, Peyton not only embraces
Elizabeth but asks Colden to accompany her to the relative safety of
New York. Although both his rival and his enemy, Peyton says in reference to the superseded Colden, "thank God it's not so rotten a world that
a gentleman may not trust a gentleman" (281).[1]

Elizabeth assigns Cato to Peyton's service for the duration of the
war, telling Peyton to "let Cato bring you back" (282) when the war

ends. Stephens barely salvages a happy ending, in fact leaving the major
characters' fates to a note. Colden goes on to serve in the South and is
reported lost at sea. Peyton, also, never returns, becoming a major but
dying at Charleston in 1780, from which latter event the author manages
to extract the dubious romantic consolation that his and Elizabeth's love
would thus never be "subjected to the wear and tear of prolonged fellow-
ship" (294) (a comment clearly in reaction to contemporary concern over
divorce as well as the need to furnish a happy ending). Only the idea of
their unity in love remains, untested by the divisiveness of ideology. His
lands forfeit, Colonel Philipse moves to England in 1783, where the still
unmarried and apparently unreconstructed Elizabeth dies in 1828. Thus
the normally anticipated joyful denouement and union is more willed
than dramatized. In the absence of a marriage, perhaps the Indian
prophet has the last word after all, a word which suggests at least a measure of America's revenge.

Personal and political motives in Robert Neilson Stephens's other Revolutionary War romance, *Philip Winwood* (1900), overlap in minimal
fashion and only in the middle chapters of the novel. Rumblings of the
Revolution are not heard until after page 100, and the war ends well
before the end of the novel. Idiosyncrasies of character preclude their
carrying obvious ideological weight. Atypical in its plot, the book follows the fortunes of lovers who marry before the war begins instead of
the fortunes of those who discover each other's personal and social
worth by noble behavior, by surviving the Revolution, by earning their
marriages. The Revolution actually separates this couple, who cannot be
reunited until the hero no longer feels that his cause "must take the place
of wife and love" (258)—the converse of those plots which *integrate*
love and adventure in a single vision rather than arrange them in serial
order—and the heroine grows disenchanted with fashionable life. Not
British military or governmental policy, but stereotypes of the British
being effete, supercilious, and culturally superior dominate the depiction
of the mother country. Despite the defeat of the British and "British"
values, compromise with the enemy in many ways marks the narrative—
the enemy's text, since the title page announces that it was written "by
His Enemy in War, Herbert Russell, Lieutenant in the Loyalist Forces."

Before—not at the same time, as would be more common in these
novels—becoming Philip Winwood's enemy in war, Russell is his rival
in love and, always, his friend. The early chapters recount the eleven-
year-old Philip's appearing in 1763 in Russell's New York neighborhood
as a penniless orphan who is taken in by the well-to-do Faringfields

when he discovers his sought-for kinsman has returned to his native England. Philip's improvident father, Oxford-bred but unsuccessful in Philadelphia as either medical doctor or bookseller, and his Edinburgh-born mother have been able to provide him little beyond a love of books. The Anglophobic Mr. Faringfield, holding grudges against England for events long past, not only allows Philip to live in the Faringfield mansion with his two sons and two daughters but also furnishes him with a job in the family's warehouse, where he copies and writes business correspondence. Philip soon joins Herbert "Bert" Russell in a special affection for the bewitching Margaret ("Madge") Faringfield and simultaneously becomes the enemy of her aggressive and possessive older brother, Edward ("Ned").

Belittled by Ned as a mere servant, Philip fears he is disruptive and offers to leave the Faringfields after the father bans Ned from the household. Madge convinces Philip to stay and Ned returns but remains habitually in trouble, managing to be expelled from both King's College and Yale and to embezzle money from his employer in Barbados. As Herbert goes through school and King's College, Phil undertakes his own course of independent studies. (Phil's special interest is architecture, to him primarily a European art, but one which he wants to adapt to American requirements—Frank Lloyd Wright's "prairie style" was emerging just at the turn of the century.) When Phil determines to travel to England to study architecture and tour the storied mother country, Madge sees her chance to circumvent her father's prohibition against England and indulge her desire to become a notable accomplished lady in London. Risen in Faringfield's employ, having saved and invested, Phil seems an appropriate match for Madge and is approved by Mr. Faringfield (whether Madge loves Phil remains ambiguous). Herbert continues working in customs, a defeated rival the point of whose rivalry is defused to a great extent by his shortly afterwards falling in love with Madge's sister, Fanny.

No sooner does the marriage take place than all plans are upset by the news from Lexington and Concord. Herbert's engagement to Fanny is postponed because of Mr. Faringfield's objection to his Toryism. Margaret is infuriated when Philip—who alone in the household takes Mr. Faringfield's side—announces that if war erupts he would fight against the king and that their June voyage is off. Madge argues that he must choose her before his country, their marriage being unsound if he chooses the wrong side or chooses patriotism before love. All the young men enlist: Phil in short order becomes a private, a lieutenant, then a captain; Herbert an ensign and a lieutenant; Ned signs up as a patriot lieutenant, with intentions of his own; the younger Faringfield brother,

Tom, serves as a British lieutenant. Even the family tutor, Cornelius, accompanies Phil as a private. Phil's life during the war is revealed mainly through the accounts sent by a captive Cornelius (Phil's own messages being frequently intercepted). Actual warfare is not rendered—as is generally the case in these novels. Cornelius later reports that during the preceding three years he and Philip were present at Quebec and had traveled on foot in winter through the Mohawk Valley, where they were captured by Indians but allowed by Sir John Johnson to join Washington at Morristown. Phil had then received promotions and wounds at many of the notable sites of the war: Brandywine, Valley Forge, and Monmouth. Shortly before Cornelius was captured and released to the Faringfields, Phil had been rewarded with an independent cavalry command. By contrast, Margaret has meanwhile enjoyed an active life in a New York occupied by the British; particularly is she flattered by the attention of the selfish, vapid, and elegant Captain Charles Falconer, who is quartered at the Faringfield home.

By the time wife and husband are reunited they have grown even further apart. Margaret, involved socially and emotionally with Falconer, wants to impress him by her plot to capture the man who in her view has sustained the rebellion, Phil's commander, George Washington. She has disclosed her plan to Falconer and secretly communicated with Ned, who has bought off several Americans surrounding Washington. On the very night when Madge's nefarious scheme is afoot, so is Phil as he eludes British sentries to arrive at the Faringfield house. Instead of being affectionate after the three-year separation, Margaret seems not only distant but distraught. Her lack of composure and his finding a novel belonging to Falconer lead Philip to conclude that he has interrupted a tryst, though Madge soon sets him straight—thinking the kidnapping already accomplished—by confessing to the plot. Her insincere declaration of love for him does not stop Phil from thrusting her from him and racing by another route back to Washington's camp, aided by a coincidental meeting with the friendly courier who has been surreptitiously carrying messages between Washington and Mr. Faringfield. (This is when he concludes that his cause "must take the place of wife and love.") Phil defeats his own wife's designs by tricking and wounding the traitorous sentry, Ned, from whom he elicits promises to disclose the names of his fellow conspirators and not to remain in the American army. Having taken the alarm, the Continentals easily route Falconer's detachment.

Back in town, Ned soon reappears at the Faringfield home, blaming Margaret not only for the ill-planned plot against Washington but also for betraying it to her husband and for being Falconer's lover. Enraged that his daughter has betrayed her husband and her country, Mr. Faringfield exiles her from his home. After a short stay at Russell's mother's home Margaret falls in with Ned's plan that they go to England so that she—believing divorce easily obtainable—may put herself in the way of wealth and/or nobility. They meet little success in London, as no aristocrats take the bait and as Ned's gambling and drinking reduce them nearly to destitution. The siblings argue; Margaret packs to leave and is struck and pursued by an angry Ned. Three men in the street save her from her brother, and install her at a wigmaker's home. Appearances to the contrary, she has not fallen to a life of shame; one of her honorable rescuers turns out to be Richard Brinsley Sheridan, who introduces her to the theater and life as an actress!

In America, private wars have been fought for the family's honor in addition to the public wars for the nation's honor—wars that provoke each other. While Margaret sailed for London, young Tom Faringfield had defended his sister's honor in a rapier duel with the irresponsible but likable Falconer, who emerges victorious. On Philip's behalf Herbert Russell now throws down the gauntlet to the trifler, this set-to to be fought with pistols. Just as the combatants face off, a messenger stops the duel with a letter from Winwood to the effect that this fight is properly his. Falconer thus gets a reprieve and both Russell and Winwood carry on their military careers. Almost incidentally, the war ends. The scene shifts once again to England when the Russells sell their home to Faringfield and take up residence in the old country; Falconer has already returned to London. Philip arrives in London with Fanny, who later marries Herbert and lives with him and his mother in England, the country for which Herbert has fought. After touring England, Scotland, and much of the Continent with Herbert, Philip stays on in London as a student of architecture.

During 1786, Philip and Herbert recognize in a "Miss Warren" a notable actress who has been playing the provinces, Margaret Faringfield Winwood. (The detail heightens our appreciation of the actress-protagonist in a realistic novel of the same year: *Sister Carrie*.) As they wait at the stage door they spot Falconer, who attempts to abduct Madge. (She spurns him and, in fact, has not even seen him in nearly three years, having gone to the provinces to escape him.) Bert and Phil thwart Falconer's designs and make themselves known to Margaret, who tells them of her life in England and that Falconer had told her that Tom had lost his life in a wartime skirmish. Chastened and contrite (changes altogether unprepared for), Madge announces her virtue and her willingness to acknowledge her marriage, since love and devotion have become more important to her than the theater, praise and admiration, London.

So much for a career. The friends must now track down Falconer, the false Lovelace, whom Philip finds in France and dispatches in the book's final duel. During their travels Winwood happens to see Ned, who has been financially supported by Margaret, being imprisoned for a robbery for which he is to be hanged. Fanny and Mrs. Russell join Herbert and the newly "remarried" couple in Paris for a brief stay.

After vacationing in Italy and Germany, the Winwoods return to New York to begin a family and establish Philip in his "Old World" career as a nonetheless American architect. (Herbert's binational orientation is reinforced by his fighting a duel—in England, no less—against a detractor of Washington's good name.) Margaret's career and collusion with the British during the war fade from memory as she finds domestic bliss in America even though her desire to see England was the actual reason for her marriage. Choosing to be a faithful wife is choosing to be an American. England's meaning in the narrative stems as much from its being morally Vanity Fair as politically a land of tyranny. Culturally, it remains the accepted standard. The war becomes a ground for the working out of a sentimentally and moralistically conceived individual destiny rather than a national destiny that emerges from national differences. Herbert, clearly Philip's enemy *only* in war, mentions no nations when in the end he hopes that his narrative may "instruct some future reader how much a transient vanity and wilfulness may wreck, and how much a steadfast love and courage may retrieve" (404).

Cyrus Townsend Brady's *The Grip of Honor: A Story of Paul Jones and the American Revolution* (1900) illustrates public social and political motives in conflict with private desires. The demands of military honor make it difficult for the protagonist to succeed in romance; for a time it seems impossible for him to remain both a dutiful officer and a gentlemanly lover. If the cultured, charming, and handsome Barry O'Neill altogether merges himself with the grand historical moment, he must become inconspicuous in the fictional love story; his conspicuous success in love would distract readers from "serious" and "actual" history. The plot of the novel resolves itself into the problem of how to retain public honor *and* get the girl. Brady's emphasis on honor as a term in his formula brings out just how conservative he is in attempting to create (more than re-create) an American virtue. In a modern perspective his "honor" seems a narrowly defined perverse fixation, and even in 1900 (and 1778?) would have seemed at least quaint and old-fashioned. His concerns are made to appear less extraneous and are put into a logical turn-of-the-century context by his dedicating the book to "Colonel John

Lewis Good, U.S.V., and the officers and men of the first Pennsylvania United States Volunteers, My Comrades in the Spanish-American War." Brady's prefatory disclaimer serves as a reminder that his contemporary reference groups believed in "exact history" and needed rationale for reading mere fiction: "The interests of the story require some slight variations from exact history in the movements of the *Serapis* and the *Bon Homme Richard* before their famous battle, for which the author asks the indulgence of the reader" (vii).

Brady circumvents the problem of how to place his protagonist on the winning democratic American side and yet make him a conventional gentlemanly, even aristocratic, romantic hero by making O'Neill only marginally American. Barry O'Neill, John Paul Jones's lieutenant, is also the Marquis de Richemont, sometime officer in the navy of the king of France and son of an Irish gentleman of high birth and rank who rose to great wealth and station in France after his lands were confiscated for his following the young Stuart in 1745. By associating Barry with France and the Stuarts, Brady is free to present him as anti-British without having to make him stereotypically and ideologically pro-American—with its suggestions of dismal social and cultural mediocrity. (Brady is not alone in using this ploy. Witness the characterization of Charles Gordon in Herbert Baird Stimpson's *The Tory Maid*.) O'Neill remains in the American service,

Not because he cared particularly for America, for democratic doctrines could never be acceptable to a follower of the young Stuart, the intimate associate of the young nobles of France; but, primarily, because he saw in it renewed opportunities to annoy and humiliate the stout Hanoverian whom he and his people hated, and from whom they had received much harm, and secondly, because he was so much attracted by the strong personality of Paul Jones. (60)

The American republic's "principles are nothing" to him; but he has "found that gardener's son a man—ay, a gentleman!" (104). Even the charismatic and democratic man from history, Jones, functions as a medial figure in the novel: a Scotsman who works for both France and America; humble and of humble origins yet "a great stickler for etiquette" (27). The major characters of *The Grip of Honor* are considered admirable to the extent that they live up to an international aristocratic code of gentlemanly behavior, a code by which honor is an abstraction, divorced from political commitment or cause. One chapter dealing with these "code heroes" is entitled "Gentlemen All." Even Jones is not the ultimate exemplar, as Brady sanctifies the code by referring to "the greatest Gentleman of them all, who had shown His breeding on a

Cross" (129)! Despite O'Neill's indifference to America, Jones reciprocates his love and "cherished the young man with all his generous heart"
(85).

Cruising off the west coast of England in April of 1778, Jones's
crew aboard the *Ranger* spots, pursues, and fires at the *Maidstone,* which
returns their fire but soon runs aground on a dangerous reef. Skillful sail-
ing brings the *Ranger* close enough to lower a whaleboat to check the
British ship for survivors. As the ship breaks up on the rocks O'Neill
scrambles aboard and finds the haughty and beautiful girl glimpsed earlier, along with her terrified maid. The women are lowered by rope to the
whaleboat, where the girl ministers to the injured O'Neill, who has
fallen in love with her at first sight. The young woman proudly declares
that she is Elizabeth Howard, "ward of Admiral Lord Westbrooke, the
governor of Scarborough Castle. I have no father nor mother" (26). Lady
Elizabeth is pleasantly surprised by the gallantry of the "pirate," Jones,
who entrusts the suddenly recuperated O'Neill with the duty of landing
the women ashore near their home. There they are confronted by three
British soldiers led by "Major Edward Coventry, a gallant and distinguished young officer, the son and heir of her guardian, Lord Westbrooke" (32), and fiancé of Elizabeth. Coventry's disparaging the
Ranger and its captain, together with his swearing in the presence of a
lady, draws O'Neill into a sword fight with Coventry, whom he disarms
but spares. Jones arrives and all acknowledge the genteel and honorable
conduct of everyone else. Military duties and a period of being feted by
the French court keep O'Neill separated from Elizabeth for a year and a
half.

Sent to scout enemy forces, O'Neill uses the opportunity to visit
Elizabeth in his persona as the Marquis de Richemont, touring England
on holiday. Elizabeth pretends not to know him, but he is identified by
Major Coventry, who makes an unexpected appearance. O'Neill nobly
surrenders his sword and reveals his military mission and his love for
Elizabeth, who has been doing her part by continuing to postpone her
marriage to Edward. She seems an entirely worthy partner for life—
although O'Neill does qualify his desire: "with youth and rank and station, it would be heavenly spent with you" (87). But her six-month
reprieve ends and she feels bound to fulfill her promise of marriage to
Edward. The most significant of the threats to honor follows, as Elizabeth's guardian offers O'Neill pardon, the ancient O'Neill lands,
advancement, and his own ward's hand in marriage in exchange for the
betrayal of Jones, the most wanted of Britain's enemies. Barry stands
firm against this temptation, and Westbrooke himself later apologizes for
offering the bribe. While this colloquy transpired, Elizabeth had been

silently listening nearby, dressed, at O'Neill's request, in clothes of "the olden time" (90). (How thoroughly the scene is a salute to tradition is also indicated by her replacing with her own portrait the figure of her mother within the frame of a canvas which had fallen and torn—a scene similar to one in Robert W. Chambers's *The Maid-at-Arms*.) Elizabeth is Richard Lovelace's Lucasta reborn as she rushes forward and almost cries "aloud for joy in this triumph of her lover's honor" (103), an honor more important than love. O'Neill can thus have her only by not having her, by rejecting her in favor of honor. In other words, he must choose Jones in preference to Elizabeth, for only thus will she choose O'Neill. She, like Barry, resents being used as a pawn "to compass the death of one poor man [Jones] to whom I owe life and honor" (108). (John Paul Jones was being newly resurrected for praise at the turn of the century. See earlier discussion of Sarah Orne Jewett's New England novel *The Tory Lover*.) In the midst of these complications Elizabeth nonetheless declares her love for O'Neill, while Admiral Westbrooke then declares that Barry must be hanged as a spy or traitor.

Jones himself, disguised as the "Vicomte de Chamillard," now reaches the castle to protest the detention of the Marquis de Richemont and to tell Elizabeth that O'Neill's only hope lies in her delaying his execution by at least six hours. Jones dramatically tears off his wig after he is recognized by Coventry, fearing he too will become a captive but finding that he is free to leave, since Westbrooke had promised the "viscount" safe conduct. A court-martial sentences O'Neill to hang at six-thirty in the evening aboard the *Serapis*, with whose captain Coventry nobly and unselfishly and unsuccessfully pleads for clemency for his rival. As O'Neill is being executed, Elizabeth approaches in a small boat, waving a reprieve signed by the admiral. The half-dead O'Neill must be cut down and revived as Elizabeth rushes aboard with the document written in a hand which Coventry identifies as that of his father— although he instantly guesses that it is Elizabeth's forgery. In another act of self-abnegation, Coventry later that night allows the lovers to slip away in her boat. When Admiral Westbrooke's barge arrives, Coventry accepts all the blame for concealing the forgery and letting O'Neill escape, explaining his actions as a gentlemanly defense of Elizabeth Howard's honor and happiness—even love becomes a form of honor. But he is now in O'Neill's earlier situation, and must face the punishment for lying, disobeying orders, and aiding the enemy. His own stern father rejects him and sentences him to prison to await trial, but allows him to participate in the impending battle.

Fiction is now set aside and "history" and John Paul Jones take center stage for the entire section of *The Grip of Honor* devoted to the famous battle between the *Serapis* and the *Bon Homme Richard*. Over-matched in all but courage and spirit—and actually sinking—the *Richard* manages to exact a surrender from the *Serapis*. Meanwhile the fictional lovers have remained physically separated from the military encounter. On their little boat Elizabeth discloses what Coventry has done for them. Since Howard is "only a woman—loving—beloved—waiting" (97), "with her, love was all" (173). But Barry feels impelled to reclaim his manly status by returning to the ship, to history, and offering to give himself up in return for Edward's release: "I am dishonored, his life is sacrificed for me!" (172). O'Neill and Elizabeth return to the *Serapis* to find Coventry fatally wounded by a blow struck by Jones in the confusion of the hand-to-hand combat. When Westbrooke now also boards the ship he finds that the British have lost and that his son is dying. He drops the charges against Coventry, "the last of his line" (243), who Westbrooke feels was redeemed by his heroic and noble conduct in the battle. The formal requirements of this artificial code are played out as Jones graciously allows Westbrooke to depart and Westbrooke declares himself a friend of Jones. Everyone has proven himself a gentleman. O'Neill's sincere willingness to reenact the sort of sacrifice made by Coventry must replace the deed, and it suffices in his being rewarded with Elizabeth. The demands of honor have been met; O'Neill can now be both a man and a lover, Elizabeth as woman remains only a lover, and Jones as history continues to represent honor. And honor becomes a form of love. Barry O'Neill can conscientiously credit the selfless acts of a forgiven Edward Coventry, "who loved you, even as I do myself" (246).

That a common nostalgic antiquarian impulse underlies attempts to realize in the present both "past" places and past times is illustrated by the National Trust for Historic Preservation's bicentennial republication of *Cliveden* (1903) by Kenyon West (pseudonym of Frances Louise Howland). The summer home of the Benjamin Chew family on the old Germantown Road, however, stands as a more evocative text, reminder of the Revolution, than does the all-too-detailed novel named after it. Just as the new turn-of-the-century genealogical societies stressed connections with the very Britain revolted against, *Cliveden* posits transatlantic ties that bind so completely that "revolution" becomes again a misnomer, and "independence" takes on only the mildest of meanings; the novel does not tolerate more than token broken ties. The connection is explicitly expressed, as well as implied by the action. The female protagonist, for example, has traveled widely, has friends in England, and feels "a comforting sense of companionship, of kinship," with that nation (13). Her brother bemoans England's fighting against her own blood in a war after all not "against the French or the Spanish or the Turk or the Indian" (374). The Americans redeem themselves by being neither too foreign nor too native. In fact, the gallant British hero reports having heard his father's friend, William Pitt, say that "the Americans are the true children of England" (250). In this view, they thus not only carry on British tradition but are, so to speak, more British than the British.

During the brief interlude between the 1777 battles at Brandywine and Germantown, Margaret ("Peggy") Murray wonders that what to her can be only temporary and superficial political differences could have led to war. She thinks of Cliveden, where she and her family are living while the Chews are in Philadelphia, as a particularly superior English country-seat. But events entangle her in the fray when her seemingly more partisan brother, Henry, entrusts her with a packet of stolen British military communiqués which he in turn had taken from the pockets of another patriot, Tim Johnson, shot after robbing a dispatcher. Henry barely has time to tell her to deliver the packet to General Washington should anything happen to him when British soldiers rush into Cliveden, and Henry ducks behind a secret panel. Margaret delays the British while Henry escapes to the stables but is set upon and beaten by the same man who had shot Johnson. Unconscious, Henry is carried back into the house by a gracious and handsome British soldier, Captain Arthur Peyton, and his friend, Lieutenant Shipton, members of a detachment that had received permission to use the stables of Cliveden, always hospitable to all gentlefolk. Our nefarious villain, Dr. Worthington, reports to Washington that the letters intended for Howe no doubt were meant to be intercepted, and that the Americans should act on that assumption. Washington, suspicious of Worthington's motives, mulls over a decision as Margaret arrives with the actual communiqués.

Cliveden achieves its Revolutionary War fame when much of the British Fortieth Regiment holes up there during an action of the Battle of Germantown. During the Americans' assault Peyton is injured and the infirm Charles Murray—father of Henry and Peggy and comrade of Washington during French and Indian War days—discloses his patriot sympathies. The American spy and friend of Henry, whom Margaret had just persuaded Peyton to release, runs from the house then returns to break into it. Peyton duels with his own Colonel Musgrave, soon to be relieved of his command, when the colonel threatens to fire upon the bearer of a flag of truce. Their movements hampered by a heavy fog, the Americans continue to besiege Cliveden instead of embarking on a better-advised advance elsewhere. The Americans' lifting of the siege finds Germantown largely destroyed, the grounds of Cliveden strewn with the dead and wounded, and the house itself sheltering the recuperating American Henry Murray as well as the injured Englishman Arthur Peyton. Peggy serves as an angel of mercy; Howe and Cornwallis visit the valiant defenders of Cliveden. The nearby town becomes appropriately, like the house, a middle ground, Anglo-American, alternately dominated by British and Americans.

Secretly a British agent but always opportunistic, Worthington, self-seeking and greedy for pennies and Peggy, uses his entrée at Cliveden to discredit Peyton by intimating that the captain has cooperated with Howe in a conspiracy against the Americans. Peyton and Peggy, trusting the ungentlemanly and licentious Worthington no more than Washington had, declare duty and honor the highest virtues but are clearly motivated by love when they decide upon an engagement. ("Engagement," of course, may connote a military as well as a marital pairing.) As Henry mends he becomes fearful of the likewise injured Peyton's presence at Cliveden, but is reassured by the information that Arthur had earlier rescued and stayed by him. But another face begins to emerge from his confusions as he tries to recall the man who had assaulted him—the face of Worthington! (The exclamation point is West's only—we are not surprised.) Washington's intention to consult Charles Murray at Cliveden gives Worthington his chance to frame Peyton with fake letters about a British plot to ambush the American general. Coincidentally, on the very night when Washington is to arrive, Peyton plans to leave Cliveden for a Philadelphia meeting with his cousin, Lord Carlisle. Spurning Peyton, Peggy rides off to warn Washington. Already forewarned by Henry of possible treachery, Hamilton and Washington have remained in camp, where Worthington advises them to punish Peyton—soon an American prisoner—as summarily as the British had punished Nathan Hale. When Henry appears at Cliveden a few hours later, however, he is pursuing Worthington, not Peyton, certain finally that the doctor had beaten him. In their ensuing sword fight Henry cuts Worthington's arm and forces him to confess his forgeries and his loyalty to the king. Peggy knocks from the doctor's hand a knife intended for her brother.

Now Margaret gallops to Valley Forge, not to incriminate but to save Peyton. The British troop which was to escort Arthur Peyton to Philadelphia takes Henry prisoner when Worthington accuses him of having stolen Howe's orders in October. While American and British soldiers fight near the Crossroads Tavern, Worthington rides in pursuit of Peggy. Winged in the wrist, she faints, regaining consciousness in the tavern, where Worthington informs her of Henry's capture. The Murrays' selfless servant, Jake, bursts into the room, holding the doctor off with a pistol and telling Margaret that Henry is back with the Americans (freed during the Crossroads Tavern melee by the thoughtful Lieutenant Shipton, secretly also in love with Peggy) and that Arthur has not been executed. Jake's success ends as British troops occupy the tavern; the doctor confidently awaits the expected arrival of Henry, but Margaret jumps him, takes his pistol and forces him to surrender knife and sword. Henry does approach, but finds no hostile reception after he explains Worthington's culpability. Corroborating Jake's report, Henry adds that Worthington had stabbed Shipton, perhaps fearing another rival to Margaret or that Shipton knew too much about his villainy. Peyton appears, embraces Peggy and forgives her for her earlier distrust.

The courtly dance, the exchange of favors and compliments that constitutes much of the plots of novels like *Cliveden*, thus concludes with proof that Worthington's name doubly misleads: he is neither worthy nor worthy of comparison with the American general whose surname his suggests. His obvious concern with self and sex makes his behavior inappropriate to either American or British gentlemen, both of whom scorn him, just as he has opposed them. But the American spy and patriot Rodney Bingham also deviates from the Anglo-American upper-class norm, especially in his disguise as Kelper (merely a "helper"?), villager turned cave-dwelling hermit. Though working for the Americans, his periodically disappearing into the wilds of Pennsylvania identifies him too completely with the American land and thus places him on the borders of the novel's concerns. The money which Margaret had given Rodney was delivered to him secretly and only through an intermediary. Primarily because of the conservative bias of the book, no contrasting but parallel figure is considered so British or aristocratic as to be similarly dismissed from the denouement.

Center stage is taken by the principals of the love story, partners in a new marriage of England and America. Arthur Peyton had actually grown up in a castle, had attended Eton and Oxford. His very errand in coming to an only superficially different America was conciliatory: to gather information for Lord Carlisle, a commissioner of peace. Peyton now wants his future wife and her father, who has welcomed the union, to settle with him in England, "your England as well as mine" (250). Margaret's early days in Virginia and her inheriting a large estate there signal a willingness to accept Arthur's offer, since the low-country Old Dominion is presented as a miniature rural England. After her engagement, albeit before the end of military hostilities, she had told her father that "England and America together can defy the world" (307). Political agreement typically enables marriages in these novels and is a motive in these instances not at all at odds with the romance convention, which demands compatible marriages rather than misalliances. General Washington, himself an American leader but also Virginia gentleman who had slept at Cliveden in the days after Brandywine, blesses the marriage and tells Henry Murray that love should triumph over earthly partisanship. He even wishes Margaret were his daughter, one who seems simultaneously a daughter of England. Only apparently strange, these are clearly not estranged bedfellows. A war for independence ironically brings combatants together; far from separating, this war unites lovers. Since the story ends before Yorktown, the author does not have to contemplate the meaning of an achieved independence. The Revolution does not have to end because in effect it has never begun.

Graphic depiction of inmates' sufferings aboard a British prison ship constitutes the only claim to novelty of Mary C. Francis's simple action narrative *Dalrymple: A Romance of the British Prison Ship "The Jersey"* (1904). Even this originality is mitigated and textualized by the author's note that the story is based upon a contemporary account of this aspect of the war written by Captain Thomas Dring, an account the "brutal frankness" of which had to be toned down to make it suitable for "modern literature" (369). (To Francis and her ilk, modern literature obviously was defined by the genteel tradition rather than the schools of Emile Zola or Oscar Wilde.) She has likewise drawn her Philadelphia scenes from a narrative by Major André. The hero's confinement on the *Jersey* is the major obstacle in the way of his union with an already Whig girl. He must survive prison life (principally by thinking of her); she must fend off various suitors thrust on her by her adoptive New York Tory family.

While Elizabeth Windham promotes the patriot cause, her guardian, wealthy and "the worst hated Tory in New York" (8), forbids his home any longer to Robert Dalrymple, lieutenant in the Continental army. Only the upper-class Tory or the British aristocrat is good enough for his "Bess" or his imposing house in a most fashionable district of the city. As Howe and Clinton close in during the days before the battles on Long Island, Robert bids farewell to Bess in language which grows "more patriotic than personal" (8). Robert joins the decimated army and a college friend, Benjamin Talmadge (classmate, as in *Brinton Eliot*, of Nathan Hale as well), on the island after carrying orders from Washington to Putnam. Robert's being hit by a bullet and by the butt of a musket becomes symptomatic of the desperate fighting, miserable state, and eventual retreat of the Americans. Suffering from his wounds and from delirium and fever, Robert is taken into the foul, dark, and cramped hold of the *Jersey*, to a life of such misery, such putrid food and sadistic guards, that the bodies of the dead are removed nearly every day to be buried in the sands of Long Island.

Nathan Hale has died and the American forces have removed to the heights of Harlem when Bess arrives to beg Washington to arrange a release or exchange of Robert. But the general pleads his powerlessness: Dalrymple remains a captive and New York embarks on a life of fashion and frivolity. The bleak prospect for the Americans is relieved by their victory at Trenton and by Robert Morris in Philadelphia backing Washington for $50,000. Likewise, Bess finds consolation in her carrying of food, drink, and clothing (sometimes in the company of the Quaker Deborah Franklin) to American prisoners at the notorious Sugar House prison. Her guardian's friend, the middle-aged Squire Elliott, has given over his suit of Bess, while Elliott's son, Paul, inspirits her with his developing patriot sympathies. Bess and Deborah unsuccessfully petition the drunken and surly British provost marshall, Captain Cunningham, for Robert's freedom, and are temporarily arrested for carrying a file and a saw into the prison. Bess does meet a man, exchanged from the *Jersey*, who assures her that Robert is, at least, alive. Peter Simpson (Bess's guardian) and his companions enter, critical of Bess but even more so of Cunningham's ungentlemanly deportment. Although she is dissuaded from actively lending aid to American prisoners, Bess nonetheless continues to furnish them the food, which is delivered by Deborah. And she continues to put off Colonel Rutherford, the Tory suitor most favored by her family, along with his offers of wealth and title.

The prisoners aboard the *Jersey* celebrate a joyless Fourth of July. Among a thousand men entombed on a ship built for four hundred, the emaciated and filthy Robert Dalrymple barely survives. Men fight for "air-holes, engaged in primitive combat in the darkness like vicious animals" (181). (This extraordinary atavism posits civilization as a thin "veneering" over "primitive instincts" [219] and thus smacks of a literary Norris- or London-like naturalism which the author otherwise spares her polite audience.) Their attempted rebirth from the ship turns abortive after officers get wind of Robert's and others' plan of escape. On a particularly stormy night prisoners had sawed through ship's planking and dropped, naked, into the sea. British boats pursued the escapees, most of whom were killed. Robert himself was struck in the left arm by a ball, knocked unconscious, and brought back to the ship, where he becomes the only survivor among the plotters. All that has changed is that now there are somewhat fewer prisoners and fewer liberties allowed by the wardens. By the time the story of the attempted break gets to Simpson, Dalrymple has been listed among those killed. Bess faints when she overhears Simpson's reporting these events.

Conditions in the city itself worsen; there is much plundering and burning, and Simpson's investments are largely lost. The grand celebration, the Meschianza, planned for Philadelphia on the occasion of Clinton's succeeding Howe as commander-in-chief, seems a welcome escape from New York. Deus ex machina in the form of a sympathetic Lord Percy's giving him a safe conduct allows Robert Dalrymple to startle all by appearing at the ball and claiming Bess, though their planned elopement is thwarted by their being separately detained. Robert is liberated by Talmadge from Clinton's retreating army just in time for him to participate in the crucial military conflict of *Dalrymple*, the oft-described Battle of Monmouth. Both sides are victimized by sunstroke, the Americans by Lee's mismanagement and cowardice. The rivalries of love and war merge as Robert and Rutherford fight and injure one another amid the din and confusion of the general battle. In spite of Rutherford's having prevented Dalrymple from being exchanged and his responsibility in having him arrested in Philadelphia, for Bess's sake the polite Robert spares him. As Robert leaves him to be rescued by the British, Rutherford simultaneously admits personal defeat and acknowledges that the spunky Americans will not be subdued. Converted by Robert's example of gallantry, the recuperating Rutherford later compliments Dalrymple's behavior, resigns his suit of Bess, and vows to return to England.

News of the battle finds its way to Bess in New York through Paul Elliott, who has joined the Continental army. Elliott suggests elopement as again her only alternative, and Robert's own plan soon arrives by way of a cooperative maid. Bess orders an uncooperative coachman to deliver her to the waiting Robert, to whom she is married even as hostile musket fire interrupts the ceremony. In flight once again, Robert and Bess outdistance Peter Simpson's men and take a boat across to the shore of Jersey, where at Monmouth the military climax had been reached.

Dalrymple's comment at book's end—"We have bagged a pretty good lot for one night, one bride and five prisoners of war" (361)—reminds us of his earlier statement that his language in talking to Bess had become "more patriotic than personal." If his rhetoric now does not become more personal than patriotic it does become both, a rhetoric in which military enemy is identified with now-dominated wife. When Peter Simpson's compeers had complained of the impulses of the Revolution, they had bemoaned its deleterious effects on women (including daughters especially), servants, and generally those who otherwise understood their justly subservient stations in life. Elizabeth had protested that she had attained adulthood, and that between her and her guardian should be declared an "armed truce" (240) about her opinions and her relationship to Dalrymple. In his affiliation with Bess, Robert now serves the social role of Simpson, having "bagged" a servitor, a wife rather than a woman: for her the Revolution is not the revolution. Her maturation frees her from parental authority apparently only for the purpose of placing her under the control of another man.

For Dalrymple, conquering a man enables the conquering of a woman; that is, war must end with marriage in romantic adventure novels about the founding of nations. Sometimes, conversely, as in this novel, his opponent's winning the woman turns the military and love rival away from interest in winning the war. Dalrymple possesses both personal and public authority as the new (male) American, for he has paid his dues in physical suffering and sacrifice for *his* country. The woman has only *supported* the man's role, while he has faced the enemy. To exacerbate her social and political offenses against progressive thinkers of her present (or, more obviously, ours), this female writer often exhibits what might be called a temporally binocular vision; that is, she sees the past and the present juxtaposed. Always to the detriment of the present, she refers to buildings and other sites which now occupy the spaces of the Revolution, the space as well as the time of the Revolution occupying her imagination. By implication, the more like the past the present can be, the better.

By 1906 the counters manipulated in these novels have recurred so often that even details reappear. Specific patterns change; the basic formula remains. *Valley Forge: A Tale* by Alden W. Quimby, for example, shares time and place with *Cliveden,* a portrait of Quakerism with *Hugh Wynne.* Its first chapter's title, "Mars and Cupid," repeats, with the terms reversed, the title of the first chapter of the Southern novel *Joscelyn Cheshire.* Once again not only do a war story and a love story coexist and parallel one another, but the two entwine to furnish a popular image, if not profound vision, of the Revolution: "How strangely war and love are blended in human experience" (87). Havard Brown's sorting through his experience to discover a proper political cause blends with his search for an appropriate wife. In both cases Havard is allowed false starts, which are later retrieved and rectified. By the novel's end Havard has made his choices, but the full range of the martial and marital options presented furnish the author's complete picture. Rejected options are in many ways invested with their own saving graces. Not only does Havard's first wife not have to be his last, but she herself changes so much that she comes to represent a wide choice of possibilities.

On the road between Philadelphia and Lancaster on the day after the battle at Brandywine, Havard Brown pauses to report news of the war to the Tory Judge Moore before he rides on to dine at the home of his girl-friend, the plain, rural, dutiful and unassuming Frances Jones. Like Frances influenced by a Quaker heritage though not technically a member of the faith, Havard loves liberty but has not actively partici-pated in the war. The blacksmith at Valley Forge repairs harness for Havard and tells him of probable Continental troop movements and of their stores hidden nearby—while William Tryon, British sympathizer and relative of the New York governor, eavesdrops. Just as Havard has now visited both Tory and patriot men, given and received information, his meeting with Frances is balanced by a conversation at the Anglican church (Quakerism is presented as simpler, thus more "American") with the polished and vain Philadelphian Ethel Thomson. As Ethel and Havard travel to the home of William Bull—a relative of Ethel—for dinner they encounter the duplicitous Will Tryon, who has long lusted for Ethel.

Though not taking up arms, troubled by whether he should adhere to Quaker principles of nonviolence, Havard does embark on a career as American scout and courier. The shy and restrained, yet manly and alert Havard poses as a sauerkraut peddler to gather at the British camp cru-cial military information, which he passes along to Colonel Dewees, who in turn reports to Anthony Wayne. The sly but not shy Will Tryon, now a personal as well as political rival of Havard, works at cross pur-poses to him by taking advantage of his acquaintance with Continental soldiers to obtain those passwords which enable the British to make the nocturnal raid on the American camp later called the "Paoli Massacre." The British torch the valley forge and the valley mill as the Americans manage to ferry their military stores across the Schuylkill on a makeshift barge. Skirting British emplacements, Havard makes for Ethel's Uncle Thomson's home, and finds himself in a woods face to face with Ethel herself, who recounts the British pillaging and burning of her uncle's house and their rude behavior to her. (Already Frances Jones had argued with Howe that the Paoli Massacre was uncivilized; we soon discover that the British have looted the Browns' farm as well.) Havard surveys the damage at Thomson's, and Ethel remains for a few days at the Browns', for her Aunt Bull's home has also been burned. Aware of a long-standing commitment to Frances and pacifism, Havard's dilemma also takes the form of simultaneously pursuing Ethel and an active Americanism. Complicating the situation is the fact that Frances is obvi-ously the woman more identified with the American land.

The Brown farm is crisscrossed by Americans and British. Alexan-der Hamilton reports on the British; Major André looks for a horse which carried money and papers which would further incriminate Tryon, and informs the Americans that Howe is willing to reimburse the losses of those not in open rebellion. An American mob led by the drunken and uncouth, threatening to despoil the honorable Judge Moore's home, makes no such conciliatory and civilized gesture; Havard and Moore together must dissuade them from a barbarism considered as grievous as that of the British arsonists. Similarly, Mr. Jones excuses Will Tryon for his Toryism but not for his savagery toward his neighbors. Frances's simplicity and patriotism seem a welcome contrast to Tryon's duplicity, yet it is Ethel who still infatuates Havard, even at a Quaker meeting attended by both girls. While Frances does not fail to perceive the feeling existing between Havard and Ethel, she remains silent. Mrs. Brown, on the other hand, openly voices her fears that Ethel would be incapable of appreciating the rural ways of her son. Despite his mother's preference for Frances and his own thoughts of her, Havard elicits a promise of marriage from Ethel by the time he accompanies her back to her home in British-occupied Philadelphia.

The title of the first chapter finds its reprise in that of the fifteenth: "War and Wedding." The enveloping action has just included the battle on the Germantown Road, during which the Americans' decisive advantage is jeopardized by their lingering to oust the British from the Chew mansion. Burgoyne has surrendered, but the British navy controls the Delaware River. Another connection between the enveloping and developing action is established when (even) Frances, on a shopping trip to Philadelphia, spots a disguised Tryon chatting with her cousin, Lydia Darrach (who played a minor role in *Cliveden* as well). Despite her Quakerism, Frances eavesdrops on Tryon, Howe, and others, eventually passing valuable military information along to the Americans. The fictional action per se, the marriage of Havard and Ethel, takes place, appropriately, in the Church of England in Philadelphia. Yet Havard still wonders whether honor binds him to Frances—and a more overtly American cause. The contrast comes home to him when he comes home, when he observes the suffering, the scarcity of food and clothing, at Valley Forge during this winter of 1777-78. (Even here, archaic renderings and amateurish poeticizing distance the potentially unpleasant and evoke nostalgia. Limbs may freeze, but the snows which drive across Valley Forge appear gentle indeed: "soon the feathery messengers fell in myriads" [185-86].) While Havard's mother takes in General Knox of the Americans to lend practical aid, Ethel for her own social amusement interacts with officers and their wives housed in the vicinity.

Seeing the foragers of Captain Henry Lee's small command taken captive by British troops, Havard outraces Tarleton and a Tory outlaw to get word of their danger to the main squad. Ethel and Havard together visit or see American notables like Anthony Wayne and Mrs. Washington and foreign ones including Baron von Steuben, Baron DeKalb, and Lafayette. But Ethel's significant merging with American place and consequent appreciation of Havard (and Frances) result quite in spite of her will, from her contracting smallpox, common in the American camp. Despite fears of contagion, Havard allows Frances to minister to Ethel. Her rival in love, Frances nonetheless tends Ethel as an angel of self-sacrifice, anointing her face with olive oil to prevent her scratching and disfiguring herself. Refraining from telling her of his earlier love for Frances, Havard discusses with Ethel their obligations to her. The example of Frances and the trauma of disease chasten and inspirit Ethel and Havard; Ethel's affection for Havard and sense of marital duty grow as she seems to recover. Apparently and symbolically weak-hearted, however, Ethel dies anyway, a fictional event which sets off a flurry of American moments in history: news of the French alliance; Clinton's evacuating Philadelphia and the British being pursued across the Jerseys; the Americans leaving Valley Forge for active duty. Havard's earlier opponent in love, Will Tryon, is likewise victimized by both history and plot, since he represents the "wrong" side and no longer has a woman to compete for and pursue: he is run down and hanged as a British spy.

Frances, predictably, comes down with the deathly illness as a result of nursing Ethel. The invalid confesses to a love for Havard that has lasted since childhood, one that therefore has roots not only deeper in American soil but is temporally more significant than Ethel's love for him. Havard, for his part, speaks of a love for Frances only superficially and momentarily interrupted by his marriage to Ethel. Mrs. Brown, eager to help Frances, informs her son that "something that thee said yesterday destroyed the disease that brought her low" (277). Suddenly hopeful, Frances quickly and not really unexpectedly regains strength and health. Havard proposes and is accepted on September 12, 1778, exactly one year after the day after Brandywine and their last walk together, described in chapter 1. Their wedding (a Quaker one, it goes without saying) takes place on September 12, 1779. Blissfully happy, the couple become the parents of a girl, christened "Ethel" at Frances's insistence, on September 12 of 1780.

Thus both Havard and Frances pay tribute to the character who seemed an incipient Tory, who in other books of this sort would have turned altogether against the idea of independence. Ethel's initial vanity, social pretension, and urban roots work against her claims as heroine. Mars and Cupid interact in a *single* story only to the extent that Ethel represents a potential enemy who must therefore be reclaimed, and Tory claimants for her (her own disposition as well as Will Tryon) defeated. Frances and Havard do their duty by Ethel (and the British traditions she represents), acknowledging her just as the photographs printed with the text acknowledge "American" houses but only as places where Cornwallis and Howe slept. Political difference to one side, the women reciprocate favors and become agents promoting each other's love for Havard: Frances makes Ethel pretty for him and inspires them by her altruism; Ethel's illness brings Frances and Havard again together. By the time, however, that Havard's first wife grows more American, the image of her earlier, "Tory" self has been fixed, described as well as commemorated. Thus, although Ethel in effect becomes Frances (and vice versa), she has already played her role and remains expendable: Havard is allowed to correct his misalliance since the author has imagined an option. Havard's pursuit of Frances would have permitted a story of Cupid, but hardly a story of Mars and Cupid conjoined in a melodramatic tale defined by at least initial and superficial personal and political conflicts and difference. Romantic plot convention has required Ethel as a wife; a political agenda requires Frances. The direction of Ethel's transformation validates the worth of Frances, but the starting point of her transformation invalidates Ethel's own ultimate worth. In the end Havard must marry Frances, for Frances has been there from the beginning, before and after Havard's infatuation with Ethel. He finds no competition in his courting of Frances. Like America, she is always available, waiting.

From the redundancy of its complete title to the incompleteness of its culminating battle, *An Express of '76: A Chronicle of the Town of York in the War for Independence* (1906) signals itself a text, and a text of its times. Although "express" is employed in the sense of "messenger" or "courier," it can also mean the message itself: an express is a chronicle. The book's introduction informs us that this particular express has been relayed to the present by means of a journal kept by the great-grandfather of the author, an express (itself and himself), however, not of 1776 but of about 1825. 1776 has been mediated. Already the text divorces itself from actual "history," an originating moment, by its being belated and itself an instance of material culture not all of which can be retrieved or reclaimed (several pages of the journal have been lost behind the weatherboarding). The turn-of-the-century monumentalizing of events is doubled by the great-grandfather's already having been furnished the opportunity to transform personal deeds into public history. At the same time, the novel suggests that (especially in consideration of the missing journal pages) history itself can never be known, is incomplete and can come to us only through texts. The 1906 writer of the novel thus retrieves pages rather than history and is himself textualized when we discover that his name, Lindley Murray Hubbard, encapsulates the names of three characters *in* the novel: Lindley Murray, Miss Murray, and Mr. Hubbard. The author has already been authored and can add no new term to a celebration of the family, the closed and enclosed world, which authored him. In other words, *An Express of '76* becomes a ritual literary acting out toward expected ends reassuring to nativist readers of 1906.

Jonathan Hubbard of Hubbardton, fresh from his only year at Harvard, has increasingly involved himself in Revolutionary activities following the death of his parents. On the present occasion he has been sent by the Boston Committee of Public Safety to deliver an important message to General Washington, but en route literally encounters the carriage of the mild and pretty Polly Murray, her upper-class New York friends, and the "strangely fascinating Lady Claremont" (3). No harm done, he soon arrives in New York, his horse exhausted because a surly character along the way had ridden off on a fresh mount arranged for Hubbard. Fraunces Tavern serves as the meeting place of military and civic notables, including Daniel Morgan, Aaron Burr, Thomas Paine, and Benjamin Franklin. Morgan and Hubbard carry the dispatch to the confident, vigorous, yet dignified Washington. The note (from the Boston Committee but a summary of an earlier note from a New York woman) discloses the identities of three men plotting to capture Washington, who now rewards Hubbard with a lieutenancy for thwarting this "Tryon Plot." Although his "mind was filled with war and kindred topics, among which no tender thoughts of petticoats had place" (84), Hubbard later consoles young artillery captain Alexander Hamilton on his lack of success with Polly Murray's lovely friend Miss Schuyler with the thought that "the war's not yet over, nor the chances for glory, fortune, and love" (76). Thus setting the terms that must be combined in the historical romance, Hubbard himself nonetheless embodies only half the formula; he remains unaware that his chance meeting with Polly Murray while on a military mission has already told the reader of his destiny in love (even if we did not know that the author's name pairs the two).

Instead of truly "expressing" himself (his self) Hubbard continues to carry others' texts of love and war. He delivers communiqués between Colonel Trumbull and Captain Webb, and a letter from Margaret Moncrieffe, daughter of a British officer, to Burr. Hubbard's duty at the ladies' "Sociable" is not to socialize but rather to keep a vigilant eye on Washington. (Hubbard asks one Captain Nathan Hale to report to Trumbull the uneventfulness of this gathering.) Though of old and titled British lineage, kinswoman of Edward Gibbon (another historical text), Lady Claremont has designed a banner for the colonials, said by Dr. Rush to personify purity and patriotism. Even as she plays affecting harmonies on the piano, Lady Claremont pleads with Washington to reinstate political harmony with England. Having again met Miss Murray and her friends, and learned more of Polly's cultivated and successful New York Quaker family, Hubbard is pressed into accompanying Burr to a boat in which he embarks with Miss Moncrieffe. Hearing others approach, Hubbard conceals himself in the shrubbery and overhears a clandestine colloquy between Lady Claremont and the British officer Colonel Simcoe, whom he recognizes from Simcoe's having been at the tavern during his own ride from Boston (another occasion when Simcoe had apparently attempted surreptitious communication with Lady Claremont). All Hubbard can report to Colonel Trumbull is his inference that Simcoe is the brother of Lady Claremont's absent husband and that some sort of anti-American plot is afoot.

Before getting involved in further military intrigues, Hubbard does deliver his own political views in a public forum. However, and significantly, his speech and his audience share a derived status. The listeners are the Sons of Liberty (not, that is, "Liberty" itself, let alone what the word refers to). Hubbard's words recall those of Paine's "Common Sense," but he insists "they were just my ideas" (159). (Hamilton, in parallel fashion, tells him that Jefferson cribbed "all men are created equal" from Judge Wilson.) The pretense that these particular words are inevitable and held in "common sense" would appear an outcome of sanctifying archives at a date well after 1776 (recall that the great-grandfather's journal dates from approximately 1825). Only during the decades after the death of the living "facts" could the words themselves come to seem as important as their meanings, the memorized subject matter of nineteenth-century schoolroom elocution and oratory—and the substance of the historical romance.

Hubbard, fascinated if not infatuated by Lady Claremont, accompanies her on a walk following which he tracks three mysterious horsemen to a nearby tavern. There he confronts Simcoe and Captain André; Simcoe fires at him just as someone else knocks him out. Burr charges in to his rescue and crosses swords with André until André and Simcoe flee, pursued by a posse of Americans. Late for assigned military duty, Burr entrusts Hubbard with the responsibility of taking Miss Moncrieffe home. Hubbard's next orders come from General Washington, who has just given Lady Claremont free passage within American lines. Washington assigns him and Count Bonvouloir the job of obtaining, through

General Clinton, boats which they must ensure are delivered from Yonkers to Jersey. The rough-hewn Corporal Cotton conducts them toward Yonkers. Meanwhile, Adjutant Reed reports that the British under Howe are landing on Long Island. Washington orders Knox's forces to Brooklyn, anticipating that the British will fortify the heights.

Bonvouloir's past and private affairs dominate the plot as we discover him to be the great love of Lady Claremont's life, a man passing as a merchant but in fact arranging a league between America and France to be implemented when America, the predestined land of the future, proves herself with a significant victory. Actually "Armand de la Rourie," he had not married the present Lady Claremont only because his family had rejected her and because she had been maliciously misinformed about his truly honorable intentions. In a fit of pique and despair she had wed her now-imbecilic English husband (which Bonvouloir only now learns). Bonvouloir's narrative is interrupted by the barging in of Burr and the Irish-French Chevalier Conway. As they drink together, Conway grows so hostile and insulting toward Bonvouloir that the latter is forced into a duel in which he proves his gentlemanly facility with the sword; each has been only scratched as Conway withdraws. As night and a storm come on, Hubbard happens upon a woman struggling to free herself from two of his earlier antagonists. He manages to save her but is knocked senseless just as he recognizes Lady Claremont. Hearing the scuffle, Bonvouloir arrives to shoot one assailant, slash the other, and take Hubbard to a nearby church where he and Lady Claremont acknowledge each other as Armand and Heloise. Bonvouloir takes the message for General Clinton from the injured and fevered Hubbard but does not travel very far when his path is blocked by Simcoe, whom he unhorses before again galloping off. Lady Claremont reveals to Simcoe the true identity of Bonvouloir.

By the time Hubbard recovers, the British have won the Battle of Long Island and the American forces are evacuating New York. Finding a stray boat, he crosses the Harlem River in the fog and is greeted by his old guide Timothy Cotton, with whom he rows south to Kip's Bay, dodging British boats all the while. Lady Claremont re-enters the story, helping to delay the British at the Murrays' home as the Americans retreat up the island, expressing faith in the colonials' cause and evidently relieved that Washington has not been captured. Colonel Knox, in effect repeating a *later* text by way of paraphrase (Emerson's "Concord Hymn"), speaks of firing a shot " 'that shall ring around the world' " (288). The entourage of Hubbard, Burr, and Conway rush safely through a band of Hessians. Relinquishing his futile search for his uniform and sword, Hubbard joins Burr in searching for and locating Miss Moncrieffe.

Ambivalent in her feelings about Burr, however, she decides to rejoin her father aboard the British ship.

American forces succeed in removing from Bayard's Hill despite British fire and having to ford a swift stream. Hubbard continues to carry documents: from Conway to Charles Lee and from Hamilton to Colonel Knox. During a skirmish Simcoe disarms and captures Conway, but Bonvouloir intervenes to take Conway back to American lines. As the battle wanes Hubbard lies quietly to escape detection, then himself heads toward camp. In his fleeing British soldiers he finds the love of woman in a final scene which reads like a ludicrous and redundant parody and caricature of Freudian symbolism, all the more striking for its tone of innocent wonder. Hubbard passes through a gorge to a cavern from which he sees Mistress Polly Murray in a boat laden with milk to be stored and cooled in another nearby cave. Much of even this encounter consists of Polly's defending Lady Claremont as an American sympathizer, verifying that the upper-class British woman can identify with the American "democratic" movement and is, in fact, a dynamic character now aligned with the colonials. (Polly herself, of course, has been all-American from the start.) With the discovery of love, the action plot also abruptly concludes, with only an allusion to Hubbard's later distinguished military career and the fates of the other principals. As Lord Stirling had earlier said to Lady Claremont in speaking of patriotism and purity, "in war, madam, as in love . . . we are never certain till the battle's won" (119). The love battle is complete. The specific military battle with which the novel ends remains incomplete, not because the battle was inconclusive but because the "story of the battle is cut short by several missing and illegible pages, difficult to follow" (335)—"follow" in both the senses of "discern" and "continue." The writer guides the reader to the pages of Professor Henry P. Johnston's history for the conclusion of the conflict. If the American victory at Harlem Heights is not a text of some sort, it simply is not.

Having portrayed the power of the American cause to convert Lady Claremont, Hubbard the novelist, in the context of his present, refers to the always-American foregone wife of Hubbard the historical protagonist: "In the Hubbard family we have a portrait of our great-grandmother, Mistress Polly Murray Hubbard" (335). The love convention is thus imperative even as an apparent afterthought about another's pictorial account-become-memorial in a book which has previously made little of a love interest for the hero. Anglophile polemics are stressed in the developing as well as the enveloping action, in both Hubbard's comment that "we are pretty much of one race of English stock" (74) and in Washington's opinion that now fighting *against* England is "the plain duty of

Englishmen" (129). Lady Claremont comes to sense the rightness of the American side while Americans consider themselves the true Britons. The city celebrated by the title is called York, not New York. Another notable public spokesperson, Benjamin Franklin, projects this decidedly conservative ideology into the future: "We are to-day setting forth an influence for the better of mankind, and this nation will have become, in another century, one of the greatest the world has seen" (40-41). Not everyone would have agreed that the United States had become a world power for "the better of mankind." But the extent to which many thought this a reassuring fantasy, in the face also of domestic turn-of-the-century social and political upheaval, is indicated by the author's stating at book's end that Franklin's vision has been corroborated by the New York of 1906.

THE SOUTH

Central to a Southern consciousness (or consciousness about the South) in 1900 was the Civil War and Reconstruction. Even in novels purportedly about the Revolution, therefore, a real subject becomes the latter conflict and its aftermath. (The War for Independence, in any case, had been viewed as, in part, a civil war pitting brother against brother and a central government against "rebels.") These books typically validate a social and political agenda so conservative as to make their dealing with a war for independence seem ironic: they implicitly declare dependence upon not just Anglo-American but also Anglo-Southern traditions of historical interpretation and literary form and formula. A passion for the past has been viewed as characteristic of both European and Southern romanticism, in contrast to the orientation to the future and possibility of the New England Transcendentalists (see Commager xxxv). Conventions of historical romance demanded a valiant aristocratic (that is, "British") hero, while the heroine—perhaps after temporary forays into a world of meaningful action—must finally resign herself to a subsidiary role in the love plot, in so doing becoming marginal and merging herself with stereotypes of the Southern belle. Forays into independence remain in the end more provisional than the however mild rebellions of contemporary Southern women in novels like the Virginian Ellen Glasgow's *Phases of an Inferior Planet* (1898).

For evidence that these writers also remained oblivious even to much earlier African-American analyses of the irony of celebrations of freedom and independence, witness the—intentional or not—lack of any expressed awareness of political statement by commentators like Frederick Douglass, whose peroration on the Fourth of July is referred to later. More contemporaneous but equally angry satire directed at the holiday includes Paul Laurence Dunbar's *New York Times* piece of 1903 (Lauter 2: 475). Knowledge of colonial African-American history was sketchy, available documents few. In the retrospect of a century, critics can discern the "1896 recognition of Paul Laurence Dunbar by William Dean Howells and the regular appearance of Charles W. Chesnutt's writing in mainstream magazines" as evidence that black writers were beginning to develop a significant and biracial readership (Bruce 11). But popular authors of the time evinced little interest in black history of the Revolutionary period—and little understanding and sympathy. Present events, like the "series of armed black uprisings in the early 1890s" and "the violent suppression of blacks, as in the 1898 Wilmington 'riots'" (Shulman 53) which Charles Chesnutt in 1901 found, sadly, at the marrow of a tradition, suffered only a relatively more calculated and pointed exclusion from white middle-class consciousness and discourse than did the African-American past. The emphasis borne out by history clearly fell upon "separate" in the separate but equal doctrine promulgated by the *Plessy vs. Ferguson* decision of 1896.

Authors' uses of the "Cavalier myth" connect the South with England so intimately that "Revolutionary War novels" strikes us as a misnomer almost as misleading as—applied to these same books—"Civil War novels." Old-time white Southerners preferred the phrase "War between the States," and these novels often dealt with the traditions of another nation—Great Britain—altogether. Civil War romances by John Esten Cooke or Thomas Nelson Page share a vision of the Old South with these novels of the Revolution in the South. An old-style Southern social, political, and literary program overrides both historical accuracy and the distinction between romances about the Revolution and those about the Civil War. The "joyous work of reconstructing the historic mansion" following the Revolutionary War, referred to in George Cary Eggleston's *A Carolina Cavalier* (1901), stands in obvious and marked contrast to the actual Reconstruction era, and can be read as a response to the supposed evils inflicted by the North upon the South between 1865 and 1877. By the author's projecting concerns associated with the Civil War onto the Revolutionary War he can fantasize a gallant participation in a war and hold on to his sentimental and paternalistic image of the Old South, a South which in this way can survive the (a) war. These Cavaliers are "reluctantly drawn into a struggle to preserve their native soil against England's tyranny, just as their descendants, in 1861, would battle against Yankee aggression" (Sutherland 184). But the British let them keep their world, a world in fact only just coming into being with the advent of the cotton gin in the 1790s; the Yankees did not let them keep their world. To us—does the writer premeditate this?—these views seem less anachronistic, or at least more fitting and excusable, in a vague and misty, because more distant, past. The formula Revolutionary War romance seemed to predicate antiquarian motives more thoroughgoing than those expected in Civil War novels of the Lost Cause. The denouement could posit a cause not lost, the paradoxical possibility of an Old South living even as the reader and writer knew it was dead. The war in the Revolutionary War novels could truly and unabashedly end with the sentiment that tomorrow is another day, a day which did not have to be bemoaned as a past gone with the wind.

*   *   *

The accommodation effected by the Revolution in Mrs. Burton Harrison's *A Son of the Old Dominion* (1897) results from a symbolic merging of its three grounds: the mountains, the Tidewater region of Virginia, and England. The post-Revolutionary settlement—treaty, marriage, inheritance—brings together characters and ideas associated with each region in a centrist vision which erases the perceived eccentricities of the first and third grounds, rounding them off, as it were, to the second. Rolfe Poythress, the "son of the Old Dominion," is a child of the West, the wilderness, who discovers his descent from British nobility. (The "daughter" or "son of" in several titles of Revolutionary War romances connotes not only dependent status but also an impulse to create a heritage *ex nihilo,* to invent a nation otherwise notable for its lacking a long past. If descendants exist, they must have come from *somewhere!)* Just as he inherits a name from John Rolfe, his future wife counts Pocahontas among her ancestors (interesting and appropriate in this context is the fact that Pocahontas died giving birth while in England). Rolfe and May are destined to marry and to possess the plantation Vue de l'Eau, which in many ways is likened to nearby Mount Vernon. The novel's title, in fact, allows the possibility of its applying to the other young male protagonist, Captain Geoffry Flower, who is altogether British, fights on the British side, and eventually returns to Britain with the Anglophile other daughter of Vue de l'Eau: he too may be considered a son of an old dominion. Still, despite the conservative and Old World traditions of the Tidewater which make the Virginians offspring of the Virgin Queen, old in a British sense implies a greater stretch of the past than "old" in a more applicable American definition.

A Son of the Old Dominion opens with the vigorous British Captain Geoffry Flower carrying his letter of introduction from colonial governor Lord Dunmore to his own Virginia kinsman, lord of the manor house and plantation Colonel Hugh Poythress. Just as he had found Williamsburg to be "England at second hand" (15), at Vue de l'Eau Flower discovers a fashionable Madam Poythress, though descended from Pocahontas, quixotically hoping to inherit a British title as the "Countess of Avenel"; the men returning from a foxhunt; the Oxford-bred Poythress's big house modeled after an ancestral British home. Flower wants, however, to experience the great and free, uniquely American wilderness, represented at this point by the spirit of the "Westerner" Rolfe Poythress, son of the dissolute and disinherited brother of Colonel Hugh. Colonel George Washington, first glimpsed at the foxhunt, embodies the "best" of both worlds: he is at once aristocratic, class oriented, and loyal, and dedicated to democratic freedoms—the godfather of the playful fourteen-year-old part-Indian Matoaca ("May") Poythress of Vue de l'Eau. It is this girl's beautiful sister, Betty, however, who becomes the heroine at the narrative and ideological center of the novel, loved by or engaged to, at one time or another, Westerner Rolfe, compromise candidate Flower, and haughty English noble the Earl of Avenel. Before the entourage from the plantation departs for Williamsburg, where the Earl joins his relatives, Flower hears from the long-time housekeeper, Judith Carnes, a confusing tale of the immoral Avenel's misdeeds in England. The match between Betty and the Earl, melancholy from the loss of his wife and son to smallpox, is nonetheless promoted by the class-conscious Madam Poythress, who is no more desirous of even seeing the West than the Earl himself appears to be.

In a Williamsburg astir with a spirit of contention the House of Burgesses meets only to be dismissed by the proud Lord Dunmore, whose Indian policy—"Lord Dunmore's War"—some think a calculated diversion from Revolutionary rumblings. Hostilities recur in the Blue Ridge and Allegheny Mountains in the days leading up to and following the murder of Logan, chief of the Mingoes. Rolfe obtains permission to absent himself from duties as a teacher in a western valley and leads a scouting detachment into the mountains. After a brief skirmish Rolfe rescues one Peggy Baker from her Indian captors but, cornered on a high riverbank, is forced to jump to evade the pursuing Logan. Safe but disabled by sprained ankle and hip, Rolfe manages to survive (for a time by feeding off a rattlesnake) until he is in turn rescued by "Mad Ann" Bailey, a wilderness messenger whose insanity is a measure of her absence from the norms of "civilized" rationality. Meanwhile the Indian war escalates as Dunmore seems determined to commit hundreds of soldiers against the now-confederated chiefs beyond the Ohio. Flower joins the western expedition; having declared his love for Betty, the girl of Tidewater title, he now has his chance to view the mountains.

Military operations center around Greenway Court, estate of strict old Tory Lord Fairfax, friend of Washington but scornful of protesting Americans. There to oppose the Indians, Flower finds himself at odds with his British kinsman, the distasteful Earl, who denigrates the patriots while announcing his own engagement to Betty. Flower threatens Avenel with disclosing his (Avenel's) part in a scheme to do away with the rightful Avenel heir, written evidence about which had been given to Flower by Judith Carnes. A common felon being no suitable husband for Betty, the Earl steals the incriminating document and flees into the night. His disappearance is complemented by the arrival of Helen Poythress,

Rolfe's mother, with a report of Rolfe's death and the disclosure that Rolfe was actually the child of a family massacred by Indians. Flower finds legal forms at Greenway Court indicating, however, that the child had been officially *adopted* by this frontier family and, putting names and other clues together, concludes that Rolfe is "the last heir of Avenel" (205), inheritor of a great principality in England! Flower writes of the results of all his familial investigations in a letter to the American branch of the Poythress family. Carnes dies soon after, still mumbling about my Lord Avenel's shameful treatment of his brother's son.

Old Colonel Hugh, with May, consults Patrick Henry, George Mason, and Washington at Mount Vernon, then, joined by the younger Hugh, visits a Dunkard religious community on his way to console Rolfe's mother. News of an imminent Indian attack sends the entourage to cover in Fort Shannon. A note delivered by Mad Ann informs Poythress that Rolfe has survived and plans to inform his mother of the fact. Hugh himself tells Helen Poythress, who has coincidentally also found refuge in the fort. Amid the smoke, noise, and confusion of the siege an argument arises over who should secure the only remaining gunpowder, hidden in a nearby house. Unexpectedly, May—like Zane Grey's later Betty Zane—dashes for the building, gets the powder, and, saved by a gallant chief from one of his own braves, returns (the fort's defenders would have shot her themselves in order to spare her from dishonor had she been caught). The fort now refuses surrender, holding out until Rolfe's thirty-man detachment comes to the rescue. Rolfe himself, however, is again surrounded, forced to jump into the river to safety. When the discredited Avenel appears at Fort Shannon, Poythress immediately informs him that the engagement to Betty is off, that she had mistaken her feelings. (The Earl's hopes are hereby doubly dashed, since he had thought the marriage would preempt further investigation into his shadowy past.) Avenel hangs on as one of Dunmore's misguided and misguiding advisers, trying to frame Flower with a manufactured military disgrace, until he dies of heart failure brought on by an American sergeant's threatening to hang him. He has been long destined, in any case, to lose an inheritance to Rolfe and a woman to Flower.

Admiration for the imposing Logan, often felt by worthy foemen like Rolfe, must give way temporarily during negotiations for a peace treaty, when Logan (whose failings are attributed to his contacts with white civilization) eloquently defends Indian rights. To the extent that opposition to Britain solidifies a self-consciously American yet Anglo-Saxon sense of being, patriots embrace for their own linguistic and actual uses those races which otherwise are rejected. The author informs us, for example, that "Americans" begins to be employed for whites rather than Indians. The name of the Native American contributes to a definition of the Euro-American while Native Americans die in battles between whites and sometime-noble Indians like Logan, portrayed as already victims of European corruptions. A part of the lineage of Pocahontas (Betty Poythress), like Pocahontas herself, reciprocates white settling of America by settling in England (see earlier discussion of *The Colonials*). But being as much victimized as victimizing does not save the race from being, at most, an integrated influence and an aspect. Images of altogether unmixed and authentic Native Americans are literally marginalized on the frontier, and excluded from discernible benefits of the Revolution.

As we have seen with books set in New England *(My Lady Laughter)* and the Middle Colonies *(The Continental Dragoon),* blacks also constitute a people who are "used" by history and by fiction and who are presented as neither notable patriots nor the "enemy" in the ritual of war. The "busy, cheery blacks" (17) who mill about the "baronial plenty" (18) of Vue de l'Eau function only as figures of speech in Washington's apprehensive discourse: "custom and use shall make us tame and abject slaves like the blacks we rule over" (35). When hostilities begin, one of the patriots' great fears is that Lord Dunmore will enlist blacks as troops rather than tropes. Since blacks are denied a shared humanity, Washington's naive comment that the new Americans might become inured to servile status carries no consciousness of blacks' just grievances. Clearly, though "tame and abject" cannot have positive connotations for whites, for blacks the phrase marks the inevitable and even felicitous. "Custom and use" have made those who have begun to call themselves Americans—in 1776 and 1897—unable to understand that other peoples may be unjustly subjugated. Though the names had not been born to the national imagination, the Revolutionary zeal of Crispus Attucks would have been less celebrated than the revolutionary zeal of Nat Turner or David Walker would have been feared.[1]

Organized colonial opposition now turns against the East, the old world represented by England, rather than the West, the Indian. The always disgruntled American General Andrew Lewis achieves his revenge by driving Dunmore from Virginia. Rolfe Poythress advances in rank to colonel and, finally, general under Washington in the Continental army; personal and national motives merge in his simultaneously rejecting his claims to the English title and estate—as well as the advice on this point of Washington and the elder Hugh Poythress—and declaring that armed resistance to the Crown is "the only cause for a true American" (332). Even Betty has learned her lesson; no longer unduly impressed by mere rank, she turns down the marriage proposal of Rolfe himself—a colonel in America and an apparent aristocrat in England. The Poythress plantation house burns, set aflame by one of Dunmore's drunken soldiers, who had mistaken it for Mount Vernon; the remaining members of the family survive the rest of the war in the overseer's house, "in sad and dignified seclusion" (340). The book takes us quickly through the days of Valley Forge and Geoffry Flower's fighting for the British in the North.

The end of the war has barely arrived when rewards, hands and lands, begin to be doled out. The Poythresses unexpectedly inherit a manor in (Old) Hampshire. Rolfe has grown to appreciate and love the now more mature—not to mention patriotic—May, whom he marries at Valley Forge even as the rest of her family departs New York for England. Although Betty does not marry royalty, she does get her Englishman; she and Flower renew their love in Philadelphia and have an elegant wedding in England after the war. They often visit America and are hospitably received at the Vue de l'Eau, rebuilt by Rolfe and May. On the one hand Rolfe has surrendered his claim to an English estate and title while on the other he has not planned to settle in the West, either. May and he simply occupy an America like England in many ways, despite or because of their proving their mettle and similarity in a war against England. (One recalls the complaints of those insurgents during the Revolution who maintained that they were being denied their rights as *Englishmen*—not necessarily as *men*.) The third ground, the Western wilderness, albeit "like Paradise before the fall of man" (293), nonetheless resists integration into this mix, May's mixed blood and Rolfe's Western associations notwithstanding. Apparently too radically alien to established Euro-American civilization, the West and its people are omitted from the final formula; no mention made of them, only the wild and fascinating spirits of Logan and Mad Ann linger. The fact of fiction itself forbids completing the stories of other spirits, texts already written, "other personages of this chronicle,—those who belong to history,—are not their names inscribed upon stones that do not lean, or split asunder, or gather moss?" (355).

A series of private/fictional and public/military enabling maneuvers constitutes the narrative strategies of George Morgan's 1897 *John Littlejohn of J.: Being in Particular an Account of his Remarkable Entanglement with the King's Intrigues against General Washington,* a tale in the end said to be a "multiplied business of knaves and true gentlemen" (280) rather than one of colonial opposition to Britain. The aristocratic title character assumes significance partly from the contrast provided by his story's being told by such an unassuming and self-effacing narrator, the rustic Asa Lankford. Although Lankford fights for the American cause along with Littlejohn, he plays no part in a love plot and is excluded from the book's title. As the story progresses from the worst days at Valley Forge to victory at the Battle of Monmouth, we are made to feel that the ultimate success of the entire American enterprise depends upon aid: the arrival of needed food and other supplies, the achieving of the French alliance, and the suppressing of misguided and insubordinate American officers.

The gain in immediacy of a first-person narrative is offset here by the loss of probability resulting from the minor-character narrator's having to be present at momentous events on which he can have little effect. For not only has Asa Lankford become the adoptive son of the poor miller at Cockfoot Mills, he has been rendered literally voiceless by an explosion aboard a fire-brig during the previous year. Other images of powerlessness abound; Asa can be affected by events but not affect them, hear but not speak. Injured, he is literally carried into the opening scene by the strong "Ortolan"—John Littlejohn in disguise. In addition to its owner and a number of Moravian girls, Quaker Hall is tenanted by sometimes mutually suspicious and bickering American and French soldiers. By way of a written note, Asa offers the information to the disaffected French that a privateer bound for the West Indies is moored near his home in Delaware. Although the American surgeon Pruitt tries to still dissension in the ranks, a duel's being arranged results when someone defames General Washington's abilities.

Also present at Quaker Hall is the vain and fashionable Alicia Gaw, Lady Gaw, who at one time had petitioned the House of Lords for title and property. She seems to recognize Ortolan and has Asa deliver a letter to him. No sooner does Ortolan receive this love note than he is challenged by Pruitt as the deserter and spy John Littlejohn. (This entire strand of the plot revolves around both friend and foe confusing Littlejohn with his uncle, the villainous and Tory John Littlejohn, of A. John later tells Asa the tale of his earlier heroism among other Americans, his having been in effect kidnapped by his violent and cynical uncle and shipped off to England, his escaping from his father's West Indies plantation and returning to America only to find himself wanted as a spy and deserter. By the by, John drops the information that his father, an aristocratic plantation owner on the Tred Avon in Maryland, has a business partner whose daughter, the childlike and simple Mary Truax, has long been his own girlfriend.) John and Pruitt preempt the planned duel by prematurely firing on each other; Pruitt falls as John escapes. Seized as a co-conspirator, Asa establishes his loyalty with a letter from the commander of his Continental regiment, then is hired by the "majestic" (48) Washington and Colonel Hamilton as a secretary.

When a Tory eavesdropper rushes forth, pushes Washington, and runs off, the pursuing Asa finds himself taken captive, bound, and thrown into an oversized oven through one end of which he forces his way, only to fall into a pit. Physically low, confined, mute, Asa remains ineffectual and can only listen, despite overhearing "the innermost secrets of the Revolution" (63), including Washington's fears of the ambition and avarice of his fellow countrymen. Lankford hears himself again accused of being a duplicitous spy and Littlejohn—in a letter from Benjamin Franklin read by Hamilton—of being a Maryland Tory sent by the British ministry to America with twenty thousand pounds in bribery money. Prisoners are interviewed in the room above Asa, and one Digsworthy Snaith promotes the cause of General Charles Lee as new commander, whispering something about Alicia Gaw's being Lee's daughter. Littlejohn again rescues Asa, cutting his bonds and calling for help. They emerge as "from the depth of the grave itself" (80), but are held as possible spies. As though his worth had not yet been otherwise validated, Asa is again found innocent by a military drumhead court. Not so fortunate, Littlejohn, unable to prove his identity, is given the dubious choice of being shot as a deserter or hanged as a spy. Asa once more becomes the passive message carrier, this time promising Littlejohn to convey his missive of love and American loyalty to Mary Truax.

Mary has not yet received John's note when she arrives at the American camp to request the release of her father and to report that the Truax home has been burned by British soldiers who suspected her of harboring an American. Further troubled at finding of the death warrant against Littlejohn, she maintains his innocence and obtains a day's stay of execution for him while she rides to York to document proof of the mistaken identity. On route with Mary, Asa is ambushed and left unconscious among some rocks, vaguely aware of having heard the voice of Snaith (John's rival for the affections of Mary). The signalman at York is shot before he can flash the message of John's innocence to the American camp. Determined to warn Mary of Snaith's ignominy and to tell Washington her story, Asa returns to discover a disguised Littlejohn, saved by an unknown friend's intervention, at an American dinner party which is, *in toto*, captured by Tarleton's British. John hears Alicia Gaw talking of cutting off supplies to the "rebels" and printing yet more Continental currency to make it even less valuable. When John confronts Alicia, denouncing her knavery and making clear that he is the captain's nephew, her defense consists of private matters: that she it was who saved him from execution, and that Mary Truax loves another.

During the excitement of a cockfight the captive Americans lower themselves from the roof by a rope and take to their heels, commandeer a British ship, and sail off, discovering several of their French friends imprisoned below board. They hide the *Bounding Bess* in the swamp near Cockfoot Mills. Asa's father is to furnish wagons to transport the captured ship stores while Asa and John ride to the Littlejohns' home, a "great white mansion" (155), where John fights his uncle and announces that he himself has displaced his father as master of the plantation. The younger John organizes the hauling of food to the American army, sending Asa to enlist similar aid on the Virginia shore from Miss Polly Leatherberry, "mistress of the vast region of Mobjack and Piankatank, with its multitudes of slaves and its unnumbered acres" (166-67). Juba, the slave who accompanies Asa to Mobjack, tells him the tale of the old and unhappily concluded love affair between Miss Polly and the elder John. Asa, along with John's letter, persuades Miss Polly, "Captain Polly," to furnish meat for the Americans. The Mobjack flotilla sails to the north, dodges a Tory fireboat, and defeats the vessel of his uncle, Captain Littlejohn, who nevertheless escapes ashore.

Meanwhile, John's wagon train, arrived at the Mills, must hide in the flume when a large detachment of British are spotted. In a variation of Odysseus's ploy, the French officer Bonfils orders sheep strapped to horses which are driven out of the flume, drawing British fire. Enemy soldiers nonetheless discover the Americans, who are saved only by the water meant to drown them throwing Hessians themselves off the waterwheel. Littlejohn's men arrive, rout the remaining British, and chase them aboard the *Bounding Bess,* which is then ignited. His wagon train then joins that of Miss Leatherberry, all converging at Valley Forge just in time to stop Washington from disbanding his dispirited army. Happiness incident upon the ratifying of the French alliance is mitigated only by a grievous injury to Littlejohn, who seems to Asa to look increasingly like his uncle, like "a smitten king" (214).

Asa hears Alicia Gaw's story from her driver, the simple-minded "Dutchman" Hance Fuchslager. During a chase it seems that her carriage, containing Mary Truax as well, had plunged off a bluff overlooking the Susquehanna, killing Alicia, "the king's intriguer" (229). Mary, for a time entangled in a tree, was taken by Hance to a home near the river. Hance, stunned, had bagged the gold being transported and thrown it—to be retrieved later—onto the rocks even farther below, near where he saw both Snaith and Captain Littlejohn viewing the scene of destruction. A sword fight between Littlejohn and Snaith resulted from each accusing the other of having stolen the gold from the carriage; Snaith stabbed Littlejohn. Snaith now returns to the Americans, acting as if nothing has happened. Mary, together with her new protectress, Polly, has been captured, but manages to send off a love letter to the recuperating John, praising his heroism. As Clinton evacuates Philadelphia and the Americans cross the Schuylkill, Polly and Mary disguise themselves in red and thereby escape the British. Soon they are sent on to Virginia.

Asa, still dumb, at least now makes noise as a bugler. In the face of thousands of British, Charles Lee orders a retreat but finds himself sent to the rear by an angered Washington, who orders a stand which becomes the Battle of Monmouth. As Molly Pitcher labors bravely on this hot day, Snaith commands a withdrawal but his subordinate Littlejohn strikes him and orders a charge, taking the enemy unawares. Snaith, disfigured by a wound, shoots himself. The injured Asa faints; however, he soon revives and, in the trauma of battle—three pages remaining!—regains his lost powers of speech. His cohort John, delirious from fever, recovers at Mobjack, attended by Mary. He and Asa go to fight together at Cowpens and Guilford Court House. After Yorktown General Washington pays his respects to Captain Polly, and French as well as American regiments attend the grand wedding of Mary Truax and John Littlejohn.

Asa's newfound ability to articulate comes too late to earn him rewards; though he is able now to make his needs known, the plot nonetheless allows him no remuneration. He has already used his "voice" to tell someone else's story, to erase himself and maximize Littlejohn's importance. The narrative contrives to furnish John with the "best" of both (British and American) worlds. Heroic, his actions at Monmouth had paralleled Washington's. But his marriage to plain American Mary and the passing of his Tory uncle have, ironically, provided him the American and Southern equivalent of the departed Alicia's desired title and property. (Remember he has grown to resemble his uncle, to suggest a king, though smitten.) His way to love cleared by the suicide of Snaith and the death of the too-thoroughly Europeanized Alicia Gaw, John settles down as John Littlejohn, of J. If aristocratic standards find validation, these standards are at least on the surface independent from Europe.

The Tory Maid: Being an Account of the Adventures of James Frisby of Fairlee, in the County of Kent, on the Eastern Shore of the State of Maryland, and Sometime an Officer in the Maryland Line of the Continental Army during the War of the Revolution (1898) reveals a great deal in its lengthy title: even though it names a "maid," the "adventures" are those of James Frisby; Kent, of course, is also an English county; and—

least obvious in 1898—the Eastern Shore's most notable nineteenth-century product was Frederick Douglass. Although little longer than a novella, the book offers Herbert Baird Stimpson ample space to praise the past and damn the present. The Revolution, for the first-person narrator, was the Great Cause; those were "stirring times that proclaimed the birth of a mighty nation" (2). "Women were brave in those days" (6); "racing was the pastime of gentlemen, and not an excuse for black-guardism and gambling, as to-day it is fast becoming" (143). After the war "dull peace" (239) arrives, so that Grandfather Frisby must now re-create "stirring times" for those so unfortunate as to "bask in the sunshine of long and dreary years of peace" (3). He takes for granted that nowadays grand deeds are few, new ways suspect.

The "nowadays" in this and other retrospective first-person Revolutionary War narratives creates a confusion in chronology which is central to the meaning of their contrasts between past and present. Apparent stress is placed on the assumed changes occurring during the period between the narrator's adventures and the time of his telling, not on those occurring during the period between his telling and Stimpson's authoring the book. The fictional narrator, eighteen years old at the time of the Lexington fight, would be in his early seventies in 1830. The story of 1830 is freed but also marred by its being the tale—another reminder of text—of an older man who embellishes, sentimentalizes, and forgets. But the author elides the seventy years between 1830 and 1900 by not mentioning them. When the narrator returns to his present, in effect he returns to 1898. If the writer lacks the Jamesian sophistication to intend an imperfect narrator whose very lapses make up an important aspect of his subject, he clearly does intend his narrator both to reassure and to damn. His narrator reassures by bringing us always back to the relatively more stable world of 1830; he damns by implying that any failings of 1830 could only be worse in 1898. By disguising 1898 as 1830 the author creates the nostalgia mentioned by Michael Kammen, a nostalgia which touches the reader because it is so indulged by the narrator himself—and compounded by the unarticulated nostalgia for 1830 felt in 1898. Since our return to even the present is a return to 1830, we conspire with the writer in a fantasy that the Civil War and the Gilded Age are not (as we also do, for example, in *An Express of '76*). But the actual old soldiers of 1898 would have been veterans of the Civil War, a war too recent to romanticize but also one whose horrors intensified the appeal of romance.

Sipping a mint julep served him by one of the many servants of Fairlee, Frisby fondly recalls a time when "gentlemen led the people" (4), when military officers were country gentlemen "of the oldest and bluest blood in the province, of wide estates and famous names" (24). He does not have to imagine the imaginary plantation Old South of romantic legend; he already lives there. His account of the Revolution must celebrate his deeds as well as explain the impact of the experience upon him, his family, his region and nation. But his saber-rattling militarism—heard from many 1898 backers of the Spanish-American War—does not really clarify the real worth of the Revolution or whether personal or national life were thereby transformed. The typical ill-defined mystique of land and pedigree overrides political and temporal differences, and crucial contrasting terms become gentlemen/rabble, women/men, and Anglo-Saxons/others.

When Frisby of Fairlee and his friend Richard Ringgold of Hunting Field canter forth to the war it is with the purpose of hunting "redcoats and fair ladies' smiles and not foxes now" (6). As though conjured up by the statement, the beautiful Jean Gordon and her father, the suspected Tory Charles Gordon of the Braes, cross their path. Although he is the "enemy," Gordon rides with the admirable "courtliness and ease" of a true "horseman and gentleman" (12). After being mustered into service as a lieutenant, Frisby thwarts an angry mob bent upon punishing Gordon for his derogatory comments about the delegates to the Continental Congress. His allowing the Gordons through a picket line and his visiting Jean result in Frisby's loyalty being questioned by Phil Rodolph, unofficial leader of the hostile Americans, who calls him "our Squire of Tory Dames" (44). In the ensuing duel, Rodolph violates the protocol expected in such affairs of honor by firing early, injuring Frisby. Frisby nonetheless is able to dispatch the base Rodolph, who, it turns out, is a part American Indian whose father (bad blood!) had cheated in a duel against Gordon fought years earlier because Jean's mother had spurned the elder Rodolph. Frisby, on the other hand, is so meticulous about proper aristocratic behavior that his duel was not fought with swords only because he had discovered that Rodolph had broken his arm—now completely healed—during the previous year. Warfare itself seems to Frisby a glorious duty for a man, but outside the now-excused ritual of battle he is just as likely to befriend and praise the British as the Americans.

The sound of fife and drum soon awakens Frisby to "life and hope again" (55). Now he must accompany the sheriff in serving a warrant against Gordon for his anti-patriot sentiments. Gordon spurns them and their document, explaining how his life had been spared through the intercession of the Duchess of Gordon when he had fought for the young Pretender in 1745, but only on condition that he no longer fight against the king, and that he leave Scotland and migrate to Maryland. (Gordon already possesses, for Frisby, a powerful charisma which comes of his being associated with the legendary and mysterious Highlands, a charisma more significant than the fact of Scottish association with the anti-British French.) After Frisby and the Maryland Line distinguish themselves in the bloody battle at Long Island, he is appointed courier to carry news of the Long Island campaign back to the authorities in Annapolis. On his route his adventures continue, this time in defense of his lady love and her father, whom he saves from a patriot posse, removing Jean first to his mother's home and then to that of her aunt and uncle, Captain and Mrs. James Nicholson. Gordon escapes to a British ship, which Frisby eludes in delivering the dispatch to the Council of Safety in Annapolis, where he stays with future governor Thomas Johnson and his two daughters. Polly and Betsy Johnson persuade Frisby to attend a horse race on his journey back north with a communiqué for General Washington. Before he rejoins the troops near Philadelphia he manages to see Jean again and to visit Fairlee. A brief argument about the relative claims of her Scottish and his English ancestry does not discourage her from presenting Frisby a miniature of herself.

Meanwhile Gordon has joined the forces of Lord Howe. Jean passes through picket lines to Philadelphia, where she is often seen with the Highland gent Farquharson and becomes a belle of the city's social season. After surviving the battles at Brandywine and Germantown and the encampment at Valley Forge, Frisby can no longer restrain himself from entering the city when he hears rumors of Farquharson's success with Jean. Disguised and accompanied by the powerful frontiersman and spy Tom Jones, Frisby gets to the city, where he sees Jean at Lord Howe's ball and, at Jean's home, interrupts Farquharson even as he proposes. An irate Farquharson is mollified by Jean's explaining that Frisby is an old friend; a duel nonetheless ensues. The gentlemanly and selfless Frisby wins the well-contested bout but stays his sword at the thought that Jean may really love this imposing soldier. In the midst of the violence of the Battle of Monmouth—graphically described, for the times—Gordon then politely spares Frisby. The exchange of civilized favors soon continues as Frisby warns Jean and a wounded Gordon of the approach of American troops. Jean, in turn, advises Frisby to flee before British soldiers come to remove Gordon—and that she does not love Farquharson. Ever prone to encounter familiar casualties, Frisby sometime later happens across an injured Farquharson, who informs him that the king has pardoned Gordon for his part in the troubles of 1745 and that he and his daughter have returned to Scotland. Frisby goes on to distinguish himself at the Battles of Camden, Eutaw Springs, and Cowpens, gaining so many "wounds and honours" (239) that by the time of Yorktown he has become a colonel. He returns to Fairlee.

Even during the war in the North the chief characters had at times returned home in spirit, as when Frisby felt that General Washington's love for his and Dick Ringgold's battle cry stemmed from its bringing him back in thought to "the Southland and the hunting fields of Old Virginia" (105). Although Frisby gains some prominence in his postwar career, becoming along with his friend Dick a member of the legislature of his state, the old excitement of this battle cry is gone. But it comes as no surprise that now his domestic life and values are established and validated by the reappearance of Jean Gordon, who has convinced her father to return to Maryland. She marries Frisby, while Nancy Nicholson weds Dick. The shift at this point to the narrator's present functions to reinforce the idea of an ongoing Southern and British tradition, a tradition projected into the future by his advising his granddaughter to marry the young namesake of Dick Ringgold and by his comment that she reminds him of "the Tory maid." Never is there an intimation that Jean Gordon has converted. For the novel's plot her Toryism simply becomes irrelevant after the war, when political affiliations no longer eventuate in armed conflict. The social and political views she represents are, however, now not only allowed but encouraged, in a novel of the Old South in which the War for Independence finally seems little more than an episode. In the book's last lines old Frisby orders his servant to serve him another mint julep. The gesture is symptomatic of the times of the novel's composition: only after the Civil War could such a South begin to be, absolved from reality and allowed to function as a time as well as a place. Only then could such a scene be offered unapologetically and yet serve the purposes of nostalgia.

Winston Churchill's *Richard Carvel* (1899) embodies his notion that the eighteenth century had traditionally been treated romantically and was intrinsically a romantic age ("Interview" 30). (A popular notion indeed, given the book's 520,000 sales in two years [Altick 224].) The narrative for the most part lacks deep-seated and irreconcilable personal and social conflicts. Issues are somewhat clouded as well by the title character's, at various times, having disagreements with at least seven men and having affairs with two quite different women. These aristocratic, pro-European men attempt to corrupt Richard's American spirit, to claim his inheritance, and to marry the woman he seems meant for. Approximately half of *Richard Carvel* is set outside America altogether, mostly in London. Much in these sections is concerned with the details of the intrigues whereby Richard's bride-to-be is urged, partly because her parents are tempted by the prospect of gentility, to marry his Lord of Chartersea.

Richard remains in London to prevent this, but while there falls in with a group of gambling and otherwise fun-loving young men. His republican sympathies finally reassert themselves after he has been insulted at an inn for not being of the gentry, after he begins to feel uncomfortable among those English who assumed airs of superiority, and especially after he must spend a short time in a debtor's prison. Although at times attracted by London life and by figures as diverse as Horace Walpole and David Garrick, he finally takes up the mantle of the future and America.

The reason Richard is in London at all is that an evil, grasping uncle had arranged for pirates to abduct him from Maryland. These pirates run afoul of a ship commanded by John Paul Jones. Richard is saved and becomes a friend of "John Paul." (Eventually he is injured in the famous *Bon Homme Richard-Serapis* fight.) Richard joins in the spirit of the *Richard*'s exploits, the exploits of a ship named for Benjamin Franklin's Poor Richard. His girlfriend later reports, for example, that in his sleep he frequently mumbles, "I have not yet begun to fight" (514)! Richard recovers in England, encouraged by Paul. Uncle Grafton uses this time that Richard is out of the way, quite like Arthur Wynne, to ingratiate himself with Lionel Carvel, Richard's grandfather and guardian, with the purpose of being named heir to the Carvel estates. Although Grafton succeeds, after the Revolution the Maryland legislature confiscates the estate and reassigns it to Richard because of Grafton's having schemed for the Tories. Richard, of course, accepts these American lands and becomes a spiritual heir to the ambitious John Paul Jones, the man with a sense of destiny.

Richard Carvel must win the heroine, Dorothy Manners, not only from Tories and her own Tory sympathies; he must also make certain that he has emotionally committed himself to her alone. The other girl in the novel is Patty Swain, for whose staunchly American father Richard works after he returns to Maryland. Patty Swain is honest, simple, helpful, and apparently in love with Richard. She seems spontaneously to incorporate the American values. Yet Richard proposes to her only because of a deathbed wish of her father, and, in fact, encourages another man to court her. The understanding Patty, self-sacrificial as usual, perceives Richard's plight and gives way to Dorothy, who shortly makes known that she has only pretended to be fond of Chartersea to avoid conflict with her parents. It seems at first glance that Patty would be the more appropriate bride for Richard than the moody, vain—and loyalist—Dorothy. This uncertainty and tension in the plot is not unique, of course, and is the consequence of the novelist's heeding the conventions of the romance. To some extent, both the heroine and the hero must be dashing and extraordinary. The tradition was well enough established that Charlotte Brontë had to make special mention of Jane Eyre's plainness. Americans seemed to lack much of the worldly sophistication called for by the romantic novel. The patriotic *American* point of the novel militates against adopting the convention. But Churchill does adopt the convention. The best he can do is compromise: the heroine is of the usual sort, but in the process of *becoming* an American.

Richard thus establishes his right to land and to a wife, both taken, as it were, from British holdings. But this domestic conclusion has been arrived at through a series of actions in which the differences between British and American have already been minimized. Being in a London debtor's prison not only leads Jones to become a participant in the Revolution, but also causes Carvel to realize that the Revolution "was brought on and fought by a headstrong king, backed by unscrupulous followers who held wealth above patriotism" (234). The Revolution could have been avoided but for "a stubborn, selfish, and wilful monarch" (449). To this way of thinking the patriot cause would have been the same for citizens of both nations. America would not have produced a new man. Richard's affection for London is "racial" and the Annapolis of the novel is said to be London on a small scale. The hero is uneasy with English aristocrats, but he also disperses an unruly patriot mob and preaches moderation. One imagines this speech, calling for restraint, addressed to the disgruntled crowd at Chicago's Haymarket in 1886—a crowd filled with those who were distinctly neither gentlemen nor Anglo-Americans. Richard does, after all, marry a not quite thoroughly reconstructed American heroine; he marries as the nation and he both begin to recover from their wounds, hoping "that the Stars and Stripes and the Union Jack may one day float together to cleanse this world of tyranny" (536).

When Amy Blanchard declared that the purposes of *A Revolutionary Maid: A Story of the Middle Period of the War for Independence* (1899) were to tell an entertaining tale and "to outline the history of the times as closely as might be consistent with a story for girls" (preface) she was signaling an avoidance of none of her prejudices or those of her turn-of-the-century readers. Definitions of what may be "consistent with a story for girls" have changed; certainly, in Blanchard's book the simpleminded, prudish, and prurient do seem permissible. Overt or insinuated sexism, nostalgia and sentimentality, racism, militarism, and pastoralism were also clearly within bounds. Escape from changing and troubled times was only one of the functions performed by these texts; the other side of the coin is that they announced themselves as statements about positive virtue and tradition. To many of the uncritical these novels furnished the right answers, and certainly answers easier than those which would result from an enlightened and thoughtful examination of the real problems of 1899. As a reviewer of *A Revolutionary Maid* quoted in the advertising apparatus of another of Blanchard's novels put it, such books are educational in patriotism. However, for most of us they define what patriotism—at least as presented by popular culture—*was* rather than *is*.

By the third chapter of *A Revolutionary Maid,* when fourteen-year-old Katherine ("Kitty") DeWitt moves from her native New York to the relative safety of Philadelphia because of the threat of war, the reader has already been introduced to the initial political alignments. Kitty's father, Paul, has become a captain in the rebel army and her young friend Elspeth Ludlow is a fiery patriot; Aunt Joanna Thompson remains an opinionated and unyielding Tory. Others begin as neutrals or even Tories and gradually develop an appreciation of the American Way: Mistress Margaret Gillespie, who has just become Paul DeWitt's second wife, and her brother—the early candidate for marriage to Kitty—Christopher Van Ness. Kitty herself, on the one hand, has just been convinced by Elspeth to sign her name in blood on a copy of the just-published Declaration of Independence and, on the other hand, must now journey to the home of her new mother's sister, the thoroughgoing Tory Mrs. Lavinia Rush. The balance of influences on Kitty is then tilted to the other side as she must escape the dangers of Philadelphia by moving in temporarily with her Jersey patriot cousins, the Gardners. Her father's, friend's, and cousins' cause becomes hers as Kitty now begins her active career for country, not king.

First, Kitty saves the life of the Maryland soldier Lloyd Holliday, a cousin of the Gardners, by having him dress in the clothes of their grandmother and later by disguising him as a girl and taking him to the home of James Gardner. Feeling shut out from meaningful participation in the war because of being female (though she does soon discover two notable female role models), her allegiance to her new nation next takes the form of escaping from Aunt Joanna's chaise to warn the Gardners of a British incursion. She earns her "red badge of courage" by way of a superficial gunshot wound suffered while she faces down a group of hostile soldiers intent on appropriating a herd of cattle. Kitty succeeds in getting through enemy lines but fails to free her captive father by using her influence with Aunt Joanna, who has married a ruddy Hessian soldier, Major von Blum. She serves as courier for various classified military communiqués and in one later episode dumps a kettle of soft soap from an upstairs window onto the heads of British soldiers below. In the city Kitty is inspirited by the work of Betsy Ross and the tale of Mary Zane about her cousin, Elizabeth Zane (Zane Grey's ancestor), and her heroic dash under fire to deliver a keg of gunpowder to American troops at Fort Henry. Kitty is present at the confrontation between Christopher, who has become a redcoat, and Lloyd, for whom she is sewing a redcoat disguise.

Lloyd's knocking Christopher down, hiding in the barn until he can escape, and attending a ball in expensive British clothing constitute some of those deeds which parallel Kitty's adventures and make him a worthy match for her. In other scenes Lloyd serves as a spy and as the author of the plot which results in the liberating of Kitty's father, a favor done in return for Kitty's having saved him. The happy reunions and appropriate marriages follow the disclosure that Paul DeWitt had not died in the Southern campaign, as had been reported, but had only lost a leg (just as Phebe Gardner's intended, John Tucker, has lost an arm—events in which all seem to take a morbid patriotic satisfaction). John marries Phebe, Lloyd marries Kitty, and Christopher has already—the new wife of Christopher and old friend of Kitty herself delivers the shocking news—married Elspeth Ludlow. Elspeth, it seems, had cared for Christopher after he was slightly injured and released from prison through the influence of Holliday, earlier the beneficiary of Christopher's unofficial and lax guard duty over the Philadelphia Tory household. She has promoted Christopher's conversion to the patriot way to such a degree that he becomes symbolically the father of the father of the country—they name their firstborn George Washington Van Ness.

The American victory and the instituting of a new national family are achieved only to be followed by a conciliatory gesture to the supposed enemy of a typical but particularly retrograde sort. Lloyd Holliday has inherited a Maryland estate and Kitty hence becomes the "mistress of a large plantation" (316). Whereas she and her mother had earlier for the most part merely feigned an enjoyment of Tory social gatherings, the dancing with André and Tarleton, to gain information possibly valuable to the rebels, Kitty and Mrs. DeWitt can now unashamedly settle down to substantially the same life: "young men in powdered wigs and with silver buckles shining . . . from twenty miles around came the company . . . with all the stateliness and dignity of the period did they tread the minuet . . . while the ceremonious bow of the squire was courtesied to by the dame" (320). The DeWitts' old New York home has been despoiled by the British and Paul DeWitt left jobless; Holliday furnishes a haven for the family and an accounting job on the plantation for Captain DeWitt. Maryland comes to the aid of New York in a restating of that Cavalier myth which equates a Southern experience—slightly modified by New South commercialism—with that of a landed English gentry.

The agrarian South absorbs the capitalist Middle Colonies in a reconciliation especially attractive to many in the decades following the sectional strife of the Civil War. Blanchard's novel concludes with a vision of a romanticized Old South which was an invention of the late-nineteenth-century American imagination and as far from the historical realities of the eighteenth century as a truly pastoral life itself was from the realities of the Gilded Age.

The casual, insensitive, and common depiction of African Americans as congenitally ignorant and happily subservient—examples to the contrary in 1899 notwithstanding—is an aspect of this vision which in the last pages of *A Revolutionary Maid* takes on a striking and virulent but unintentional irony. One of the slaves reports the reason for the bonfires and cannon shots on the plantation: "Dat—dat—Fort July, Miss Kitty" (319). For us the episode contrasts with Frederick Douglass's 1852 oration about *your* Fourth of July celebration, a day of mourning for him (Lauter 1: 1704-23). (The equation whereby the political and cultural relationship between America and Africa America mirrors that between Britain and America, noted by Prince Hall even in the eighteenth century, defines a relevant issue: a nationalistic militancy is modified by the thought that African Americans are being denied their rights as *Americans*—hence, Martin Luther King Jr.'s insistence that his movement was essentially conservative—just as the Americans insisted that they were being deprived of their rights as *Englishmen*.) Blanchard is unaware of her own unawareness of the meaning of freedom day here and in a scene in which an old slave named Moses plays "Yankee Doodle" on the fiddle for the holiday makers; not only does she employ simple-minded stereotypes in her portrayal of blacks, but she also has no notion of how the name of Moses might be invoked as the sign of a leader to the Promised Land (and *had* been so invoked by the authors of spirituals, by Mark Twain, and by Harriet Tubman long before appropriations of the name by Booker T. Washington and Marcus Garvey). In 1776 the slaves did not have to be free; a guilt and a fear could be voided by mainstream writers in 1899 imagining that African Americans at that earlier time did not even want to be free. Blanchard's Independence Day is singularly tribal, as the book begins with a dedication to her "dearly beloved mother whose ancestors fought in the Maryland line" and concludes with the thought that, while a new day is supposedly dawning for everyone, "the fires of liberty still burn, and the light of peace enfolds the homes made free by the blood of our sires" (321). If "homes" is meant to be inclusive, "sires" clearly is not. Blanchard's maid becomes another instance of the Revolutionary who is far from revolutionary.

The movement southwards from the New England of *A Girl of '76* continues in the third of Amy Blanchard's Revolutionary War romances, for
the entirety of *A Daughter of Freedom: A Story of the Latter Period of
the War for Independence* (1900)—the novel does not really treat a substantially later period of the war than the earlier two—is set in the territory between Williamsburg and Savannah. The author has arrived at a
place and a time of heart's desire, and the text describes not just the contrast between Britain and America, but also the preeminent part played in
the war by the South: without the South's imposing aristocratic leaders,
"without these, and without those brave militiamen who, without clothing, without pay, without even encouragement, fought with such courage
for their southern homes, where would have been independence for the
colonies?" (287). An encomium on the South is delivered which makes
the book's magnolia-adorned cover altogether appropriate. Again the
region is idealized in a portrait which includes the South seeming a new
rural England and African Americans being pictured as comic and ignorant, fearful and superstitious. Southern black and lower-class white
speech is marked as nonstandard and substandard by its content, by
spelling and punctuation, while no such indicators of dialect occur for
the speech of upper-class Southern whites, whose no-less-regional
modes of speech are taken as normative. As in *A Girl of '76* and *A Revolutionary Maid,* a thirteen- or fourteen-year-old female matures to nineteen or twenty, in a story in which her adventurous career reflects and
responds to sectional and national events and which ends with her marriage signifying the beginning of a new(?) American order. The heroine
passes through adolescence along with the nation.

The varying fortunes and threats of war drive the daring Byrd
Graham—her brother's name is Beverly, another time-honored Virginia
name—in a large circle beginning at her family's home near Charlotte,
North Carolina, continuing through Williamsburg and Norfolk, thence to
Charleston, and finally back to North Carolina and Tidewater Virginia.
Her first stop is at Cousin Becky Tucker's, where all are saved from hostile troops by a timely warning from Indigo, the young slave who Byrd
insists always accompany her. (This is the first of several instances when
Indigo rescues his mistress from difficulties in scenes which nonetheless
portray him as a trembling and merely amusing buffoon.) Lord Dunmore's bombarding of the city forces Byrd and her mother—her father
had died in a military engagement before formal hostilities had been
declared—to leave Norfolk, where they have been nursing an ill Beverly,
who is now in the patriot army. Off they go to the Virginia plantation of
Grandfather George Page (note the reference to the surname of the con-

temporary author of nostalgic Old South romances like *Befo' de War* and *In Ole Virginia,* Thomas Nelson Page), the Tory holdout who lives with his rebel sister, Aunt Tryphena Page. Here at Heathworth Beverly and Byrd become acquainted with their cousins, the gentlemanly and politically neutral Conway Saunders and the coquettish and Tory Champe Saunders. Confronted by another group of British soldiers while she is riding, Byrd strikes out at their commander and gallops off shouting "The Tories are coming!" (77). Cornered again, she pulls a pistol on the soldiers as Indigo butts one of the most aggressive. Soon overpowered nevertheless, Byrd is disarmed, bound, and stashed in a tobacco barn.

Beverly soon introduces the family to his army friend, the natty and well-mannered Monsieur Amboise DuBois. At about the same time, Byrd, having escaped from the barn, displays her anti-intellectualism by spurning her William and Mary tutor, whom she tells to join the army. She cannot, however, avoid all education, as Mr. Page has now determined to send her and Champe to Mrs. Minor's finishing school near Norfolk, an alternative to superior but now unavailable English schools. As their boat descends the James toward Norfolk they are set upon by a British ship to escape which they go ashore, where Byrd shoots a redcoat who is grappling with her grandfather. Indigo also shoots an enemy soldier, but another slightly wounds Byrd; abandoned by all but Indigo, she can only surmise that Champe and Mr. Page have been captured by the British. Friendly fisherfolk arrange for her and Indigo to board the *Matilda,* a merchantman bound for Charleston, still an American stronghold. Here she of course meets her brother, who advises her to stay with Major, Mrs., and Mercy McKay. Indigo overhears a Tory scheme fomented by Francis Piper, whose motivations include jealousy of Beverly's success with Mercy. The household is thus enabled to thwart the Tory ploy and capture several British soldiers, among them a former attacker of Byrd who tells of Champe and Mr. Page's having been released. Redcoats yet again invade the house, and in the ensuing melee Mercy is struck by a blow intended for Beverly. The British are routed by a group of dutiful blacks led by Indigo, after which Byrd binds Piper's injured foot and takes him to safety on his promise no further to oppose the patriot cause. Beverly is ordered to Savannah; after Mercy mends, Byrd and the McKays head toward the Graham's home in North Carolina.

Coincidence and Byrd's incredibly bad luck continue as her entourage falls in with Francis Marion's men, including her brother's friend, DuBois. No sooner do her friends save a man from a tar and feathering than she and DuBois are themselves captured at the end of an improbable impromptu horse race. DuBois avoids suspicion by pretending to be a mental incompetent, while a courteous Captain Hardy Dawson defends Byrd from soldiers who try to seize her horse. Byrd returns the favor by allowing Dawson to escape when the British foragers are later taken. Arrived back in Charlotte, Byrd finds herself attracted by both DuBois and Conway Saunders, the latter of whom also now meets the necessary requirement of having become a patriot soldier. News gets through that Beverly has been taken prisoner in Charleston and that Cornwallis is marching toward Charlotte. The Grahams again vacate their home and travel to Virginia, where George Page has finally converted to the rebel side. Conway is feared dead in one of the bloodiest Southern battles. Beverly returns safely home with an account of being in prison and on a British prison-ship, from which he was freed through the interposition of a former Tory beau of Champe. At a grand fete honoring the Marquis de Lafayette, Conway dramatically appears and tells of being furnished an escape by Dawson, whom Byrd had aided. The grandfather, unable to restrain himself longer, enlists. The final bit of stage business is a comic version of the conflating of political and personal motive: Champe saves DuBois by dressing him as the maid and Byrd saves Conway by riding away with him to the secret tower room. (Mercy's version of the equation was her belief that she would die for only two causes: her country and the one she loved.) The surrender at Yorktown occurs and all joyously follow Washington to Fredericksburg.

The political and military conflicts ended, justice is now meted out in the related personal and social spheres. All along an essentially social and personal view has been superimposed on what has passed as a military and political problem. Being thwarted in love has caused political animosity; political animosity has preempted the possibility of love. Yet England remains the privileged social model for places with ersatz English names like Heathworth. The ladies return to the wearing of those silks and satins once considered "Tory," and the gentlemen return to their foxhunting. The many favors now and earlier proffered and returned are exchanged among upper-class characters of both "sides." Although Conway Saunders notes the bravery of John Sevier and his uncouth mountain boys, compared to whom he feels a mere dandy, they are depicted as eccentric, true but not blue-blooded. The old-liner, Grandfather George Page, had begun to turn away from his dedication to the king under the influence of a British soldier's particularly rude behavior toward Byrd, which he considered vulgar, the actions of "some low white trash desiring to rob those better than himself, and no English officer," "a hireling" (83). These wars, he feels, should be affairs among gentlemen, not concerns of the lower or commercial classes. And not just the "genteel" in general, but "men" in particular: Page's initial and misguided anti-patriot stance had stemmed, "more than anything else," from "Aunt Try's constantly aggressive attitude" (87).

The old Southern world is reconstituted as the major characters are disposed of in marriage. Aunt Tryphena Page marries Colonel Isidor Carter—yet another name from the roster of First Families of Virginia—after decades of courtship. (Aunt Try's "aggressive attitude" will no doubt be finally curbed.) Beverly Graham pairs off with Mercy McKay, with whom he soon settles on the Graham homestead with their son, Amboise Louis Gilbert Des Meaux DuBois Graham! The representative of the Old World himself, Monsieur Amboise DuBois, weds Champe and moves to Tidewater Virginia after briefly revisiting France. Byrd Graham, of course, marries Conway Saunders, the upper-class Southern gentleman who has at the same time sworn allegiance to the new American democratic experiment. (A Frenchman, DuBois apparently cannot serve as this sort of husband—he is not the compromise candidate necessary to an American heroine compounded of the Old World *and* the New.) As the American—and Southern—icon, George Washington adjourns to Mount Vernon; Byrd and Conway retreat to their plantation, Maiden's Pleasure, parents now of George Washington Saunders. The War for Independence has not freed them from dependence upon what is presented as a British/Southern heritage. Even the name of the plantation carries this flavor of superficial archaic innocence—a maiden ignorant of the world's realities.

Blanchard's homage to the homeland can only be construed as a defensive response conditioned by the fact of the Civil War: "The South had borne the brunt of the war, had suffered more wrongs, had lost more property—ruthlessly destroyed by marauding parties—than any other part of the country" (287). The new nation is seen as owing its very existence to a South which that apparently ungrateful nation itself would later not allow its (the South's) own way of life. As in a later war, these Southerners are rebels as much against change—the loss of prerogatives—as against the injustices of a status quo. The veiled references to the Civil War mark *A Daughter of Freedom* as a late-nineteenth-century novel. The fantasies of 1900, for example, include the projecting onto the past of the idea of self-sacrificing African-American peasants so much more concerned with their masters than with themselves that they would spontaneously go out of their ways to defeat—and reject the bribes of—Tories in a War for Independence which in no way would alter their own dependent status. The final scene of the novel communicates for a last time the myopia endemic to these fantasies. While the births of the heroes' and heroines' children, "the first free-born American citizens in the family," are being celebrated downstairs, upstairs their mammies "Aunt Dilly and Tyky, crooning their weird songs, rocked on their knees the two little ones, each fast asleep" (312). But these lullabies are after all no more "weird" than Mr. Graham's final injunction to Byrd before he rode off to lose his life in a pre-Revolutionary skirmish against the British: "be always on the side of the oppressed" (25).

The very title of *A Carolina Cavalier: A Romance of the American Revolution* (1901) by George Cary Eggleston signals that it is yet another Anglicized American book, and Southern Civil War novel disguised. Though "a romance only," the novel purports to make accurate use of historical details in its validating of themes associated with a romanticized South as England/England as the South: "Patriotism, and an unflinching sense of honor—love and heroic devotion" (9). (Eggleston's better-known brother, Edward, became a somewhat more modern and scientific social historian as well as more realistic writer of regional fiction.) As if in conscious parallel to the diplomatic dealing during the Civil War, wherein the Palmerston ministry was secretly sympathetic with the South but failed to recognize the independence of the Confederacy, Eggleston posits an American world identified with aristocratic British traditions and "still"—in 1901 rather than 1779—dependent not so much on the North as on Britain. It is altogether in keeping that, as Thomas A. Bailey writes in *A Diplomatic History of the American People,* "British unfriendliness toward the North during the Civil War was concentrated in the upper classes" (320). Noting that "the facts of history are here mentioned only in so far as they gave rise to the incidents recorded in this romance, and may serve to explain its events" (285), Eggleston fails to note that his antiquated story line "explains" a vision of the history of the Gilded Age as well as the Revolution. The unappreciated enthusiasm and selfless zeal of these late-eighteenth-century Southern soldiers are worthier "than all the virtues of our commercial age can ever be!" (167). Tawdry trade, the modern and the Yankee, thus become contemporary targets for attack as surely as they were for romantic Southern poets like Sidney Lanier or would be for the Nashville Agrarians.

A Carolina Cavalier opens with an Anglicized American "invading" his own land. After seven years at Eton and Oxford, spending summers on the Continent, Roger Alton of Alton House must take up with a mysterious compatriot and navigator in order to sail from the Bahamas back to South Carolina and avoid British-controlled ports—for young Alton is, of course, a true American patriot even though he at first seems to others "an Englishman of the upper middle class" (13) with "the stately manners of the time" (12). His new friend, Thomas Humphreys, steers the boat through Gulf Stream and storm, deposits Alton safely ashore, and tells him to forget that they ever met (Alton guesses that he must be a pirate). Roger sets out to visit the nearby home of an old acquaintance, Mrs. William Vargave, whose tomboy daughter, Helen, has become a "radiantly beautiful young woman" (57) and heiress with whom Alton immediately falls in love in spite of earlier improprieties committed by her reportedly dead father. The Vargaves inform him that the British have taken Savannah and that the war has been divisive, creating a great deal of treachery and distrust, especially due to selfish and opportunistic Tories. Alton returns to the boat to find Humphreys and his belongings gone, but a note telling him that bullet-lead is secreted in the bottom of the boat. On his way to Alton House, Roger stops at a country inn, where he is forced to strike a man for insulting his father.

Alton House and its thirty-thousand-acre estate have prospered under the management of Roger's twin sister, Jacqueline (otherwise "Jack"), who is engaged to Roger's young aristocratic friend Charles Barnegal. Alton's father, Colonel Geoffrey Alton, has called a meeting of distinguished patriots at Alton House, a meeting which includes Francis Marion and John Rutledge, the governor, who appoints Roger a captain. At the Charleston headquarters of Commander Rutledge, Roger again meets Humphreys, who has been working as an American spy. As the troops move out Alton and Humphreys are fired at by Tories and escape to the swamp, to the American General Lincoln, thence on to Orangeburg with a dispatch for Rutledge. Indecisive, the British commander, Prevost, halts midway between Savannah and Charleston, starts a retreat, and fortifies the sea islands. In Swamp Fox fashion Roger's troops harass and effectively distract the British, though Roger is hit in the shoulder by a bullet. Suffering from Barnegal's extraction of the bullet and from subsequent fever, Alton journeys to the Vargaves, soon after to Alton House, to recuperate. Roger's band enjoys continued success in their swamp-based sorties against the Tories. They are called upon to free Jacqueline from the clutches of the Tory squad organized by Charlie Barnegal's evil uncle, though they are unable to save the home of the Vargaves from destruction. In a final showdown, Roger and Barnegal's band route the British at Alton House but fail to save the building from the flames. Captain Roger now joins the resistance in the northern part of the state and is twice promoted, becoming a lieutenant-colonel.

What we might consider the author's guilt-ridden compensatory fantasy of significance leads him to present domestic and domesticated women and African Americans who through momentary and decisive action in a war for "independence" nonetheless perpetuate a polity of dependence. At least the moment of *gaining* victory embraces the full cross-section of Southern society. Helen and Jack, with "the most patriotic little band" (320) of youthful blacks imaginable, fend off the Tories from their homes long enough for the menfolks to come to their rescue. Earlier a belle dressed "for masculine inspection" (59), Helen now heroically dashes forth to set fire to an outside log kitchen which Tories were using for cover, becoming the tomboy of her preadolescent days. Particularly susceptible to reverses in love, "a woman without a man's resource of participation in the troubled life of the time" (200), Jack yet asserts that women can fight, organizes her squad of devoted slaves, and bravely undergoes her brief captivity with the British. Events like these depart from the social norms portrayed and, if carried too far, would destroy the historical novel's balance of practical action and love interest; women finally become victims of dated ideology and literary genre. Even though the love plots parallel a larger world, by book's end the women are always there at the disposal of the very men whose actions eventuate in keeping women at their disposal. More nearly a balance of motives functions for male characters in the historical romance: "However pressing may be affairs of state, especially to enthusiastic young men engaged in a war for all that human nature holds dear, affairs of a nearer and dearer kind insist sometimes upon their superior claim to attention" (238).

The unwonted participation of black slaves in schemes to maintain a system of peonage stems from the author's nostalgia for an antebellum but post-Revolutionary War South. (This notion takes added point from historians' emphasis on statistics and polemics which show that at the time of the Revolution itself the South was not unalterably committed to slavery.) Blacks are seen to be defending a benevolent economic and social system and to be protecting themselves from the horrible fate of being captured by the British, who would send them to the West Indies "into a servitude more cruel than any the American mind at any period in history has tolerated" (250), to a servitude unredeemed by pity or sentiment, "a slavery inspired solely by greed of gain" (392). The blacks possess a world worth defending and a fear of being sold "down the sea"—analogous to being sold "down the river." Eggleston sounds an elegiac note of 1901 in his desire "to say one word in favor of the institution of slavery,—now dead and done for,—with all its possibilities of evil": "how closely the ties of affection were knitted between them and their kindly masters, and how great the pride of servants was in their dependence upon families of distinction" (120). The prime case in point of the submissive and sycophantic stereotype in *A Carolina Cavalier* is Roger's "man" Marlborough, who under orders and on his own goes out of his way to aid his white folks. He even becomes a soldier—though innocuous because still a servant. (We are informed that blacks by law could constitute only up to half a military company, could be therefore only underling soldier-servants at best. Fear of an armed underclass, of course, figured in Southern military strategy during the Civil War.) He finds his identity in his dependence on Alton: "I am proud to belong to you, Mas' Roger" (119). Marlborough can act with intrepid bravery, but his utter mental slavery disallows freedom: "I'se Marlborough Alton now. If you sets me free, I'll be just Mulborough nothing—or may be just Jake. For the Lawd's sake, my mastah don't set me free, but jes' lem me be your own pussonal servant as I is now" (120).

In many passages of Eggleston's novel the enemy ceases to be an England which would whisk away happy slaves to the West Indies and becomes a later North which would impose upon them the heavy burden of freedom ("Mis' Jacqueline" has been educating "her" blacks):

The laws making it a penal offence to teach negroes to read were enforced only when the abolition of slavery became a subject of political agitation, filling the people of the South with apprehension of negro revolt and the massacre of their families. Those laws were regarded solely as self-defensive measures in the face of a great danger. Until that danger was threatened, it was deemed the high duty and privilege of the white people to instruct and civilize the blacks, many of whom, in the Carolinas, were native African savages, of recent importation. (106)

Eggleston has more than his facts wrong (by the time of heated controversy over abolition, significant numbers of Africans were no longer being brought into the South); to him, no gradual or immediate change seemed called for. The Old Plantation becomes a middle ground between "bad slavery" in the West Indies and the emancipation of the abolitionists, the novel a fictional war against Britain (i.e., a Revolutionary War romance) and against the North (i.e., a Civil War romance) in its defense of a status quo. In fact, the usual picture of the Revolution as itself a civil war emerges as divisive partisanship, treachery, and opportunism (especially of Tory sympathizers) replace "armed conflict between the soldiers of two nations" (63)—in other words, an affair of honor among traditional gentlemen. Twice Eggleston mentions a civil war as the "cruelest of all things" (63 and 311). The British have failed in not being "British" enough, to the extent that Tarleton, Cornwallis, and others possess a "brutish insensibility to honor." The British commanders' considering the patriots "criminals," "vermin," and "rebels" (recall the 1860s context) (284) stirs Roger's anger and "made of him not so much a soldier with a duty to do as an insulted gentleman bent upon resenting and resisting in vindication of his personal right" (298). Just arrived from England, he wants to be a gentleman *in* America. American fiction continued to fight civil wars—and wars about civility—even in nominal Revolutionary War novels.

Before the "new" society can be reconstituted on the old models and the appropriate marriages take place, all marks against family honor must be erased. It turns out that Humphreys is actually Helen's father and had feigned his death in order to hide the shame of having forged the elder Colonel Alton's signature. He has been blackmailed by Charles Barnegal's uncle even though the colonel himself has kindly refused to incriminate Mr. Vargave. Vargave has atoned by working hard to repay the "loan" and by opposing the British. He dies at peace with himself and forgiven by a Colonel Alton who, in another of the book's obvious fantasies, says that Vargave's past is forgotten just as there is "no history back of the republic's birth" (366). The knowledge of the crime dies with William Barnegal, and Roger is free to marry Helen Vargave (he could never have wed the daughter of a known forger). The jealous and villainous "Wild Bill" Barnegal, alcoholic and still angry that years earlier he had lost possible brides to both Colonel Alton and Charlie's father, proves to have lied as well in telling his nephew that he (Charlie) was a bastard (the idea that Charlie's father was already married to another woman when he was born is refuted by documents showing that this first wife was herself already married!). Charlie Barnegal can now marry "Jack" Alton—Jacqueline again, no doubt. In the last chapter, "which brings the war and the story to an end," Helen sends Roger off to fulfill his obligations to his first mistress, "Liberty," before she marries him. The end is all that Geoffrey Alton, a stickler for formalities, could have wished. The singular world achieved by the war and by the story conspicuously parallels the world before the war—either war—as Roger rejoins Helen to begin "the joyous work of reconstructing the historic mansion in all the glory of architectural adornment to which its sturdy walls invited its new master—for Roger was its master now, Col. Geoffrey Alton having passed away, full of years and of honors" (447-48).

These novels focus so clearly upon disparate claims—war and love, the public and the private, male and female, America and Britain—that their dual vision and commingling of terms must finally result in a picture slightly out of focus. The terms in the title of the first chapter of Sara Beaumont Kennedy's *Joscelyn Cheshire: A Story of Revolutionary Days in the Carolinas* (1901), for example, can meld only through an unmotivated denouement. "Cupid and Mars" (see discussion of Alden W. Quimby's *Valley Forge* in the Middle Colonies section) drive forward their separate plot lines until an unconvincing resolution is interjected in a belated attempt to stay the martial and give birth to the marital. Whereas the Continental soldier Richard Clevering of Hillsboro'-town, North Carolina, is "as gallant a figure as ever melted a maiden's heart or stormed a foeman's citadel" (1), his beloved Joscelyn Cheshire has only the option of melting a man's heart. His career is depicted in similes which mix the military with romance: he goes forth to a tryst with an American scout, "as eager as a lover to meet his mistress" (47). And, even here, the hero's exploits in war merely *qualify* him to be later considered worthy of the girl who still may choose another; in fact, his deeds are performed at the time on behalf of her "enemy," the Continental side. A partisan political agenda cannot be easily configured because gallantry and courage in themselves render the hero worthy of being accepted by the women of either political side, both of whom inhabit historical romance and Anglo-American tradition. War is necessary to the plot, but essential reasons for war are frequently washed out by the necessity of bringing man and woman together in love. The discourse fights an uncertain war of independence for its plot lines, hardly a revolutionary battle against British ways or the conventions of costume romance.

At the beginning of *Joscelyn Cheshire* Richard Clevering acknowledges his love for Joscelyn, but also acknowledges that he must subdue this Tory girl just as he must subdue the British. He must in the meantime exhibit his love of the Tory but not of Tories. His patriot sister, Betty, also faces the dilemma of love for a Tory, in her case the dashing aide to Cornwallis, Eustace Singleton. Upon its first departure, for the desolation of Valley Forge, his regiment is dissuaded by a concerned Richard from firing at Joscelyn's house, even though she remains contentiously pro-British and his own father becomes a casualty of war. Bored by the monotony of camp, Richard joins an American scout in dressing as a workingman and entering British-occupied Philadelphia, where he and the scout are hired to row a boat to the landing near which a grand fete and tournament are going forward in honor of the departing Howe. Richard recognizes a familiar face, that of the striking Ellen Singleton, look-alike cousin of the North Carolinian Mary Singleton (Eustace's sister, who feels Eustace would be the appropriate match for Joscelyn). Disguised in a British military cloak, Richard provokes Ellen into revealing the details of a British plan for a detachment under her lover, Grant, to capture Lafayette's forces, whose movement from Valley Forge has been detected. Richard and the scout narrowly escape detection themselves as they return to Valley Forge and warn Lafayette's troops to turn back immediately.

As the British later evacuate Philadelphia they are pursued by the Continentals, who fail to follow up their advantage decisively because of the indecisive command of Charles Lee. American fortunes improve when an inspiring Washington overrules Lee and when the redoubtable Molly Pitcher takes her dead husband's place at the cannon during the Battle of Monmouth. Richard Clevering's own fortunes turn downward when, suffering from a head wound, he is taken prisoner. His scheme to escape proceeds smoothly after he picks and chews his rope apart, but ultimately fails because he feels sorry for the naive young North Carolinian Billy Bryce, and decides to take him along; only Bryce now escapes, and returns to his home colony to report his misadventures and news of the battle at Monmouth and to communicate Richard's love message to Joscelyn.

Richard is taken with Clinton's army to New York, from where he is removed to a British prison-ship (the notorious Sugar House prison is full—see the depictions of Sugar House and ship in Mary C. Francis's *Dalrymple*). Depressed by the absence of Joscelyn, the foul air and scant rations aboard ship, and the sight of dead prisoners being buried in the sand nearby, Richard is befriended only by a sympathetic British artilleryman, James Colburn. After receiving a letter from Colburn informing her of Richard's plight, an only apparently reluctant Joscelyn cooperates with Betty in writing a letter to Eustace telling him to use his influence with Cornwallis (an old friend of Joscelyn's father) to promote an exchange of prisoners, if not an outright freeing of Richard. The flailing of an elderly prisoner who had merely stolen a pear meanwhile arouses Richard from his mental stupor, inspiring him to plan a mutiny, which goes awry when another prisoner attempts to lead a rash and premature insurrection. Richard's next ploy is to feign death; put in a body sack he is taken ashore and buried—but previously provided by a friendly prisoner-sexton with a bit of driftwood over his face and a reed for a breathing tube. Eerie as he rises from his shallow grave in foggy and stormy weather, weak but desperate, Richard succeeds in strangling a patrol soldier and throwing him off a nearby cliff. Directed by a poor fisherman to the peddler Dame Grant, a grateful Richard is allowed to use her passport and accompany her to the Jersey shore.

News of Richard's "death" and escape precedes his return to the South, to which the theater of war also shifts. Still presuming that Joscelyn will ultimately be his, Richard entrusts to her the gold piece which was given him by Colburn and rejected by the generous Dame Grant, informing her that it will later be made into a wedding ring. During the weeks after Richard rides off again, Hillsboro' serves as a stopping place for both the Americans under Gates and the British under Cornwallis. Joscelyn becomes the "Royalist Rose," a favorite of the young British officers, especially Captain Barry. Her coquetry and flattery had also just defused the hostility of a pair of American soldiers who had intended to reprimand her for not flying the American colors. Eustace Singleton survives a storm at sea, and visits his girlfriend, Betty. Secretly back in town, a spy and passing as a Tory soldier, Richard saves Joscelyn by restraining her runaway horse. Later that night the British cut off his flight to safety and he must abandon his own steed and climb into an upstairs window of Joscelyn's home. While the occupying army hosts a party downstairs, Joscelyn hides Richard in the attic and excuses his knocking over a flower pot as the deed of a cat. A still-suspicious Tarleton insists on searching the entire house for the missing spy, but finds nothing. Joscelyn furnishes food for Richard and finally recants from her requirement that he no longer convey military intelligence to the American commander as a condition of her helping him to escape. Her "accidentally" knocking over a candle in the attic creates a confusion which allows Richard to escape. He feels relieved by no longer having to inconvenience or incriminate Joscelyn, but still worries at the continued presence of Captain Barry near her. Soon, however, the British remove from Hillsboro', as open harassment of the Tories increases.

Richard marches on to South Carolina and Georgia, but Joscelyn is briefly held by the Americans, under an accusation of espionage because of letters she has received from Cornwallis's camp—actually love letters from Barry. Love interest and war interest continue to intersect when Richard becomes the mortally injured Barry's nurse after a particularly bloody skirmish. Coincidence is compounded by Richard's discovery that Barry is the man for whom Ellen Singleton had mistaken him— hence, disclosed secrets to him—in Philadelphia. The opposing soldiers' images further merge for the reader when each acknowledges the other's gentlemanly qualities and when Richard in praise and strict honor writes to Joscelyn of Barry's death. By the time of the surrender at Yorktown the Tories back home have come in for even harsher treatment, some of their property being confiscated: Mr. Singleton flees to Canada. Richard, wounded, resolute but not so aggressive, arrogant, or self-confident as earlier, returns to ask for Joscelyn's surrender. The war has altered her as well, made her more dignified and sober, less impetuous, but she nonetheless does not capitulate at a lovers' private Yorktown.

Several specifics of the denouement go into the making of the usual tepid Anglo-American brew. Eustace Singleton and Betty Clevering obviously will marry. The English Colburn writes that he wants to become an American. Tory haters become less adamant and Richard defends Joscelyn against her maligners by emphasizing her "American" heroism in hiding him in the attic. The final melodramatic touch comes when Richard, slipping on ice, fractures and lacerates his already injured arm so badly that it must be amputated. Whether this endows him with a necessary sign of bravery, and therefore success, in the war plot (though on her enemy's side), or signals an unmanning that renders him harmless as antagonist, Joscelyn now appears with the coin which he said would become a wedding ring, telling him that "the war is over, and I surrender myself" (338). Cupid and Mars are able to mingle to the same degree that Richard's losing an arm suggests a loss of potency in love and war—disarmament with a vengeance. As lover and as soldier he is no longer marked as different, the opponent; or, rather, his state symbolizes the inevitability all along of his becoming reconciled to his marital and martial partners. Such a reading, at least, saves the narrative from an altogether too abrupt and inconsistent ending.

Both lovers in this action-filled novel have now performed deeds which show that they deserve not only each other but also the social and psychological security of an ethnocentric world. The very wedding ring used in the American marriage belongs to Britain. Richard Clevering has protected Joscelyn *from* Americans, and he himself has both befriended and been mistaken for his British rival, Captain Barry. Richard's rising from the sands of the beach therefore does not become a rebirth into a new democratic and egalitarian spirit. Joscelyn's dilemma has been whether to follow Tory ways or those of her non-Tory friends; she wants to betray neither, and to her intimates she is known as "loyal, though a Loyalist" (227). As a woman excluded from the war plot, she performs only her token bit for the British during the actual conflict. Along with the denouement of the love plot, she must for the most part be held in abeyance while the war lasts. But when the love plot recommences, her presence can dictate the personal terms of the war's ending. However, when neither party undergoes a significant conversion in already similar political attitudes, the lovers must meet at the only acceptable place, the place where received social traditions and literary traditions become one.

Hallie Erminie Rives's rendition of the Revolution, *Hearts Courageous* (1902), plays fictional variations but not new themes. Her old-style Virginia and her conventional lovers exist between an egalitarian Western ideal and the most antiquated of Old Worlds, though she pays passing homage to both. Her use of a French Huguenot romantic hero, Louis Armand, both a noble and a republican, enables her to reinforce the image of an Anglo-American New World beset by neither the corruptions of monarchy nor the violence and uncouthness of the frontier. From Rives's perspective, the future and excessive and destructive French Revolution looms in the background even though it is in her narrative's future, and it serves as contrast to the much different American War for Independence. If only the Virginians were not denied their rights as Englishmen—a breed that instinctively loves freedom—all would be well. The heroine praises the pioneers of the new settlements but in speaking of the courtly planter class mentions that "Virginia was first settled by gentlemen" (105) and was unique in being colonized "by a single people" (135). The Virginians love the virgin land but also the Virgin Queen, their foxhunts, and "still sent their sons to Eton and Oxford to be educated, and spoke of England as 'home'" (25).

Although some of Rives's outlanders people the extremes of the political and social spectrum, her portrait of colonial Williamsburg itself is so skewed that her conservatives become centrists. What so strikes her—but a fact necessary to her calculated ideological agenda—is that Williamsburg, though "the miniature copy of the Court of St. James, aping the manners of the royal palace," was nonetheless "the Heart of the Rebellion" (216). That a traditional and responsible aristocracy could and should lead was a circumstance that allayed fears of social chaos in America in 1902 (and could be projected as an implied desired fate into the France of 1789); that aristocrats could also be rebels merges Rives's picture of the Revolution with a common view of the Civil War:

It is a thing to note, since rebellion commonly springs from the people rather than from the quality, that it was contrary in Virginia. There the aristocracy was not Tory. There were few enough like my Lord Fairfax, who, born noble, held nobly to their loyalty. Those who held with the king, besides the toad-eaters, were for the most part the lower classes, office-holders, tradesmen who looked for sales, lawyers just over from London. (216)

The antagonists to the ideal society of the late nineteenth century are thus transmuted and displaced to the late eighteenth century: Southern nativist hostility to the immigrant and to Yankee capitalism suggests itself. From the same ship that brings Armand to America "the gangway was thrown down for the herded human cattle that had thronged the lower deck" (87). (Our own most vivid "picture" of just this scene is Alfred Stieglitz's photograph of "huddled masses" of immigrants taken in 1907, *The Steerage*.) Those who "held nobly to their loyalty" could be redeemed by their personal code, so that Fairfax is a "splendid old man" (20) despite his representing "the masterfulness of birth, the pride of

"Colonel Tarleton, of the British Legion, at your service." Illustration, by A. B. Wenzell, for p. 323 of Hallie Erminie Rives's *Hearts Courageous* (Indianapolis: Bowen-Merrill, 1902).

power" (23). On the other side, although politically a contrast, Patrick Henry, "a forest Demosthenes," functions as one of nature's noblemen, a gentleman but no dandy, embodying "the new spirit of the new land, eager, thoughtful" (23).

As the novel opens, eighteen-year-old Anne Tillotson of Gladden Hall, in a rare show of American independence, argues with her aunt that she will marry whomever she pleases and defends the good name of Patrick Henry, whom the local gentry have branded as little better than "a low-country demagogue, half the time dressed in buckskins" (9). The pleasures of life in the Old Dominion include the foxhunting and banqueting of these First Families, but complaints are beginning to be heard that the king has taken to denying these local gentlefolk their rights as British citizens. The monarch has even been foisting superfluous slaves upon the colony. Meanwhile, Anne's eventual spouse arrives from London aboard the *Two Sisters*. Armand has been working as secretary for the "Marquis de la Trouerie," who en route has died of the "flux." On a coin toss, Armand wins from the brutal Mr. Rolph the services of a poor Italian indentured woman—there is our token new immigrant!— whom he had earlier befriended aboard ship. Not really knowing what now to do with her, he turns to an interested bystander—Anne—and suggests that she engage the unfortunate woman for the period of her indenture. At first offended by Armand's presumption when they had not even met before, Anne hears the bondservant's story, relents, and agrees to take her. Armand praises Anne for this display of noblesse oblige and for so politely apologizing to him for her initial coldness. Though not quite as sisters, Anne's and the Italian woman's fates are joined in a pairing of rich and poor, American and immigrant, servant and supervisor. Anne falls in love with the other immigrant, Armand, even before he saves her from a limb that falls on their carriage. He celebrates that he now possesses all a man—and the plots of these novels—must have: a cause to fight for and a woman awaiting after the fight.

Uncertainty about which cause Armand in fact fights for gives rise to the mysteries and complications of the plot. Captain Foy, aide to the new and unfeeling royal governor, Lord Dunmore, reports a rumor that the Marquis de la Trouerie is in America as envoy of the French king, intending to assess the American situation and the possibility of French aid crucial to the Americans. Knowing that the marquis died aboard the *Two Sisters,* a Captain Jarrat bribes Louis Armand to impersonate the marquis and inform the French monarch that the Virginians are loyal to the British Crown. Armand plays along but becomes involved in a duel with Captain Foy when Foy insults the reputations of two gentlemen— George Washington and Washington's old friend, the Tory Lord Fairfax. Adept at swordplay, Foy finds himself nonetheless losing to the even more talented Armand when the duel is stopped by an emissary sent by the governor. During the confusion occasioned by the emissary's appearance Foy takes unfair advantage by stabbing Armand, who for several subsequent weeks is tended at Fairfax's Greenway Court by Fairfax himself and by a concerned Anne. Shortly after Armand tells her a story whose point is that love should conquer all, the governor tells her that Armand actually is Monsieur le Marquis de la Trouerie.

Henry's "give me liberty or give me death" speech galvanizes patriot feeling in the colony, Philip Freneau's verse incites rebellion, and news of the Lexington fight proves there is no turning back. Jarrat's jealousy of Armand leads him to expose Armand as an impostor and conspirator against the peace of the colony, but before he is captured Armand entrusts Anne with important papers which she must deliver to Benjamin Franklin in Philadelphia. To prevent the papers being seized by Jarrat, Anne tosses them to the redemptioner woman, who is struck by Jarrat but succeeds in hiding them—hiding them so well that even Anne does not find them for days. By the time she secures the papers and makes her way to Philadelphia, Armand concludes that Anne has betrayed him: Franklin has received no packet from a young lady of Virginia. Armand is himself at liberty on his promise to the British authorities, his life otherwise forfeit, to deliver to Congress a false message containing no encouragement for the Americans. Almost simultaneously, Anne finally places the authentic message from France into the hands of Franklin, Armand wounds Jarrat and attempts to break into the chambers of Congress with an improvised and accurate message, and the bells of Philadelphia announce the Declaration of Independence. A man of his word, Armand returns to his British captors with the declaration that he would not have presented their message to Congress in any case. The demands of honor discharged, Armand jumps from the British ship, escapes, and goes on to a notable military career with the Americans. Anne, too, has her successes, like warning the Virginia Assembly meeting at Charlottesville of the approach of British troops and obtaining a release from Cornwallis for her faithful retainer, John-the-Baptist.[2]

During the warfare in Virginia Anne liberates a captive Armand by making use of the written form which Cornwallis had actually signed for John-the-Baptist. Their escape to Gladden Hall is secured by the appearance of troops led by the imposing Lafayette. Lafayette's disclosure to all—surprise of surprises?—that Armand in fact is the Marquis de la Trouerie, that he has therefore fooled the British by "pretending" to be who he really was, is complemented by Anne's assuring Armand that she too has been straightforward and has never betrayed him. In the final chapter, "The Passing of the Old Regime," the British surrender at Yorktown (an event coterminous with the death of Fairfax, true to his king to the last) and the daring and pride of the New World—Anne Tillotson—weds the nobility of the Old—Louis Armand. For now, albeit fictive and temporary, the author can have the old regime both pass away and remain; the friend of Marie Antoinette has become an American revolutionary who is aware that in France a "storm is gathering," "the people look with hatred upon my order." "France is not ready for liberty," Armand declares; "The blood of her best must flow first" (406). Louis Armand, Monsieur le Marquis de la Trouerie, had earlier praised Anne for being indifferent to "grandeur and titles" (208)—but she finally does marry a titled noble, one on the "American" side. If a British aristocrat cannot be assimilated, since at least militarily and temporarily he was the enemy, certainly a French one may be, since he was part of a French alliance no matter how class-conscious his nation. If America should not be an aristocracy, an aristocrat of Armand's stripe can yet find a niche in Rives's Virginia. The newlyweds can live neither in the land of the imperious British opponent nor in that of the future Reign of Terror. They cannot even live in a changing egalitarian America, but must take that middle ground which, according to a letter by Franklin, had been referred to by the king of England himself as the most important of the Southern colonies, that land settled by gentlemen—Virginia. Hero and heroine pay tribute to their land and to each other in the final words of *Hearts Courageous:*

"Here, and here alone upon this earth, is Liberty! And to Liberty my life belongs!"

"To Liberty," she whispered, smiling, "to Liberty, and—to me!" (406-7)

A historical novel in which a horse can play a major role would seem slight indeed. Such is the case in Joseph A. Altsheler's 1902 offering, *My Captive: A Novel.* The horse, in fact, has the best of it. Old Put—named after General Putnam—in many ways is more noble and valiant, more useful and enlightened, than the priggish yet presumptuous first-person narrator, Philip Marcel. Marcel's career records the intersecting of the desire for power and the power of desire, the chauvinistic and the male chauvinistic. That he would not be *taken* captive creates no empathy with her he would *take* captive. Metaphors of war are used to define the male role in love, while those same metaphors render the woman powerless. Thus, it is presumption in women to "meddle with war" (1), but show toward them a "stern, unyielding temper, and they submit at once" (17). Their place is to be captured—and to want to be captured. (Altsheler either had not read Aristophanes' *Lysistrata,* with its "war shall be the concern of women!" or had read it to little effect.) The American male's asserting control over the British merges with his asserting control over women. Applied to narratology, this allows the historical novel to tell a single story, as the British disappear but women remain. The author unwittingly describes the divided and perplexed yet, in this sense, unified status of the romantic protagonist of historical fiction: "With a battle on one side of him and a woman on the other, what is a man to do?" (1).

The almost compulsively repeated series of captures and escapes which makes up the plot of *My Captive* creates the impression of a story which does not advance; clearly, first and last, the heroine is "my captive," no less so as eventual wife than as military prisoner from distant Devonshire. At the close of a battle, Julia Howard, saucy and anti-American daughter of a soldier in Tarleton's legion, falls into the hands of South Carolina gentleman Philip Marcel (a central character in Altsheler's *In Hostile Red* as well). About to be delivered into captivity in Morgan's army, she mounts and abruptly spurs her horse, strikes Marcel's riderless one, and races away. Marcel regains the superior Old Put and, before she can dodge into the forest, overtakes her. She so praises his horse that he allows her to ride Old Put—and she escapes again, whipping Old Put on until Philip remembers he can call the horse back with a loud whistle. This time he ties her hands. Around the camp-fire, they share a meal and Julia talks and sings of marrying a loyal English soldier, one who would mind "no other thing" but "the ladies or the king" (53). Growing drowsy as she sings, Marcel is easily overpowered and captured by Captain Crowder's men, who Julia evidently knew were in the vicinity. However, these soldiers' rowdy singing and dancing, their drinking themselves into a drunken stupor, so offend her that she defends Marcel from an imminent hanging by telling them that the young American possesses valuable information. Later that night she even cuts the straps that confine him, and together they canter off. As Julia's stolen horse is shot from beneath her and Old Put bites and tramples one of Crowder's men, Julia and Philip manage to gain the relative safety of a recently deserted cabin.

Crowder's crew, nonetheless, sets up camp within view of the cabin. Confident he can fight off Crowder, Philip fails to fight off sleep, but succeeds in shooting the first of the men who break into the building. Donning the dead man's red coat, Philip along with Julia flees to the tangled darkness of the forest. Julia rides Old Put and Marcel plods on half-asleep toward Morgan's camp (a wasted trip in Julia's perspective, since she is confident Tarleton will soon take Morgan's force, in any case). When they encounter British troops Philip continues in his role as a Tory soldier. Although Julia plays along, wishing he were not a "rebel," she draws his own pistols on him, ordering him to go to Tarleton's camp. Ambivalent in her feelings toward him by now—and wishing that American and Briton could compromise—she is relieved that the shot from the accidentally discharged pistol misses him, but nonetheless leaves their camp during the night. More apprehensive that the lawless Crowder will find her than that she will find Tarleton, Philip discovers his fears well founded: Julia is again with the wild bunch. Shots are exchanged, and Marcel's sword fight with Crowder ends with Marcel's victory when his opponent slips. Male potency and dominance in war as well as love join in a single image: Julia promises not to run off again, and after an hour of silence exclaims, "quite suddenly," "Oh Mr. Marcel, what a swordsman you are!" (172).

When Philip and Julia arrive at the up-country plantation house of one Sinclair Harley, they are understandably taken for husband and wife. Marcel, suspicious when he sees one of Crowder's desperadoes outside, correctly infers that Harley is an impostor—he is actually Flournoy, Crowder's commander. To protect Philip, Julia casts aside her modesty, dances alluringly before Flournoy, and promises to become his "queen" if he will release Marcel (of whose real identity Flournoy has been informed). Knowing that Julia is terrified of Flournoy's advances, Marcel rejects her sacrifice and wants to dispatch Flournoy, now drunk and asleep. The ex-minister Clymer intervenes and shows some residual virtue by arranging for Philip to go to Julia's room that night and flee with her. The plan succeeds until the revived Flournoy draws on them, an interruption which proves temporary when Flournoy and Clymer argue, and shoot and kill one another. Julia again astride Old Put, Philip walking alongside, each compliments the valor and faithfulness of the other. She proves herself again when she snatches up the sword of a British scout Marcel has shot and slashes the shoulder of another hostile horseman, running him off. As Julia resuscitates Philip, who has taken a glancing bullet blow to the head, she declares her love.

Finally at Morgan's camp, Philip tells of Tarleton's movements and entrusts Julia to the American ladies. Though outnumbered three to one, the American soldiers dig in for a battle at the cow pens (Cowpens). All is smoke, blood, confusion, and violence as the British charge the lines of Americans led by South Carolina and Georgia riflemen and cavalry. As Philip strikes one trooper, Old Put saves him from another by biting his arm. The gloriously victorious Continentals lose only twelve men. The joy of Julia's rejoining her father is lessened by his becoming a captive, though Philip informs him that he will soon be a captive of a happier sort, since he is to live with his daughter's new family after her marriage. (Her regaining her father thus chronologically merges with her gaining a paternalistic husband.) "These," says Marcel, "were resounding boasts for a young soldier to make, but they all came true after Yorktown" (281). (The last word, as discussed earlier, a possible pun with "Yoketown"—marriage following surrender.) Marcel in coopting the father's place validates his own manhood as an authority figure, having previously declared that a major reason for the entire war was for Americans to prove that they are not provincials.

More than its subtitle makes Alfred Henry Lewis's *The Story of Paul Jones: An Historical Romance* (1906) a novel. This is the story (i.e., text) of Paul Jones, not his life. In it the American Revolution serves as more than a mere episode in an account of Jones's whole career. The crossings of love and war communicate a vision of the issues of the Revolution which challenges credibility, but perhaps no more so than in the preponderance of these novels. Conscious of social class and apparently insecure about his own initially humble status, Jones in this simple pseudo-biography legitimizes his achievement through alliance with

European royalty, not through celebrating the potential of the lower orders or criticizing the arbitrariness of birth as the measure of merit. If "between love and war his heart was formed to swing like a pendulum" (278), the—subliminal or not on the writer's part—reasons for his liaisons relate directly and simultaneously to the social and political perspectives perceived to be at issue not only in this conflict but in the French Revolution as well. As his heart swings between love and war, his and his maker's minds swing between commitment to the aristocratic and the democratic, the native and the foreign, 1776 and 1906. The author has inherited an egalitarian and American revolution made iconic through texts, but in 1906 discovers ample appeals of an American ancien régime. Obviously as ambivalent as Jones himself, Lewis gropes with Jones defining himself and with how these same social, political, and national concerns could be resolved in his contemporary world. In particular, Lewis haltingly approaches issues germane to African Americans, for whom the Civil War would seem logically to function as a War of Independence.

John Paul, twelve years old, of Scottish peasant stock yet possesses a patrician appearance, resembling—significant rumor has it—the laird for whom John's dull gardener father works. Promoted by the laird for his precocious nautical skills, young Paul is permitted to sail to Jamaica and Virginia (where his older brother, William, operates a plantation), his first vessel a slave ship chartered between West Africa and Kingston. So affected by the brutality of the Middle Passage and slaves' fates in the cane fields of Jamaica that he sells his one-sixth interest in the *John O'Gaunt,* John Paul at the same time believes that blacks are safer and happier on plantations like his brother's than as "savages" in Africa: his notion of the good and bad, American and foreign, slavery parallels that depicted in other novels of Southern apology of the period like George Cary Eggleston's *A Carolina Cavalier.* The British ship on its voyage back to England carries him as well as the Jamaican yellow fever, which claims many on board, including the captain. Well before the *King George's Packet* reaches England John Paul takes charge as self-appointed acting captain, characteristically insisting on the necessity of discipline and order.

Rewarded by an English shipowner with the captaincy of a cargo vessel, the *Grantully Castle,* Paul sails many seas piling up profits while studying languages and becoming—like Edwin Arlington Robinson's Richard Cory—"admirably schooled in every grace." Through this self-education he develops two nearly distinct personalities. Putting down mutinies and inspiring loyalty (despite a quick temper) as a sailor, as a man of society he accommodates himself to circumstances: "the darling of colonial drawing rooms, he is also the admiration of the men" (71). "He ever remembers the ladies" (128), though he develops no meaningful romantic involvements until somewhat later, remaining for some time "not a marrying man" (69). Yet in male dialogues at sea he indulges in a sexist lingo which forces at least some connection between his selves, an erotic language of possession and commodity: "a sailor loves his ship as though it were a woman" (217). Paul's first American "vessel," the *Ranger,* possesses a shape "as delicate as the lines of a woman's arm!" (126). This ship's flag is made from the dresses of New Hampshire girls, "quilted of cloth ravished from their virgin petticoats" (128). Perhaps rustic rural Americans do not have to be accommodated, but rather exploited like the American land or American slaves. Even when he labors in the name of the American Revolution John Paul employs the rhetoric of an upper class and master class, as this class is contradistinguished from both "mistress" and "slave." Therefore the very tropes meant to unify his personality and careers in love and war serve to bring forth further contradiction and inconsistency. The moment when Paul's next ship, the *Alfred,* runs up its flag is sanctified with an emotional and national significance, but no one seems aware of the eighteenth- and nineteenth-century paradox and irony of the banner's motto being "Don't Tread on Me." If this sailor bravely resists being tread upon, he cannot always resist treading upon others or allowing others to be tread upon.

After his stint on the *Grantully Castle,* as captain of yet another ship John Paul sails to Virginia and finds his brother dying of "lung fever." John Paul inherits the plantation and a name—by a cousin's proviso inheritors of the estate had to adopt his name, Jones—and settles down for two years as a prominent planter. He leaves this life when the argument over colonial rights begins, when he himself argues with an obnoxious British soldier and travels to New York and Boston, where he hears of Lexington and Concord. Taking everything personally, Jones inevitably utters words we would expect of a Civil War-era planter addressing the Union: the British "can now call us 'rebels' and, calling us 'rebels,' they will try to reduce us—for all our white skins and freeborn blood—to the slavish status of Hindostan" (85). He considers "rebel" objectionable because it implies a deviation from the right and the normative. Despite the near alliance between the Confederacy and the British in the 1860s, the British as imperious enemy who would make slaves of those who own slaves and send the actual slaves to a "worse" and impersonal slavery based solely on market-driven greed here serve as surrogate for the Yankee. Many unreconstructed Southerners continued to insist on states' rights and on the proposition that Northern capitalist wage slavery was the worse evil. When Lord Dunmore lays waste his plantation, the sentimental paternalist Jones first thinks of his slaves rather than of being made a slave: "My poor blacks!"—"the plantation was to them a home, not a place of bondage." He bemoans the fact that they might now face disease and the lash "in the cane fields of Jamaica" (108) that he knows so well. One recalls passages from, say, *The Old South* (1892), in which Thomas Nelson Page, while acknowledging that slavery brought on a national tragedy, concludes that to Africans themselves it was a blessing which brought to the race the only "civilization" it has known. Read most cynically, therefore, Jones's American Revolutionary project (for us, if not for 1906, a Civil War project as well) is to ensure that Virginia become "not a place of bondage" for him, but rather for others.

Putting his plantation business in order and contributing three thousand guineas to American patriot coffers, Jones joins the new navy, soon being promoted from lieutenant to captain. After serving under two incompetent officers, he is given charge of his own ship, the sloop *Providence;* with him on this microcosmic American world are "his faithful blacks, Scipio and Cato" (103) and the Indian Anthony Jeremiah. Later, as captain of the *Ranger,* Jones's duties are to harass and preoccupy British ports and shipping; in so doing he encounters, outmaneuvers, and defeats a larger British ship, the *Drake.* After Burgoyne's surrender—the French are always reported to have been waiting for a significant American victory before throwing their weight on the American side—Jones carries important dispatches to France, where he meets Benjamin Franklin as well as local royalty. Having avoided the snares of sundry colonial dames, he almost immediately falls prey to romantic entanglements in France (whose upper classes are more worthy of his social aspirations?). Kin to the king, the married Duchess de Chartres becomes enamored of Jones and promotes his cause so well that the king orders him a ship, the *Duras,* which Jones renames, in Franklin's honor, the *Bon Homme Richard* (thus figuratively combining the gift of European birth aristocracy with hard-working and "natural" American aristocracy, just as the duchess being the instrumentality of his obtaining the ship brings together military and romantic narratives). The newly outfitted *Richard* sails north past Ireland, then down the east coast of Scotland, where she engages the *Serapis.* As the ships exchange fire, two of the *Richard*'s three eighteen-pound guns explode, killing several men. The vessels lashed together broadside, sailors grapple in hand-to-hand combat. Even as his ship is sinking from the water required to douse the flames, at the Big Moment Jones's spirit carries the day: he has just begun to fight. The *Richard* does go down, but exploding hand grenades ignite powder on the *Serapis,* which strikes her colors.

Jones for the rest of the book steers a middle course between the claims of peasant and patrician, hero and lover, the French and the American. He takes the *Serapis* to Holland, where the Dutch and British bicker over whether Jones should be treated as "a rebel, a pirate or a disagreeable guest" (223); he fails in provoking a duel with a traitorous French naval commander. The ship which he sails toward England is driven by storm and winter to a French port. An old friend, the Marchioness de Marsan, introduces Jones to her godchild and ward—also kinswoman of the Duchess de Chartres (herself mother of Louis Philippe) and, in fact, an illegitimate daughter of the old king—Aimee Adele de Telison. John Paul immediately "forgets the blue of the ocean in the blue of Aimee's eyes" (257). He intends a characteristic, if perverse, view to be the highest praise of the tender sentiments: "love is even sweeter than war" (259). Aimee reciprocates with "his glory, is as dear as his love" (267). The duchess gives a grand banquet in Jones's honor, at which she relinquishes her claims on him and he histrionically turns over to her the sword of the captain of the *Serapis*. She and the marchioness arrange the marriage. But then Jones's plebeian and foreign roots return to haunt him: Aimee, a Bourbon, would be driven from the court for marrying a peasant. In such a case being a wife constitutes permanent ignominy, whereas being a mistress does not. Jones and Aimee nonetheless wed in a secret ceremony. For a time "the surrender of the *Serapis* is forgotten, as a thing trivial and transient, in the surrender of this girl with the glorious red-gold hair" (267). Then the combative John Paul sails for Philadelphia. His bid to fight a duel with the cowardly Arthur Lee for mentioning his lower-class origins is squelched by Washington, who assigns him command of the *America*—a ship of state, indeed. But Jones's ambitions are soon doubly thwarted; he is disappointed in both love and war when his and Aimee's infant son dies and when the Revolutionary War concludes.

At loose ends, Jones becomes in effect an international mercenary, a sailor of fortune. First with the French fleet in the West Indies, where his health suffers, he then joins the navy of the Empress Catherine of Russia, who rewards him handsomely for routing the Turkish fleet on the Black Sea. As his other financial interests flourish, suddenly but not surprisingly he develops "no more heart to own slaves" (288)—he sells the Virginia plantation. Technically on a leave of absence from Russia, Jones returns to Paris, remaining coolly neutral amid the contending factions but becoming acquainted with Robespierre, Danton, Mirabeau, Lafayette, and Thomas Paine. In this charged environment, "Admiral Paul Jones, while a republican, gives his sympathies to the king, in whom there is much weakness, but no evil" (291). Jones does find evil elsewhere, and breaks his neutrality in comments about using guns to convince the "mob" to support "conservatism and justice": "as though a ship were better for being keel up" (293), in his nautical jargon. After Mirabeau's death, he comments, "the animals are without a keeper" (295). Jones officially resigns from the Russian service when Washington sends him a commission as admiral in the American navy to fight the "Barbary pirates": "The prospect of a brush with the swarthy freebooters of the Mediterranean animates him mightily" (301-2). (Considering earlier themes, one is not certain whether these men transgress in being freebooters or in being swarthy—or both.) Jones's death prevents his participation in this exploit. A surprising final half-page depicts Napoleon contemplating his own megalomaniac designs and sadly ruminating, perhaps because of shared propensities and because Jones could have furthered those designs: "Paul Jones did not fulfill his destiny" (308).

John Paul Jones's fame ill matches this almost pathetic end. He falls short of a military accomplishment deserving of enduring note, just as the fruit of his love dies at birth. He is not allowed final battles; Aimee effectively disappears from the book. The author does not align him altogether with either love or war, democracy or monarchy. Yet Jones has his American moment and monument as skipper of the *Bon Homme Richard.* And the very divisions and paradoxes in his character reflect the sort of American Revolution imaged in these texts. Forever at sea, as it were, as an inarticulate life force, he possesses an authoritarian personality appreciative of aristocratic power and privilege and at odds with the supposed agenda of the American patriots; the lowly John Paul marries the daughter of a king. American fascination with royalty is expressed. But he finds no final satisfaction in this life either, and is drawn to the life of action typified for so many in 1906 by Theodore Roosevelt. At times he identifies with the plight of the underclass—at its broadest the class of Parisian revolutionaries, women, Jamaican field hands, not to mention his own earlier self—and at other times seems callous toward it. If Americans at bottom felt that the democratic impulse had been sanctioned and sanctified by history, they still indulged fantasies of power over emergent and possibly insurgent groups, however much these fantasies connoted insecurity, bigotry, or criticism of their own status as commoners. History had already appropriated Jones's national moment. The writer was left, therefore, with developing the sketchy irreconcilable aristocratic option in his compound portrait. In holding together contending motives, Lewis furnishes an image of the Revolution typical of the times, and an image of an early-twentieth-century America in which even his own divided protagonist could find a text and a home.

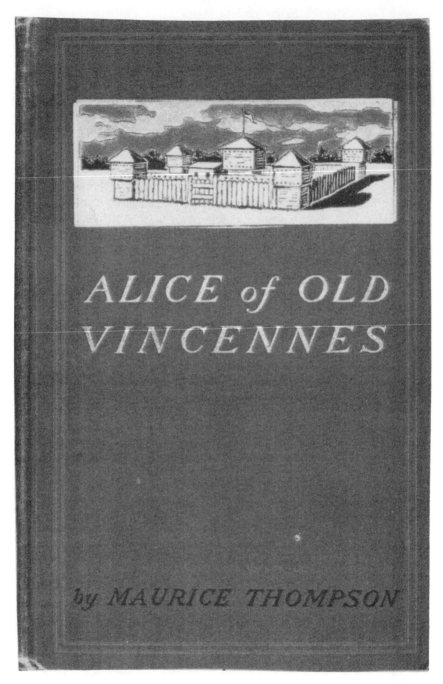

Cover of Maurice Thompson's *Alice of Old Vincennes* (Indianapolis: Bowen-Merrill, 1900); see pp. 173-75 below.

THE WEST

The myth and mystique of the great American forest, the Eden of the new Adam, would seem to make it the land of a genuinely new beginning, a land where a revolution could produce an unprecedented dispensation. A unique America could spring from the uniquely American. These Revolutionary War novels depict the region from the Mohawk Valley to the Old Northwest and southwards, and in so doing couple the fact of the war with early pioneering in the West and with turn-of-the-century manifest destinarian and imperialist agendas. As the actual old West was transmuted into images of a desired Old West it, too, became a time as well as a place (see the introduction to the section on the Middle Colonies). But, at the same time, subtext and escapist impulses implicitly address the present of these novels. Even the contemporary West as depicted by the romantic heirs of Bret Harte seemed an exotic and picturesque enough land, and Stephen Crane's portrayals distinctly cynical and revisionist.

By 1893, the frontier thesis had defined an indigenously national influence, true, but simultaneously the frontier was declared closed as a viable reality. The frontier was now a safely distanced past. The Far West of the formula Western long continued to be, typically, an immediately post-Civil War land. Setting fiction between 1865 and 1890 enabled a revisiting of the "frontier" past and West, freeing characters to do so because the nation farther east had purportedly resolved its own intersectional squabbles (though contention based on North-South conflicts were, in fact, carried over into the West). It seemed the West's turn to be described and defined. Yet that era also witnessed migrations to the West from the East and from Europe and Asia, the completion of the transcontinental railroad in 1869, and other transforming influences which were national and present rather than regional and past. After 1890, Revolutionary War romances set in an older West suggested another way of preserving a fantasy West, while commemorating national events and national purposes. Versions of a past *that* safely distant would possibly not be held to literary or historical standards of the present. Analogously, conserving yet circumscribing physical spaces of the West became a studied agenda in the days between John Muir's founding of the Sierra Club in 1892 and the founding of the National Park Service in 1916.

History, including literary history and historiography, in stressing the *idea* of the West had denied the region/time status as an ontological ground long before modern hermeneutics, but the tendency to imagine the West as an originating and definitive national locale continued. Preeminently, it was considered ground. While the West was being demythified and demystified in the face of late-nineteenth-century Native American uprisings, exposés of hardship and drudgery on the prairies, and the railroad's victimizing of wheat growers, the region's appeal as myth—partly for these contemporary reasons—grew. The myth prospered as the "West" receded into time and the frontier faded distantly beyond actuality, becoming appropriate subject only for historical fiction (the genre, in this sense, of most modern Westerns set, as most are, immediately after the Civil War). In addition, harking back to the eighteenth century allowed Eastern romancers to reclaim a West spatially *in* the present East, just as Southerners could imagine an Old South in the New. Making western colonial New York the frontier meant that novelists could portray appropriate "frontier" virtues in their own world yet one not yet touched by urbanization, industrialization, and the new immigration, by what some—including these same authors in other moods—would have called progress. Expressions of an escapist psychic necessity were caught in the apparent contradiction of relegating to an innocuous and romanticized past a land otherwise associated with the future and real possibility.

Whether conscious of doing so or not, these writers parallel contemporary American colonialism with an eighteenth-century and earlier colonization *of* America. But they do not posit an American victim now becoming a victimizer; the worst of the eighteenth-century British remain villainous while modern Americans dominate Native Americans, foreigners, and others for their own good. Naivete becomes a function of national chauvinism. The novels deal with the appropriation, in the name of America rather than England, of "pagan" lands and peoples. The nation formed of these lands could be radically Other only by absorbing the ethos of the Other. This, of course, never happens. The new country born of the Revolution is based on the same Euro-American principles which were by the close of the nineteenth century being exported to the Philippines and the Hawaiian Islands. Nativist nationalistic fervor was being expressed in both texts—the American and the foreign, the past and the present, the already written and evolving accounts of "current events." Indian (to use these novelists' designation: "nativist," a word similar to the more recent "Native American," ironically *excludes* the Indians) peoples in these novels of the West—their presence, to Leslie Fiedler, definitive of the Western just as African Americans are neces-

sary to the "Southern" (see *The Return of the Vanishing American*)—
function through their military alliances as adjuncts to the whites on both
sides. They, in the most derogatory sense of the word, serve.

Yet there are moments in these books when even the Anglo-Saxon
feels and nearly succumbs to "the spell of America" (an "Indian" and
almost mystical oneness with the wilderness described in Harold Frederic's earlier Revolutionary War novel *In the Valley*). "In Massachusetts,
in Virginia," as Robert Frost has it, "still colonials,/ Possessing what we
still were unpossessed by," "we found out it was ourselves/We were
withholding from our land of living." The only "gift outright" consists of
"salvation in surrender" "To the land vaguely realizing westward" ("The
Gift Outright" 145). This merging would lead to the seemingly laudable
and long-sought goal of defining American difference. But by the turn of
the century, if not by 1776, such a fulfillment and gain clearly implicated
loss for the Native Americans—clearly not included among Frost's
"colonials"—about and for whom whites had reservations. A people
already possessed the land; a land already possessed a people. A self-
conscious "primitivistic" posturing is revealed as just that when contrasted to phenomena of 1890 and 1891 like the Battle of Wounded Knee
and the recrudescence of the Prophet's (Tecumseh's brother) vision of
pan-Indian opposition to the encroachments of the whites: the Ghost
Dance. One chant intones, "a nation is coming, a nation is coming"
(Lauter 2: 744), a nation reclaimed from Euro-American expansion.
Such a nationalism would not have set well with these novelists had they
known of it: nationalism was for "U.S." By the end of the decade, the
Creek journalist and poet Alexander Lawrence Posey complained that
"the immemorial hush/Is broken by the rush/Of armed enemies/Unto
the utmost seas" (Lauter 2: 493). His fears were borne out by the failure
of the 1905 convention at which Posey and others proposed the creation
of Sequoyah, an Indian state formed from Oklahoma lands.

*   *   *

Despite its being set on the fringes of the frontier, Joseph A. Altsheler's
The Sun of Saratoga (1897) is shot through with images of compromise,
of mediation and the medial. Not only does the American army to which
Richard Shelby belongs occupy the ground in New York between the
British armies of Burgoyne and Clinton, Dick Shelby often visits the
"enemy" camp and is on one occasion accused of being a Tory sympathizer (Shelby speculates that the Tories may even have comprised the
majority of the American citizenry). Dick saves a number of Tories from
hostile patriots; the heroine, Catherine ("Kate") Van Auken, proves her

Americanism only after a period of apparent Toryism as a member of a Tory family; she makes the "right" choice of a husband following what seemed to be an engagement to a British soldier, Captain Ralph Chudleigh. The half-Tory Dick will marry the half-Tory Kate. Altsheler's use of the retrospective first-person narrative creates the usual sense of immediacy but at the same time its retrospective nature allows him to place his narrator in time between the Revolution and the time of his writing and to suggest thereby the persistence and worth of an ongoing British tradition which in no way ended with the war—and therefore by implication can be extended to 1897 as well.[1] The author's problem would seem substantial: how in these circumstances to create a protagonist nonetheless dedicated and partisan, American and instrumental in a war for independence. That it does not become a problem is a measure of the typically and essentially conservative stance of the genre.

The American troops in northern New York have gained a significant military advantage over those of the British General John Burgoyne to the Americans' north. In addition to defeating Burgoyne, it has become crucial to the American strategy to prevent word of Burgoyne's plight from reaching the forces of Clinton, to the Americans' south. A weak point in the security of the American line is said to be the Van Auken house. Captain Martyn's relieving Dick on guard duty and a moving light in a window of the Van Auken home are the first indications that the British are plotting to get messages through to Clinton. Suspicious of Martyn, Dick orders his men to remain nearby. They confront Martyn as he attempts to ride away; he fires at them, tears up his traitorous message, and shoots himself. In the next skirmish Americans capture several British soldiers, but Dick's friend, Sergeant Whitestone, is injured by a shot directed from the Van Aukens' upper windows. When a figure that looks like Kate tries for the second time to escape to the south and is stopped by Dick, she shoots at him and they grapple—only for Dick to discover that it is her disguised brother, Albert Van Auken. A forgiving Shelby allows Albert to return to the house, from which he again tries to escape by dressing in the Continental uniform of the ill Lieutenant Belt, who has replaced Dick as commander of the guard. Although he knows that Albert is unrepentant and in fact a conspirator with Martyn, Dick releases him to go to Burgoyne's camp and escorts the rest of the Van Auken family there as well. The American generals suspect treason to themselves and increasing danger for those remaining in the house.

The next episodes take place with Dick stranded in the British camp. Officers ply Dick with drink to induce him to disclose important information. Failing in this, they apologize for their ungentlemanly attempt. The roster of the many sick and wounded grows ever longer as another battle breaks out before Dick can return to American lines. "Why should men filled with mutual respect," thinks Shelby, "be compelled to shoot each other?" (77). A heavy toll is exacted by American sharpshooters in a pitched battle which Burgoyne sees as his only chance short of being reinforced by Clinton's army. The strength of the American army has grown and is moving closer to British lines. Albert seems to be returning earlier favors by showing Dick a way out of the British bivouac; actually his guide turns out to be Kate "disguised" in her own clothes. Before he can make good his escape, Dick is shot at and accused of being a spy by advanced troops from both the British and American camps: "Was I to dance back and forth between them forever?" (89). During the fury of the Battle of Saratoga Albert himself saves Shelby from a Hessian bayonet, a favor Dick immediately returns by returning an injured British soldier to his fellows. Kate exhibits her continuing concern for Dick by making inquiry of his and Whitestone's fates in the recent battle. Dick recalls a childhood fondness but otherwise articulates no special connection between him and Kate.

Dick Shelby's next duty is to scout Clinton's forces and return with news of their strength and whereabouts. Stopped by British guards, he and Whitestone pretend to be Tories and report that the British are winning and that Clinton is already moving north with a strong fleet and an army of five thousand men. The following quixotic episode finds Dick and Whitestone manning a battery of four cannons overlooking the river and with well-placed shots harassing the British fleet. After leading the British to believe the battery is a veritable American stronghold, Dick and Whitestone flee to the north and furnish the American army the requisite information.

Their assignment now is to bring back, dead or alive, an escaped prisoner who may attempt to deliver word of Burgoyne's sad situation to Clinton. The escapee—Ralph Chudleigh, of course—masquerades as a farmer and for a time eludes Shelby, Whitestone, and Private Adams. Soon realizing their error, they regain Chudleigh's trail and he wheels and shoots Whitestone in the leg. Dick alone pursues Chudleigh and finally takes him prisoner after a hand-to-hand fight in a river. Without his comrades or weapons, Shelby ushers Chudleigh back to an American detachment, where some soldiers discover Chudleigh's identity and conclude he should be hanged—and that the protesting Dick must be secretly a Tory. This impression is heightened later by Chudleigh's rescuing Shelby after he falls from a log on the river, strikes his head, and nearly drowns: "I am a gentleman, Mr. Shelby," Chudleigh explains (165). After falling in with Whitestone and Adams again, Dick obtains a

British uniform from Americans who have taken prisoners. Although Dick tells the Americans that the uniform is for an American who intends to become a spy, it is actually to be worn by Chudleigh to protect him from the treatment he would receive as a British spy not in uniform. Although Dick proudly conducts Chudleigh to his American colonel, Chudleigh is soon sent back to the British camp in an exchange of prisoners. The meaning of Kate's response to Shelby's preserving Chudleigh escapes Dick—even if Chudleigh himself has not: "Dick, you are a fool!" (171). Patriot military fortunes also rise as the Americans win in a confrontation mainly between cannon.

Meanwhile, a messenger from Clinton has been taken with dispatches announcing that Clinton is advancing nearby with seven thousand troops. When Dick discovers that this messenger is reported to be Albert Van Auken, he tells his generals of an attempted deception: he had seen Albert less than a day earlier in *Burgoyne's* camp. Considering Albert at this point little more than a nuisance, the American authorities release him and, accompanied by Shelby, he goes back yet again to Burgoyne's encampment. An entire chapter is now devoted to British attempts to cross a no-man's-land to the river for necessary water. As each soldier approaches the clearing he is picked off by American backwoodsmen, who appear to enjoy the practice, since it is "in their line," though Dick is repelled by it. These sharpshooters are even prepared to fire at the women, including Kate, who now appear with buckets. Shelby must restrain the Americans. While the terms of Burgoyne's surrender are being negotiated, Albert tells Dick that Chudleigh has been wounded and is being nursed by Kate. Dick apprehends a British soldier with an actual message from Clinton to Burgoyne telling him to hold out for certain rescue—but Burgoyne has in any case already officially surrendered.

The title of the final chapter, "Capitulations," makes the usual reference to both the public and private spheres. But neither the public nor the private surrenders are unconditional. Major characters have all along trod a middle physical, political, and social ground between the American and the British. Supposed enemies have shared clothes and been mistaken for each other. They frequent each other's camps and commiserate about the lack of civilized principles of frontiersmen and Native Americans. After one of his sojourns in Burgoyne's camp, Dick had concluded that he "was fast getting to be at home in either camp" (193). Shelby feels that a major cause of the war had been the chafing of Americans under the accusation that they were "the degenerate descendants of Englishmen" (216) but further opines that "the great English race is still the great English race" (217), even improved since—and because of—

the Revolution. The Americans have now both proven their worth and been identified with an English tradition. Dick's British rival mends nicely as Kate declares that her engagement to Chudleigh was a plan of her mother, who was "fond of people of quality, especially when the quality was indicated by a title" (69). Kate's initial refusal of Shelby's abrupt proposal is put down to womanly capriciousness and will be followed by a marriage which thus becomes the private concomitant to and validation of the public military surrender.

Maurice Thompson declares in the preface to the quaintly titled *Alice of Old Vincennes* (1900) that he intends to make "the connection between Alice Roussillon's romantic life . . . and the capture of Vincennes by Colonel George Rogers Clark." Thompson's particular indulgence in romantic historical nostalgia garnered "the first full-page advertisement in trade history" (Altick 223). Instead of emphasizing the unique virtues of a hybrid form, Thompson apologizes for what his readers might find to be the failings of the historical novel: the book "to those who care only for history will seem but an idle romance, while to the lovers of romance it may look strangely like the mustiest history" (dedication). History thus has significance, but is boring; fiction is exciting, but frivolous. (Although elsewhere he admits that history is often picturesque and fiction tame.) "The mission of the poet and the romancer" is to transcend the "refractory and unlovely realities and give in their place a scene of ideal mobility and charm" (55-56). The book can be at best only a supplement to William H. English's historical account, Thompson's source: read with English's book it makes the Revolution both "vivid *and* authentic" (420, emphasis added). If they can be "connected," the texts of history and fiction nonetheless cannot be reconciled. Thompson either considers each discrete or insists that fiction's "mobility" must transcend the "refractory and unlovely realities" of history. To us, however, his novel functions as a single fictional/historical discourse "about" the eighteenth as well as the nineteenth century, neither history nor fiction— and both. Thompson's very impulse to define and discriminate as well as to write the genre manifests values of 1900 America and serves as a commentary on popular contemporary views of literature and history. His becoming part of the fad exhibits in itself the appeal of the money motive in his time.

Thompson's creating a fictional figure who herself is an avid reader of romantic fiction—as was Janice Meredith in the Middle Colonies novel of that name—marks a compound removal from the standards of realistic fiction. The author legitimizes his novel's worth by thus grounding it on other texts which substitute for "real life" and which free him to write about the "brave, heroic men and beautiful women, and war and love" (9) which Alice reads about. Likewise, the hero's later acceptance of captivity does "not comport with her dream of knighthood and heroism" (187). The writer's own text can at least be based on *something* (an extra-personal source, an origin not in print) and can thus be "authentic" as well as "vivid" in portraying his vision without the supplement of English's text. In calling attention to the textual, Thompson unintentionally textualizes even English's "history" and subverts his own apology for fiction. The plot of the book depends upon the reader believing that Alice gradually realizes her impact on "actual" events; she must leave the romantic nonsense of her fictions in order to live her own self-defined life and thereby enter history—a history already textualized by the references to English's book. She inhabits a fiction, and to the end is part and parcel of a work which closely follows turn-of-the-century conventions of the historical novel of the American Revolution.

Alice plays a central and symbolic role during the stressful yet glorious days of the Old Northwest Territory. Like her sister heroines she is an accomplished and spunky girl who after proving her worth settles down in the instituting of an American family. She is a "child of the American wilderness" during those strenuous yet bracing "days when women lightly braved what the strongest men would shrink from now" (4). She takes an aggressive lead in defeating her future husband at mock swordplay (in a later tilt, he wins), in spurning the advances of a licentious British soldier, and in devising patriotic plots against the British attackers of Vincennes. In what Thompson intends to be scenes of high drama Alice is identified with the new American flag itself, which she lets "droop over her from head to foot" (74). She helps to sew the flag; she saves the flag and hides it from the British during the time they control the fort. After George Rogers Clark and his men conclude their heroic march through wilderness and icy waters from Kaskaskia to Vincennes and liberate the town, Alice triumphantly appears with the flag and hoists it in victory as old "Oncle Jazon" screams, "Long live George Washington! Long live the flag of Alice Roussillon!" (375).

An ideal of the new American family (i.e., the *United* States) will be born of the Revolution. But both hero and heroine think the other is dead and are therefore equally startled by the apparent rebirth in the recognition and reunion scene. A shot from the British commander Hamilton's pistol had indeed accidentally hit Alice, but struck the Indian charm-stone given her by Long-Hair for caring for him when he was injured; although the romantic hero had been a captive of one of the tribes, the scalp seen earlier near the town turns out not to have been the young American's. The people of the land thus have a hand in magical preservation. The young couple's life together is coeval with the American annexation of the Northwest Territory: "On the verge of a new life, each to the other an unexpected, unhoped for resurrection from the dead" (378).

This American family nonetheless has the characteristic ties to an Anglo-American tradition. After withstanding their military siege, the Americans succumb to British social if not political example. The worth of the enemy is asserted more than that of the ally. Even the French are damned by faint praise in the novel's denouement. Despite living in a French and Catholic town, having a French name and temporarily a French boyfriend, and being befriended by two priests, Alice finally discovers that she comes of an Anglo-Saxon Protestant clan named Tarleton, "daughter of an old family of cavaliers" (135). In marrying Lieutenant Fitzhugh Beverley of aristocratic Virginia she has literally met her match. In a reflex movement to the east, Alice and Fitzhugh settle on the Virginia estate which Alice has inherited from her own ancestors. (In the next generation Alice's debt to the West and to her adoptive French family is partially paid by her daughter's marrying an Indiana officer, a token tilting of the balance back to the American and Western side of the Anglo-American equation.) Yet the novel celebrates the novel—the unique and radically new as well as the fact of fictionality. We are reminded that the author is indebted to other texts and cannot therefore posit a true and uninscribed origin welling from the Western soil and the Native Americans themselves. The women of the Revolution, these "heroic souls," gained for us "not only freedom, but the vast empire which at this moment is at once the master of the world and the model toward which all the nations of the earth are slowly but surely tending" (183); "the glory and the value" of the period "must forever be kept sacred by the descendants of heroes" (420). These boasts of American independence and superiority carry a significant ambivalence because of our knowledge of generic convention and our perception of the unarticulated and racist xenophobic fears of the turn of the century.

As though conscious of the parallels between the personal and the national, the narrator of H. A. Stanley's *The Backwoodsman: The Autobiography of a Continental on the New York Frontier during the Revolution* (1901) announces on page 22 that his "story again opens" in April of 1776. Prior to this moment the growth through adolescence of Peter Diehl has been established as an analogue to the rebellion against Britain. The orphaned Peter has asserted his rights and independence against his abusive guardian and supposed uncle, Hans Diehl. Similarly, both he and his uncle are among those treated like "niggers" by the latent Tories possessed of unearned "riches, glory and power" (5): Sirs William, Guy, and John Johnson and the Butlers. Before the pro-British can be opposed the symbolic killing of the father is carried out by a blood-besmirched, ugly, and unsavory stranger named Benjamin Beacraft, who in the forest immediately after the murder of Hans Diehl tells Peter that he (Beacraft) is rightfully a Diehl and that his (Peter's) name is Ehlerson. After purchasing the deer just shot by Peter, Beacraft and his mystery disappear into the woods, so that Peter returns to his cabin bloodstained and carrying coins. Evidence against him, Peter rushes by the sheriff and flees. Befriended by the "queenly" (16) Molly, wife of Sir William Johnson and sister of the Indian leader Joseph Brant, Peter escapes to the West, the wilderness, to live for nearly two years among the Indians as "Quedar." A renewed acquaintance with a white missionary, the Reverend Samuel Kirkland, apparently prevents him from identifying altogether with his Native American family, his father, Skenando, and his sister, Owaimee.

In his Indian garb Peter attends a great council where Brant—a Christian and newly returned from London—argues for war and alliance with the British. The staid Skenando's minority view for conciliation and peace becomes dissent, and he must lead his braves to safety, Peter and Owaimee to hiding. Nonetheless, the nefarious Walter Butler, his designs on Owaimee already thwarted by her father, shoots and kills her and captures the wounded Peter. Skenando appears, vowing revenge against Butler. Though a partisan belligerent, Brant conveys to Peter's captors orders that Peter not be burned at the stake but, rather, released after his recovery. Peter now determines that his services would be more useful in Pennsylvania, sells his furs, and heads south with Murphy, his uncouth Irish sidekick. Still weak, Peter is taken in and employed by a wealthy Quaker merchant in Philadelphia, Jason Horne, about whom he had been told by the Reverend Kirkland. The influences of the city, the Hornes, and their beautiful young niece, the Southern belle Edith Darrah, lead to Peter's being transformed "from an awkward backwoods giant to a gentleman" (106). Kirkland has twice become the agent of balancing Peter's life, of saving him from "savagery" and showing him "civilization."

Competition in love arrives in the person of Captain Mordaunt Woolsey, a handsome Continental soldier who nonetheless "looked like an Englishman of the better class" (110). His wealthy and landed North Carolina connections and his father's monetary favors to Edith's father have made Woolsey the arranged future husband of Edith, as indeed he is by the terms of Mr. Darrah's will. Simple and jealous "Quedar" seems an outsider, particularly since "the lines of social status were very sharply drawn all through the colonies in those days. Especially was this true in the south and in Philadelphia and New York" (116). This marriage appears inevitable despite Woolsey's upper-class indulgence in vices like drinking and womanizing. Peter feels excluded as he decides to serve on the New York frontier again, although Edith does entrust him with a miniature of her and a braid of her hair.

Near the Delaware River Peter is surprised to see Woolsey—who had said he was going south—a captive of Indian braves. He and Woolsey are thrown together when a second party, this time of Senecas, captures Peter. After Skenando and Peter's Indian "brother," Hon Yerry, free him and Woolsey, Peter goes on to a varied career as a Continental irregular. Hearing Hon Yerry's report of the Battle of Oriskany and seeing scalped and mutilated bodies for himself, Peter reports to Gates's army ten miles above Albany. Disguised as a Dutch farmer and undeterred by the possibility of being recognized by his hometown sheriff, he serves as a scout and spy, delivering to Burgoyne's army false information designed to provoke an open engagement. When the Second Battle of Beamus Heights breaks out, Peter scrambles back to American lines. Burgoyne soon after surrenders his army of 5,763. Mordaunt Woolsey continues to snub Peter and, in fact, directs "friendly fire" at him during one skirmish. Peter is, however, reassured by letters from Edith and the Hornes telling of her spurning of the will's provisions and Woolsey's suit (just as he later receives a missive from her assuring him that she considers slanderous a note circulated by Woolsey implying that Peter is a sly and drunken spy). Persuaded by friends to remain in the army, Peter spots hostile Indians from whom he is saved by the half-white, semi-legendary, and supposedly insane Tamalaqua and his great wildcat. Days later, as he looks out for the advance guard of Sullivan's army, Peter witnesses Beacraft stabbing Tamalaqua, but not before he hears Tamalaqua declaring that Beacraft had stolen Quedar and murdered Hans Diehl, his own father. Brant expresses his willingness to tell all he knows, but will not release Beacraft to be interrogated by Peter about the mystery of his parentage.

Dodging war parties of Senecas and Onondagas, Peter rejoins his army in its push westward. A skirmish escalates into the Battle of Newtown, followed by the panicked retreat of the British. During furious hand-to-hand combat Peter again falls captive to Butler, who orders him strapped to the torture post. As arrows and hatchets strike the post Peter remains unflinching, confident of the aid of Indian friends, one of whom, unseen, cuts his cords and tells him to run. The location of provisions, guns, and the best trail have already been furnished him by Little Aaron.

Peter turns back on the pursuing Beacraft, frightens away his nemesis's companion, and captures Beacraft. When Beacraft—who, after all, had furthered Peter's rite of passage by freeing him of a false parent—develops a serious case of smallpox, he is cared for and pitied by Peter. Adversity and gratitude loosen the gruff Beacraft's tongue enough that he reveals that Peter is actually Duncan Christopher Fisher, whose father, Judge Donald Fisher of Fisher's Corners near Staunton, Virginia, had owned about nineteen thousand acres, stock, and slaves. Beacraft goes on to disclose that Peter/Duncan's parents had died of smallpox themselves in the 1750s. When Duncan's guardian, his uncle Major Fisher, had ordered a beating for two of his workers—Beacraft and his reprobate father—who had stolen from him, for revenge the hands had kidnapped Duncan and taken him north. Major Fisher had soon afterward died, without an heir. Beacraft murdered Tamalaqua because he knew of the kidnapping. Murphy verifies these details, for he, too, had known the Fishers, among the "noblest blood" (322) of their region. Duncan's mother had, in fact, tended the Murphys during the smallpox epidemic. His story told, Beacraft recovers.

At Schoharie Peter receives orders to proceed to Philadelphia. After a tearful parting from old Skenando, Peter enters the city to tell his much-affected Aunt Sally Fisher of his identity, to be promoted to captain, and to be reunited with Edith—to take upon himself, in other words, the mantle of "name and fortune" (350). For, ideologically, the titles of chapters 36 and 37 are the same: "I Meet George Washington" and "Edith." Duncan Fisher, no longer the Native American "Quedar" or the Germanic "Peter Diehl," marries a supposed radical, a "rebel," yet a member of one of the "best and oldest" families of the South, an heiress. Duncan insists he not be given preference in the military because of Washington's knowledge of the Fishers' good reputation. But after his marriage Duncan Fisher goes to the "patriarchal surroundings" (369) of a Mount Vernon-like estate in Virginia, greeted by numberless fawning blacks, to found his own sector of the new nation.

The irony of his end altogether escapes Peter Diehl/Peter Ehlerson/Quedar/Duncan Christopher Fisher. Possessed of a plantation which he cannot earn but only inherit, he forgets his earlier scorn of the title and status of the Johnsons and Butlers; his gangs of slaves serve as no reminder of his youthful revulsion at being treated like a slave. Fisher has in like manner bid farewell to a native American influence as well as to Skenando. The love letter from Edith which declared her preference for him over any prince (a safe gesture considering that in the author's mind Fisher is already in some sense an American equivalent of a prince) contrived with Kirkland's influence to prevent Peter's ever again becoming a backwoodsman, "half-Indian" (325). Like Cooper's Natty Bumppo he preserves his white and Christian "gifts," but unlike Bumppo does not otherwise wed the wilderness. The war itself, according to Duncan, voided the possibility of Iroquois peoples' settling peaceably and intermarrying with whites. Duncan forgets that the same licentious Walter Butler who had lorded it over Peter had also threatened rape of his Indian "sister," and later shot her. Owaimee, by the novel's conclusion, is dead to Duncan in any case; even the idea of marriage to her kind is unthinkable. Duncan has become neither backwoodsman, New Yorker, nor revolutionary. It is as though establishing oneself as the new American consists of certifying one is neither black nor red nor even German and of finding an appropriately Anglo-Saxon-American parent, name, and wife. This identity as a Southern gentleman furthers the Cavalier myth usually associated with Southern Civil War and Reconstruction—but also Revolutionary War, as we have seen—novels. While the book ends with a new beginning of honors, riches, and children for Duncan and Edith Fisher, their dynasty has all the marks of a continuation of an old Anglo-Southern tradition. And Duncan, the first-person narrator, can savor his nostalgia as well: he mentions in passing that the events told here happened nearly sixty years before the time of his telling. The reader's sentimentalizing of the Revolutionary period is augmented by her or his perception of the narrator's own sentimentalizing of the period and by the reader's own nostalgia for (even) an antebellum 1835.

The Son of a Tory: A Narrative of the Experiences of Wilton Aubrey in the Mohawk Valley and elsewhere during the Summer of 1777 (1901), "edited" by Clinton Scollard, purports to be personal and plain in order to lend reality to a story of a time "when our beloved land was but a nursling in the family of nations,—she who is now fast growing to such full stature" (viii). Insofar as the title character functions as an image of this new nation, the "nursling" has great difficulty birthing, indeed. Beginning with his initial perusal of *"The Gentleman's Magazine,* fresh from London" (11), and continuing for more than half of the book, the protagonist acts, if he does not believe, as a Tory. The momentum he gains as a "Tory" carries him well past the point where he has lost most ideological or personal reasons to be one. Typical moderation marks even his post-Tory phase. He remains, by reason of the title and in any case, the son of a Tory in a text said to be "edited," formed and reformed of written materials, rather than derived from the actual and radical (Henry David Thoreau, who declared his independence by moving to

Walden Pond on the Fourth of July, enjoyed the pun on "radical," etymologically "root").

Wilton Aubrey had promised his dying mother that he would never
desert his father, that he would never upset his staunchly Tory sire by
disclosing his own patriot proclivities. Prevented by ill health from
having pursued a military career, Mr. Aubrey is now nonetheless eager to
join the British invasion from the north led by his old Cambridge friend,
Barry St. Leger. Before the Aubreys, Van Eyck, and other Tories can flee
to the British army, they must dodge unfriendly neighbors and provision
a boat; Wilton is challenged as a Tory and defeats Heinrich Herborn in a
street fight. (Neither Herborn nor Wilton's father knows that Wilton is in
love with Herborn's half-sister, Margaret Wells—just as his actual political attitudes are concealed from them.) Feeling, however, that he must
warn Whig friends of the British invasion and see his girlfriend before
he departs for Oswego, Wilton returns to the Flatts, where he is spotted
and chased, hides and escapes, and is believed drowned. Unable to get
word to Margaret that he has survived, Wilton along with the other
"Tories" weathers a thunderstorm and arrives at Oswego. There they are
soon met by detachments of the unpleasant Sir John Johnson and the
prideful and alcoholic St. Leger, who makes Mr. Aubrey an aide and
Wilton a secretary. Their new duties have not rightly begun when
Wilton's father dies in his sleep.

Although it might "appear strange" (131) to others, "it did not occur
to [Wilton] that night, nor indeed until some time afterward, that there
was now no sacred duty that bound [him] to the side of the king" (120).
Inertia and the aftershock of his father's death so dull his thought that he
goes on to guide Lieutenant Bird's reconnoitering party and deliver a
message to Colonel St. Leger. Aubrey has all along functioned as an
uncommitted imaginary space between adamant partisans. While (appropriately, for him) at King's College (later Columbia University) he had
become a friend of the patriot Alexander Hamilton; on the other hand,
although not "really" a Tory he is forever the son of one. His predisposi-
tions as a British-style gentleman lead him to decry British alliances
with Native Americans, whose raids constitute not war but "sheer butchery" (19). In this one instance he verbalizes opposition to his father's
point of view, finding a voice to suggest that the British have affiliated
themselves too closely with those whom he would never think of considering the real Americans: the British have gone too far, as far as the
(white) Americans themselves, in leaguing with "savages." Indians are
poor allies, adds the Tory Van Eyck, since to them "a white man's a
white man" (82). Wilton's showdown with the Whig Herborn balances
the later duel with the British Lieutenant Hamilton (whose name paral-

lels the patriot Alexander Hamilton's), brought on by Hamilton's impugning the bravery of the common American folk—and being challenged by Wilton as no gentleman himself. Wilton is winning the fight when St. Leger and Johnson stop it and arrest Wilton for raising a sword against an officer. His knowledge and appreciation of Benedict Arnold's talents and later fate allow Aubrey to "feel the sincerest pity and regret that so brave and capable a soldier" (285) could become an ignominious turncoat.

In the weeks after his rebirth from his apparent drowning after the fight with Herborn, Wilton also becomes an incomplete transition in time between the old and the new, as his old family dissolves and he notes the need to establish a new, American, family with Margaret. He feels in any case that personal grudges as much as ideological differences have prejudiced Tories against him: the hostile Johnson, who knows that Wilton knew Alexander Hamilton in New York and that he knows of Johnson's own earlier cowardly flight to Canada, is probably plotting against him and turning St. Leger against him; Lieutenant Hamilton was apparently manipulated by Johnson as well as jealous of Aubrey's preferment. Aubrey sneaks out of his tent to warn the Americans of a British ambush and finally is able to join the Whig forces, enlisting in Captain Von Benschoten's company. A rushing sortie from the fort surprises the British, whose colors are surmounted by the brand-new American flag. One of a party going for reinforcements, Aubrey is separated from his fellows, views the carnage left after the ill-fated Battle of Oriskany, and overhears Tory plans for a mass gathering. He gets through to Fort Dayton with the news of the British strategy. Butler and other Tories are captured (although Aubrey convinces his personal friend Van Eyck to flee) as the Continentals begin an expedition of their own. General Benedict Arnold arrives, ordering a trial for Butler and the others and selecting Wilton to deliver a message to Colonel Gansevoort that his troops will come to the rescue as soon as his forces have gained sufficient strength. Arnold's tactics succeed so well that the British raise their siege of the fort and retreat; St. Leger will from this time be unable to aid Burgoyne.

After Aubrey joined the Americans and told his tale, he had obtained news about Margaret. Following his reported death she had been ill and distraught for weeks, accusing her brother of being the murderer of one not really a Tory after all. (Heinrich Herborn and Aubrey soon agree, however, to end their grudge when Aubrey finds Herborn, thought to be a casualty at the Battle of Oriskany, wandering in the woods.) Taking time out from his military duties (Wilton acknowledges that re-enlisting will not be very attractive after he finds Margaret), he returns to the Flatts to find only a report that Margaret had recovered her health and that she and her mother are away on a journey. Herborn suggests that they have probably gone to a brother of his stepfather in Albany, where he and Aubrey now follow. Slowed by the unexpected size of the town, they finally locate Margaret and her mother. The joyous reunion is succeeded by the standard union. Aubrey is to reclaim a heritage by moving into his Tory father's home. More than the son of a Tory, himself an ex-Tory who has often behaved on the basis of personal values and expediency, he settles down in gentlemanly fashion with the woman of Whig family. Again lovers' fates mirror an incomplete revolt from Britain.

Winston Churchill's panoramic and patriotic treatment of American Manifest Destiny, *The Crossing* (1903), deals only in part with the Revolution. In this follow-up to his Southern novel *Richard Carvel* Churchill declares and signals by his title that he intends to range over most of then-settled America and to indicate the development of the nation from the Revolution to the Louisiana Purchase. (The book briefly extrapolates to 1903—the centennial of the Louisiana Purchase.) The major sections of the saga are set in the Appalachians and the territories of South Carolina, Kentucky and Indiana, and Louisiana. Scattered through the narrative are Western heroes from the early national period: Daniel Boone, Andrew Jackson, George Rogers Clark, and Simon Kenton. Churchill describes "the beginnings of that great movement across the mountains which swept resistless over the Continent until at last it saw the Pacific itself. The Crossing was the first instinctive reaching out of an infant nation which was one day to become a giant" (596). His emphasis is to be on those qualities of the pioneers "that go to the conquest of an empire and the making of a people" (115). The hero's race, in those days when "a man was a man" (92), brings liberty with a sword: "the best is fought for, and bled for, and died for." Written, but written on the veritable mountains bordering the Wilderness Trail, "upon that towering wall of white rock, in the handwriting of God Himself, is the history of the indomitable Race to which we belong" (96). Despite being unappreciated, George Rogers Clark nonetheless is possessed of an epic vision of the Northwest Territory being "filled with the cities of a Great Republic" (145). (Clark also commemorates an Independence Day with a vision, a vision of America's stretching to the Pacific and becoming "the refuge of the oppressed of this earth" [157]. Although in these equations "race" may be read as "nation" and the oppressed theoretically include any race, in the context of 1776 the white English-speaking hero would not have been surrounded by non-whites or immigrants who peopled America long after the Revolution. The race of 1776 is celebrated in this genre, and Winston Churchill is far from being Emma Lazarus.) Surely here will be an imagining of a radically originating ground.

Only book I of *The Crossing,* "The Borderland," deals primarily with the Revolutionary period. Like *Alice of Old Vincennes,* it culminates with the American capture of Vincennes. During this third of the book the adolescent hero, David Ritchie, matures and becomes famous as Clark's drummer boy, playing his instrument as well as a heroic role during the expedition from Kaskaskia to Vincennes. Ritchie is both an active participant in significant events and commemorator of them, since he is the first-person and retrospective—thus at times nostalgic—narrator. Although from childhood he longs to visit Kentucky, "The Land of Promise" (7) across the mountains made so attractive by the stories told him by Daniel Boone, Davy Ritchie and his father first leave their cabin in the Blue Ridge Mountains for Charleston, where Davy is left with relatives when his father goes off to fight the Cherokees. Davy's aunt and uncle, the Temples, prove to be low-country Tory aristocrats with sumptuous homes in town and on the Ashley River. In the early days of the war John Temple must flee because of suspected Tory activities. Davy experiences plantation life, observes Mrs. Temple, as selfish and wicked as her gallants or her husband, and develops a friendship with his dashing young cousin, Nick Temple.

Davy turns once again to the mountains and the West after the death of his father in the Indian wars. Soon adopted into the family of old Mr. Ripley and his plain but spirited granddaughter, Polly Ann, Davy arrives in frontier Kentucky where Polly Ann's boyfriend, Tom McChesney, has been active in wilderness warfare. Davy, too, kills a man in defending Polly Ann, scalps a hostile Indian, and is injured in an Indian attack. Now initiated into the frontier and frontier combat, Davy is ready to enlist in the army of Colonel George Rogers Clark, who has vowed revenge against the British commander in the Northwest Territory for allegedly bribing tribes to take American scalps. Clark's men reach French Kaskaskia, which pledges allegiance to America, and smoke the peace pipe and gain the friendship of "the forty tribes in the Northwest country" (208). The celebrated march to Vincennes, undertaken by fatigued and hungry men through icy waters, ends triumphantly with the American flag being raised over Vincennes and Clark commending young Davy for his bravery.

The remainder of *The Crossing* concerns David Ritchie's post-Revolutionary career, which takes him from Richmond, where on Clark's advice he studies law, to Kentucky, St. Louis, and New Orleans. New characters are introduced but several major characters from book I reappear. While established as a lawyer in Louisville, Davy meets Nick Temple again. A professional political mission takes Davy to New Orleans, where he finds that Mrs. Temple has been taken in by the very people he is to consult. This family furnishes a love interest for Nick in the person of Antoinette de St. Gré and the opportunity for him to be reconciled to his now contrite and no longer beautiful mother, whom he has always felt to be a morally corrupting influence. It is Ritchie's romantic life, however, not Nick's and not his own professional career alone, which adds a new element and extends the scheme of book I and thereby illustrates the "logical" fate of the Revolutionary War hero. This final dispensation is Ritchie's marrying a relative of the St. Grés, the thoroughly French Hélène de St. Gré, Madame the Vicomtesse d'Ivry-le-Tour, pictured on a locket given Ritchie long before. Hélène becomes the confidante of Sarah Temple and nurses Ritchie back to health after he is infected with the yellow fever which is fatal to Mrs. Temple. Hélène combines the "best" of the other two women in Ritchie's life, Sarah Temple and Polly Ann. (Polly Ann's role as the all-American girl who is nonetheless not the heroine—because she is all-American from the start—was played by the simple, unassuming, democratic Patty Swain in *Richard Carvel*.) Hélène is as self-sacrificing and pure (American) as Polly Ann, as self-assuredly upper-class (European) as Mrs. Temple had once been. Her Americanism will save her from Mrs. Temple's fate.

Even in this novel of movement to the west, an American ideal cannot be imagined apart from an Old World norm. Although Ritchie fears he may be beneath Hélène, he disapproves of the French Revolution and acknowledges that she deserves her title and would have continued a brilliant and politically influential life in France had that Revolution not occurred. He does not hold to even an egalitarianism from which his own original social class stands to gain. Land acquisition rather than revolution parallels romantic plot as Louisiana is ceded from Spain to France before being purchased by the United States, "ours inevitably" (593). Likewise, Ritchie acquires the Frenchwoman, and in marrying her replaces the now-deceased French husband she had by an arranged marriage. The "crossing" comes to seem more appropriately a nineteenth-century Mendelian genetic phenomenon which results in a new hybrid species rather than an eighteenth-century sign for a grand progress across the continent. After their wedding, Hélène and David return to Kentucky, repossessing the land of George Rogers Clark and Polly Ann McChesney. We are scarcely as surprised as Monsieur Gratiot, who concludes that "the strangest of all is that Clark's drummer boy should have married a Vicomtesse of the old régime" (595).

Zane Grey's long career as a popular novelist began with a historical novel set during 1782, *Betty Zane* (1903). The story deals more obviously with frontier life and Indian border warfare (hence, is in an important sense Grey's first "Western") than with the Revolution per se and is based upon legends of Grey's own eighteenth-century forebears, a story continued for the post-Revolutionary years in *The Spirit of the Border* (1906) and *The Last Trail* (1906). *Betty Zane* begins with the pioneering efforts of the five Zane brothers in the region of the latter-day tristate area of West Virginia, Ohio, and Pennsylvania, and climaxes in the siege of Fort Henry (Wheeling), in which "the British Rangers under Hamilton took part with the Indians, making the attack practically the last battle of the Revolution" (xii). Despite being based on fact and treating the war only tangentially, *Betty Zane* follows a familiar pattern as fiction and "history." For example, in making melodrama of the past, it adopts a hortatory tone toward the present. Grey complains that "in this busy progressive age there are no heroes of the kind so dear to all lovers of chivalry and romance" (viii). The novel is dedicated "to the Betty Zane chapter of the Daughters of the Revolution" (vii) and commemorates a commemorative monument which stands in Wheeling. The imperatives of romantic narrative convention, antiquarianism, and sentiment and nostalgia conspire to bury any Revolution conceived as actual. The actual, rather, is the text itself, the present accretion upon an increasingly distant and spectral past.

The Indian/wilderness/freedom congeries of forces figure significantly in the picture of the land which was gaining political independence. The new Americans absorb this tradition along with an Old World one. All the Zane brothers as youths had been held captive by the Indians for two years. Ebenezer ("Colonel Zane" later), Silas, and Jonathan were ransomed while Andrew was killed while attempting to escape. The remaining brother, Isaac, now presumed dead, has escaped and been recaptured several times; he loves and is loved by Myeerah, the beautiful half-French daughter of Tarhe, chief of the Hurons. Colonel Zane's household presently includes Elizabeth ("Betty") Zane, who has joined her brother after having been reared and educated by a now-deceased aunt in Philadelphia, where Betty had "luxury, society, parties, balls, dances, friends, all that the heart of a girl could desire" (69). She, however, grows to appreciate the frontier and the simplicity, honesty, and hard work of its folk, and has become the typical willful, spirited, mischievous, physically accomplished heroine.

The romantic hero also possesses Eastern, if not European, roots transplanted into the wilderness. After his father's death Alfred Clarke leaves behind "the stately old mansion" in Virginia, the "plantation, slaves, horses" (169-70), in his search for adventure and fortune as a soldier on the frontier. He too has been educated in Philadelphia, and spent two years at Princeton Theological Seminary. Meeting the spunky and assertive Betty forms part of his adjustment to life in the settlement. When the handsome and polished Clarke first encounters her, he must restrain a rebellious Betty from riding beyond safe limits around the village. He regains her good graces by rescuing Isaac, the long-lost brother that resembles Betty, who has once again escaped from the Indians, this time to warn his family of an imminent attack by Indians and British. Clarke seems indifferent to Betty but "happens" to be nearby to help her after she sprains an ankle. He then again offends her by impulsively kissing her and not apologizing (though he later explains to a temporarily incensed Colonel Zane that she had run off too quickly for him to do so).

After military duties on the frontier, an injury or two, and a trip to Virginia to see his dying mother, Clarke returns to Fort Henry and a scornful Betty. All is smoothed over when it is revealed that Sam, a black servant who had taken a dislike to Clarke, had kept a letter of apology and proposal of marriage which he was to deliver to Betty. Betty and Alfred marry and thus assimilate each other's Eastern and Western heritage which has been theirs separately already. To a greater extent than the protagonists of most novels in this group, they give themselves to a Western world which by 1903 was also becoming a time, the past. When Clarke speaks of the frontier's "free, wild life" and the pioneers' being "honest and simple and brave" (68), he could just as well be referring to the turn of the century's image of an American past. As in Grey's later novels of the Far West, this Western place/time becomes therapeutic for both protagonists and readers (we have mentioned, for example, *Wanderer of the Wasteland* [1923] and *The Call of the Canyon* [1924]).

The uneven course of this love story is played out against the backdrop more of Indian-white than British-American relations. Betty herself is identified with the Indians by being mistaken for one and by her similarities with Myeerah, who eventually marries Isaac, Betty's look-alike. (Grey's sympathy for the Indians and criticism of white corruptions and government policies were to become much more thoroughgoing and polemical in such later novels as *The Vanishing American* [1922].) This Zane brother, Isaac, is torn between the white and Huron worlds, and although he convinces "the White Crane" to marry him under white forms, he also agrees to live among her people. Grey leaves little need for the reader to extrapolate social and political messages from this

Romeo and Juliet plot device, as he has Clarke say of Myeerah—who already has a dual heritage—that she "is the first link in that chain of peace which will some day unite the red men and the white men" (210). Betty's and Clarke's acts of conspicuous heroism occur in scenes in which the final destructive Indian attack is prevented, yet the author concludes the book by mourning "that the poor Indian is unmourned" and that "no more will his heart bound at the whistle of the stag, for he sleeps in the shade of the oaks, under the moss and ferns" (291). (During the Revolutionary period itself, the poet Philip Freneau had already envisioned the Native American presence as an absence, the specters of "The Indian Burying-Ground.") This ambivalence toward the Indian, the Indian's world, and its meaning for the new settlers, is also figured forth in various white characters. The determined woodsman Lewis Wetzel (a character reminiscent of Robert Montgomery Bird's Nick of the Woods), whose tender feelings for Betty do not quite suffice to "civilize" him, carries out a vendetta against the red men, but is presented as a true spirit of the forest. On the other hand, the villainy and barbarity of characters like Simon Girty and Ralfe Miller is defined by their being renegades from (even) an Indian world. Again the newly independent white American's identity is compounded of a simultaneous accepting and rejecting of elements of both the American West and Western (i.e., European) civilization.

A concern with the role of women also places *Betty Zane* with many of the Revolutionary War romances of this period. Women often take an aggressive, but temporary, lead. Myeerah saves Isaac in a number of scrapes. The heroine gives her name to the book even if she is not always the central character. Despite being in fact an independent and self-sufficient spirit, Betty envies a man's independence and self-sufficiency. And she must, paradoxically, lose her independence so that America may gain its independence. The family of a new nation includes a wife who has been tamed, just as Clarke restrains Betty's ramblings in their first scene together. However striking and meaningful her sacrifices for the American cause, when the nation—family—is established, she knows her place, as though she early on asserts her independence only that she might later lose it. Grey acknowledges that the times must have tried the souls of "those grand, heroic women" (263) more than the souls of men, yet leaves Betty at the end a wife and grandmother reduced to telling tales of her early adventures. Fantasies of female freedom no doubt had a greater appeal for insecure men in 1903 than female freedom itself. But in Betty's memories and our text she forever dashes through enemy fire with the bag of gunpowder that will save the fort.

Although set far from a major military front, *Felice Constant, or the Master Passion: A Romance* (1904) by William C. Sprague dramatizes combinations and concatenations of elements on other fronts. The love and war linkage, the fact of multiple and competing male and female lovers, the relative influences of the French, the British, the Native American, and the "American"—all these figure importantly in the narrative. In resolving conflicts among particular but representative characters, the novel's denouement leaves the reader with an image of a new national self. Whereas the war itself usually precipitates and resolves conflicts in these novels and thereby creates the possibility of a new world, here the effect is gained without the actual depicting of massive military confrontation. The actuality of the Revolution as backdrop suffices, as it offers the author the opportunity to manipulate his markers toward his foregone conclusion. In his tale "of love and war" (22) characters insist that "love truly unfits men for war" and, on the other hand, that a soldier "loves only the cause he fights for" (138), unfitting him for love. Resolution comes only when the conditions necessary for establishing a lasting love and for defining that love (including its ethnic and national dimensions) are made possible during and as a result of the war; political revolution creates romantic resolution, just as the romantic resolution communicates a vision of the outcome and purposes of the revolution.

When the British occupied Detroit, the land of the old Frenchman Pierre Constant was declared forfeited and his cabin burned; his wife soon after died of exposure. On his daughter's pleading Constant was exiled instead of executed, and resettled in isolation on Grosse Isle with Felice and their Indian workingwoman, Marmjuda. This world of American nature becomes Felice's sphere, contrasting to another world she hears of in her father's tales of courtly La Belle France. Neither the Americans nor the French, but rather the British threaten liberty, just as they have already largely destroyed with rum and bribery the intimacy once existing between the French and the Indians.

As the story opens, Felice meets an (Anglo-)American foe of the British in the person of Lieutenant Robert Norvell, on a one-man scouting expedition for George Rogers Clark following the American victory at Vincennes. At one time a *courier de bois* and later a soldier in the British army, the ardent lieutenant now serves under Washington. A man inured to danger, he eludes his pursuers in a canoe furnished him by Felice, to whom he gives his mother's ring as a token of appreciation (and infatuation). At the cabin of Constant's compatriot, Jean Guion, to which he has been directed by the girl, Norvell discloses the rest of his past. When a child at the village of Detroit, Norvell had escaped harm but his father and, perhaps, his sister had been killed by a murderous Frenchman now only vaguely remembered by Robert. Later the confused and defenseless boy was taken by Indians, with whom he lived for five years before fleeing to the settlements and going east as trader, trapper, and guide. In Virginia he learned of colonial grievances and "caught the spirit of the men of Virginia" (40) like Colonel Clark, whose regiment he joined.

Jean tells his own tale of having once been a profligate at the French court (where his father and grandfather had been masters of the king's hounds), but of having come to America as to a new beginning, living as an Indian in pre-British days and marrying Mintinao, mother of the surly young Jacques. This laconic and uncouth French-Indian aspirant for the hand of Felice, willing even to murder Pierre Constant to obtain her, intuits the threat presented by Norvell but loses in the initial fight into which he goads the American. Biding his time, Jacques must meanwhile do Norvell's bidding and travel to Detroit, from which he returns with news of a British plan to kill Guion and burn his cabin. Robert organizes a defense against this exigency before he implements his own plans to continue serving Clark, find a way into Fort Detroit, and determine the whereabouts of his sister if she still lives.

A grand ball for Detroit fashionables hosted by the British at the village of Sandwich on the Canadian side of the river furnishes Norvell the opportunity to gather military intelligence. But even before he enters the festival hall he must save a free-spirited young woman, Doris Cameron, from the licentious advances of the dissolute British Lieutenant Philander Doremus Skelton, "born and bred in London, pet of society" (170). Norvell knocks out Skelton, and ferrets from Doris the scheme of Skelton and two comrades to join a band of drunken Indians and kill Guion. Tricking both the Englishman and his friends, turning them against one another, Norvell foils their designs. At the dance itself he reports Guion's safety to Doris and tries to disembarrass her of her father's violent prejudice against patriot rabble. Already partly persuaded of the justice of his cause through perceiving his personal sincerity (and attractiveness), even after he identifies himself as a veritable patriot she agrees to lower a rope for him from the stockade at Detroit. By the time Norvell paddles back to Guion's cabin, Jacques has taken his boat to Constant's, where he leads Pierre to believe that Felice has entered into an unsanctioned liaison with Robert. The morose young Guion so offends the fearful Felice that she declares her loathing for him. Jacques rushes out of the cabin, threatening Robert's life.

At Detroit, Norvell locates the site where his father's cabin had stood, and observes the British under Captain Richard Lernoult further enlarging and fortifying the post. Doris does lower a rope from the walls, but even as he scrambles into the stockade Norvell begins both to question Doris's sincerity and to have second thoughts about taking advantage of her helpfulness—too late, since once he is inside she tosses the entire rope outside the enclosure. She exhibits notable ingenuousness in finding a haven for Robert in the home of the French pro-Americans Antoine and Annette Moreau, on ground forbidden her by her rebel-hating father. To this French couple she discloses her love for Norvell. But Parks, one of Skelton's accomplices, disabuses her of optimism by telling Doris that he knows of Robert's spying and of his ongoing affair with Felice Constant of Grosse Isle. Apparently not jealous, Doris warns Robert and tells him that the impending return of a British expedition would furnish the requisite confusion for his escape. Her plan seems to prosper until Jacques, already having informed on Robert, confronts him and is again beaten. Robert retreats for the moment to the home of the Moreaus.

To celebrate the return of the British forces and to reciprocate for the festivities at Sandwich, a ball is to be held at Detroit. Having heard of Felice's beauty and desiring to make Doris jealous and even to humiliate her, especially since he has concluded that Doris is a traitor in collusion with Norvell, Skelton invites Felice to the dance, thereby becoming the third—the British—competitor for her. He bribes her to attend with a letter which promises an interview with Lernoult, the upshot of which she hopes will be amnesty for her elderly father and his being permitted once again to live in Detroit, near doctors and his church. Skelton also hints at pro-American feeling even among the soldiers. Hesitant to leave her wild flowers and birds, wanting the best for her father and Norvell but suspicious of the British, Felice arrives at Detroit to find that Skelton has not so much as spoken to Lernoult of her father's plight. The "accomplished libertine" (204) flatters her and suggests that she employ her charms to gain her ends with the commander. Offended and outraged, at the ball Felice nonetheless temporarily warms to the dancing and the compliments. Regaining her composure, however, she spurns Skelton for his love talk and his deceptions, and spots Marmjuda, who informs her that Robert is present at the ball. By chance the couple with whom Felice takes refuge from Skelton turn out to be Doris and Robert. Felice hurriedly whispers to Norvell of Skelton's scheme to give her a key with which she is later that night to let herself back into the stockade. Her personal pride hurt by the only man she has ever found truly interesting, the man for whom she has in effect renounced her country, Doris must be content with Norvell's escorting her home.

Later that evening, when Skelton attempts to force not only the key but also his attentions upon her, Felice cries out—the prearranged signal for Robert to spring forth and bash Skelton. Exchanging vows of love, Robert and Felice flee in Marmjuda's waiting boat. But there is to be no happy ending as yet, for when Norvell meets the failing Pierre Constant on Grosse Isle he immediately recognizes him as "Michel Deshon! Coward! Murderer!" (244)—the face he recalls from childhood as the killer of his father. Felice, incapable of believing this ignominy of a man who had just encouraged her to rescue Norvell, orders her lover to leave. Pierre, however, admits to his daughter that he is in fact Michel Deshon, long since grown contrite for his misdeeds and desirous of begging Norvell's forgiveness. (In his increasing delirium, Constant's mind, too, returns to the time of the crime, and he mistakes Felice, wearing her mother's dress, for his own young wife.) The king's army with its Indian allies reaches the cabin. Skelton agrees not to harm those inside if they will give Norvell over to justice; but as Pierre accepts this deal Skelton adds the proviso that Felice must marry Jacques. She grandiloquently denounces these terms, opting for honor even though she is a defenseless woman now alone in the New World wilderness. Her response results in Pierre's being shot and his cabin set ablaze. Norvell, who has expected this attack and remained near, now enters the fray, first carrying Constant inside as he asks the old man's pardon and as the expiring Pierre confesses his guilt and its expiation, his change of name which signaled a change of heart. Failing to fend off all his assailants, Robert agrees to surrender in exchange for a British offer to allow Constant Christian burial.

As the flotilla of canoes carrying the British and their captives progresses toward Detroit a violent thunderstorm arises and scatters the boats, dashing that of Robert and Felice on the rocky shore. The two find cover in a rude fish-house, and soon after give Pierre Constant proper burial. The world seems washed clean by the electrical storm, and Robert feels unburdened of the past and the spirit of revenge. Back in Detroit Skelton defends his actions to his superiors, while Doris admits her respect for Norvell and his cause to a Neill Cameron enraged at hearing of her part in rebel schemes. So angry is he that Cameron spurns Doris as not even his true daughter; he had long ago rescued her and bought her "from an Indian for a jug of whiskey" (298). The distraught daughter rushes to the Moreaus, where Madame Moreau confesses that she knows Doris's true identity and that this knowledge has been the real reason for Doris's of late being forbidden the cabin: she is Doris Norvell, Robert's long-lost sister. No longer bitter toward Felice and having an additional motive for saving Robert, Doris takes to her canoe but is shot in the back by Parks, who had been ordered to see to it that she stay in Detroit. Witness to this shooting and to the attack on Constant's cabin,

Jean Guion takes Doris to his place and fetches a doctor from Sandwich, who, it comes as no surprise, pronounces her wound mortal. Traveling to the village to seek his son and an explanation for the recent violence, Guion happens across Robert and Felice.

At first taking Doris's weakly muttered word, "brother," metaphorically, Robert then glimpses the truth and "held her close as if they were one" (320). With her dying words she requests that "Robert-tell-them-I-too-fought-for-the-cause! Tell-Felice-Constant-I-love-" (321). Whether her statement was complete or, if not, what her concluding word would have been is left unsaid. "Robert"? "Felice"? "The cause"? The possibilities of love and war merge as do the siblings and the lovers. Actors in this family romance finally sort themselves out into their prescribed roles, "heaven" now having furnished Norvell everything, a wife and a sister. Love no doubt remains the "master passion" (or the master's?), but the third term in the book's title—"romance"—indicates imaginative fictional narrative compounded of Eros *and* Ares, though no further reference is made to Norvell's role in the rest of the Revolutionary War.

What Robert and Felice have already gained is a new life resulting from elements of the old. Their alliance becomes the French-American alliance written small. Norvell had earlier explicitly cast the French in the New World in the role of explorers (though in the Old World capable of the most excessively effete and corrupt lives), the British heritage if not their current practices representing to him established community and religious and political freedom (and, recall, the British were portrayed as those responsible for interrupting the close and too "exploratory" ties between the French and the Native Americans). Old Guion, appreciative of this new Eden, had realized that the French flag was destined not to fly here, though the French influence will make itself felt on the new figuration, the composite American who had not yet been born when the other peoples involved had contended in the French and Indian Wars of the 1750s. The Americans, as both Robert and Doris had mentioned, are true Britons to the extent that they are carrying forward the resistance to oppression, even if it be the tyranny of the British ministers and the king themselves. But neither can the individual aborning be altogether British: there exists a political and social rationale for Doris's giving herself for Robert and for the prohibition of the complete identification which is incest. She and the Britishness her family represents must form only *one* aspect of Robert's new existence as he works through influences which must sometimes seem at least moderately external.

If the American is to be the person of basically British traditions affected by traditions of the French, she or he is also the person imbued with an—however ersatz—ethos of the Native American, the definitive non-European factor which claims (and reclaims, since both lovers have had earlier lives in the forest) its own in the name of the American wilderness but which cannot be wedded in body (the fruit of miscegenation is here the sullen Jacques Guion). The Indian stands witness, and the Indian who stands witness to the departure of Felice and Robert by canoe onto the lake south of Detroit reports seeing "the spirit of the river going on to meet its destiny in the great ocean" (322). The mystique of Native American lands goes with them. The plot of Felice Constant thus becomes not so much the general and explicitly described conflict *among* these groups as the discovery of the value *in* each to the end of creating a national being, the worst in each constituting the enemy and the best defining the truly American self made necessary and compulsory as a consequence of a War for Independence.

Among the many and popular romances of Robert W. Chambers, three dating from this period deal with the Revolution: *Cardigan* (1901), *The Maid-at-Arms* (1902), and *The Reckoning* (1905). They make use of many of the same locales and some of the same characters, but treat various periods of Revolutionary history. *Cardigan* begins with a typical apology that, whereas the romance thrives on the emotional, sentimental, and nostalgic, the history texts from which the romance draws are "more profitable" (preface). The events narrated in the novel begin in May of 1774 and culminate with the Battles of Lexington and Concord in 1775. The sixteen-year-old Michael Cardigan's coming of age early on becomes an emblem—however "unprofitable"—of a limited revolt from British rule. Cardigan's youthful rebellions (against the schoolroom and Mr. Butler, learning, tradition—thus Britain?) indicate and adumbrate his later stance as a patriot. Although he lives with his admirable and conscientious titled kinsman, Sir William Johnson, Cardigan nonetheless identifies with the outdoors, freedom, and the native American—both anything indigenous and the "Indian." That there are conservative tendencies in Cardigan's finding a place in a not-quite-new America is signaled throughout the book through a variety of means.

First of all, Cardigan has grown up with an unquestioning trust in the mother country's methods of ruling the colonies. He has been left alone with America by the death in childbirth of his mother and his father's losing his life with Wolfe at Quebec. Cardigan must reconcile his desire to carry on this military tradition with his impulse to thwart injustice and personal insult, which results in his accepting the tradition but rejecting misuses of it; he becomes an American soldier. He can become a true soldier, and one in a true cause: "'Let us, who are Americans,' says the rebel Colonel Cresap, 'imitate our fathers by fighting for America'" (207). Although Sir William has intimated to him a fear that eventually he will have to choose between king and country, Cardigan (we come to expect this) is able to embrace both country and, symbolically at least, king as well. Chambers's hand is heavy, so to speak, during the scene in which a recuperating Cardigan is informed by his doctor that the stab wound delivered by an unprincipled royalist was not fatal only because the blow's force was blunted by a folded British flag which Cardigan had salvaged from Cresap's fort, a flag which "flew for centuries above free men" (398). Cardigan reports that he "shall always honour" that flag, though not necessarily "the men who bear it" (327). In like manner he puts aside the uniform which he had so thankfully received along with a "commission as cornet of horse in the Royal Border Regiment of irregulars" (45), when he had vowed to serve "God and King and country" (46). As he later puts it, "true hearts can beat as freely under a buckskin shirt as beneath the jewelled sashes of the great" (338). That the triumvirate of God, king, and country fragments for Cardigan is only illusory; God finally aligns himself with a country which has absorbed a temporarily misguided king.

As in *The Maid-at-Arms,* the new Americans are pictured as an outcome of a sometimes unconvincing interplay between the Indian and the British, the land and an Old World cultural tradition. Michael Cardigan's guardian, Sir William Johnson, is both a "Baronet of the British realm" and "superintendent of the Indian Department in North America" (49), highly trusted by the tribes of the Six Nations as an honorable man. Yet Sir William's prime objective is to guarantee Indian neutrality in what he hopes will be a "white man's war" "between two civilized peoples, and not a butchery of demons" (114). Apparently balancing this and similarly racist stereotypes is another fantasy of amalgamation: Sir William is married to "Aunt Molly," sister of Joseph Brant (Thayendanegea), chief of the Mohawks, and by her has two sons (this mixed family also figures in H. A. Stanley's *The Backwoodsman* of the same year). Sir William has sympathy for imposing and noble Indians like Logan and Quider, who saves Cardigan from being burned at the stake, but, on the other hand, in his vision of their lands the Tryon territory becomes a greater Devonshire. His ward and our heroine, Felicity Warren, has upper-class connections along with her childhood pseudo-Indian name, Silver Heels. (Felicity's faithful blubbering black maid Betty and the peddler Saul Shemuel illustrate that Chambers's negative ethnic images take in African Americans and Jews as well as Native Americans.)

Cardigan's romantic, political, and social careers take their appropriate Anglo-American course after those moments when he cares more for the woods than for "King or rebel or any woman" (129). Pastoral wishes of 1900 are clearly implied in his preferring the forests to the "cities, where solitude is in men's hearts!" (61). The responsible and priggish Cardigan even feels fascinated at times by the impudent, careless, fun-loving woodsman and highwayman Jack Mount, "Catamount Jack," who rescues him from hostile royalists during Cardigan's mission to assess Indian unrest near Pittsburgh. Royalists on the frontier, including Cardigan's rival in love and war, the villainous Walter Butler, had covertly attempted to provoke the Indians to ally themselves with the king in any future conflict. It is here that Cardigan discovers that Cresap is just and patriotic and where he consults the tribes about their concerns. Border warfare breaks out between the Cayugas and the settlers following the royalists' massacre of Logan's family, which has already been corrupted by strong drink. A brief skirmish occurs between the king's soldiers and those settlers who now understand royalist misadministration on the frontier. The remainder of the plot concerns fights between whites and Indians, rebels and royalists, replete with captivities and escapes, as Cardigan works his way back east to Lexington and Concord and Felicity and an appreciation of an American cause made clear to him by the cameo appearances of Patrick Henry, John Hancock, and Paul Revere.

Complications in the related love plot arise from both hero and heroine having rivals. Early in the novel Felicity Warren dislikes her informal Indian name and means "to wed a gentleman of rank and wealth" (72). After possible marriage to Walter Butler seems precluded by Sir William Johnson's dismissing him as secretary and suitor, Felicity apparently becomes engaged to the effete and foppish Lord Dunmore; she appears the destined "first Lady in Virginia" (220). Even though Sir William has now agreed in principle that Michael Cardigan and Felicity may wed, the marriage is prevented by her own plans and by what is intended as Michael's startling melodramatic disclosure: "I can't have you, and—and my country too. Silver Heels, I'm a rebel!" (231). For the marriage to eventuate the author must endow the heroine with an appreciation of the land and democracy, the hero with at least the trappings of a titled nobility. Both happen. Disillusioned by the royalists, no longer wishing to be a countess, Felicity attends Michael as he recovers from his wound and declares that her love for him began "on the day when you first wore your uniform, and I saw you were truly a man" (286). She writes Michael a letter in which she recalls "a child called Silver Heels, whose mad desire for rank and power crammed her silly head, till, of a sweet May day, love came to her" (395). Butler and Sir John Johnson plot to have Felicity disinherited by providing spurious evidence that she is not Sir

Peter Warren's niece. Convinced that she is the daughter of Jack Mount's friend Cade Renard, the "Weasel," Felicity befriends and lives with this man for a time. The Weasel has for several weeks, in his growing derangement, confused Felicity for his own long-lost daughter. (Interestingly, the Weasel is the man for whom Michael is mistaken when he is imprisoned with Mount.) Before proof arrives that she is actually Captain Warren's own child rather than his niece, Felicity has been forced to save the life of her "father," a commoner and accused thief, at the price of her virtue. The culpable Butler continues to pursue her to Lexington, where Cardigan contemptuously dismisses him to live in dishonor until they may meet on the field of honorable battle and where Felicity marries Michael and sets busily at work casting bullets for the rebels.

Felicity, however, has little competition for the affections of Cardigan. Only Mrs. Hamilton, a childhood friend with whom Michael has a brief flirtation taken more seriously by Felicity than by him, stands in the way. Michael is finally so disgusted by Mrs. Hamilton's becoming the pathetic mistress of the royal governor that he prefers risking his life attempting a flight through British lines to obtaining from her a pass to Lexington and Concord. But Cardigan's fate with Felicity is not to become a frontier commoner, let alone an imitation Indian. Michael and Felicity are willed money and Tryon lands by Sir William Johnson. Cardigan also inherits the title and lands of his Irish uncle, Sir Terence. Silver Heels and Michael have become My Lady and Sir Michael Cardigan. They can retain aristocratic status while rejecting aspects of the same heritage: Michael next joins Mount and the Weasel for further Revolutionary battles against Britain. Felicity later sings a lullaby to her children in which she laments that courts are full of flattery and the city full of wantonness. Although now more alienated from the wilderness, the Cardigans are graced by the Indians with a new identity: they are the "People of the Morning, Tierhansaga" (502).

The accommodation of apparent social, political, and national oppositions is once again worked out in the personalities and actions of the major characters of Chambers's *The Maid-at-Arms* (1902). The daughter of Sir Lupus Varick seems initially an unsophisticated country lass, capable even of swearing and drinking, who defeats her husband-to-be, George Ormond, at hatchet throwing. By the end of the book, however, she has become a reincarnation of her European ancestor, Helen of Ormond, "Royal Maid-at-Arms" (15), and has become conspicuously beautiful and well mannered. Dorothy Varick must break her engagement to Sir George Covert (whose "secret" surname logically makes him a stand-in for the unnamed George, king of England), to whom she has in the event not absolutely signed away her "liberty" (137). Only then could she marry the young Floridian hero who has traveled to New York to consult with his kinsman, Sir Lupus, about the issues and anticipated course of the Revolution. (This George's name connects him with the American George, George Washington.) Sir George Covert voluntarily frees Dorothy from any earlier pledges; he has long since fallen in love with a relative of Joseph Brant—the part-Mohawk prophetess Magdalen Brant, who has herself been educated in London and can physically and socially pass in a white beau monde. George Ormond adjusts to life in northwestern New York and enlists in General Philip Schuyler's army, soon being promoted from captain to colonel and becoming Dorothy's lover and hero.

Classism, sexism, and racism again impact the values emerging from the Revolutionary War. Sir Lupus, who as a neutral is propagandized by both sides, hopes to maintain his social and economic position. A major evil to both Tories and patriots is not being gentlemanly and honorable in love and war, not being, in other words, the heroes proper to Anglo-American historical romances. The most thoroughgoing loyalist is another relative of the Varick/Ormonds, Walter Butler, a sullen fanatic in several of these novels and one who is eventually captured. The behavior of patriots is sometimes just as reprehensible. The Battle of Oriskany (portrayed in several period novels and very much differently in Harold Frederic's *In the Valley)* becomes such a bloody and shameful defeat for the forces of Congress because General Herkimer is influenced by an overly eager, undisciplined, disputatious group of officers and men. Whereas Benedict Arnold makes clear to George Ormond that he is offended at being passed over in promotion (he does nothing else in the novel), General Schuyler takes the correct course in writing to George that even though General Gates has been unfairly promoted over him, the cause they share remains all-important. Self-seeking egoism has no part in honor.

Tories are not following the rules in making use of "savage" Iroquois for their own dirty work; Ormond's men hang the renegade Danny Redstock, who has been selling rebel scalps to the Tories. Earlier, Ormond's troops had been sickened by the atrocities committed by white men dressed as Indians. The rebels, too, treat the Native Americans as undisciplined, simple, superstitious, violent, and sexually promiscuous, as in the scene where a half-naked Magdalen Brant appears at an increasingly orgiastic religious ceremony. In another episode a disguised Magdalen plays on the fears of tribes allied with the Tories and frightens them away by ranting of the reappearance of a legendary "Stonish

Giant," in reality the armored Dorothy Varick, who by this ploy releases George from captivity. At the same time and as usual, the associating of the Native Americans with the body of America means that they must be imaginatively possessed and taken seriously as a major element of the life of the new nation. Thus, we are presented typical perfunctory fantasies of amalgamation: Magdalen's being half-white, helping the side of Congress, and marrying Sir George, as well as incidental details like both hero and heroine knowing at least one Native American language.

The Reckoning (1905) concludes Chambers's series of novels on how the war "affected the great landed families of northern New York" (vii). In fact, these American families occupy only the geographical and conceptual center of the book; most of the actual narrative is set either in New York City or in an upstate New York from which many of the rural aristocrats have already been displaced by the war. In the last half of the book, action takes us altogether beyond the estates and settlements into the northern forests. That Chambers would assert, in the face of the preponderance of its real materials, that the book deals with "the great landed families of northern New York" gives away the idea that his declared subject must be in some sense an "averaging" of the extremes which are in fact presented: the city and the wilderness, Europe and America, the white and the Native American.

Yet the first-person narrator embodies and enacts the reconciling of these extremes in a book whose Anglo-American social and political vision is apparently and finally defused of much of its point by the discovery of more profound underlying and symbolic—if uncalculated—psychological and sexual motives. In the preface the narrator can only imagine a future (but a future existing well before 1905, we conclude) and providential embracing of an England in whose name atrocities have been committed: "God knows; and yet all things are possible with Him—even this miracle which I shall never live to see" (xx). But in the end Carus Renault does embrace England, in the person of a relative of the royal governor of Canada. The protagonist seems simply unaware of the symbolic meaning of what he has done, just as the author seems unaware of the notion that the psychological and sexual can encapsulate and explain the superficially rendered social and political. But here our very sophistication may lead us away from treating the historical romance on its own terms. We naively empower ourselves as readers by rushing past history and authorial intention and literary convention and in effect blaming Chambers for not knowing that the year of *The Reckoning* was also the year of Sigmund Freud's *Three Essays on the Theory of Sexuality* and Albert Einstein's early work on relativity. In our perspective all things do seem possible by 1905—except knowing what 1905 seemed like *in* 1905.

Carus Renault, if we do not employ the system of averaging opposing terms also appropriate to *Cardigan* and *The Maid-at-Arms*, would appear an impossible self-contradiction: in various manifestations he is at once altogether European and altogether Native American. He has some English blood but is more French; his parents live near Paris on his great-grandfather's estate. For four years he has served as private secretary to his kinsman, Sir Peter Coleville, in New York, a city unique in being "the great hearth of the mother-land where the nation gathers as a family, each conscious of a share in the heritage established for all by all" (11)—a progressive egalitarian thought until one remembers that the narrative present is 1781 rather than 1905. Carus loves Coleville's family though he is opposed to their cause, and makes a point of saying that many in even the better classes in the city are committed to the cause of liberty. On the other hand, he had arrived in New York "fresh from the frontier" (2) of upstate New York. But he is not simply a backwoods baron of the Judge William Cooper stripe; he is also an adoptive Indian like Cooper's son's Natty Bumppo, having replaced a departed war-chief: "I can be a barbarian, too, for I am by adoption, an Oneida of the Wolf Clan, and entitled to a seat in Council" (19).

Carus longs for a return to the settlements of his childhood rather less than he chafes under the inactivity and dissembling imposed upon him as an American spy. Although he is sure he performs a necessary service well and that his "Excellency," George Washington, always spoken of with reverence but never present, has assigned him his duty for sufficient reason, Carus still prefers the open and manly combat associated with the country to the hypocrisy of covert listening and conveying messages to his fellow patriots in the city. His role becomes more galling when Lady Coleville's kinswoman, the attractive and initially childish Elsin Grey, arrives for a visit from Halifax, where her relative, General Sir Frederick Haldimand, serves as governor of Canada. The Colevilles' plans to match Elsin with Carus seem thwarted by her mystifying references to Walter Butler, a leader of British troops and Indian irregulars in Carus's Tryon County and infamous (again) instigator of the Cherry Valley massacre. Renault's fight and flight instincts both continue to be suppressed because of his forced duplicity. When he hears at a dinner party that Butler, Butler's father, Sir John Johnson, and Colonel Rose are to rendezvous with their men at Niagara and a place called Thendara, he can only hope to get the word to others working for His Excellency. Walter Butler himself soon arrives in town, advising Clinton to pursue an aggressive and bloody strategy against the Americans and their allies on the frontier and along the Hudson—a plan nixed by Clinton, which angers Butler. Carus meets Butler, now his prime enemy in love and war, appropriately, at a cockfight heavily wagered on by Sir Peter but not by Carus himself, who saves money partially out of abstemiousness but more from his desire to furnish funds to suffering American prisoners. The handsome, fascinating, superficially gentlemanly Butler apologizes to Carus for his Indians having in error burned the Renault frontier home. Carus lacks firm evidence of Butler's ignominy, and therefore cannot openly confront him and thereby prove his own manhood. To make matters worse, Butler is to escort Miss Grey back to Halifax upon her being recalled by Haldimand. She clarifies nothing by stating that she likes Carus more than she does Butler, but loves Butler more.

Renault sends communiqués about Butler's plans to Colonel Willett and Washington, and holds a clandestine meeting with rough-hewn patriots the "Weasel" and Jack Mount, from whom he hears a rumor that Butler already has a wife, or at least a mistress. Butler recounts to Carus a tale of having been—like Carus himself—adopted into the Wolf Clan (though of the purportedly less virtuous Delawares), and Carus is struck by the anomaly of their being "two white men, gentlemen of quality," having their "very individualities sunk in the mystical freemasonry of a savage tie which bound us to the two nations" (90-91). Onehda (Carus's Oneida name) avows that his allegiance to the tribe is second only to his allegiance to his not-yet-independent country, and vows to warn his "people" of impending danger. He is further incriminated in Butler's eyes when Butler discovers in a cupboard a blotted copy of part of Carus's letter to Washington. Word that Butler evidently is not married to his Tryon County mistress—thus not a would-be bigamist—prevents an impending duel between him and Sir Peter, but Butler's accusing Carus of being a spy makes future confrontation between these two inevitable. Elsin saves the day by claiming to have written the note—in Carus's handwriting no less—as a prank and by charging Butler with inappropriate behavior for having stolen the note. Butler expresses his regrets, but Elsin knows that he knows she was lying and covering up for Carus. Before he returns to the safety of rebel lines, Carus tells Elsin that he is indeed a spy. Elsin, inexplicably, removes and crushes a miniature of Butler under her heel. She now obtains from Clinton a pass to the north for herself and Carus by again lying, saying that she plans to elope with Carus, though plighted to Butler.

As soon as he exits from the city Carus feels joy, "a free wind blowing from that wild north I loved so well" (154), though as yet unfulfilled by that most "magnificent activity": "to be hurled pell-mell among the heaving, straining melee, thrusting, stabbing, cutting my fill" (185). Escaping pursuit, meeting up with Mount and the Weasel, Elsin and Carus gain the Continental lines, where Colonel Hamilton conveys to Carus Washington's praise of his work as a spy along with his regrets that Carus's rashness prevents his receiving further intelligence assignments. Partners in adversity, Carus and Elsin declare their love for one another, but she still insists she can be everything but not a wife to him. It seems that when she was little more than an impressionable child struck by his romantic image, she had not only become engaged to Butler but had actually married him—nevertheless he has never so much as touched her. Although he recognizes the primacy of honor and public duty, Carus realizes that his private problem would be solved either by killing Butler or by proving he was already married when he wed Elsin. (Describing courtship as "the pretty combat for supremacy" [119] is the sort of figure of speech which links the public and the private, love and war.) Carus receives timely orders to stop Butler's military depredations in the north so that a surprise British invasion and massacre of the Oneida Nation might be prevented. After getting through to West Point by boat, Carus finds that he has been appointed captain of the Tryon Rangers. Not sure of the possible dangers of a British attack, he brings Elsin with him to Albany, and on to Schenectady and Johnstown.

The farther he presses into the wilderness, the more Carus must surrender a white European moment. When Colonel Willett assigns him duty as a scout and spy, he must leave Elsin behind. Selecting an Indian male, Little Otter, to accompany him on this mission, Carus entrusts Willett with his watch and money. (Carus thus anticipates Faulkner's Isaac McCaslin's having to give up the three "lifeless mechanicals" before he is vouchsafed a vision of the bear. Ike and Sam Fathers, Chingachgook and Natty Bumppo, Ishmael and Queequeg, Huck and Jim— the fantasy of men of different races uniting in and with a state of nature existed long before Leslie Fiedler's famous 1950s explication.) The "Thendara" where the tribes are to convene, Carus informs Willett, is merely a name for any place where certain sacred ceremonies are enacted: "Thendara *was,* and *will be,* but is not" (273)—as though the brooding American land will reclaim its temporary and merely recent inhabitants. He feels that unwarranted Indian ferocity was acquired from untoward Tory example, and that true brutality is exhibited by the "horse-riding savages of the West" (273)—one suspects this evaluation stems from the fact that when the book was written the Eastern tribes no longer constituted a viable threat. Simple generalizations about Native American life are further challenged for Carus when he sees the part-

Indian Christian Carolyn Montour rummaging through papers at the old Butler home. She seems to him very "civilized," considering that she is the daughter of Catrine Montour, the "Huron witch" and "fierce temptress of the forests" (297). Startled by Carus, Carolyn soon calms down enough to tell him that she had been searching for a record of her marriage to Walter Butler, for to be shunned by a husband would make her an outcast among the Iroquois. (Her having once been dubbed the "Cherry Maid" links Butler's unbridled sexual lust with his blood-lust as the villain of Cherry Valley.) Carus informs her of Elsin's supposed marriage to Butler.

At the council fires of Thendara, the male symbol—the pipe—is passed among the men in "the most sacred rite of the Iroquois people" (305). Astutely, persuasively, passionately, Carus pleads for the preservation of the Great League of the Six Nations, for the Oneidas not being singled out as vulnerable belligerents deserving punishment. After the council disperses, a lone horseman approaches the fire—Walter Butler, too late to have a voice as one of the absent and discredited Delawares. Butler immediately recognizes Renault despite his Indian garb, and their argument and fight ends with Butler diving into the river, but not before he calls to the Royal Greens to pursue Carus, "Lyn" Montour, and Little Otter. Carus alerts the countryside to flee to the relative safety of Johnstown (although he also takes narrative time out—significantly during this late autumn—to lament the passing of the forest and the Indian in a tone that would seem to have more point a century later). The harassed threesome rush back to the defense of the town, where Carus's frantic search for Elsin turns up only a note in which she announces that she feels conscience-bound—partly because of Renault's own example of self-sacrifice—to return to her husband and try to persuade him not to brutalize at least the helpless and the old. During the early stages of the ensuing battle at Johnstown, Elsin is with Butler in Johnson Hall.

The Americans at first retreat and lose their cannons, the rallying point of their military might, then regroup and regain their artillery. The British are routed and Butler and his men are pursued into the cold heart of a darkness which, like Joseph Conrad's a few years earlier, suggests social and psychological meanings as well as geographical ones (and, in an American context, the Crèvecoeur/Cooper notion that the regeneration made possible by the wilderness can, if perverted by a license masquerading as freedom, become degeneration). As the insolent libertine flees to the sublime rather than beautiful fastnesses of the north (yet another almost compulsive repetition of what had just happened to Carus) he becomes one with the environment, id becomes (id)entity:

And the Red Beast must be done to death. What fitter place to end him than here in the wild twilight of shaggy depths, unlighted by the sun or moon?—here where the cold, brawling streams smoked in the rank air; where black crags crouched, watching the hunting—here in these awful deeps, shunned by the deer, unhaunted by wolf and panther—depths fit only for the monstrous terror that came out of them, and now, wounded, and cold heart pulsing terror, was scrambling back again into the dense and dreadful twilight of eternal shadow-land. (366)

Butler is brought to bay as he kneels at a spring (a natural source suggestive of the elemental) and, before Carus's censoring voice can stop them, two frontiersmen shoot Butler and the Oneidas scalp him, rendering him a "battered, disfigured thing" (371). Meanwhile Elsin, the worse for wear, has rejoined the Americans and been befriended by Lyn Montour. Her conscious mind shrinking from acknowledging Butler and her own dilemma, she nonetheless remains fascinated by the man who lacked redeeming social value as she marks herself with widow's ashes: as the fire dies and "the black curtains of obscurity closed in" sparks briefly illuminate "the naked bodies of the Oneidas, sitting like demons" (374-75). She excuses Butler, thinking his powerful animal instincts had overrun socially acceptable limits and even a perception of human individuality: "I think his reason was unseated when I came to him there at Johnson Hall—so much of blood and death lay on his soul" (376-77). His own men had feared him; he did not seem to recognize Elsin. In the delirium of her recovery she calls Carus "Walter"; though the husband of her youth has died, she is left with a slight limp as a reminder of him and her forest journey.

The trip back to Albany is the couple's rejoining of a social and political world, through fields "all golden in the sun" (380), where they are greeted with the news of Yorktown: "Butler's dead, and Cornwallis is taken!" (382). The future wedding between the virginal Elsin and Carus signals an acceptance of social forms as their union also means that a new society emerges from the violence of its own begetting. Those with still some conspicuous wilderness in them, Jack Mount and Carolyn Montour, pair off. (This "other" wife of Butler has also been freed by his death, and her French surname—also suggesting "mount"—links her with Jack in any case.) A miniature of Washington sent from him to Elsin in effect replaces the one of Butler she had destroyed. The voice of Washington has all along been the voice of duty and social responsibility. As Colonel Willett has it, "God and his Excellency know best!" (276). Washington's orders made Carus a spy, prevented him from exhibiting a significant aspect of his true self and living a life of action.

On the other hand, as an agent of aggression Carus shares with Butler membership in Indian tribes. This fact binds him to Butler and to Native American lands, and finally makes the Revolution's "European" political and social purposes seem trivial, temporary, or mere exhibitions of "deeper" motives. Once of the Wolf Clan, always of the Wolf Clan (though Butler's degradation had taken him to "deeps" even "unhaunted by wolf and panther"). Stereotypes of the nobility of Native Americans and their identity with a life-giving soil merge, in the old paradox, with images of the destructive savagery of their conduct. The savage in the new (white) American must be tamed; Butler does meet his fate. Carus Renault and Elsin Grey confront Butler but cannot dismiss him: they had reckoned with Walter Butler as an enemy in love and war, the enemy of *Cardigan* and *The Maid-at-Arms,* but not with the Walter Butler in themselves.

The last of our interrelated novels, Frederick A. Ray's *Maid of the Mohawk* (1906), offers a reprise of expected narrative lines and, in specific, repeats settings of Harold Frederic's *In the Valley* and Robert Chambers's romances. "In this story of love and war" (2), Tory and patriot brothers compete as soldiers and as prospective husbands for the heroine; after a period of apparent Toryism, the heroine's American sympathies are disclosed and she marries the democratic hero; the notable deeds of the Revolution are depicted as examples of purpose for the present. Ray begins by declaring that his intention is to relate a simple tale which may serve as a message to those who wish to "know of the valiant sacrifices made by our people of the Mohawk [Valley]" (1), to bring "out the parts played in that great drama by my own people, the Dutch of the Mohawk" (2). The first-person retrospective narrator is so old that he can be, in effect, his own Revolutionary forefather: in celebrating the drama of the Revolution and his own part in it, contrasted to his calm and uneventful present, Henry Van Horn implicitly contrasts the dedicated Revolutionary generation to the more divided and confused generation of 1906. Ray's hagiographic social and political agenda rarely becomes as explicit as it does in the passage which mentions that "the generation of the time I am writing had best not know the sins of their fathers" (36).

Shortly after Henry Van Horn's family had settled in the Mohawk Valley, Henry's father lost his life in the war against the French. His mother had then married James Hastings, a widowered employee of the British Land Agency. James's son Gilbert predictably becomes the dashing, handsome, well-dressed and well-mannered, educated rival of Henry for the affections of Jeanne Mortier, the French "maid of the

Mohawk," beautiful in mind and body. The social-climbing Madame Mortier intends Jeanne for Gilbert and takes her off to the supposed safety of New York City when war threatens. Henry fears, after he enrolls in the Tryon County Militia, that Gilbert will become "brave enough to lay siege upon the fortress of a woman's heart" (107). Henry's increasingly important role in the military begins with his being one of the three scouts sent to Fort Stanwix to deliver the message that its forces are to join with those of General Herkimer in a concerted blow against the British. (Another of the scouts is the representative back-woodsman of this novel—the long-haired, rough-talking, Indian-hating, unkempt, and coonskin-capped Timothy Murphy.) They deliver the communiqué only to discover that his impetuous and jealous aide, Colonel Cox, has goaded Herkimer into a premature attack which becomes the bloody and disastrous Battle of Oriskany. Meanwhile Gilbert has obtained an undeserved lieutenancy in the British army and spends much of his time gambling and escorting Jeanne in New York and Philadelphia. The forgiving Henry's later allowing Hastings and his entourage, including John André, through colonial picket lines does not impress the nefarious Gilbert, who puts a price on Henry's head. Henry becomes an adviser to General Washington and with the Sullivan expedition returns to the valley. His old friend Paul Manning, about whom had always existed suspicions of ill-got wealth, entrusts Henry with a mysterious note to Washington which becomes the deus ex machina of the story.

The next scenes find Henry a spy in New York City working with the publisher of the *Royal Gazette,* James Rivington, who despite his journal's title is a faithful patriot. The causes seem lost after the hardships of Valley Forge and Gilbert's taking Jeanne to the altar. But all is salvaged as Washington accepts Manning's contribution of eight thousand pounds, which rekindle "the fires of liberty" and restore "harmony and satisfaction" (230), and as Jeanne feigns fainting to stop the ceremony's being concluded and soberly toasts the Unknown Benefactor of the Americans (Manning) at a drunken Tory revel. Jeanne then convinces André, another of her suitors, to liberate the imprisoned Henry, just as she had earlier persuaded Henry to free André and Gilbert. The argument between Gilbert and André which follows results in Gilbert's being released from duty and being imprisoned so that he cannot subvert André's secret mission to West Point, where rumor has it that a disgruntled and traitorous Benedict Arnold is to cede the fort to the British. Jeanne tells Henry of the plot but he is unable to prevent André's arriving at West Point before him; although André is captured and executed, Arnold escapes to the British. Henry's military duties now take him to Yorktown.

Abruptly, the novel reports that the war has ended. Two years pass and Henry has returned to his farm in the Mohawk country. During a visit from General Washington, a dying Paul Manning tells his life story, including accounts of his unhappy marriage and how he obtained the gold treasure through his buccaneer grandfather. Following her mother's death, Jeanne announces her acceptance of Henry's marriage proposal. Gilbert has already died, possibly a suicide, miserable and perhaps insane. The centrality of these Revolutionary period events in the careers of the hero and heroine (and, by extension, the careers of those turn-of-the-century readers who identified with them) is reemphasized in the final reminder of the novel's narrative technique. These have been the "principal events of our lives," "we knew these things were true" even as we find ourselves "believing for the time that memory had played tricks, that phantom shapes and ideas, coming from so remote a past, had beguiled us" (339). The past in all these novels has been recalled, not just remembered but called again, called forth, conjured, re-created in the telling. As in Shakespeare's Sonnet 116, if the discourse is not "true" then no man ever wrote—but the narrative is itself the writing which finishes the equation and thereby "proves" its own truth. Knowing "these things were true" is a statement which the reader supposes is the inevitable consequence of an unspoken "these things were"; the former statement calls the latter into being. The story places us in a narrative moment in need of a memory that does not play tricks, yet within the lifetime of a still-living and therefore "real" narrator. This narrator's story thus has a perceived worth despite his existing in a time which itself could only be a memory to a reader of 1906. The narrative is in this way self-validating.

CONCLUSION

The land becomes ours but we not the land's, to paraphrase Robert Frost. Though supposedly imaginings of a regenerate nation which could spring from the soil of America, could define itself through opposition to the Old World, these novels present a congeries of motives. Their pointing to both the past and the present, Europe and America, embodies an impracticable desire for the resolution of cultural conflicts, a desire which had such a marked appeal in troubled times that it was also expressed in other literary genres and in historical novels covering other periods, as well. We have also mentioned the defensive responses of cultural texts like genealogical societies and American foreign and domestic policy. Many phenomena of turn-of-the-century America can be "read" using an interpretive template which yields the sorts of messages so evident in the novels discussed here.

In a sense American Revolutionary War novels were retrospective treatments of the "international theme" so favored by the Henry James who scorned the historical romance. In the James formula, too, the young American girl finds her identity in the interplay between domestic and foreign, even between the worlds represented by Henry Adams as the modern dynamo and the archaic Virgin. In defining American values and possibilities intrinsically and not by national contrasts, "country life" and regional novels like those of James Lane Allen and Edward Westcott also "recalled a simpler, purer idealized society whose image appealed powerfully to the times" (Nye, *The Unembarrassed Muse* 36). Perhaps most suggestive is the concurrent vogue of the historical romance and the utopian novel (both, we are free to say, forms of science fiction in their involving time travel).[1] The historical novel has, in fact, been viewed as an "inverted utopia" in its escapist functions and its illusion of entire self-contained societies (Henderson 13). (Brian Aldiss, in *The Trillion Year Spree,* calls this period of science fiction "The Flight from Urban Culture.") A historical novel which envisions American destiny—as many of these novels do—must typically contend with or flee the realities of the era of its composition, must appear therefore either troubled or parochial. Other modes of expression perhaps stem from a combined and "irresponsible" psychological and social sublimation, but the utopian novel altogether abrogates this responsibility to history, since "pure romance really belongs to the future, which is absolutely cut off from any possible reference to truth of fact or truth of sensation" (Scholes and Kellogg 228). Utopian novelists like Edward Bellamy and arch-realist William Dean Howells exhibited a serious concern for contemporary social ills and projected their future disappearance. The future, in their texts, is always the future; it cannot be proven false by its countermanding history. Even the sophisticated reader tends so to privilege history and to separate it from its literary constructs that he or she comes to feel the historical fictionist more irresponsible, innocuous, or false in her or his "utopian" project than the historian of the future, to whom she or he grants imaginative license. But what nevertheless belongs to the past, add Robert Scholes and Robert Kellogg, is not mimesis (the present) or romance (the future) but myth, which can embody the images and values by which we live (228).

The often explicit call in these novels for a rededication to national principles makes for what at times seems a didactic tone. Since they are re-creations as well as recreations, we are not only entertained by the doings of fictional and historical luminaries but are also asked to possess their patriotic zeal. A simple sense of nationalism and providential destiny was expressed "in a society more thoroughly given over to the norms of exploitative capitalism than any other in the history of the world" (Berthoff, *The Ferment of Realism* 186). Even though this stance might seem a protection against reality, a continuation of the bankrupt American idealism of the genteel tradition, a questioning of unknowable authors' motives yields silence and is thus beside the point. What we do know is that these historical novelists were in any case so popular that their influence, if nothing else, must be taken seriously. As Cary Nelson puts it, "it can be taken as axiomatic that texts that were either widely read or influential at key moments need to retain their place in our sense of literary history, whether or not we happen, at present, to judge them to be of high quality" (Elliott 914). William Gilmore Simms, whose own novel *The Scout* (1854) describes the rivalry of Whig and Tory half-brothers for the favors of the same girl, had expressed himself strongly on this subject: "A national history, preserved by a national poet," Simms had written, "becomes, in fact, a national religion" (*Views and Reviews* 54). He also thought that "it is the soul of art, alone, which binds periods and places together" (36). Hervey Allen in 1944 wrote in a similar vein: "Since what people believe about the past largely fixes their action in the future, the responsibility of the historical novelist is actually a great one" (120). Critics continue to discover that such novels have significant practical influence: "Historical novels have undoubtedly been the single most important source of information about, and awareness of, the American Revolution" (Kammen 145). Thus, "good historical novelists can reshape the skewed map of the American past in the public mind" (Fleming 20). In their effects these novels may as well be history in its traditional definition, instead of particular and dualistic narrative texts. In this sense, reader response has and had already made history and fiction one, just as, in Charles Molesworth's words, "reading habits, themselves the result of historical periods and styles, must invariably have their impact on the total 'production' of the literary text" (Elliott 1026).

Together these novels present a regionally diverse composite portrait of the nation. They are much less dissimilar in narrative strategy, theme, and tone, sharing many characteristics with historical novels of the Revolution not written during this era. Yet their particular adaptations of metaphor and the conventions of romance, their pointed if implied critiques of the contemporary world, illustrate that their authors used historical fiction and were used by it in ways consistently characterizing the period. Novels and history alike "merely substantiated conventional opinion and left undisturbed the simplifying accretions of popular memory" (Berthoff, *The Ferment of Realism* 186). (The possibility of what might be called revisionist historical fiction had been explored by writers like Melville, in whose *Israel Potter* the grand effects of Israel's meeting the august Dr. Franklin are lost when that worthy happens to be looking the other way.) Turn-of-the-century romancers inherited the impossible task of wedding individual characters to generalized political meaning and fiction to history, not just hero to heroine.

In creating images of stability and a meaningful Revolution, these novels also joined their past with their present. The history that had intervened between the Revolution and the late nineteenth century had eventuated in a world in need of the assurance of these images. Partly by trying to make the Revolution real to us by conceiving it in our terms, we destroy its essential nature. Each new reinterpretation becomes an aspect of later ones, all of them influenced by passing events. The Civil War, especially, made the Revolution more distant and its issues simpler to the fin de siècle than they actually were. Incarnations of the national/heroic seemed easier to discover in an antebellum America sheltered by time, before that era the actual sufferings and sectional and sectarian confusions of which were present to memory. Familial conflicts in the Revolutionary War novels could be resolved with the creation of a united American family already consecrated by time and the magic of "1776." The emphasis on separate loyalties, even within families, can be seen as a parallel to the divisions of the Civil War; the shared heritage a salve for its wounds. Coincidentally, that war had ended with an Old World/New

World familial trope: *Our American Cousin*. (Not without effects which are worthy of further investigation is the fact that several of these writers—S. Weir Mitchell, John W. DeForest, and Winston Churchill among them—also wrote novels about the Civil War.) Inevitably, "in some instances the complications of a later day have been imposed on the plot; that is, modern concepts of which the forefathers were unaware have been read into the struggle" (Leisy 113). Whereas later novels about the Revolutionary War often express a "sense of bewilderment over changing conditions" (Leisy 113), no such sense was expressed at the turn of the century. Representative historical novels of our own time include Howard Fast's *The Hessian* (1972), a challenge to mindless patriotism and a calculated literary utilization of the Vietnam War and the trial of Lieutenant Calley.

Thus we turn again to our final context, our present (not *the* present, the present of the reader to whom this book is itself an artifact of the past). Roy Harvey Pearce is right as far as he goes in his opinion that a literary work is "a kind of statement which can never be dissociated from either the time in which it was made or the time in which it is known" *(Historicism Once More* 17). In our present, the present which affects our readings of any texts, the novelist and critic Raymond Federman calls attention to writers like Joseph Heller, Thomas Pynchon, Kurt Vonnegut Jr., Jerzy Kosinski, and John Barth producing fictions which question "the official versions of historical events" and ironically remake all periods of American history (Elliott 1150-51). I would go further. Our readings, our notions, of turn-of-the-century American Revolutionary War novels come generally by way of our not reading them. The mere reciting of other titles from the period is itself our commentary on these historical romances (an indication of our values, our limitations, our agendas—our canon): *The Red Badge of Courage* (1895), *The Theory of the Leisure Class* (1899), *The House of Mirth* (1905), *Sister Carrie* (1900), *The Souls of Black Folk* (1903) (if not *Up from Slavery* [1901]). Or, for other reasons, we might suggest an alternate list: Jacob Riis's *How the Other Half Lives* (1890), Abraham Cahan's *Yekl, a Tale of the New York Ghetto* (1896), Charlotte Perkins Gilman's *The Yellow Wallpaper* (1899), Kate Chopin's *The Awakening* (1899), Pauline Hopkins's *Contending Forces* (1900), Upton Sinclair's *The Jungle* (1906). When we do approach books like the Revolutionary War novels in our supposedly enlightened present, we grow acutely aware of the justice in modern critics' remarks that we cannot really read them in the precise spirit in which they were written, let alone revisit the American Revolution.[2] On the other hand, "ignoring the pastness of past works of literature is possible to conceive of but impossible to do. The choice is really between reading with a sense of the past that is derived casually and unreflectively and reading with a sense of the past that is arrived at deliberately and methodically" by critics who "must blot from their mind as much as possible whatever may have happened after the literary work they are criticizing was published" (Jackson 63, 72). Since the unfamiliar is always described in terms of the familiar, "the unavoidable displacement of the nineteenth-century environment by our twentieth-century one affects our understanding both of the nineteenth-century environment and of the eighteenth-century environment to which the novel addresses itself" (Jackson 45, writing of Sir Walter Scott's *The Heart of Midlothian*). (An inevitable sense of formal literary anachronism also stems from our knowing that the modern historical novel's beginnings postdated 1776—that these fictional creations were not options to that world.) Whereas the historical novelist may wax imaginative, the historical critic is held to a standard of thoroughness which includes historical research even when the borders between past and present, fact and fiction, are eroded by hermeneutic approaches which posit interpenetrations of fiction and history. Recent novelists themselves are in some cases aware of the paradox. In writing his award-winning *Middle Passage* (1990) Charles Johnson reports of months of research on the slave trade and nautical terminology yet speaks also of using the past as a metaphor for the present. Especially when considering the historical novel, the critic must guard against allowing his or her subject altogether to flee either to geography and history or to the ground of its generic counterparts of other times and places.

Well before poststructuralist and postmodernist thought began to affect literary and historical studies, American history had been scoured as the definitive subject of a national literature. (The United States's lack of a unique and autonomous language preempted defining its literature linguistically in the same way that Western European and other countries have. A declaration of independence from the English language seemed impossible, and America's native languages, known by relatively few, represented mostly oral cultural traditions) Whereas the earliest theories of American literature were framed by departments of history, departments of English had "themselves been founded to help realize the antique dream of America as the manifest destiny of Anglo-Saxon progress" (Spengemann 16). In his useful elucidation of the history of American Studies, William Spengemann unwittingly addresses the very issues at play in turn-of-the-century American Revolutionary War novels and in their cultural matrix. Not only does American Studies investigate subjects like these novels, but the history of the discipline of American Studies itself reveals a course of development corresponding to implications of our subject. "Just as," writes Spengemann in *A Mirror for Americanists,* "the popular interest in colonial American history arose in the nineteenth century from nationalistic motives," so the twentieth-century study of American literature emerged "to help justify the separation of American from English literature by creating a native tradition for our national treasures" (31-32). In other words, the Revolutionary War novels fall chronologically between an American self-consciousness about national history and an academic consciousness about national literary tradition; the period's historical romancer felt no special hesitation in utilizing national history in an English genre, even in the writing of novels about rebellion against England. What we read as mixed signals come not only from a pervasive and defensive Anglophilia but also from the circumstance of literary content (America) and form (British) being parallel, coexisting, but intertwined appropriations of what in his study of American Studies as a discipline Spengemann calls "the quaint pleasures of self-regarding anglophilia and misplaced American patriotism" (123). These novelists could have it both ways. In fact, they wrote on the eve of the period, World War I, after which literary works of Britain and America tend to be studied together as instances of an international modernism. The Revolutionary War novels anticipate this bifocal view, but hardly in its modernism, just as, on the other temporal side, they recoup a passé and self-conscious Anglophilia fashionable among some classes.

The Revolutionary period itself marks the beginning of our typical dividing of English literature from American literature courses, as though our curriculum itself declares independence. Consequently, "from the time of the American Revolution to the rise of international modernism after World War I, American and British literature are customarily viewed as inhabiting two almost totally unrelated realms" (Spengemann 123). Twentieth-century academics did not always accept Emerson's 1837 pronouncement that Americans had "listened too long to the courtly muses of Europe": a retroactive notion of an even earlier and yet clearly American literature had been formulated. The Revolutionary novels bring these conceptual realms together; their subjects signal the time when the realms had grown apart. This period from 1775 until 1918, continues Spengemann, was partially defined by a shift from emphasis on the formal to an emphasis on formless energy in creative literature (another indication of the atavism perhaps inherent in the formulaic historical novel by the end of the nineteenth century).

After World War I the historical school of American scholarship gained ascendancy, associated as it was with a championing of American uniqueness, freedom, and progress—and subjects like the War for Independence. The later critical school, "on the other hand, emerged in a period of spreading uncertainty about the value, if not the reality, of political, social, and material progress in America" (Spengemann 18). Darling subjects of progressive liberalism—or regressive conservatism—met a cynical reception, and emphasis was placed, in any case, on form, not content. A myopia resulted whereby older historical views were themselves considered historically limited, whereas the critical school's own formalist views were somehow timeless. In fact, all theories find themselves in history; their practitioners discover themselves affected by cultural context and refine their arguments on that basis. At least now we no longer arbitrarily separate or think we can separate the historical from the critical. The critical approach cannot override distinctions of time and place; the historical approach has cast off "positivist assumptions and scientific pretensions" (Spengemann 155). These modes of interpretation lose their independence but become components of a new strategy at once historical and textual, a strategy born of revisionist historiography and poststructuralism. It is a theory of time and in time. If we know a past moment well enough, we can sensibly and convincingly explain what texts meant at that time; our arguments can possess internal consistency. But as far as we are otherwise concerned, these texts exist for us, now.

A single passage from one of the turn-of-the-century American Revolutionary War novels can serve to illustrate the point that many of a historical novelist's announced or apparently conscious contemporary purposes may have become altered or irrelevant in becoming text, that authors can unwittingly write—better than they know—that history is text and that the moment of writing and the moment of reading are both in history. Thus, *Rereading the Revolution*, too, possesses its own historical context. (The referenced novel's mere inscription of the boyhood nickname of the scholarly book's author appeals to someone's present.) A child's naive blunder during an imaginary Revolutionary War becomes the humor of 1902 and becomes serious literary theory of the late twentieth century. The episode occurs in *The Maid-at-Arms:* " 'I see I must teach you history, cousin,' she said. 'Father tells us that history is being made all about us in these days—and, would you believe it? Benny took it that books were being made in the woods all around the house' " (29).

NOTES

Introduction

1. The account of the exposition presented here is based on chapter 1 of the profusely illustrated sourcebook written by Lally Weymouth and designed by Milton Glaser, *America in 1876: The Way We Were*.

2. Perhaps most to the point is Foucault's "History, Discourse and Discontinuity." For recent treatments of these concepts in works not otherwise referred to here see Jerome McGann, *Historical Studies and Literary Criticism*, and Harold Veeser, *The New Historicism*.

3. These critical crossings and recrossings remind us that "conceptual framework" always connotes a mixed trope: concepts seem reasonable and necessary, whereas "frame" suggests limits and limitations.

4. See, for example, Budick, Morris, and Gossman.

5. See Berthoff, "Fiction, History, Myth" 271ff.

6. In line with revisionist views of canon formation, little distinction is made here between what used to be called popular culture and elitist art. In actuality, little distinction was made among historical novelists in 1900 between what later may have been considered alternate modes or strategies. No matter its degree of artistry, the historical novel (like the early modern novel itself when contradistinguished from "the more self-contained artifacts of lyric poetry") is "the child of the market place." Exclusions are no longer often based on class, race, or gender. We tend to find disquieting the idea that relative access to and appreciation of "high" Western art is determined by possession of leisure as well as available training and consequent notions about the nature of literature (see Dickstein 33–37), even though these phenomena, too, constitute revelatory aspects of the historical contexts of the art. Ironically, the new historicism has contrived with an apparently ahistorical poststructuralism—though new historicism also subsumes poststructuralism—in validating the status of formerly marginal texts. Language becomes definitive in any case and across genres, including any form which has been traditionally considered more as social commentary, "particularly historistic" and no longer lived than the "lifetime of its immediate audience" (Pearce, *Historicism Once More* 85), than as artistic achievement. This conflation of high- and lowbrow, historical and literary, places texts on an equal, if not yet fully articulated, footing as expressions of time and place, whether "time" and "place" are themselves constituted only by texts here being beside the point. The impulse and inducements to write the

popular historical novel were so strong around 1900 that the genre found practitioners in both canonized writers like Sarah Orne Jewett and pop cult favorites like Zane Grey, writers who in this instance endorsed very like formulas, an endorsement which itself speaks to the nature of the age. Unavoidably, logically drawing from our critical views, we respond favorably to Russell Reising's desideratum: "Without an expansion of the canon, there can be no real opening, no freshness, no democratization of American literary studies—there will only be new critical tools applied to the same old texts" (222).

7. See, for example, Leisy vii, Hart 203–4, Earnest 144, and Van Doren 216. Michael Kammen cites the period from 1933 to 1948—a time obviously notable for an economic depression and a war—as the third and last of these periods. He concludes that this periodization "provides an important index to the rhythms of American culture" (148) but that the impulses at work during each era were different. The earliest vogue for the historical novel resulted from nationalistic fervor, whereas novelists between 1933 and 1948 were driven to an "assessment of our national character, and especially its origins in formative times" (Kammen 165), with a stress on economic and social motive, civilian life, the "seamy" and the Tory side (Woodress 389). The first of these three periods has been treated by Ringe 352–65.

8. Quoted in Conn 241. His project in fact included the integrating of American popular music and allusion to American literary expression in his compositions. Unlike the novelists, however, Ives had to contend with the prejudice against the use of American materials in serious Euro-American musical art.

9. Following upon Freud's analysis of the motives of (male) power and the (female) erotic, John Cawelti has delimited adventure and romance as separate "moral fantasies" (*Adventure, Mystery, and Romance* 41–42). What any historical novel makes possible is a simultaneity of these drives. Since adventure, war, is "history" and the love plot is romance, the victorious hero's rewards must usually include both winning the war and getting the girl, bringing together history and fiction as reciprocal influences in the portrait of an epoch.

10. Elaine Showalter has recently employed the late nineteenth century as a template by which to read gender roles of the late twentieth century (and/or vice versa?) in *Sexual Anarchy: Gender and Culture at the Fin de Siècle*. Interestingly and appropriately enough, Barbara Bardes's and Suzanne Gossett's book on women and political power in nineteenth-century America is entitled *Declarations of Independence*.

11. The following bibliographies were useful: Baker, *Guide*; Jones and Ludwig; McGarry and White; VanDerhoof. Many novels not identified in these sources were located by way of advertising in contemporary novels.

New England

1. Because these novels generally conclude with the end of a war which marks the beginning of a marriage, it becomes more relevant than clever to stress the phonetic identification of "Yorktown" with "Yoketown" (just as we are free to link Eliot's given name with "Briton" or "Britain"). Male dominion displaces and replaces British dominion over America. Having struggled against and defeated the "mother," the American man is empowered to have his way with the now-demure wife. The possibilities of the woman's revolution *end* at Yorktown, and again the gaining of independence usually means for her a consigning to dependent status.

2. More appropriate to the latter West, the belated West which we compulsively portray as an originating ground, would be Hart Crane's Pocahontas, "the mythological nature-symbol chosen to represent the physical body of the continent," in *The Bridge*. "The nature-world of the Indian," Crane continues, is a living part of "the Myth of America"; Powhatan's daughter is "the woman with us in the dawn," "the flesh our feet have moved upon" (248–49, 57).

The Middle Colonies

1. Being a deserter or a coward, therefore, does not disqualify one from being a gentleman. What does preempt that standing is made abundantly clear in a lengthy statement (only part of which is quoted below) relegated to a note but obviously at the center of the author's 1898 consciousness. Nostalgia turns vicious and contrives with a political agenda in the attempt to retrieve the American land principally for the Anglo-Saxon. The contention which took place in the Philipse manor house during the Revolution fades to insignificance in the face of the edifice's present consecrated status:

The building is closely hemmed in by sordid signs of progress. Ugly houses, in crowded blocks, cover all the great surrounding space that once was a thick forest, fair orchards, gardens, fields, and pastoral rivulet. The Neperan or Saw Mill River flows, sluggish and scummy, under streets and houses. A visit to the manor-house, now, would spoil rather than improve one's impression of what the place looked like in the old days. Yet the house itself remains well preserved, for which all honor to the town of Yonkers. There is in our spacious America so much room for the present and the future, that a little ought to be kept for the past. It is well to be reminded, by a landmark here and there, of our brave youth as a people. A posterity, sure to value these landmarks more than this money-grabbing age does, will reproach us with the destruction we have already wrought. Worse still than the crime of obliterating all human-made relics of the past, is the vandalism of nature herself where nature is exceptionally beautiful. To rob millions of beauty-lovers, yet to live, of the Palisades of the Hudson, would bring upon us the amazement and execration of future centuries. This earth is an entailed estate, that each generation is in honor bound to hand down, undefaced, undiminished, to its successor. In order that a clutched wallet or two may wax a little fatter, shall we bring upon ourselves a cry of shame that would ring with increasing bitterness through the ages, shall we invite the execration merited by such greed as could so outrage our fair earth, such stolid apathy as could stand by and see it done? Shall an alien or two, as hard of soul as the stone in which he traffics, mar the Hudson that Washington patrolled, rob countless eyes, yet unopened, of a joy; countless minds, yet to waken, of an inspiration; countless hearts, yet to beat, of a thrill of pride in the soil of their inheriting? (292–93)

Much could be said of this passage and its self-consciously high rhetorical manner. The linking, for example, of "wallet or two" with "alien or two" exhibits its anti-Semitic stance; in the writer's fantasy the very numbers of new immigrants are minimized while descendants he values are "countless."

The South

1. It hardly comes as a surprise that Constance Cary Harrison, though active in the New York high society about which she also wrote, had family roots in Virginia and had been for over three decades the wife of Burton Harrison, the private secretary of Jefferson Davis during the Civil War. While it is true that, as Daniel Sutherland has written, *A Son of the Old Dominion* extrapolates the conflict against the North to an earlier one against England, Yankeedom and the modern seem more pointedly the target of Mrs. Harrison's fiction than England and the past, more destructive of the Old South of which she "painted such a deliciously languid picture" (Sutherland 183). The romanticizing of the Lost Cause possible by the 1890s allowed her to reconstitute by novel's end just the sort of Vue de l'Eau which eighty years after the Revolution must inevitably confront change and the outsider. Although her novel of manners, *The Anglomaniacs* (1890), satirizes the new rich of New York for aping English aristocrats, her Old Southern aristocrats reflect the same prejudice, thereby reminding readers of Mark Twain's quip that Sir Walter Scott was a major cause of the Civil War.

2. This John-the-Baptist points the way to no savior, no brighter future. Blacks in the novel present the usual images of sycophancy or become the objects of the disguised fears of a later day, as when we are told that British leaders like Cornwallis were "sowing insurrection among the faithful blacks" (317). The British become anachronistic abolitionists. Applying to blacks the idea and ideal of revolution is subverted by reducing arguments to the absurd. Anne, for example, belittles John-the-Baptist for asking whether the Revolution will mean that whites will become black and blacks become white. She scorns

to answer the simple-minded question which Rives has made John-the-Baptist ask. *That* would be too great a revolution for Miss Anne to contemplate. Blacks are thus dismissed as so far outside *any* social and political scheme that the rationale for their exclusion is self-evident.

The West

1. As in Stimpson's *The Tory Maid* and Frederick Ray's *Maid of the Mohawk* the technique opens the narrative to contrasts available only through wider temporal scope. Here, the narrator compares the Battle of Saratoga with the "recent" Napoleonic Battle of Austerlitz and frees the reader to imagine the narrator's nostalgia for 1777 and to indulge his or her own nostalgia for both 1777 and 1805. Publishers' merchandising techniques also sometimes furnish and remind us of a wider scope. The 1971 paperback reprint of *The Sun of Saratoga*, for example, attempts to erase the effects of history of the period from 1897 to 1971 by not indicating the original publishing date and by carrying just the sort of sensational romantic cover expected in the latter year. The publisher interprets by pretending that 1897 *is* 1971. This period of unwritten "future" history from 1900 to the present is always very real to these novels, a crucial determinant of their "content" insofar as—which is very far indeed—we perceive only those meanings which are available to us. The intervening history of which we are cognizant and our critical apparatus give us new books and imply a history of modes of reading which follow the publication of the books themselves.

Conclusion

1. More than a spate of books on feminist and other utopias have appeared in the last few years. Some that cover the turn of the century include those by Jean Pfaelzer, Carol Farley Kessler, Thomas Clareson, Howard P. Segal, and Frances Bartkowski.

2. Dominick La Capra usefully contrasts an ahistorical and all-consuming "presentist" view with an equally false and fantastic empathetic "teletransportation" to the past (9–10). See also Jackson 3–4.

BIBLIOGRAPHY

I. Primary Sources

Altsheler, Joseph A. *In Hostile Red: A Romance of the Monmouth Campaign.* New York: J. B. Lippincott, 1897.

——. *My Captive: A Novel.* New York: D. Appleton, 1902.

——. *The Sun of Saratoga.* 1897. New York: Grosset and Dunlap, 1971.

Blanchard, Amy Ella. *A Daughter of Freedom: A Story of the Latter Period of the War for Independence.* Boston and Chicago: W. A. Wilde, 1900.

——. *A Girl of '76.* Boston and Chicago: W. A. Wilde, 1898.

——. *A Revolutionary Maid: A Story of the Middle Period of the War for Independence.* Boston and Chicago: W. A. Wilde, 1899.

Brady, Cyrus Townsend. *The Grip of Honor: A Story of Paul Jones and the American Revolution.* 1900. New York: Charles Scribner's Sons, 1908.

Burroughs, Edgar Rice. *Tarzan of the Apes.* 1912. New York: New American Library, 1990.

Chambers, Robert W. *Cardigan: A Novel.* New York and London: Harper and Brothers, 1901.

——. *The Maid-at-Arms: A Novel.* New York and London: Harper and Brothers, 1902.

——. *The Reckoning.* New York: D. Appleton, 1905.

Churchill, Winston. *The Crossing.* New York: Grosset and Dunlap, 1903.

——. *Richard Carvel.* London: Macmillan, 1899.

Crane, Hart. *The Complete Poems and Selected Letters and Prose.* Ed. Brom Weber. Garden City, N.Y.: Doubleday, 1966.

DeForest, John William. *A Lover's Revolt.* New York: Longmans, Green, 1898.

——. *Miss Ravenel's Conversion from Secession to Loyalty.* 1867. Ed. Gordon S. Haight. New York: Holt, Rinehart, and Winston, 1955.

Devereux, Mary. *From Kingdom to Colony.* 1899. Boston: Little, Brown, 1908.

Eggleston, George Cary. *A Carolina Cavalier: A Romance of the American Revolution.* Boston: Lothrop, 1901.

Farmer, James Eugene. *Brinton Eliot: From Yale to Yorktown.* New York: Macmillan, 1902.

Fast, Howard. *The Hessian.* New York: Morrow, 1972.

Ford, Paul Leicester. *Janice Meredith: A Story of the American Revolution.* New York: Dodd, Mead, and Company, 1899.

Francis, Mary C. *Dalrymple: A Romance of the British Prison Ship "The Jersey."* New York: James Pott, 1904.

Frederic, Harold. *In the Valley.* New York: Charles Scribner's Sons, 1890.

French, Allen. *The Colonials: Being a Narrative of Events Chiefly Connected with the Siege and Evacuation of the Town of Boston in New England.* New York: Doubleday, Page, 1902.

Frost, Robert. *Poetry and Prose.* Ed. Edward Connery Lathem and Lawrance Thompson. New York: Holt, Rinehart and Winston, 1972.

Glasgow, Ellen. *Phases of an Inferior Planet.* New York: Harper and Brothers, 1898.

Grey, Zane. *Betty Zane.* New York: Grosset and Dunlap, 1903.

——. *Call of the Canyon.* 1924. New York: Simon and Schuster, 1975.

——. *The Last Trail: A Story of Early Days in the Ohio Valley.* 1909. Lincoln: U of Nebraska P, 1996.

——. *Riders of the Purple Sage.* 1912. New York: Pocket Books, 1980.

——. *The Spirit of the Border: A Romance of the Early Settlers in the Ohio Valley.* 1906. Lincoln: U of Nebraska P, 1996.

——. *The Vanishing American.* 1922. New York: Simon and Schuster, 1982.

——. *Wanderer of the Wasteland.* 1923. New York: Simon and Schuster, 1968.

Harrison, Mrs. Burton [Constance Cary]. *The Anglomaniacs.* 1890. Ed. Elizabeth Hardwick. New York: Arno P, 1977.

——. *Good Americans.* New York: Century, 1898.

——. *A Son of the Old Dominion.* Boston, New York, and London: Lamson, Wolffe, 1897.

Hubbard, Lindley Murray. *An Express of '76: A Chronicle of the Town of York in the War for Independence.* Boston: Little, Brown, 1906.

Jewett, Sarah Orne. *The Country of the Pointed Firs.* 1896. Garden City: Doubleday, 1956.

——. *The Tory Lover.* Boston and New York: Houghton Mifflin, 1901.

Kennedy, Sara Beaumont. *Joscelyn Cheshire: A Story of Revolutionary Days in the Carolinas.* New York: Doubleday, Page, 1901.

Kirk, Ellen Olney. *A Revolutionary Love-Story.* Chicago and New York: Herbert S. Stone, 1898.

Lewis, Alfred Henry. *The Story of Paul Jones: An Historical Romance.* New York: G. W. Dillingham, 1906.

Mackie, Pauline Bradford. *Mademoiselle de Berny: A Story of Valley Forge.* Boston, New York, and London: Lamson, Wolffe, 1897.

Mailer, Norman. *Armies of the Night: History as a Novel, The Novel as History.* New York: New American Library, 1968.

Melville, Herman. *Israel Potter: His Fifty Years of Exile.* 1855. New York: Warner, 1974.

Mitchell, Silas Weir. *Hugh Wynne, Free Quaker: Sometime Brevet Lieutenant-Colonel on the Staff of his Excellency General Washington.* 1896. New York: Century, 1905.

Morgan, George. *John Littlejohn, of J.: Being in Particular an Account of his Remarkable Entanglement with the King's Intrigues against General Washington.* Philadelphia: J. B. Lippincott, 1897.

Page, Thomas Nelson. *The Old South: Essays Social and Political.* Chautauqua, NY: Chautauqua P, 1919.

——, with A. C. Gordon. *Befo' de War: Echoes in Negro Dialect.* New York: Charles Scribner's Sons, 1888.

Quimby, Alden W. *Valley Forge: A Tale.* New York: Eaton and Mains, 1906.

Ray, Frederick A. *Maid of the Mohawk.* Boston: C. M. Clark, 1906.

Rives, Hallie Erminie. *Hearts Courageous.* Indianapolis: Bowen-Merrill, 1902.

Roberts, Charles George Douglas. *Barbara Ladd.* Boston: L. C. Page, 1902.

Robinson, Rowland Evans. *A Danvis Pioneer: A Story of One of Ethan Allen's Green Mountain Boys.* 1900. Rutland, Vt.: Charles E. Tuttle, 1933.

——. *A Hero of Ticonderoga.* 1898. Rutland, Vt.: Charles E. Tuttle, 1934.

Rodney, George Brydges. *In Buff and Blue, Being Certain Portions from the Diary of Richard Hilton, Gentleman of Haslet's Regiment, Delaware Foot, in our Ever Glorious War of Independence.* Boston: Little, Brown, 1897.

Scollard, Clinton. *The Son of a Tory: A Narrative of the Experiences of Wilton Aubrey in the Mohawk Valley and elsewhere during the Summer of 1777, now for the first time edited by Clinton Scollard.* Boston: Richard G. Badger, 1901.

Shipman, Louis Evan. *D'Arcy of the Guards, or the Fortunes of War.* Chicago and New York: Herbert S. Stone, 1899.

Simms, William Gilmore. *The Scout.* 1854. Ridgewood, N.J.: Gregg, 1968.

Skeel, Adelaide, and William H. Brearley. *King Washington: A Romance of the Hudson Highlands.* Philadelphia: J. B. Lippincott, 1899.

Sprague, William C. *Felice Constant, or the Master Passion: A Romance.* New York: Frederick A. Stokes, 1904.

Stanley, H. A. *The Backwoodsman: The Autobiography of a Continental on the New York Frontier during the Revolution.* New York: Doubleday, Page, 1901.

Stephens, Robert Neilson. *The Continental Dragoon: A Love Story of Philipse Manor-House in 1778.* Boston: L. C. Page, 1898.

——. *Philip Winwood.* Boston: L. C. Page, 1900.

Stimpson, Herbert Baird. *The Tory Maid: Being an Account of the Adventures of James Frisby of Fairlee, in the County of Kent, on the Eastern Shore of the State of Maryland, and Sometime an Officer in the Maryland Line of the Continental Army during the War of the Revolution.* New York: Dodd, Mead, 1898.

Taylor, Mary Imlay. *A Yankee Volunteer.* Chicago: A. C. McClurg, 1898.

Thompson, Maurice. *Alice of Old Vincennes*. Indianapolis: Bowen-Merrill, 1900.

Tilton, Dwight (pseud.). *My Lady Laughter: A Romance of Boston Town in the Days of the Great Siege*. Boston: C. M. Clark, 1904.

West, Kenyon (pseud. of Frances Louise Howland). *Cliveden*. Boston: Lothrop, 1903.

White, Richard Grant. *The Fate of Mansfield Humphreys*. Boston: Houghton, Mifflin, 1884.

II. Secondary Sources

Aaron, Daniel. "What Can You Learn from a Historical Novel?" *American Heritage* (October 1992): 55–62.

Aldiss, Brian W. *The Trillion Year Spree: The History of Science Fiction*. New York: Atheneum, 1986.

Allen, Hervey. "History and the Novel." *Atlantic Monthly* February 1944: 119–21.

Altick, Richard D. *Writers, Readers, and Occasions: Selected Essays on Victorian Literature and Life*. Columbus: Ohio State UP, 1989.

Bailey, Thomas A. *A Diplomatic History of the American People*. 10th ed. Englewood Cliffs, NJ: Prentice-Hall, 1980.

Baker, Carlos. "The Novel and History." *Delphian Quarterly* 24 (1941): 15–20.

Baker, Ernest Albert. *A Guide to Historical Fiction*. New York: Argosy-Antiquarian, 1968.

Bardes, Barbara, and Suzanne Gossett. *Declarations of Independence: Women and Political Power in Nineteenth-Century America*. New Brunswick, NJ: Rutgers UP, 1990.

Barnes, Margaret Ayer. "The Period Novel." *What Is a Book?: Thoughts about Writing*. Ed. Frances Lester Warner et al. London: Allen and Unwin, 1936. 213–19.

Barthes, Roland. "Historical Discourse." *Introduction to Structuralism*. Ed. Michael Lane. New York: Basic, 1970. 148–68.

Bartkowski, Frances. *Feminist Utopias*. Lincoln: U of Nebraska P, 1989.

Baumgarten, Murray. "The Historical Novel: Some Postulates." *Clio: An Interdisciplinary Journal* 4 (1975): 173–82.

Bennett, David H. *The Party of Fear: From Nativist Movements to the New Right in American History*. Chapel Hill: U of North Carolina P, 1988

Bercovitch, Sacvan, ed. *Reconstructing American Literary History*. Cambridge: Harvard UP, 1986.

Berthoff, Warner. "Fiction, History, Myth: Notes toward the Discrimination of Narrative Forms." *The Interpretation of Narrative: Theory and Practice*. Ed. Morton W. Bloomfield. Cambridge: Harvard UP, 1970. 263–87.

——. *The Ferment of Realism: American Literature, 1884–1919*. New York: Free P, 1965.

Braudy, Leo. *Narrative Form in History and Fiction*. Princeton, NJ: Princeton UP, 1970.

Bruce, Dickson D., Jr. *Black American Writing from the Nadir: The Evolution of a Literary Tradition, 1877–1915*. Baton Rouge: Louisiana State UP, 1989.

Brumm, Ursula. "Some Thoughts on History and the Novel." *Comparative Literature Studies* 6 (1969): 317–30.

Budick, Emily Miller. *Fiction and Historical Consciousness: The American Romance Tradition*. New Haven, CT: Yale UP, 1989.

Carter, Everett. "Realism to Naturalism." *Theories of American Literature*. Ed. Donald M. Kartiganer and Malcolm A. Griffith. New York: Macmillan, 1972. 379–405.

Cawelti, John G. *Adventure, Mystery, and Romance: Formula Stories as Art and Popular Culture*. Chicago: U of Chicago P, 1976.

——. "The Concept of Formula in the Study of Popular Literature." *The Study of Popular Fiction*. Ed. Bob Ashley. Philadelphia: U of Pennsylvania P, 1989. 87–92.

Churchill, Winston. "Interview." *Boston Herald*. August 27, 1899: 30.

Clareson, Thomas D. *Some Kind of Paradise: The Emergence of American Science Fiction*. Westport, CT: Greenwood, 1985.

Colie, Rosalie L. "Literature and History." *Relations of Literary Study: Essays on Interdisciplinary Contributions*. Ed. James Thorpe. New York: MLA, 1967. 1–26.

Commager, Henry Steele, ed. *Britain through American Eyes*. London: Bodley Head, 1974.

Conn, Peter. *The Divided Mind: Ideology and Imagination in America, 1898–1917*. Cambridge: Cambridge UP, 1983.

Daspre, André. "Le Roman Historique et l'histoire." *Revue d'Histoire Litteraire de la France* 75 (1975): 235–44.

Dekker, George. *The American Historical Romance*. Cambridge: Cambridge UP, 1987.

Dickstein, Morris. "Popular Fiction and Critical Values: The Novel as a Challenge to Literary History." *Reconstructing American Literary History*. Ed. Sacvan Bercovitch. Cambridge: Harvard UP, 1986. 29–66.

Elliott, Emory, et al., eds. *Columbia Literary History of the United States*. New York: Columbia UP, 1988.

Earnest, Ernest. *S. Weir Mitchell: Novelist and Physician*. Philadelphia: U of Pennsylvania P, 1950.

Ferguson, E. James. *The American Revolution: A General History, 1763–1790*. Rev. ed. Homewood, IL: Dorsey, 1979.

Ferguson, Robert A. "'We Hold These Truths': Strategies of Control in the Literature of the Founders." *Reconstructing American Literary History*. Ed. Sacvan Bercovitch. Cambridge: Harvard UP, 1986. 1–28.

Fiedler, Leslie A. *The Return of the Vanishing American*. New York: Stein and Day, 1969.

Fisher, Philip. *Hard Facts: Setting and Form in the American Novel*. New York: Oxford UP, 1985.

Fleming, Thomas. "Inventing Our Probable Past." *New York Times Book Review* July 6, 1986: 1, 20–21.

Foote, Shelby. "The Novelist's View of History." *Mississippi Quarterly* 17 (1964): 219–25.

Forbes, Esther. "Why the Past?" *What Is a Book?: Thoughts about Writing*. Ed. Frances Lester Warner et al. London: Allen and Unwin, 1936. 223–33.

Foucault, Michel. "History, Discourse and Discontinuity." Trans. Anthony M. Nazzaro. *Salmagundi* 20 (1972): 229–33.

Garner, Stanton. *Harold Frederic*. Pamphlets on American Writers, No. 83. Minneapolis: U of Minnesota P, 1969.

Gossman, Lionel. *Between History and Literature*. Cambridge: Harvard UP, 1990.

Greenblatt, Stephen J. "Shakespeare and the Exorcists." *Contemporary Literary Criticism: Literary and Cultural Studies*. 2d ed. Ed. Robert Con Davis and Ronald Schleifer. New York: Longman, 1989. 428–47.

Greene, Jack P., ed. *The Reinterpretation of the American Revolution: 1763–1789*. New York: Harper and Row, 1968.

Haight, Gordon S., ed. *Miss Ravenel's Conversion from Secession to Loyalty*. By J. W. DeForest. 1867. New York: Holt, Rinehart, and Winston, 1955.

Hart, James D. *The Popular Book: A History of American Literary Taste*. New York: Oxford UP, 1950.

Henderson, Harry B. *Versions of the Past: The Historical Imagination in American Fiction*. New York: Oxford UP, 1974.

Hofstadter, Richard. *The Age of Reform: From Bryan to F. D. R.* New York: Vintage, 1955.

Holly, Flora Mai. Review of Sarah Orne Jewett's *The Tory Lover*. *The Bookman* 14 (October 1901): 195–96.

Hutcheon, Linda. *A Poetics of Postmodernism: History, Theory, Fiction*. New York: Routledge, 1988.

Jackson, James Robert de Jager. *Historical Criticism and the Meaning of Texts*. London: Routledge, 1989.

Jones, Howard Mumford. *The Age of Energy: Varieties of American Experience, 1865–1915*. New York: Viking, 1971.

Jones, Howard Mumford, and Richard M. Ludwig. *Guide to American Literature and Its Backgrounds since 1890*. 4th ed., rev. and enl. Cambridge: Harvard UP, 1972.

Kammen, Michael. *A Season of Youth: The American Revolution and the Historical Imagination*. New York: Knopf, 1978.

Kantor, MacKinlay. "The Historical Novelist's Obligation to History." *Iowa Journal of History* 59 (1962): 27–44.

Kartiganer, Donald M., and Malcolm A. Griffith, eds. *Theories of American Literature*. New York: Macmillan, 1972.

Kennan, George. "It's History, But Is It Literature?" *New York Times Book Review* April 26, 1959.

Kessler, Carol Farley, ed. *Daring to Dream: Utopian Stories by United States Women, 1836–1919*. Boston: Pandora P/Routledge and Kegan Paul, 1984.

Krieger, Murray. "Fiction, History, and Empirical Reality." *Critical Inquiry* 1 (1975): 335–60.

La Capra, Dominick. *History, Politics, and the Novel*. Ithaca, NY: Cornell UP, 1987.

Lauter, Paul, Juan Bruce-Novoa, Jackson Bryer, et al., eds. *The Heath Anthology of American Literature*. 2 vols. Lexington, MA: Heath, 1990.

Leisy, Ernest. *The American Historical Novel*. Norman: U of Oklahoma P, 1950.

Leitch, Vincent B. *American Literary Criticism from the Thirties to the Eighties*. New York: Columbia UP, 1988.

Levin, David. *History as Romantic Art: Bancroft, Prescott, Motley, and Parkman*. Stanford, CA: Stanford UP, 1959.

——. *In Defense of Historical Literature: Essays on American History, Autobiography, Drama, and Fiction*. New York: Hill and Wang, 1967.

Light, James F. *John William DeForest*. New York: Twayne, 1965.

Lukács, Georg. *The Historical Novel*. Trans. Hannah and Stanley Mitchell. Lincoln: U of Nebraska P, 1983.

Marcus, Steven. *Representations: Essays on Literature and Society*. New York: Random House, 1975.

Martin, Jay. *Harvests of Change: American Literature 1865–1914*. Englewood Cliffs, NJ: Prentice-Hall, 1967.

McGann, Jerome. *Historical Studies and Literary Criticism*. Madison: U of Wisconsin P, 1985.

McGarry, Daniel D., and Sarah Harriman White. *World Historical Fiction Guide: An Annotated Chronological, Geographical and Topical List of Selected Historical Novels*. 2d ed. Metuchen, NJ: Scarecrow, 1973.

Michaels, Walter Benn. *The Gold Standard and the Logic of Naturalism: American Literature at the Turn of the Century*. Berkeley: U of California P, 1987.

Morgan, Edmund S., ed. *The American Revolution: Two Centuries of Interpretation*. Englewood Cliffs, NJ: Prentice-Hall, 1965.

Morris, Wesley. *Toward a New Historicism*. Princeton, NJ: Princeton UP, 1972.

Nettels, Elsa. *Language, Race, and Social Class in Howells's America*. Lexington: UP of Kentucky, 1988.

Novak, Barbara. *American Painting of the Nineteenth Century: Realism, Idealism, and the American Experience.* 2d ed. New York: Harper and Row, 1979.

Nye, Russel B. "History and Literature: Branches of the Same Tree." *Essays on History and Literature.* Ed. Robert H. Bremner. Columbus: Ohio State UP, 1966. 123–59.

——. *The Unembarrassed Muse: The Popular Arts in America.* New York: Dial, 1970.

Pearce, Donald. *Para/Worlds: Entanglements of Art and History.* University Park: Pennsylvania State UP, 1989.

Pearce, Roy Harvey. *Historicism Once More: Problems and Occasions for the American Scholar.* Princeton, NJ: Princeton UP, 1969.

——. "Romance and the Study of History." *Hawthorne Centenary Essays.* Ed. Roy Harvey Pearce. Columbus: Ohio State UP, 1964.

Pfaelzer, Jean. *The Utopian Novel in America 1886–1896: The Politics of Form.* Pittsburgh: U of Pittsburgh P, 1984.

Reising, Russell J. *The Unusable Past: Theory and the Study of American Literature.* New York: Methuen, 1986.

Renault, Mary. "History in Fiction." *Times Literary Supplement* March 23, 1973: 315–16.

Ringe, Donald A. "The American Revolution in American Romance." *American Literature* 49 (1977): 352–65.

Sabatini, Rafael. "Historical Fiction." *What Is a Book?: Thoughts about Writing.* Ed. Frances Lester Warner et al. London: Allen and Unwin, 1936. 23–39.

Scholes, Robert, and Robert Kellogg. *The Nature of Narrative.* London: Oxford UP, 1966.

Segal, Howard P. *Technological Utopianism in American Culture.* Chicago: U of Chicago P, 1985.

Showalter, Elaine. *Sexual Anarchy: Gender and Culture at the Fin de Siècle.* New York: Viking, 1990.

Shulman, Robert. *Social Criticism and Nineteenth-Century American Fictions.* Columbia: U of Missouri P, 1987.

Simms, William Gilmore. *Views and Reviews in American Literature, History, and Fiction.* 1845. Cambridge: Harvard UP, 1962.

Smith, Herbert F. *The Popular American Novel: 1865–1920.* Boston: Twayne, 1980.

Spencer, Benjamin T. "Regionalism in American Literature." *Regionalism in America.* Ed. Merrill Jensen. Madison: U of Wisconsin P, 1965. 219–60.

Spengemann, William C. *A Mirror for Americanists: Reflections on the Idea of American Literature.* Hanover, NH: UP of New England, 1989.

Steuber, William F. "Using History for Fiction." *Wisconsin Magazine of History* 43 (1960): 245–52.

Strout, Cushing. *The American Image of the Old World*. New York: Harper and Row, 1963.

Sutherland, Daniel E. *The Confederate Carpetbaggers*. Baton Rouge: Louisiana State UP, 1988.

Swados, Harvey, ed. *Years of Conscience*. New York: World, 1962.

Titus, Warren I. *Winston Churchill*. New Haven, CT: College and UP, 1963.

Unger, Irwin. *These United States*. Vol. 2. Boston: Little, Brown, 1978.

VanDerhoof, Jack Warner. *A Bibliography of Novels Related to American Frontier and Colonial History*. Troy, NY: Whitson, 1971.

Van Doren, Carl. *The American Novel 1789–1939*. New York: Macmillan, 1940.

Van Tassel, David D. "From Learned Society to Professional Organization: The American Historical Association, 1884–1900." *American Historical Review* 89.4 (1984): 929–56.

Veeser, Harold. *The New Historicism*. New York: Routledge, Chapman, and Hall, 1989.

Weinstein, Mark A. "The Creative Imagination in Fiction and History." *Genre* 9 (1976): 263–77.

Weymouth, Lally, designed by Milton Glaser. *America in 1876: The Way We Were*. New York: Vintage, 1976.

White, Hayden. "Fictions of Factual Representation." *The Literature of Fact: Selected Papers from the English Institute*. Ed. Angus Fletcher. New York: Columbia UP, 1976. 21–44.

——. "Interpretation in History." *New Literary History* 3 (1973): 281–314.

Woodress, James. "American History in the Novel: The Revolution and Early National Periods, 1775–1815." *Midwest Journal* 8 (1956): 385–92.

Young, Thomas Daniel, Floyd C. Watkins, and Richmond Croom Beatty, eds. *The Literature of the South*. Glenview, IL: Scott, Foresman, 1968.

Ziff, Larzer. *The American 1890s: Life and Times of a Lost Generation*. New York: Viking, 1966.

INDEX